THE VERMEER EFFECT

Frank J Ryan

For my Sophia Celeste
May the wind always take you
May you forever soar free

COPYRIGHT

Cover art by Jorge Santos
Cover design by Red Raven Book Design
Hillary Avis Editing

First Printing: 2017 ISBN 978-0692905562

www.frankjryan.com

PROLOGUE

The first rays of the morning sun pierced blood-red through the rolling fogs of Boston Harbor, scintillating over the calm waters of the Charles River. The early morning breezed through the open archways of a nineteenth-century palace situated on Evans Way, as high above a white dove glided past the dense trees of Back Bay Fens toward a glass-paned roof and the cloistered nest she called home. A lone tail feather had found its way free, floating and wafting through the archways leading into the courtyard.

A little hand reached across the pavement. A boy with round cheeks and curious brown eyes picked up the snow-white plume. His mother had dressed him in a light blue polo and beige golf shorts, brand new sneakers, and blue striped socks pulled up to the knee. It was his first field trip to the local museum. He stared at the white feather between tiny fingers and wondered at this grand place, a magical place of beauty and spirit.

Shafts of sunlight broke through the parted double doors behind him, casting their warm glow onto the marble woman atop her pedestal at the far edge of the inner courtyard. Surrounded by palm trees, delphiniums, and hydrangeas at the mosaic center of the courtyard, Persephone, Daughter of Zeus and Queen of the Underworld, beckoned the boy into her garden.

He stole a glance at the adults at the far end of the corridor. Their whispers echoed along the vaulted ceilings above while the other kids played jacks on the

1

stone-paved floor. But something else on the far side of the courtyard caught his eye. Shiny orbs stared at him from the shadows and blinked. With a neigh, a tiny four-legged beast pranced and hooved just beyond the far entrance across the garden, the rider pulling on its reigns. The strange creature, no taller than half his height, spun around and fled from sight.

Through the trees, past trickling fountains, the little boy ran after them as fast as his pounding heart would take him. Up the far staircase he sprung and capered, disappearing into the secret rooms of the Isabella Stewart Gardner Museum. Persephone broke a grin from atop her permanent place in the garden. She'd waited a long time for that intrepid little boy.

The air was cold but somehow cozy, like a blanket hanging over the place. The prancing hooves echoed beyond the bend. He pattered through the corridors, catching a glimpse of a fluttering cape vanishing through a doorway. After it he went, bursting into one of the many rooms, this one with green, patterned wallpaper and dark, wood-paneled walls. The bronze chevalier and his steed stood perched atop the room's doorway in their permanent pose. He smiled at the boy scurrying across the red clay-tiled floor; if he would have only turned around. The boy came to a stop at a writing table by a lancet window facing the outer gardens. Peeking through the blinds, he searched for the adults below.

Nothing.

The little boy popped away from the window when she caught him. At a small corner of the room there she hung, the painting in her gilded frame. Soft morning light captured the oiled canvas: young girls in their yellow and blue dresses, playing and singing to the silent melody of the harpsichord. The checkered floor beneath their slippered feet, bathed in its own light from inside the canvas, gleamed as the sun seeped through the edges of the folded blinds. But what stopped him stone-still was the man in the painting. The man sat with his back to him, sash draped over his broad shoulder, strumming a stringed instrument in the rust-orange chair. The mysterious man whose face he could not see called his name.

"Richard!"

He drew a sharp breath as long fingers vice-gripped around his arm. His mother pulled him back to the present. His heart pounded, but it wasn't she who frightened him. There were secrets inside that painting. The performers whispered them to him. He could hear their silent melody of light and color.

"Don't you ever do that again! You could have given me a heart attack," snapped his mother, catching her breath as she pulled him away.

"Who is that, Mommy, that man in the painting?"

"I don't know. Let's go."

He took a last look back at the man, hoping to catch a glimpse of him, hoping he would turn around, when the walls around Richard began to bend. The steady hum of the air conditioner was replaced by a distant buzz of something very different, something that should not have been there, when his eyes met another's at the far side of the room.

Deep inside a second canvas, the Stranger waited. From his fishing boat, in the heart of a terrible storm, the thirteenth man, a hand on a line and the other on his hat, reached out to the little boy. The Stranger begged to be saved, to be delivered from the tempest that raged in the painting and in the madness of his own mind. But it was too late for Rembrandt—as it was for that little boy. The calendar on the table marked March 17, 1990, and time had stopped for both of them...

The distant buzz had become a deafening roar.

I

DANGEROUS BEDFELLOWS

Twenty-five years later…

T hey always told him to think pleasant thoughts at times like these, they did, those little voices in his head; anything to distract him from the gonad-seizing terror clawing up his belly. The more Richard Robles tried not to think about it, the further those little gonads pulled upward. He loosened his white-knuckled grip on the edge of the bench beneath him and let out a smile.

I shoulda never, really. Oh, shit!

The butterflies in his belly made him double over. The buzz in his ears was again the familiar deafening roar. His memory fled to that faraway place where he first heard it, but his ass was still stuck to the seat. On his black visor, bathed in the red light from the overhead bulb, was the reflection of the black-clad skydiver who sat across from him.

Way out of my league. This is so crazy! Anja Robles somehow always made him do such crazy things.

A deck plate vibrated beneath his black boot to the whir of the engines outside. He gripped the bench as a loose canister suspended into the air along with the contents of his stomach.

Ah, the feeling of zero-Gs.

"Sorry, a little rough patch. Great night for jumping though," came the gruff bellow from the big-bellied jumpmaster at the back of the plane.

Richard leaned over. He could see Anja's shoulders give that little hunch and her feet that little bounce every time she laughed. Seeing him scared shitless was the cutest thing ever, she would say. Touching visor to visor, he took her gloved hand as the red overhead light went green. The fuselage door slid open as the jumpmaster pulled back the handle. The freezing wind whipped through the plane with the deafening roar of the turboprops.

"We ain't got all night, girls. You wanted thirty-eight thousand; you got 'em!"

Richard let go of the bench as his gloved fingers clicked a red button on the inside of his wrist. The LCD telemetry display on his forearm went dark, suddenly reappearing over his right eye. He stood and grabbed the handle overhead, his wingsuit fluttering under his arm. Beyond the open door was nothing but cloud-covered blackness, haloed in distant lightning. He could feel the cold wetness of the storm through his suit and something else a bit warmer between his inner thighs—and maybe a bit moister, too. He took a look back at Anja, thankful the jumpsuit kept everything in. If she knew what just happened, he'd never live it down.

"Robles, you are one crazy son of a bitch," shouted the jumpmaster, his beard sprouting from under the edges of his oxygen mask.

If he could only see the expression behind Anja's opaque visor, he thought, as he took an intrepid last step toward the open door. Words could do no justice to the things she did to him. Richard pitched backward into the black expanse beneath the plane, shooting the jumpmaster a polypropylene-clad middle finger. Anja slid forward and, without a moment's hesitation, jumped into the darkness after him as the plane banked away from the tempest below.

***

David Bradford stared out the window of the rear passenger seat of his Audi A8 as they wound along the river. The streetlamps high above gleamed off her metallic black body paint as she slipped beneath an arched overpass. In the rearview mirror, the desolate city street extended behind them.

"You think two bottom-feeding, slime-eating senators from Kentucky and Mississippi matter? They're the least of my worries. Tehran and the president will deny the existence of any side agreements to our accord," said David to the young man directly opposite him.

James Fenway was his Deputy Secretary of State. He was young and polished in his fresh suit, cropped hair, and clean shave, typical of the Ivy League graduate and what David had come to expect from him. The young man possessed guile and ambition that would serve him well in Washington. David appreciated the quickness with which he learned and his lust to apply those lessons as ruthlessly as would be needed.

"The Republicans will block its passage in Congress," said James.

"It's already approved by the UN and the threat of the Security Council withdrawing support will curb their enthusiasm. Sometimes it's best to put the cart before the horse, especially if the cart is full of shit, and the path leads back downhill. Don't you worry, James, the Speaker will make sure it passes. We just need to give the *people* some good theatrics in Washington and let the media circus play out," said David.

As he spoke, there sat another among them with piercing eyes of iridescent yellow set in angled cheekbones beneath a boney brow and white-blond shorn hair. His face was pallid, with a deep scar beneath the left eye. The albino carried himself with a straight back and squared shoulders, the bearing of a cut-and-dry military man.

"Have the arrangements been made?" asked David.

"Yes, Mr. Secretary," said the albino.

"Today you're in Khartoum, slated to meet with President al-Bashir," said James.

"The security detail has been nixed, as requested," concluded the albino.

He was a man of few words and David liked that. The less most people spoke, the better.

"Good," said David. His eyes followed the length of the river as the vehicle reappeared from under an overpass.

"Rumors speak of your Nobel Peace Prize, sir," said James.

"That's one less the president will have over me. We'll both be Nobel laureates in the esteemed company of such fine personalities as Joseph Stalin, Adolf Hitler and the son of the soil upon which we're now present, Benito Mussolini. Did you know that Stalin and Hitler and, yes, Mussolini were all nominated for the Prize, albino?"

"No, sir. I did not."

"See, there? An honest answer. You are now duly informed," said David.

"Yes, sir."

"Gandhi, of course, was never awarded such an honor," he added, turning his attentions squarely back on his Deputy Secretary.

"Don't you worry about a thing, James. Distractions of this sort make for the best entertainment. Especially when they take the eye off the real prize," said David with a facetious smile as the black Audi streaked over cobbled streets toward the domed cathedral in the distance.

***

The winds swirled above the storm clouds as the black-suited skydiver spread hands and feet like a flying squirrel, catching the upward lift. Richard loved the tingle of adrenaline through his fingertips and the rush of gelid air past his suit. The darkness flashed stark white as lightning cut through the cottony clouds, and condensation crystallized over his tinted polycarbonate visor. The strobe lights at his ankles flashed as expected as he adjusted to the GPS bearings over his right eye. Dipping into a new angle of attack, he headed straight for the storm clouds below.

Anja focused her sights on the blinking strobe light in front of her. Even in her layered wingsuit, thirty-eight thousand feet was still cold. She sucked in breaths of mixed oxygen from her hip canister, keeping focused to task. It was moments like these she remembered why she married the man, and it was time for a little fun. She closed her arms and legs and plunged into the storm cloud after him.

Richard punched through, out the other side, through the ice crystals of a mushroom cloud, skimming along the stalk like a base jumper would down the side of a cliff, ionized air prickling his skin. The lightning was getting too close when she dropped onto him, clamping to the rear straps of his harness.

"I missed you," said the raspy voice over his earphones. Anja'd latched on to his back.

She wants to play.

He closed his arms, scissor locked his legs into downward acceleration, and barrel rolled left. The sudden jolt ripped her off his back.

"You asshole!"

In six seconds, they'd dropped another thousand feet.

The alarm rang in Richard's ears and flashed red over his right eye; *not enough altitude, horizontal distance too far.* The computer was recalculating the safety drop. With the press of a button on his forearm, he overrode the system.

"We're adjusting our drop, how copy? Anja?"

Like a dense star cluster, millions of lights suddenly twinkled in the gaping darkness beneath him. Sprawling pockets of light, tiny dots shimmering on a black canvas, radiated out in a huge web. The glowing city beneath him reached out with her sparkling tendrils. Richard could see the craggy outline of the coastal highway beneath his feet.

"Anja, how copy? Anja, can you hear me?!"

No response. He rolled onto his back. Nothing above, nothing behind him, nothing around.

Out of time, he spun back around toward the city lights. Nosing down into a near-vertical descent; the wind roared past him, the ground rising fast, the drop zone blackening into a gaping chasm. The free fall raced through his veins. He pulled the cord. The harness cut into his flesh, tearing the skin beneath the suit. The drogue chute flared out behind him. His legs flung forward from underneath him as the canopy slammed the brakes on his downward motion. The ram-air parachute mushroomed above the streets. He angled forward, feet dangling over dark apartments and empty rooftops.

Richard swooped in just above the buttressed perimeter wall as Saint Peter's Basilica disappeared beyond the wooded hilltop. Toggling the air brakes, he skimmed over the open grass, past a fountain, and came to a running stop at the edge of a forest. He stood on the grounds of Vatican City, but there was no Anja.

***

The pavement was moist with the remnants of the passing storm as rolling thunder echoed in the distance. Viktor Kletnov looked over an empty plaza surrounded by gray, buttressed walls and baroque arched windows. The cold pressed against his bearded face. His breath blew warm in the freezing night. Steam emanated from his shoulders as he stood, in a trench coat and a fedora hat, next to the purring Mercedes S550.

From the uppermost floor, a single, candlelit lancet window looked down upon him. Viktor was the first to arrive, his Mercedes rolling through the arched entrance, the gate already pulled open. There were no guards to be seen, their absence a testament to the security itself. The Syndycate didn't meet often face-to-face.

He noted the distances across the courtyard from the echoes of the trickling waters of its central fountain. In the darkness he made out the outlines of the corner alcoves. The night was still when the sound of approaching tire treads interrupted his musings. A tinted, long-bodied vehicle entered the plaza from beneath the archway, circling around the far side of the fountain. He stood his ground as the fog lights enveloped him. His hand played with the thing in his left coat pocket. The Audi came to a stop two car-lengths away, and the right passenger door opened. From the corner of his eye he saw movement in the far alcoves. A glint of light appeared as quickly as it vanished.

Viktor was pleased with himself. He hadn't lost his eye. There was something—or someone—in the shadows after all. The man from the car, dressed in a black suit and blue tie, approached him. The American delegation had arrived.

***

From his niche among the far alcoves, Giovanni Battista watched the cars file into the plaza under the cover of night. The heavens had been accommodating, blanketing the sky in thick clouds. The rank smell of the sulfurous storm bit at his nostrils. Giovanni had lived in the service of the pontiffs and this Syndycate for many centuries, his sole function the protection of his pope and the defense of these hallowed grounds. His pencil-thin, upturned mustache, bushy salt-and-pepper hair, rail-thin limbs, and creased countenance beguiled those unaware of his kind as to the truth of what he was—a truth few in the Syndycate, and only the pope himself knew. In all his years of service as Inspector General to the Holy See, and in all his ages present behind these walls, this was a first. He was a Sicaari, and Sicaari would never dare intrude on their masters, but the Secretariat had personally confided in him this task.

"You will be my eyes and ears, Giovanni. You are to speak of this to no one." Giovanni never got used to his Polish accent when speaking Italian.

"Many, both inside and outside these walls, depend on this," he'd said, and with that the Secretariat, the second most powerful prefect in the whole of the Diocese, was gone to tend to his duties.

On this night, neither Vatican Police nor Swiss Guard patrolled the Belvedere Courtyard. They had called on his Sicaari to provide special protections, and from the shadows, they watched. Nothing would get near the conclave they did not allow. Giovanni scanned the plaza with a critical eye as the men in suits approached the entrance to the Papal Library and the robed figure who awaited them. Even from here, he could tell the guests did not kiss the signet ring on the right hand. The pope would not greet these men openly this evening; the deniability was by design. Giovanni stepped away from the rooftop parapet and whisked away into the night, set to purpose. He learned long ago God did not always do as he wished, but as he must.

***

Richard dragged the open canopy up the hillside and into a clearing between the trees, away from the paved path. He unclipped the oronasal mask, pulling the visor and helmet from his head and gulped in air. Beads of sweat rolled and dripped from the tip of his nose. His wild dark eyes were scanning the horizon for the silhouette of a falling canopy when the fluttering rush of air through nylon caught his ears; a shadow radiated out from beneath his feet. He lunged aside. Anja crashed between snapping branches, crumpling onto the ground where he'd stood. He sprung to his feet, digging into his side pouch for the aid kit. In a single motion, he activated her canopy retrieval system, unclipped her mask, and removed her visor.

"You asshole," Anja gasped, not caring who heard her. She could barely complete her sentence, but her expression finished the thought. She was hyperventilating.

"I love you, too," whispered Richard, holding the paper bag over her mouth and nose. Anja's blue eyes burned with defiance that slowly gave way to serenity as the edge of the bag began to stain red. Richard pried her grip from his hand. The blood wasn't coming from her mouth or nose. He breathed a sigh of relief until he felt a throb pulse through his palm. He pulled back his glove, revealing a gaping gash. The edge of a splintered branch protruded from his flesh.

"Give me that. I can handle it. Give me that," demanded Anja, taking the aid kit from Richard's good hand.

"We have to get out of sight," Richard urged.

"This will take a minute," said Anja. The grounds of the Vatican were desolate, too quiet for Richard.

"Ah, that hurts."

"Stop whining like a little bitch." She ripped the thick splinter from the wound. He gritted his teeth as she applied the alcohol with a glint in her eye.

"We should have seen guards by now," said Richard. The hoot of an owl somewhere in the trees broke the silence.

"This serves you right, you and your world record," said Anja, wrapping a bandage round his hand.

"As I recall, you suggested thirty-eight thousand feet."

"Yeah, except for the fact that we're jumping into a winter fucking storm, it's freezing fucking cold, and you're playing chicken with the ground, yeah, it was a great idea."

"After what you did up there, don't get me started. Surprised you're not dangling from the Vatican's radio antennae."

"If you hadn't been such an asshole, maybe I'd have come down just fine," said Anja

"You ride the stallion, you're bound to get bucked off."

"You mean gelding." Anja tied the bandage with a final and very painful tug. "That should do it. I—"

Richard pressed his bandaged hand hard over her mouth. A twig snapped somewhere in the trees. The grounds had been too quiet.

***

Father Fleitas thought he saw something. There in the gardens of the Vatican, he thought he saw something. He pressed thumb and forefinger between his eyes, an old habit to clear his sight and thoughts. A black shadow had fallen from the sky. But it couldn't be. A glass of the good stuff and a Last Judgment manuscript were a dangerous combination. A man

15

could take to imagining things, crazy things. Still dressed in his clerical robes, white collar unbuttoned and hanging from his neck, Father Fleitas could not sleep.

Why me, for the love of God?

He stood at the narrow window of his narrow quarters, the bottle of Scotch in his hand, tasked with deciphering the one-page letter from the Carmelite nun.

Just a bunch of garbage to rile their conspiracy-theorist spirits.

But it was dangerous garbage. He gulped down another shot.

Yes, he saw something. Another half-empty bottle stood at the edge of the varnished old table. Old parchments, leather-bound tomes, and scrolled manuscripts overflowed from the shelves. Piled in a mess on the floor, atop the table, and on the bed, they took up most of the living space in his cramped quarters. A single candlelit lamp flickered dangerously close to the parchment.

The smell of ancient paper and burnt candle would have suffocated lesser men. But Father Fleitas was dedicated to his cause. He hadn't been outside in three days. A small pile of bottles stacked in a corner served as testament to his dedication. The fluids kept him clear to focus on the message of the secret archive. But of all the works, he was handed *the secret*. He would have politely declined if given the choice. But Cardinal Scarlatti wasn't much for giving his clergy choices. It was an honor to serve in the Congregation for the Doctrine of the Faith, and a curse.

There were plenty of others in the Biblical Commission to choose from. Why me?

He stared at the parchment on the table, sealed in a clear plastic, written in the gentle curving script of a woman's hand. It was the untranslated text, the very document handed to the Bishop of Leiria almost seventy years prior. Unlucky for him, Portuguese was one of his strong suits.

He turned back to the gardens and saw it there again, a black shadow falling from the sky. Pinching the bridge of his nose, he shut his eyes.

Virgem Maria.

He took in a deep breath of musty air. He could taste the candle wax as he slowly opened his eyes. The gardens spread out peacefully beneath him. The bottle in his hand was empty. He began to sweat. He needed another one. He poured from the other, but that too had gone dry. The pile in the corner was getting bigger. The candle was burning out. The room was suddenly heavy with the nauseating smell of old parchment. The words throbbed in the back of his head: *the black shadow descended from the east.*

"I need air."

He gently placed the glass on the table.

To think these people could take this seriously.

The fresh air would do him some good. Father Fleitas scooped up his cassock as he staggered to the door. He fumbled with the handle and stumbled into the hallway. Back in the room, under the flickering candlelight, the yellow parchment containing the *Fourth Secret of Fatima* lay quietly on the table.

***

The clearing between the trees on Vatican Hill lay silent; not a mouse stirred. The owl blinked as it watched and waited. A breeze brushed the treetops when the man first appeared at the edge of the small clearing. He moved into the open as he scanned the area ahead. Like a cat in the night, he made hardly a rustle through the soft underbrush. At this range, Richard clearly made out the weapon hoisted on his shoulder.

Why were Swiss Guard dressed in night camouflage and goggles, sporting TAR-21 assault rifles?

His contracting scrotum again clawed back up his stomach into his chest.

Lucky for Anja she didn't have a pair... Well, maybe she did.

A second shadow appeared as the first moved slowly to the middle of the clearing. The second guard scanned the grounds until the first man's hand suddenly came up, signaling a halt. The owl leapt off its perch into the clearing. Spreading its wings, it soared into the dark.

The guard slowly lowered his hand as he rose from his knee. The two men continued forward across the clearing, passing between two trees. *Thank God they didn't look up.* Embraced against intertwined branches above them, Richard and Anja watched as the guards melted into the night.

Elsewhere in that dark forest, Father Fleitas wheezed and cursed, his legs burning from the uphill slope.

Cursed devil, I didn't come here for a workout.

He pressed against his legs as he fought to climb up the hill when he froze like a deer in headlights. He saw it again, something, this time slinking across the roadway.

It must have been a fox.

He reached in his overcoat. He always carried a little reserve for difficult moments. Popping the cap, he took a swig. The burn refreshed his body.

"Ah, that feels good…" He gulped in a breath.

What if that wasn't a fox?

He looked around, realizing that Vatican or no, this forest was no safe place. He stumbled back the way he came, or so he thought.

***

It had been twenty-five years since the Syndycate last met. They tried so hard to fit into this world, each of them aging with the times to compliment the games they played. They were so obsessed to be just like one of them, like the humans, that the mere utterance of their truer nature was punishable by death. The fear the Syndycate lived under and their obsessive lust for greed and power was still the same, whether twenty-five or two-thousand years later.

Some things just never changed. Viktor spent the whole of two minutes with David, and he needed an escape. He absconded into the shadows and managed his way here, to one of the four reception rooms that made up the papal apartments, the Rafael Rooms. After all this time, David was still an asshole, Viktor concluded, as something caught his attention and made him forget for a second just how much of an asshole David Bradford really was. A winged cherub held an inscribed message on the gilded dome above his head.

Suum Cuique. May all get their due. David Bradford would get his due.

Viktor needed to gather his thoughts before the Council convened, before the final guests arrived. The Gallery of Maps guided his way here. A vaulted ceiling of ornate Mannerist frescoes spanned the length of the corridor, and elaborate maps of sixteenth-century Italy lined its walls, giving Viktor the sense of how Gregory XIII saw the vastness of the world during his time.

No wonder such a man would establish a new calendar.

Through the Room of Fire, past the fresco of the Crowning of Charlemagne, Viktor made his way, the walls echoing his every step. Neither guard nor alarm stopped him. He finally stood at what had once been the supreme tribunal of all Christendom, *La Stanza della Segnatura.*

This world had many gifts, many gems to offer their kind. Great art at the hands of humans was one such gift; one that few of his world cared for and fewer still could master or even understand. It was a legacy unique to humans.

Before him, beneath an arch of golden swastikas, was the council of thinkers by Rafael, *The School of Athens.* The great philosophers, mathematicians, artists, and military men of Classical and Hellenistic thought stood preserved by the great master himself. In all his years as a collector of priceless works, this was the first time Viktor beheld Rafael's great masterpiece. Plato and Aristotle stood rightly at the center of all Western thought. The search for the soul, the *Eudaimonia,* as Aristotle would have put it.

Man's happiness truly was inversely proportional the size of his ego. The same held true for his own kind; the greater their ambitions, the greater their agony. Whatever power, gain, or wealth they earned for themselves, it never mattered, time had proven it was never enough.

Viktor pulled the thing from his pocket, a small six-pointed benitoite stone that pulsed a cobalt blue. The stone in his hand was something the Syndycate had not seen in centuries, an artifact lost to memory, and one that if discovered would cost him his life right where he stood.

Viktor never quite understood the Argylians' terror of being discovered, nor the need to live in secrecy among humans. They were a species stranded on this planet by their own doing, struggling to survive the inhospitable clime of this world and the war that raged between themselves and the others they brought here with them. But they adapted, learned to survive, and in time became part of this world.

Human legends grew and with them came many names, some of which he rather enjoyed. The Romans had referred to them as *Praeter hominem*. Their medieval descendants morphed their legend to that of *Cambions*. Viktor kind of liked the idea of himself as a child of human female and incubus. The Greeks termed them *Vrykolakas*, monstrous vampires. His favorite was what the Japanese believed of them, the *Obake*, and definitely the closest to their reality. The more recent myths of Nordic Aliens and Zeta Reticulans were a more boring personification and not of any interest to Viktor.

Each legend held a bit of truth, and yet there was so much more to them that humans would never know. But the term the Syndycate had chosen for itself at the last conclave was by far the final straw. Even among themselves, they'd taken to political correctness: *Exohumans*. The idea turned Viktor's stomach—so modern, so boring. Viktor even preferred the old Basque term for them, *Basajaun*. As insulting as it was to be thought of as a hairy, forest-dwelling savage, it was *oh* so much more fun.

Viktor pressed the stone deep into his hand as he studied the image of Archimedes frescoed on the wall and wondered.

So this is where Richard got his idea.

The stone was the centerpiece to a device of incredible power, one of thirteen Armillary Spheres. Together these thirteen conjured the *Ilythiium*, a creature so powerful none of their kind could ever fully control it. The *Ilythiium* nearly destroyed them before it was banished by the Guija—creatures who could move through time as easily as Viktor walked through the Gallery of Maps—one of the many races brought to this world following the Great Schism and the destruction of their home worlds. Once cast from this existence, the members of the Syndycate forbade even their own kind to possess the slightest knowledge of her. Those memories were eradicated from their consciousness, conserved by only a select few that did not include Viktor Kletnov. But he woke to the truth of what had been hidden from them for so long. The thirteen of the Syndycate were the last of their race, and without the *Ilythiium's* power they would wither and die. Whereto she was banished, he could not be certain, until now.

Richard Robles was Guija. He had masterfully hidden the secret of the *Ilythiium's* whereabouts in the colors and contours of an oil painting so many centuries ago. *But which one, which painting?* It was a question Viktor could not answer. He wasn't even sure how he knew it was a painting. His instinct and the stone—an awareness to time that perhaps even he did not fully grasp—guided his pursuit. Viktor pocketed the benitoite stone and gazed over the painting before him. He would possess the *Ilythiium* again, and this time bend her, bend the Syndycate, to his will.

"I do not take kindly to eavesdropping, my apologies. But I take less kindly to interlopers."

Viktor spun around. Giovanni Battista stood at the entrance to the room, his hands in his pockets. Viktor was more surprised at the fact he had not heard him approach than at the intrusion.

"My apologies in kind. I got caught up playing the tourist."

"I ask you return to your delegation. This place is off limits."

"The guards were nowhere to be found. Perhaps you're their replacement," said Viktor mockingly.

Giovanni tensed like a cat about to prey on a mouse. "Perhaps you should take your cue from the fresco behind you, *The Cardinal Virtues,* and prudently see your way back."

"Very clever of you, Mr. Battista. As I see you are temperate, I will be prudent. If you'll excuse me." Viktor smiled as he left Giovanni to ponder the question of how he knew his name.

***

No movement came from the structure before them; the gardens inside the outer walls were temptingly quiet. They bade their time moving silently along the wall, careful to stay out of the garden lamplight and the sight of unwelcome eyes, when Anja suddenly stopped them in their tracks with her patented *tsst*.

Richard searched with nose and ear, and nothing. He hoped those guards they met weren't downwind of them.

They both released their packs from their backs and drew out black rope and a grappling hook. Richard handled the pneumatic launcher; setting a three-pronged hook into the tip, he pushed it in with a faint click.

Anja produced a flat panel from her pack. A touch, and the display illuminated in a soft red backlight. She swept and prodded her finger across the screen as the area schematic of the entire Vatican City displayed before them. She hit an icon to a drill-down map. With thumb and forefinger she expanded the view. The building's external perimeter and walled-off garden appeared on her screen. A red intersecting network overlaid the whole of the courtyard and the Pinacoteca.

"A ten-year-old detection grid is a thing of beauty," said Anja, as she clicked a series of icons, the red bands of the grid suddenly going green.

"Now just don't let them see you." She closed the display and gathered her line and hook.

The rope uncoiled like a black serpent and whisked upward into the night. The barb at its end wedged into the stone. The line creaked beneath the strain of Richard's gloved grip. He pressed a boot to the wall and pulled himself up the side of the building. His hand throbbed as friction burned through the field dressing around his palm. Hand over hand, he tugged forward, his strained breaths louder and louder in his own ears. Reaching the top of the wall, he hoisted himself onto the roof and looked back.

Richard gasped for air as Anja now tested the line. The barbed fang held fast in the rock. He watched as, hand over hand, she drew her body up the building.

Damn, she's hot!

Thought vanished to the sharp crack of snapping steel. Richard lunged unto the falling rope and the severed eye of the hook still attached to its end. He lay face flat to the side of the wall, arms outstretched like an upside-down Christ. Feet crossed, he lodged his boots into a crevice between two stones at the rooftop's edge, one hand coiled around the broken hook, the other around the rope as Anja dangled and twirled beneath him, midway between rooftop and ground. Muscle and sinew strained to keep his chest from ripping apart.

"Climb," begged Richard, with what breath remained him.

Viscous blood rolled down the rope and over her gloved hand. Richard's blood. The wound had reopened. Anja braced a foot on the wall. Richard swallowed the pain. She gripped her way up the sticky blood-soaked rope, terror on her face. As she climbed, blackness closed in around Richard. His arms relaxed; his sight left him as Anja pulled the last of herself over the edge and reached back, somehow seizing his harness at the last minute in her own grip of desperate strength. She dragged his crumpled body back over the edge of that wall, and collapsed onto the rooftop.

***

Deep in the recesses of the Secret Archives, within her vaulted rooms filled with ancient tomes and scrolls, globes, and astronomical contraptions of every

25

sort, the Syndycate of the Thirteen gathered. Frescoed upon the ceiling, powerful angels and great men of the cloth, wrapped in red-laced gold and ancient Latin scripts, gazed down upon them. Viktor looked to his watch. Two minutes past two and only ten of the thirteen had arrived. In silence they waited, each at their respective place in the semicircle around the ornate high chair that faced them, empty, at the center.

Dark and musty, claustrophobically small to any other mortal not of the Syndycate, this place would have been otherwise overlooked and forgotten as an unkempt cobwebbed corner deep in the bowels of this ancient library. But this night had made something different of this place. This night, it was spacious and elegant, a place only they—and those invited into their presence—could reach. But two were absent, Salil Jawadi and Christian Huygens, a fact not lost on Viktor, or any of the others for that matter. They each had their agendas. Everything had a purpose. Nothing was happenstance.

Viktor took notice of each around the semicircle. Their roles in society had changed with the times, and it was fascinating to see what had become of each since the last conclave. They hadn't aged a day, except for how it best served their need for obscurity in the waking world. Wilhelm Gottfried sat opposite him near the other end of the semicircle. He peered through thin glasses and had thin lips, an even thinner head of hair, and a slender build. In his tailored gray double-breasted suit, he sat as upright as Viktor last remembered him, a stern and implacable Lichtenstein banker.

Next to him sat Yusef Rahim, chairman of BNC Internationale, the largest retail bank in the world.

Through similar eyewear as his fellow financier, the Saudi-born banker stared at Viktor with droopy, unblinking, calculating eyes.

Nathanial Brandenburg, chairman of Spancore Industries, and Roger Bannister, head of Bannister Media Holdings, took their places alongside the American delegation. Viktor knew the two Brits to be under David's thumb, friends since their days together in the Skull and Bones Society at Yale. After all, Bonesmen always saw themselves a step above the rest.

The most curious was Avi Ben-Gideon, the Israeli Prime Minister, seated only a chair's length from David. Ben-Gideon was a hawk, and yet an advocate of maintaining a powerful Iran — with a caveat of course.

The world must perceive a powerful tiger in a toothless old cat.

Viktor remembered the words of the prime minister. They made for great conversation at the last dinner meeting with the Persians.

Charles Saint-Michel, one of the twelve Undersecretary Generals to the United Nations, was also present. The man had placed himself between Ben-Gideon and Viktor. Saint-Michel was the head of the Internal Oversight Services. He would be vital in helping them leverage the UN.

The two men at each end of the semicircle were the first to rise. Cardinals Paulus Lubinski and Luigi Pierini were outwardly pious and inwardly ruthless. Their devotion to their faith and their pontiff made them, in Viktor's estimation, of limited use and highly dangerous. They all played their human roles so well they almost forgot what they really were and spared no pain to avoid the very mention of it, even among themselves. So powerful and yet to live in such fear of the humans; it was an irony that Viktor could not embrace.

He turned his attentions to the far entrance as the arched double doors parted and those gathered rose to greet the red-robed cleric who appeared soundlessly, gliding over the ornate stone floor etched with the Crescent Moon and Thirteen Stars of the Syndycate. The Secretariat of State to the Holy See, Cardinal Domenico Scarlatti entered the space. Viktor peered at David, knowing the ambitions that lured his heart. The hubris that once nearly destroyed the Syndycate lay hidden beneath a veneer of tolerance and control among her members. Their voices had fallen silent while David paved his ascent to power behind closed doors and secret meetings. He had requested them all here this night with his solution to the Persian question—what Viktor knew to be a first step to consolidating his power over them and their order of things. But his ambitions needed them. His ambitions needed Viktor. *Did David know of the Ilythiium?* Somewhere in David's intentions this night, Viktor would have his answers.

***

Richard sucked in deep, gradual breaths as Anja wrapped his torn right hand yet again. In an instant, he had lost it all and the next he lay cradled in her arms, the nightmare of what could have been replaced by someone who made life so worth living. He cleared a strand of hair from her ear with his good hand as she tenderly finished off the dressing.

28

"That's twice. I'm not doing a third," said Anja, with the usual twitch of her nose and a grateful smile for saving her life.

"We're a half hour behind," said Richard.

"Twenty-eight minutes, to be exact."

"The guard shifts in less than an hour." Richard rolled to his feet.

"I know, I set the schedule," said Anja.

They made their way in through the rooftop entrance just as they planned. The easiest way into a museum was always through the roof, especially when they had inside help to unlock the door. They moved along one of many interlaced hallways, past stained-glass panels now dark from the night. The museum was pitch black with the occasional light above an exit, just as it should have been.

Richard followed Anja until they came to a stop at a sealed doorway. She took out her touchscreen and a small case. The security grid reappeared on the screen and the red light on the door scanner suddenly went green. She turned the handle and the door gave way.

"Who loves you?"

Beyond the doorway, behind a faux wall panel, were a pair of square black felt bags and two cardboard tubes, each as tall as Richard, standing on their ends. It had been no easy task to plant these inside the building, or at least that's what Anja told him.

They toed their way down a stairwell, spiraling deeper into the bowels of this eerie place. A chill prickled his skin as if the walls themselves teemed and crawled somewhere beyond the darkness. They counted their paces and stopped. Richard shone the light. They found the marked door.

"You have the honors," said Anja.

"Here we go," said Richard. Turning the handle, they slipped past into the darkness beyond.

***

Viktor had always been wary of the wolf-eyed little man in the red zucchetto and fringed shawl. Cardinal Domenico Scarlatti was a squirmy little rat of the most treacherous sort, and Viktor's dislike for him was only outdone by his hate for David. He couldn't help but notice how the Cardinal had grown weary from the years within the labyrinths of this place, how the veneer of patience over him had thinned. Two of their thirteen had failed to show and those who would make their whereabouts known were already at work to seek them out. The Cardinal addressed the ten men seated before him.

"We are humbly obliged by your presence this evening, gentlemen. Mr. Huygens and Mr. Jawadi regret to inform they could not be in attendance this evening. I will serve to cast their votes as Convenor of the Council." Viktor knew full well they hadn't informed anyone of anything.

"If you will allow me, Secretariat, I would like to address the Council directly," interrupted David.

Scarlatti's smile pleased Viktor. Hardly a word spoken and the battle lines had been drawn.

"By all means, Mr. Bradford. As chairman, and a guest in our home, you carry the floor."

David was Deputy Chairman within the federated network of the Syndycate, but Scarlatti held the office of Convenor among the Council. The Deputy Chairman led the Council, but the Convenor held

30

standing veto. The Convenor had the authority to cast a deciding vote on any proposal brought before a Council session and speak for those not present. This evening he carried a voice for three. It was a fact lost on neither Viktor nor David.

"Good morning, gentlemen. Each of you is aware of our agreement this week with the Iranians and all its stipulations on sanctions relief and their nuclear program. As expected, the document has produced great distress in Washington, while the rest of the world has all but consented to our agreement. The president already received approval for ratification with the UN, thanks in no small part to Mr. Charles Saint-Michel, seated with us here this evening."

None round the semicircle gave even the slightest acknowledgment. There was no need to thank someone for something expected of his subservient role.

"I welcome you thus to Annex Number Five of our accord, a separate and stand-alone agreement between the Syndycate and the Republic. I present it to you for final ratification this evening."

Viktor laughed deep down inside. The Syndycate lived in terror of the humans and yet for so long they thought themselves above all others who shared this world with them, striking their own side agreements to the benefit of only those worthy enough to sit among their kind. These ten decrepit men, deciding the fate of nations, served only to confirm where his heart and loyalties lay. The Syndycate had not always shared a common ambition in the past, and that was a dangerous prospect for the man who now addressed their circle. A game of mortal chess had begun, and David Bradford had opened with the first move.

Viktor's eyes gleamed with the lust of his own ambitions while another gazed down upon them from the arrow slits cut out of the ancient dome high above. Viktor glanced up from his place in the semicircle, giving whoever was there a grin. His sixth sense was never wrong. He turned his attentions back to the ongoing discussions before him. He hadn't missed a nuance of the conversation, as he was certain none of them had either.

"So you give the Iranians a clear path to a *bomb*, and then corner public opinion with an agreement from the UN before we can stand up to the piece of shit document you put together. I underestimated you, David."

"Come now, Avi. There's no need for aggression. We all fight a common cause," said David, his words laced with cynicism.

"You threaten all we've done to create the peace we now have," retorted Avi, with an unwavering stare at David.

"You call Palestine and Gaza peace?" asked David with a near grin.

"The idiocy of your government with your incursions into Iraq; is that what you're referring to? Would we have seen an Arab Spring, a disintegration of Syria, or a birth of the Caliphate if not for you?"

"All has played in our favor and none have enjoyed it more than you," said David.

"You're a fool, David, who still trusts too much," said Avi.

"I trust no one," retorted David — rather sharply for a politician, Viktor thought. This wasn't the David he remembered. For some reason the Jew was getting under his skin; too easily, in fact.

"The balance of power is shifting, and we must shift with it to our favor," said David, this time with a more measured tone.

"Recall 1939 and what that meant for this Syndycate. We did things this world should have never seen. Exposed things they should have never known. He, too, stood before us and spoke of a new balance of power, much as you do now," said Cardinal Scarlatti from his high perch at center.

"You cannot compare the War to this. There are others who this very minute jostle against us, who shift the very order of things beneath our feet with eyes set on what we've fought to preserve for so long. I am proposing a new direction, one that maintains our advantage. One that most benefits you, Avi."

"You're right, David. There are many who now move against us. That is the very reason a shift in power as you propose is too great a risk for us to bear," said Yusef, the other banker beside Wilhelm. Viktor delighted in seeing David struggle with his own sweet-tongued argument turned against him by his supposed allies. Even the Saudi banker agreed with these naysayers.

"Our survival has always depended on our ability to adapt to change and lead at its forefront, as we must do now," said David.

"Neither your time here, nor what's become of us has dampened your hubris, David," said Wilhelm, the otherwise quiet Lichtenstein banker.

"Do not be fooled, any of you," boomed David with sudden force. "Greed and decadence have made you fearful and weak. A new power is forming, greater than in 1939. You speak of our secrets, and yet the Syndycate is whispered of in hidden corners and

33

closed boardrooms by those who should have no awareness of our existence."

"If that were true, the Sicaari would know of it," retorted Cardinal Scarlatti—a bit less sharply than before, Viktor noted.

"You all speak of hubris? There is no greater hubris than willful ignorance. The Russians and the Chinese are forming an alliance against all we represent. They are reshaping the future of Central Asia from the borders of Europe to the South Pacific, and Iran is the centerpiece to that strategy—a strategy that does not include us!"

"You will not fool the Iranians. At the first hint of treachery they will strike out with such speed and vengeance that none, not even this Syndycate will be able to stop them. Will any of you be able to control the Ayatollah, or their mullahs, or any of the other countless men who can so easily bring your plans to chaos?" retorted Avi, refusing to back down from David's onslaught.

"The treachery has already been committed. It is the fear under which you live. You betray yourself when it is us who should wield the power," said David, sounding like a father speaking to a petulant child. He rose from his place as the wall panel pulled away to reveal the same thirteen stars and crescent moon of the Syndycate etched into the stone floor beneath their feet.

"We will look to the Persian to preserve our interests in Tehran," said David, turning to each man seated at the semicircle, his eyes coming to rest upon Viktor. The coat of arms on the screen had been replaced with the blank stare and hardened face of an imperious man.

It was only a matter of time before intentions would make themselves known. Salil's absence this night was by David's design. But Christian Huygens's absence was still another matter, one that would become apparent soon enough.

"Salil Jawadi?! We will never allow him such power. The delusion that you hold power to command such over this Syndycate is a luxury lost on you, David. All here see your ambitions for what they are and stand united against what you've become," said Avi rising from his chair.

"Then may the vote be cast and the voice of this Council be final arbiter," said David, staring fiercely at Ben-Gideon as a wolf would a suckling fawn.

From behind the arrow slit high above the chamber, unwelcome eyes still watched. Viktor knew the intruder's attentions and loyalties lay with the wolf-eyed cleric at the center of the coven, observing with his steepled fingertips and pursed lips. The Convenor would decide their fate this evening, and Viktor found it in his heart to share its possibilities with their unwanted guest.

The men of the coven vanished. From his perch high above, Giovanni heard the clangor of steel and wails of agony. Someone else's memories flooded him with a glimpse into the past and the terrible possibilities of what was yet to come. Viktor glanced up to the dome and smiled as he toyed with the strings of Giovanni's mind.

Down below, each moved to cast their vote. Viktor turned his focus back to the wolf-eyed cleric staring at the image of the man upon the screen. He watched the cleric glance to the empty chairs at the end of the half-crescent circle before him, at the chair belonging to that man projected on the wall, the face of the hardened man they all knew as Salil Jawadi.

***

Through dark corridors, deep into the very penetralia of this forbidden place, past the security system and the guards, they'd come for their prize. Each would get a chance at a painting, but of the two, which one? Anja pulled her lucky Walking Liberty half dollar and gave Richard the luxury to choose. It was all part of the fun. Richard picked tails. Anja won. Of the two paintings, there was only one he really wanted. It felt good giving in to him. It was Richard's birthday, after all.

The game was simple. They split in opposite directions, each toward their painting. Whoever finished most masterfully and fastest would set the reward; the winner determined the after-prize. If Richard won, Anja hoped it would have something to do with her wrists and ankles. It was *his* birthday, after all.

Anja arrived first at her destination, with the cylinder and felt bag over her shoulder. She stood before the painting she selected, shining her black light onto its canvas. Her eyes dilated with euphoria as the black light revealed just what she wanted to see. There was almost no inpaint, nothing added to the canvas since its master first brought it to life. There were no lines, no glue, only the light luminescence she expected from the pigments of that century. The Caravaggio before her was a pure original and in near-perfect condition. Christ was the central figure, dead in the arms of his followers. The aged face of Mary

36

Magdalene, the loss of hope, was dark and raw. The *Deposition of Christ* was a punch in the mouth to the ideal of Caravaggio's day. With this piece, he cemented chiaroscuro as the style to be emulated. He was a ruffian, a brawler, a rock star.

"He was so fucking hot," Anja said under her breath.

"I heard that," whispered Richard into the microphone that connected them.

He moved along a corridor into another room, coming quietly to a stop just beyond a sphere of light. A crate laid open in the center of the space, the painting inside exposed for anyone to see. Richard needed no black light for this one. The *Blinding of Samson* was just as he'd seen her only four months earlier at the Städel Museum. His client had become impatient, so arrangements were made to bring her here. There was no greater satisfaction for Richard than stealing this Rembrandt from right under the noses of those he most despised – the Syndycate – and getting paid most handsomely for it.

Richard emerged from the darkness, gliding across the cold stone, his soft-soled shoes pressing into the Arabian rug in front of the crated canvas. He stood before her in his black bodysuit, in stark contrast to the light upon the canvas. Placing the black bag and cardboard cylinder onto the matted carpet beneath his feet, he got to work.

He trailed his finger along the edge of the painting. The frame was still firmly in place. He guessed it was from shortly after the War, and it hadn't been removed since. Precision and a light touch were needed; not a fleck could be removed from her canvas.

He pulled the painting toward him, resting its weight gently against the stone dais upon which the crate lay. One by one, he unclasped the holders behind the frame. Richard could see where the paint was weakest. Pressing the corners of the canvas gently, he split the oil away from the old wood, and the painting came free of the frame. The oil paint around the edges remained pristine and intact. He unsealed the cylinder and opened the black felt bag. In few quick motions, he lay the new stretcher bars flat on the floor before him. They matched the exact dimensions of the painting. Samson glared at him with his one eye.

"How goes it on your end?" asked Richard, adjusting his earpiece.

"Working the frame off the wall now," said Anja. She hadn't the heart to tell him she was practically done.

The chiaroscuro canvas now lay on the floor, its stretcher bars removed. From this angle, even in the darkness, she could appreciate how imposing this masterwork was. She slid it slowly into a casing of sorts: a collapsible, impact-resistant, rollable frame made of a lightweight aluminum polymer designed to the unique specifications of this individual painting. She rolled it up, slipped it into the cardboard tube, and clipped the lid shut. *It fit like a glove.* She stepped back in momentary admiration of her own work. Caravaggio's *Deposition* still hung on the wall as it always had, or so it seemed.

"Exquisite," she whispered. Suddenly the proximity detector rang in her ear.

Guards!

There was no way he could finish. The two Samsons agonized next to each other. Richard glanced back and forth between the canvases, sweat rolling down his cheeks. The open cylinder and tool kit lay sprawled on the floor, a little messier than usual. Footsteps approached. His creation was still halfway out of the frame; Rembrandt's original lay halfway in the polymer aluminum case.

Pain speared through his belly, up his spine. The urge was sudden, the need to survive. Primal instinct surged into his brain.

"Anja, I'm losing control."

"Richard, don't do it!"

The walls began to bend, and the deafening roar of the tempest filled his ears. The echoing footsteps, resounding ever louder, came to a sudden stop.

"You'll destroy everything, I beg you." Anja's voice was the last thing he remembered.

***

Giovanni stepped through the doorway from the main reception hall into Room XVI. Rarely did he come to the Pinacoteca in the dead of night. But rarely, too, did any of their guests. A crate stood empty before him on a rug spread in the center of the room. Men cautiously mounted the new acquisition onto the far wall as the curator directed the work.

"Piano, contra il muro," he shouted, clearly exasperated at their inability to get the painting hung just right.

Giovanni had come from the Hexagonal Room. The humidity there had been a bit off, higher than usual for the museum. His flashlight traced the walls, stopping at the Caravaggio. He gave the canvas a long look before parting the black curtain facing the courtyard,

39

scanning the edges of the glass double doors. He focused his beam on the door handle, bending down for a closer look.

"Is everything all right, Signore?" asked the curator, drawing Giovanni's mind back from what he just witnessed, where he'd just been.

"Yes, of course." Giovanni smiled beneath his upturned twirly mustache, concealing his weapon under his blue tunic. He had been in the Hexagonal Room, and in the blink of an eye he was now standing here. If there was ever an expression of contempt for the ineptitude of it all, it was the scowling face of the curator as he resumed pleading with his workmen.

Giovanni felt a sudden nauseous claustrophobia. *It happened again.* His senses defied logic. He was in that other room with that other painting and the curator, yes, Room XVI, and suddenly he was again here, at the balcony of the Hexagonal Room, aware of what was about to happen, before it happened.

He scanned the courtyard, his eyes stopping on the marble handrail. Droplets of thick red crimson confirmed his suspicions; the blood was already starting to coagulate. Whoever had bled here was long gone.

Giovanni rushed from the balcony, sealing the glass door shut behind him, moving as fast as he could toward the light at the end of the hall where he discovered the curator at work on this unusual painting, the curator he hadn't yet met, but somehow already had.

"Is all well, my children?"

Giovanni recognized another voice before he could turn around, as if time played games with him, one moment overlapping the next, jerking his awareness from one place to another, one second to the next. Maximilian Schmitthenner, otherwise known to the world as Pope Paul VII, shuffled into the room, still dressed in his pajamas. Cardinal Scarlatti, David, and Viktor followed, as the remainder of the guests, just moments before locked away in the papal libraries, now waited in the entrance hall to Room XVI. Giovanni glanced around at all those faces oblivious to the déjà vu that only he seemed to notice.

"I could not sleep and wished to greet our new arrival," said Pope Paul, as he quietly approached the massive painting resting against the wall, Cardinal Scarlatti and David at his side. "I meant the painting, of course," he added with a warm smile.

"Your Holiness, we will have it up immediately for you," insisted the curator.

"No need. I will enjoy it as is."

"Yes, Your Holiness." The curator bowed, stepping away.

Aged and bent from years of toil and service to the church, Pope Paul's body was mangled and slight, but his essence commanded. With a cold gaze, he studied Samson's fate at the hands of the Philistines.

"Delilah believed she could blind Samson to her complicity. I may be frail of body, but God makes me a billion strong," the pope murmured. He turned to David and settled his trembling hand on the American's shoulder. "My Secretariat has informed me of the decision…"

Giovanni was unable to capture the rest. The pope turned his attentions back to the Rembrandt and raised his voice. "The painting is beautiful. Thank you for this most gracious gift. I pray the subject matter does not imply your true intent. Else it may be you who finds himself hanging from Blackfriars Bridge," said the pope in a gentle tone. The last was not something Giovanni expected from the frail old man, or David for that matter.

Pope Paul blessed David with a sign of the cross before he turned from the painting and slowly shuffled his way out. The guests followed suit, leaving Viktor alone before the Rembrandt as its preparers returned to their duties of hanging the canvas.

So this was why Christian Huygens had not joined the Syndycate this evening.

Viktor approached the oiled linen. Huygens and Richard had other plans, plans for the painting that hung on this wall, or at least the one this forgery replaced. He studied her rich browns and cool tones, the intricate lines, and the bold brushstrokes splashing across the huge canvas. Viktor had a keen eye. He could spot a forgery down to the brush hairs dried into the paint, and this one was a fake.

Huygens was after the *Ilythiium* as well. *Did he believe its secrets were somehow in this painting?* Richard was its guardian. He would never give the secret of the *Ilythiium* over so willingly to any of the Syndycate. No, Richard's secret lay in another painting, one that only Richard could give him, and it would take more convincing than just money for Viktor to possess it.

Viktor clasped the small six-pointed benitoite stone, pulsing a bright cobalt blue, in his hand. He sensed the imperfections in the stone, and in the glitches of his memory. The stitching in the tapestry of time had somehow been torn and patched back together. Few Argylians would notice the effects of what only a Guija could do. Perhaps this Giovanni might sense it too, though unlikely he would know what was happening to him. He'd likely never met a Guija, until now.

Viktor couldn't help his satisfaction. His instinct once again proved him right. He held the burning stone tightly for none to see. He somehow knew to bring it this night, as if a glimpse into the future. Richard likely sensed the stone and didn't even know it. His own instinct would have been too much for him to subdue, the temptation too great to resist. Even one stone without its Armillary Sphere was powerful enough near a Guija to do things to time none could ever fathom. The last thing a Guija would want is to unravel and restitch time so messily. Even the smallest moment, the smallest tear in the grand tapestry could have profound, unintended effects. Time had indeed been altered. Richard had been here.

"Intriguing, isn't it?" asked Giovanni.

Viktor didn't turn from the image. "There's so much to capture the imagination. You always discover something new, something you didn't see before."

This Giovanni was too curious, a trait perhaps in Viktor's favor. A subtle suggestion of the mind might once again be in order; *perhaps for Giovanni, or perhaps for those he works for. The Sicaari will deal with Christian Huygens.*

Viktor let his instinct once again guide him. He sensed a new and sudden clarity. *Huygens was after the wrong painter.* How could Viktor not have known till now? His instinct whispered to him; the very stone in his hand amplified his vision. He would get Richard to do once again what only a Guija could do. Viktor was suddenly aware of her presence; the *Ilythiium* was near. He could see the long-ago memory, like an echo from the past whispering where Richard had hidden his secret—the unintended effects of even the smallest tear in the grand tapestry of time. The secrets Viktor sought were hidden within the brushstrokes and imagination of the great master of light. Indeed, Richard Robles would bring him Johan Vermeer.

"Gentlemen, if you'll excuse us," interrupted the curator.

"Have someone clean your floor. It's rather dirty," whispered Viktor so only Giovanni could hear him. At Giovanni's feet was a crimson drop of fresh blood. His head snapped back to the canvas, but Viktor was already gone.

***

Father Fleitas ran and ran, breath spewing into the cold, wet night. He stumbled and crashed through brush and thicket; oblivious to where he started or how long his legs had pushed him. He clenched his side to keep his liver from bursting out of his skin. The terror wouldn't let him look back.

I need a drink. My throat is burning.

His eyes watered, his nose was dry; he'd lost his bottle. He plunged headlong through trees, tripping head first, into the foliage. Knees and hands dove into clammy mud and wet leaves. Thorns and branches pricked and scratched his face. He tried to get up when he saw a shadow cast on the ground before him. Someone—or something—stood behind him. He glanced back and warmth released from between his legs. Beneath the overhanging branches, *it* stood. Darkness stared at him from beneath black cloak and veil. Across an impossible distance, a hand, a long and slender tendril with translucent, acicular fingernails,

44

streaked out and wrapped itself around his throat, cutting off the scream before he could form it. Blackness where a face should have been approached him.

"Where is it?" hissed a serpent voice from behind the black cloth, as a squeezing pain seized his chest.

Elsewhere, a silhouette by a window stared out over the gardens. The Basilica's dome stood prominently in the foreground. The symbol of Catholic power reached into the sky as a tempest roared through his thoughts. The cardinals sat waiting in his chamber, but Pope Paul bade his time at the window.

"What word have we of Francisco?" asked the pope in his gravelly whisper.

"Father Fleitas has been in his study for three days," said Cardinal Scarlatti.

"Could David Bradford be the one written of?" asked Scarlatti as he thumbed his sleeve, consumed with the weight of what the Syndycate had decided.

"You needn't worry about the American. But Salil Jawadi, he is another matter."

Pope Paul had heard the plans of ambitious men many times before. He considered the distant lightning beyond the cupola of Saint Peter's. He considered the doubt he felt in his heart and the clarity of thought at what must be done.

"Summon me Father Fleitas. I will have words with him. And summon the Sicaari," ordered Pope Paul, as he shuffled over to his small cot and laid his head down to rest, his pupils dilating black as he gazed up at the wood rafters.

The corridors of the Vatican lay silent as the one of the black cloak and veil found her way in. The sharp tendrils that had closed around the priest's throat slowly turned the knob to a door. The candle wicks faltered as she glided through the desolate bedchamber of Father Francisco Fleitas, her shadow casting itself upon the parchment atop the writing desk. In the end, Father Fleitas could not control his bladder, or his tongue. He gave away exactly what she was after, the whereabouts to what her master tasked of her. Her long-nailed, desiccated fingers reached across the desk. A black sleeve swept over its surface as the parchment beneath her robes vanished. The lantern by the window flickered, pitching the room into blackness. The one of the black cloak and veil vanished, and with her, the *Fourth Secret of Fatima.*

II

NEPTUNE'S TRIDENT

March was always such a beautiful time to visit Washington, D.C.. Vadim loved the cool breeze of the city blowing the last breaths of winter and the scent of the coming spring. This was a quick trip and then back home. The *Nowruz* holiday was not far off, and he looked forward to seeing his wife and girls again after being away for so long. The airlines had just resumed direct flights between Washington and Tehran, a result of the recent accord. Vadim appreciated the added convenience.

The gray turtleneck felt comfortable this morning. His black wingtip shoes snugged his feet. The brown leather briefcase in his hand was as polished as the gray-striped, single-breasted suit was refined. The clothes helped him blend in with the D.C. style. He could have been an employee at any one of the agencies inside the Triangle.

He kind of liked the clean-shaven look in the mirror. His wife would be shocked by how young it made him appear. The briefcase strained the muscles in his arm and shoulder as he stepped off the curb onto the crosswalk. He'd carried her twenty-kilo weight over three kilometers. He didn't ever remember his rucksack being this heavy during his training with the Revolutionary Guard. Better to think of the burn in his shoulder than of his handler this morning.

Vadim walked past the busy crowd. Some were on their cell phones, while others focused on their path, counting the steps to their cubicles. Others still chased taxis or, like him, obsessed over their must-have morning coffee.

He held the door for a memorable young woman at the coffee shop and lost his place in line. Some things he just couldn't shake, like his sense of Persian chivalry, but no one would notice that. The young woman certainly hadn't. He ordered his latte and waited patiently by the counter for his name. He didn't need to make a show of it. He'd seen his contact at the corner table by the window with his open laptop and cup of coffee.

"Roberto!" called the barista. Vadim raised a finger and snatched his cup off the counter.

He walked on over to the rear of the shop and sat down in front of the man with the laptop, placing the heavy case beneath the table between his knees. Andrei Birkin had been waiting for him for some time.

"Could we make this any more obvious?" asked Vadim in smooth Russian.

"Don't worry, if they knew what's in that case, you wouldn't have laid a foot at Reagan," said Andrei, taking a sip of his coffee. Vadim at least respected a man comfortable enough to sip coffee with a nuclear bomb nestled between his thighs.

Andrei Birkin was tall, blond, fit, self-assured, and well connected. His thin frame and features made him raise eyebrows and turn heads—and not only of the female persuasion. His contemporaries in the American intelligence services had already noticed him. He was the youngest director to ever serve with the Russian Foreign Intelligence Services (SVR) in Washington. He worked out of the Russian embassy as the head of operations reporting to the Director

General in Moscow. All the spooks had their eyes and ears on him. No wonder Vadim wanted to pass on this assignment.

"The last thing I wanted was to be here having coffee with you. Don't get me wrong, I love this city, and you're a great guy, but I want to know why Viktor pulls me out into the open like this."

"The eyes on you have no idea who you are. Besides, your shadow is a personal friend. I asked her to give you some space, let you enjoy the city for the day. The National Gallery is a good place to go, if you haven't been. They'll be putting on a new exhibit in the next few weeks. Too bad you won't be here to see it. A young man, his name is Guillermo. He'll be waiting for you there. You will leave him the briefcase. I have to get to the embassy, so I have to cut this short."

Andrei took a sip of his coffee as he turned the page of his morning paper.

"Viktor has one more request of you, so enjoy your coffee. It's freezing where you're going," said Andrei with a smile.

Vadim wished he could wipe it from his face.

***

It was a winter-gray night like so many before on the Murmansk Peninsula. The four men in their crisp, blue uniforms and coats were not here by chance; another had sent them. From far away, he had requested them, and they answered his call of duty. Captain Dmitri Borei strode briskly through the long dark corridor with his two commanders and lieutenant. The gold stripes on their jacket sleeves clearly marked their ranks. The rhythmic echo of their footfalls pounded in his ears. From beneath the brim of his black hat bearing the gold emblem of the Russian Navy, Dmitri focused on the steel door at the end of the hallway. Sweat beaded above his brow. Square-jawed and bent-nosed, he looked more like a mariner than an officer. Dmitri came from the easternmost parts of Russia, along Kamchatka's coast, but one would have thought him from deep in the Caucus Mountains instead.

Dragging from his cigarette, he stared out into the night through the ice crystals forming around the edges of the window pane, wondering how memory could so warp with the passage of time. The perimeter lights to the Nerpichya Naval Base on the Zapadnaya Litsa River were out. Not a guard patrolled the sea wall leading to the three finger piers. The dry dock was desolate. Only the skeletal remains of a frigate laid up for repairs stood on its pylons. He strained to forget old friends, now only ghosts, bearing the heavy pain in his jaw from the sadness he must swallow. These men could never see weakness.

The frost forming on the window reminded him of the fireside warmth of Christmas nights so long ago. Soft laughter filled his heart again. His boy Sasha clung to his mother's neck, curly rust-blond hair and her same big blue eyes shining in the firelight. The old laughter faded with the exhale of his cigarette. The memory was replaced by the dank wetness and freezing cold within these walls. With renewed resolve he flicked the butt onto the floor, crushing the embers underfoot. He pushed past the door and stepped out into the wind, his three officers following right behind him.

Bushov had already been here an hour longer than he wanted, standing watch behind the frosted glass of his tugboat cabin, shielded from the cold, whipping wind. He puffed warm air onto his gloved hands to ease the tremors beneath his bundled windbreaker. As the captain to the *Europa,* one of four tugboats assigned to this place, he knew not to ask too many questions. This wasn't the first time he'd been asked to pull a ship out this late at night. But it'd been a long time since he serviced one of these. He was awed by her massive size. The tug looked like a tiny seahorse latched onto a sea monster's back.

He waited for the signal from the other tugboat at the far end, maneuvering the *Europa* with a slight thrust to port and then to starboard to keep her place against the current. Bushov was cold and wet, and hungry, and not up for the duties of the Northern Fleet this evening. He took a swig of the vodka and a chunk of the fatty white *salo* by the telegraph wheel and waited.

Bushov lived in Zaozyorsk; a gray place, forbidden to outsiders, a place where everybody knew everyone else's dirty gossip. His wife left him for a younger sailor on another one of the tugboats, and he would be damned if he'd lock himself down again with one of the harpies from this dreary town. Now it was just him, his collie, and his boat, and he was going to make sure it stayed that way. The less he dealt with the likes of everyone else, the better.

A white strobe flickered in the distance as the fog began to lick its tendrils over the water. First one, then another—two flashes had been the signal. He revved his engines and slowly pressed the throttle forward as the little tugboat lurched toward her duties and the looming structure ahead.

***

Dmitri's eyes had long adjusted to the darkness. The taste of the cold night made him only hunger more for that next cigarette. He stopped to listen as the mist crawled over the ominous shadow before them that jutted forth from the sea. Her rounded upper hull and large deck house towered over them like a sentry in the night. It had been eight years since their last patrol, and far too long since he laid eyes on her — far too long, indeed. Yet, there she stood, once again ready for him to command.

Dmitri forged ahead, dead set on the walkway at the far end of the finger pier. Their only chance lay at the other end of that walkway. The lieutenant looked back and around for anyone unexpected. An uninformed guard might prove costly to them — and the guard.

Meanwhile, a few miles southeast of the naval base, Admiral Vasily Nygev sat at his desk, the lamplight and a glass of vodka to keep him company. As the commander of the entire Northern Fleet, he dealt with a flotilla falling apart at the strakes without the resources or manpower to keep up with the changing times. The world he once knew had been a much safer place.

As a young officer at the height of Soviet naval power, he rose quickly up the ranks, first with the Black Sea Fleet and then north in Murmansk. He lived through the catastrophe of the crumbling of the Wall, watching the events from his home in Severomorsk. He was a relic of another time, as outdated as the ships of his rusting fleet. He remembered that night the Berlin Wall fell, the impotence with which he watched those moments. It was a night much like this one.

He downed a swig of liquid fire from his shot glass and poured himself another. He'd suffered the bureaucrats and their cutbacks, the oligarchs and their new money, these so-called men of peace and their economic treaties. They created a new Russia for themselves, one where men like him had no place. He kicked back another swig, this time to the portrait of the proud officer hanging on the wall.

Gone were the days of old glory on the Barents Sea. Instead, he'd been left with his ships to rust in the cold and drown in the overflow of nuclear waste; the only reminder of his once-great armada was the occasional accident that leaked out for the world to read about. He'd been given orders; the daily mishaps, the leaking fuel rods, the cracking containment chambers, the slow quiet stuff, he obscured from the world's view. After all, he was an officer, and he did as he was told. Fire burned down his throat as he poured himself another.

Nygev stared at the file folder open before his desk and nervously rolled the felt pen between his fingers when the rap of knuckles on wood sounded at the door.

"Enter," he bellowed, as a junior lieutenant opened the door.

He stood before Nygev at rigid attention. He was so young, so smooth of skin, so young. If only to be that way again, with so much time to make it right. The young man looked away after a few seconds of Nygev's stare.

Nygev signed his name to the order with a decisive stroke, closed the file folder quickly, and handed it back to the junior officer. With a crisp salute and bow, the young man stepped out and shut the door behind him. Nygev had deeply instilled the old protocol in his adjutants. If he only stayed a moment longer, perhaps peeked into that order, demanded of him what he had done. Maybe it would have been easier if the 12th Directorate knew what Viktor had commanded and what he had agreed to: the theft of a Typhoon-class submarine. Perhaps the inevitable consequences would have been swifter and less painful.

Nygev rose from his desk and walked to the window. The cruisers *Piotr Veliky* and *Ustinov* stood at their pier, ready for their orders. It was unfortunate that this night, the stroke of his pen had not been for them. But soon it would be. Soon the whole of the Northern Fleet would be called upon again to take up the fight, and they would be ready. By God and Mother Russia, they would be ready.

***

Vadim had waited for hours in this frozen wasteland. He should have known Viktor would do this to him, send him to the most forsaken place on the planet. Washington, D.C., was supposed to be the last assignment. He delivered the package to that Russian and done just as he was told, handing the briefcase to that young man at that museum, the one named Guillermo.

It seemed like Andrei had enjoyed telling him about this last one, this last assignment before Viktor promised he could go home. How he wished a well-

54

placed blade would slice the smug smile from that Russian's face. If Vadim could only get close enough to Viktor, he might place one there, too. But he wished to see his wife more, and this was the price he paid for a life that had chosen him more than he'd chosen it. Soon he would be home and done with all this, and Viktor or any others of their cadre would never find him again.

From the high ground on the frosty hillside, he had a clear view of the naval base, its three piers and dry dock with her buildings in their state of neglectful disrepair. The Northern Fleet couldn't fix a few buildings or have a few guards on duty, it seemed. The base stood in total desolation.

Vadim traveled north from Moscow. He made sure to stay out of notice of any crossing his path. He spoke to no one, traveling only by car, sleeping in remote hotels when the luxury allowed itself. He paid all in cash and stayed away from mass transport. The ways into Murmansk were treacherous.

He crouched just inside the rusting perimeter fence of the naval base. Moored at the nearest pier was the *Donsky.* She was Russia's most advanced Typhoon-class submarine and supposedly the only one of her type left in active service. He heard rumors at the Ministry of Defense of two more returning to duty. Until now, those had just been rumors.

His attention turned to the other vessel sitting at the third pier. She was of the same size and configuration, a Typhoon like the *Donsky.* His infrared night goggles zoomed in on her port bow. The intelligence had been correct. He slowly scanned across the anechoic rubber tiles on her outer hull, used to dull passive sonar detection. The Russians must have revived one of the five submarines decommissioned after the fall of the Soviet Union.

But which one?

He adjusted his goggles. The lenses captured the images. Enhancing the resolution, Vadim brought up the traces of what he'd been looking for. He found her hull numbers. She was the TK-12, the *Simbirsk*. He zoomed out from the hull to get his bearings. Still, there were no guards and no movement from anywhere except the Navy's blue-crossed white flag whipping high above the nearest building. The *Simbirsk* was the same sub that collided with the *HMS Splendid* back in 1991. According to defense ministry records, the vessel had been scrapped at *Zvezdochka* shipyards in 2007.

Then how was she here?

Interested parties would pay good money to know. Viktor wouldn't be the only one; Tehran might also have an interest. But these thoughts mattered not. He was done with this. His family mattered more than any money such information might bring. He must convince himself of this. Ambitions turned into obsessions, and obsessions were their jailers, as much for Viktor as for Vadim. He couldn't blame Viktor or anyone, only himself. He carefully made his way down the hillside to the open ground below, toward the monster at the far end of the docks.

***

The fog rolled in over the river's surface and blanketed the pier. Only the deck house now jutted above the white mist covering the naval base. A spotlight shot through the dark and silhouetted the vessel. Dmitri was advancing to the gangway when a man's shape suddenly emerged from the shadows, followed by two others in trench coats. The outlines of AK-47's checked Dmitri's advance. His officers went for their pistols.

"*Nyet*," Dmitri commanded. A man in a swishing trench coat approached, the light revealing his face when he was an arm's length away.

"Misha Andreev," said Dmitri, relaxing. Misha Andreev had been Dmitri's executive officer on his last deployment and weapons officer on their last tour aboard the *TK-12*. This time he would once again resume his duties as XO to the captain.

"We have completed departure protocol. The crew is at station, awaiting your orders, sir," saluted the gaunt-faced man. "Then let's be on with it," said Dmitri.

Without returning the salute, he motioned Misha up the gangway as the other officers followed suit. He took a last look back down the pier and into the darkness behind him.

***

Vadim watched the four men disappear into the rolling mist, everything once again silent. They had made no effort to conceal their arrival. They moved past him so close he could smell their aftershave. He recognized the lead officer. The reports, the rumors were true. Dmitri had been released from Kolyma military prison.

How would Viktor have known to order Vadim here? Either Viktor was after the Typhoon or he knew someone else was.

Vadim crept across the open ground, waiting for a shout or a rifle crack. Loping into a full gait, he sprung with all his strength off the pier's edge into the air as far as his legs would take him, crashing onto cold steel with a clang that echoed through the bow of the ship.

The climbing putty worked. Like a tiny insect, his hands and knees stuck onto the side of her massive tubular hull, nearly six-hundred feet long and seventy-five feet wide. He hung above the water line as the hull plates above him curved out of sight. He reminded himself of his daughter waiting for him back home. He gathered himself and climbed until he lay a speck atop the deck.

As he rose to his elbows and knees, somewhere across the base in the near foothills an infrared lens zeroed in on him with a crosshair and distance readout. From over a kilometer away, the shrouded figure watched Vadim make his way along the bow of the vessel.

***

Bushov approached the Typhoon as he had hundreds of times before, angling in to hook the line to the mooring cleats. The flashing strobe from the other tugboat at the bow signaled maneuver and speed. His own crew stood with lines and hooks ready to attach to the giant hull, as two men atop the submarine appeared, throwing the heavy ropes to them that would tie the tug to stern.

Where are the rest of them?

Usually there were eight or so submariners at each end working the decks just before departure. Strangely, he noted no more than two.

Poor bastards. The Navy couldn't even afford a proper crew.

His boatswain signaled attachment to the *Simbirsk* as their seaman was still working to lock in his end. Bushov waited, and the strobe flashed again. *Release from the moorings, aft one-quarter*, read Bushov, his Morse a little rusty. He looked back as the seaman gave the ready signal.

About time.

He placed the engines in reverse and pushed the throttle forward one-quarter. The boat dug into the water as the props churned hard beneath her. The Typhoon began to pull away from the pier.

***

Still in his uniform, dress shirt undone, Admiral Nygev held the portrait in one hand and a glass of vodka in the other. He stared at the image in the frame; he could see his own glossy-eyed reflection faintly in the glass. An officer's life was abstinence from loved ones. He paid a heavy price for a country that had all but forgotten him.

He put the frame back onto the shelf over the fireplace, placed the already-empty glass next to their picture, and took out the Makarov pistol from his hip holster. He looked at it for a long moment before turning the barrel to his face, unafraid of the fingertip resting comfortably over the trigger.

How much would it hurt?

He hesitated. He placed the pistol down at the edge of his desk and began to undress.

How quick would it really be?

Across a corridor, past a sealed door, a bright overhead lamp reflected off the bathroom mirror as a fine hand placed a folded, white towel with soap and aftershave next to the sink. Nygev would be there soon to soothe body and mind in the solitude of his nightly hot shower. Viktor's orders had been explicit; Nygev was not to see another sunrise. The figure loomed large against the tiled wall as her hand reached up, her black coat sleeve pulling back to reveal the edge of a stylized tattoo in the form of a lion, scripted in a forgotten language up the length of her forearm. The Hashishin understood his death must be appropriate to the circumstances. The rest had been left to her creativity. She quietly undid the showerhead and went to work on her craft.

***

Vadim hid against the edge of the submarine's giant conning tower, standing on steel the length of almost two soccer fields. The men, who cleared the deck, had not seen him. He could hear the growl of the tugboats somewhere out in the fog and could feel the slow movement beneath his feet as the giant hull distanced itself from the dock.

Twenty submarine-launched ballistic missiles, over two hundred nuclear warheads, each capable of traveling almost halfway around the world, delivering an explosive yield five thousand times that of Hiroshima, stood in the belly of this thing.

He dropped down at the base of the deck house, pulling a black, plastic-encased device from his pack. He peeled away the bottom and stuck the KGAN satellite terminal to a deck tile as he powered up its command and control touch screen. He activated the asymmetric cryptographer and inserted a flash drive into its side. With an almost instant satellite link, the upload bar began to track the progress of a file transfer. He'd been given the device with specific instructions to upload the data he collected to the Kandinsky Global Area Network system and do so only from the vessel itself. He needn't ask why the peculiar request. Now it all made sense to Vadim. The data transfer was more than just what he collected here. Viktor wanted to know the whereabouts of this vessel and this device would assure that. The data of course was meant for Viktor alone but there was no way Vadim could allow that. He thought of his daughter, that beautiful toothless smile and that soft coo when she was but a baby. How much he loved her, he could never explain. He should have never gone to see the Russian in D.C. He should have never accepted this. He should have never come here. But it was too late for regret.

On a second interface, a configuration panel appeared as his fingers typed commands he never should have entered, meant for someone who never should have seen this, because of something someone should have never done. *His daughter will not live in world such as this.*

Vadim looked back; the boat was now lengths away from the pier, the gap impossibly far to jump across. He would brave the freezing waters for his little girl. He set his sights on the shore, when dark blots splattered against the screen. What had been his chest was suddenly a gaping hole, spewing glutinous blood. A second hole appeared, blasting bits of flesh against his goggles. This time, the shell knocked him back onto the anechoic deck plates. His eyes began to fill red with blood. His vision was leaving him. The cold was taking over, his body going numb.

Vadim reached out, fingers barely at the keyboard. Anguish tasted of blood and regret. He would never see her again, his little girl. The one who waited for him for so long would never know everything he had ever done. Everything had been for her.

From across the base, on the crest of a small mountain, the shrouded figure pulled away from the rifle-mounted scope. Crystal-gray eyes looked on from beneath hooded fatigues. The sniper considered his hit. He was disappointed in himself. It had taken two shots. That really bothered him. The dead man far below lay crumpled, a tiny speck on that cold steel deck, while the tugboats slowly turned the *Simbirsk* toward the mouth of the *Zapadnaya Litsa* River.

III

NEW FRIENDS, OLD ACQUAINTANCES

Every morning, Danny came up with a new game. This morning, he buzzed through the hallway and crashed into Richard like a kamikaze pilot as he flew from room to room. All his friends liked computer games, but Danny liked to dream instead that he was a great adventurer on a quest to a far-off land or a pirate in search of long-lost treasure. Richard just grinned. Danny definitely got that from him.

This morning he was the Red Baron. The housekeeper, Clara, dreaded the Red Baron, chasing Danny around the house, picking up after him. She tried to duck out of the way as he flew, arms apart, right at her. The buzzing sound should have prepared her for the machine-gunner spittle from his mouth. She probably would have preferred bullets to the saliva spraying in her eye, Richard thought, as she wiped her face and Danny disappeared around the corner.

Richard stood at the full-length mirror as he adjusted his lavender-striped tie. He liked getting that perfect, V-shaped knot. He pulled the tongue in, over, and through, tightening it snugly. Gingerly, he finished it off. His right hand still throbbed beneath a fresh bandage.

The pain was a constant reminder of the night at the Pinacoteca. He had created an orb of sanctuary, a bubble in the way this human flesh perceived time. To a Guija an orb of sanctuary was a way to hide within the passing current of time itself, but only for an instant and with terrible effects on the human flesh he now inhabited. But this orb of sanctuary had been especially powerful, and that frightened Richard. There was no way of knowing what such a thing could do to their continuum, the reality he and Anja had created for themselves. Something so simple could have such dire and unintended effects. Richard looked around the room. Everything was still as he remembered. Anja hadn't said a word since their return and that perhaps was strangest of all. Time dysplasia was forbidden. It was the promise they made for each other, and for Danny, long ago.

No more games with the Syndycate, Richard swore to himself. *This stunt at the Vatican was the last one!*

The sound of crashing plates stopped his musing. His sense of adventure, Danny got from him, but his streak of mischief, *definitely his mother.*

The reflection of the painting hanging on the wall behind him caught his eye in the mirror. Richard turned to *The Storm on the Sea of Galilee*. The Stranger stared at him as he always did from the edge of the tiny fishing boat caught in a tempest.

"Laugh all you want; nothing a few brush strokes won't fix," said Richard, taking a brush from a jar by the night table and inching it close to the canvas.

Richard swore the Stranger frowned at him, almost. He smirked back, dropping the brush into the jar, and left the room for the menace in the kitchen.

"Once again the Baron goes down," said Richard, scooping up Danny with his good hand as Danny squealed with joy. "What do you think you're doing destroying this house?"

"Dad, I'm in a dogfight."

Richard looked up at Clara with sympathy for her woe. Clara scowled at the boy from behind the kitchen counter. Danny made a mess of her cleaning duties. She'd have to stay at least an extra hour this morning.

"*Señor Ricardo, Daniel es incorregible.*"

"*Mil disculpas, Doña Clara,*" said Richard in perfect Spanish, as he placed Danny back on his feet and gave him a menacing look.

"I missed you, Dad."

"Destroy the kitchen to get some attention, is that it? Maybe you have a crush on Doña Clara."

Clara laughed. Danny gagged. Clara stopped laughing.

In her late forties, with dark eyes and sharp features, she said her looks made it harder to find house-cleaning jobs around town. Thank God for Anja. His wife had picked the help. That's how confident she was in herself. And besides, if he ever even thought about any funny business, Anja would have his balls skewered on a frying pan, she so lovingly whispered in his ear the first night they hired Clara, and Richard most definitely believed it.

"Let's go, Danny," said the tall redhead with long legs, standing at the front door in high heels and a Monday-morning power suit. Anja smiled at him. Richard still couldn't take his eyes off her after all these years.

"Time for school."

Not far off, on the campus of Georgetown University, young men and women in basketball jerseys, carrying signs and emblems of the great bulldog and their slogan *Hoya Saxa*, bustled and brayed as they made their way to the gymnasium or the dorm rooms. It was the opening day of March Madness.

The campus was wild this morning, and no one was going to class—except, of course, for Mike Freeman and the rest of the students taking Middle East: A Geopolitical Analysis.

What did geopolitics have to do with an engineering degree anyway?

A lot, Professor Robles would say. There was a lot Mike would like to say to Professor Robles right about now. He had scheduled a midterm exam on the first day of March Madness. Sitting beneath the clock tower, surrounded by the thick gray walls and arches of Healy Hall, Mike Freeman and the other students waited at their desks for their professor who was, as usual, late. Mike could barely get out of bed this morning from the headache and the debauchery of the night prior, and this morning the party went on without him.

A text popped up on his phone.

Hoya Saxa. Good luck on your test, sorry not sorry.

A picture of his buddy—wide-eyed, tongue out, and wearing a Hoya game jersey, a beer in one hand and Melanie Ann's perfectly formed boobies in the other—smiled at him from his phone. This struggle was real. The heavy stones and aging window panes were a prison this morning. Sure, he could leave—if he wanted to fail the class and lose his internship at the NMIC, the National Maritime Intelligence Center. How he hated responsibility on perfect days like today that should be nothing but beer, babes, and basketball.

The prof strode in briskly, looking relaxed. They all turned to him with a mix of gloom and resentment. Mike could have sworn the cynical bastard was trying not to laugh.

He's actually laughing at us.

"So, the events leading to the American Hostage Crisis in Iran," said Professor Robles, breaking into a lecture without even a good morning.

"Sir, aren't we taking a test?" asked Janine, the raven-haired girl who sat at the front.

Richard smiled and kept on lecturing. Mike Freeman hated himself. Even now, after the bastard scheduled the test on opening day, the guy had a way about him that Mike hated to love.

"Three days before, on November 1, 1979, Prime Minister Mehdi Bazargan met with US National Security Advisor Zbigniew Brzezinski—I can never get that name right—in Algiers. You taking notes?" asked Richard, looking right at Mike.

"Iranian television finds out about it. The Ayatollah is outraged, condemns the meeting, fires Mehdi, and three days later, students, like yourselves—except they didn't care about March Madness—take sixty-six American hostages. Nobody get any ideas, alright?"

"We take no prisoners," said Mike, from his perch at the back of the room.

"No, you do not, Mr. Freeman. Melanie Ann can certainly vouch for that, yes sir, she can," said Richard, struggling to keep a straight face.

How'd he know about Melanie Ann?

"I have my sources, in case you're wondering," said Richard as he opened and closed his bandaged right hand. "Fourteen were released, and what followed was the longest-standing hostage crisis in American history, culminating with the failed Operation Eagle Claw that left eight servicemen dead. Finally, after 444 days, the Algiers Accord was signed just minutes after Ronald Reagan was sworn into office. The moral of the story: read between the lines."

"Just put one between my eyes, please," whispered Mike, low enough that no one could hear except the political science major who sat next to him.

"When it comes to foreign relations between the US and Middle East, conspiracy and intrigue abound, as do the endless sands of the Persian desert. God, that's poetic," said Richard as he looked up at the wall clock.

It was only five minutes into class and things could look no direr for Mike.

"See you all next Tuesday," Richard tossed his book onto the desk. The class was silent, momentarily shocked at the announcement.

Leaving no time to deliberate or ask questions, Mike was the first one out the door. He rushed headlong around the corner, out the front of the building and onto the campus grounds with a giant leap, not setting a single foot on the steps of Healy Hall.

Richard watched him go from the window out the campus gate as fast as his legs would take him. He couldn't blame the kid. If he were his age, he'd run that fast after Melanie Ann, too. Perhaps the night at the Pinacoteca hadn't changed a thing after all. If that young man were any indication, reality and time were exactly as they should be. Richard exhaled with relief as he squeezed his right hand to ease the pang that once again pulsed down his arm.

***

Karl Downing sat at his desk with a fresh pot of black coffee brewing in the corner and a hot cup in hand. It was a gray, overcast morning. He looked out past the thick glass window to the sprawling buildings, parking lots, and wooded hills beyond. He watched the long chain of slow-moving congestion that made up the Baltimore-Washington Parkway's morning rush hour and sipped his coffee. Boy, was he glad he wasn't in that mix.

Karl had served as Deputy Director to the National Security Agency for the past two years, having served as Executive Director for four years before that. As the largest signals-collection agency in the world, the NSA was an around-the-clock operation tracking everything from low-level radio emissions and telephone chatter to multispectral photography, satellite imagery, microwave communications, Internet, and e-mail — just to name a few. Crypto City — insiders' loving nickname for the sprawling NSA campus — was always on, taking everything in and never letting anything out. That is, until one of their own decided to take it upon himself to disclose most everything they did. The fact the world knew the names of their programs and their dirty laundry didn't bother Karl so much. It was *how* they knew that was the problem. It made tracking targets that much more difficult, and the targets who paid attention, the ones who adapted their ways, that much more dangerous. This morning he was reading a report on some of the president's proposed changes to their data collection processes and efforts.

Just more red-tape bullshit.

None of it would change anything at the NSA, anyway, and that was a good thing. They'd keep up their collection efforts and practices as they always had. In fact, the congressional committees charged with their funding and oversight would appropriate more monies to his agency under the auspices of cleaning it up. Of course, they'd leave him to decide what the job of *cleaning it up* might look like. Yes indeed, sometimes red-tape bullshit was a good thing after all.

This morning, he savored his black coffee with a touch of sugar, one pack of Florida Crystals organic, and a quarter slice of lemon. A simple frame stood atop his desk, holding the images of two handsome teenage boys, a classy blonde with a warm smile, and a yellow Lab named Appleton. Next to her was a younger, less stressed, healthier, and happier version of the man who now sat in the leather, high-backed chair.

Karl grew up in Lincoln, Nebraska, with dreams of joining the military. Fresh out of high school, he enlisted in the Air Force, where he found himself assigned as a tail gunner to the 72nd Strategic Air Wing out of Andersen Air Force Base. For all that happened since then, he was still known around these halls as the guy credited with one of only two MIG-21's shot down over Hanoi by a B-52 tail gunner.

The things they found interesting in Crypto City.

Those were memories he would rather not think about, especially during these rare moments of peace and quiet. But for some reason, they came calling this morning. A knock at the door startled him from his reverie.

"Enter," called Karl, as the polished, beech wood door slowly opened.

Brian Reese, Senior Operations Officer at the National Security Operations Center, entered the room. Unlike Karl, who dressed every morning for work in a black, blue, or gray flannel suit, Brian was more laid back. In slacks and loafers, with the sleeves of his button-down shirt rolled up, he looked the part of the overworked and underpaid intelligence officer. Behind him, two more gentlemen entered the room, both of whom Karl had never met before.

The first was dressed in the impeccable blues of the US Navy. He wore the silver leaves and three yellow sleeve stripes of a naval commander. The second, in khakis and dress shirt similar to Brian (only much thinner and younger), wore thin-rimmed bifocals and stood uneasily before Karl. Badges hung from their necks, with the large, red letters "PV" stamped across them. Each had a file folder in hand.

"Should I break out the antacids?" asked Karl, looking at his watch. Not even 8:00 AM and he already had unknown visitors to his office. That rarely boded well, especially on a Monday morning. "Boy, how I miss the weekend already."

"Good morning, Karl," said Brian, as he closed the door behind him.

"I guess I don't need to tell ya to have a seat. Might as well make yourselves at home."

"Thank you, sir," said the commander, as he approached one of two leather chairs, the thin young man taking the other. Brian pulled up a third chair

71

from the small conference table at the other corner of the office.

"Karl, this is Commander Robert Madison from the Office of Naval Intelligence, liaison to Central Security Services," said Brian.

"That's quite a job description, commander."

"Thank you, sir."

"This is Jonathan Fraker from Special Collection Services," said Brian, turning to the thin, bespectacled gentleman.

"Now I know something's really wrong when they let SCS out of the basement."

"It's good to get out every once in a while, sir," Jonathan said, relaxing.

"At least you have a sense of humor about it," said Karl.

"It's not hard when I have so much material to work with."

"I would offer you some coffee, but I want it all for myself this morning. What can I do for you gentlemen?"

"Last night we received a report from one of our field operatives at the Yulin Naval Base in Hainan," said Brian.

So that was the reason for the visit.

"The underground submarine facility?" Karl asked.

"Yes, sir. He's tracking the development of the new 096 Tang-class submarine. Two weeks ago he intercepted a high-level, encrypted communiqué regarding an incoming shipment of plumbing hardware for the base's urinal facilities."

"Excuse me?"

"We thought the same thing when we deciphered and translated the text." Jonathan adjusted his black-rimmed bifocals. "The shipment arrived last night. Our operative was able to gather imagery and text regarding the content of the urinal freight."

"You're coming in here to talk to me about urinals and toilet bowls on a Monday morning? Really? Shit me."

"I wish I could shit you, sir," said Jonathan.

"That sounded really wrong," whispered Commander Madison to Jonathan.

"Apparently our cargo was not toilet bowls, but components that make up the R-39 Sturgeon submarine-launched ballistic missile," said Brian.

"Those are the old Russian missiles on the Typhoons."

"What would the Chinese want with those old pieces of junk?"

"We do not know, sir. Their subs use the JL-2s, much smaller and more efficient than the Sturgeons. And even if they wanted to use them, it's unlikely they have the D-19 launch system needed to operate the missiles anyway," Commander Madison said.

Karl exhaled slowly. He hated a report that left more questions than answers. Then again, he hated most reports. "I'm going to need an Enigma machine to decipher this."

"That's not all, sir. The shipment was accompanied by a detachment of special operations marines out of Nanjing, the Flying Dragons. Ten steel crates were loaded last night onto another freighter flying a Pakistani flag. This one named the *Amplify*. It's the same freighter we tracked in South Africa under a Hong Kong flag, four years earlier, loading British built Bladerunner 51 speedboats using the name *Diplomat*.

The freighter is actually the *Mufateh*, part of Iran Shipping Lines," said Jonathan.

"IRISL?" asked Karl.

"Yes, sir."

Karl remembered those Bladerunner 51s well from a night long ago he'd much rather soon again forget. That freighter could no longer exist, Karl was certain of it. It had been sunk the night of the Peter Cole incident. It could no longer exist, it just couldn't.

Lighthearted and laid back. Lighthearted and laid back, Karl.

Jonathan opened the file folder and handed him the cryptanalysis report.

"So this is where you remind me why we keep you signal intelligence guys locked up in a basement somewhere."

"Yes, sir. Forget the fact that it's all in Chinese, and forget the — plumbing terms, as we'll call them. The message was packetized and delivered over Tianlian satellites using KG-84A encryption. It was mounted over general traffic in and out of the naval base and dispersed over several repeating and seemingly randomized intervals. The signals did not originate from Zhengjian, Dinghai, or Qingdao. They didn't originate from anywhere inside China. Very purposeful. Asymmetric. Sophisticated. We suspect the Chinese don't even know the message traffic is there. Their intercept operations are weak at best," said Jonathan.

"What about the Chinese special ops guarding the shipment?" asked Karl.

"They looked Chinese. They were dressed Chinese," said Commander Madison.

"Around here, if it looks like a dog, walks like a dog, and barks like a dog, it's usually a fucking cat," said Karl.

"Sir, we are going to need more surveillance to determine who and what is at play here. We can't say if it's the Chinese for sure right now," said Brian.

"Yeah, yeah. We have to quintuple-check something before we get it right. Nothing new," said Karl. A long silence followed. Karl couldn't take them staring at him like that. "Alright, fucking say it. Which one of you's got something on my wife?"

Brian's chuckle was cut short by the content of his message. "Several smaller steel crates were also loaded onto the *Amplify*. They were highly shielded from the inside and matched another set of boxes we were able to identify. We suspect them to house the R-39 MIRV warheads for the Sturgeon missile—one-hundred-megaton nuclear warheads. We estimate at least twenty of 'em."

"Jesus Christ!" Karl threw the report onto his desk. *Lighthearted and laid back, my ass.*

"Brian, do me a favor. I'll need a whole pack of antacids from downstairs, or maybe three or four." He popped two tablets into his mouth and took a swig of the still-steaming coffee. "I just knew I shoulda asked you to leave the moment you got here."

***

Ramin Ramjani swirled a small spoon through his steaming cherry blossom tea as he took in the early morning colors of the spring sky over the Alborz Mountains just north of Tehran. The rays of the rising sun slowly spread across the snowcapped peak of

75

Mount Tochal in the distance as he brought the hot tea to his nostrils, taking in the aroma of cherry blossoms and the whisper of the breeze in the oak tree high above.

"Good morning, *vanak*," whispered Ramin over his tea to his little oak tree.

His grandfather planted the tree over seventy years ago when his family first moved into this home, situated north of Darakeh Square on one of the many winding side streets that sloped into the foothills of the Alborz. The oak tree now stood high over the walled rosebush garden his father had planted.

The creaking of the screen door behind him announced her arrival. Soraya Ramjani's small, soft, sandaled feet stepped lightly onto the patio deck as she carried out the morning tray filled with dates, apricots, mulberries, and naan surrounding a steaming pot and cup of cherry blossom tea. Dressed in the red flowing gown with the blue dragon pattern that Ramin had bought her on his trip to China, Soraya glowed with her usual early morning energy.

Ramin couldn't help thinking that she was the ideal of Persian beauty. Her small stature was offset with her large personality—and even larger belly that was hidden under the tray. She was in her last trimester of pregnancy, and she could be as fiery as she was now sweet. Even with achy ankles, back spasms, cravings, and the occasional upset stomach, she was a good sport about it. She was as proud of their baby as she was of her husband, especially on this, his day at the university.

"They are exceptionally beautiful this morning. A gift from Allah for my husband," said Soraya of the blooming roses along the wall.

"The sunrise, the flowers, and you," said Ramin, approaching his wife as she placed the tray onto the garden table beneath the oak.

"I should be first," said Soraya. She shot him a serious look up from under her long eyelashes.

"I save the best for last."

"You are such a thief of the heart. *Delbar-am*." said Soraya as she pulled him down by his shirt, placing a tender kiss on his cherry blossom–flavored lips.

"We have a dinner gala this evening at the university."

"I kiss you and that's what you say?"

Ramin knew Soraya hated these formal events. She wasn't one for dealing with all of the political and influential types that came with his work. She lived through enough of that during her father's days in politics. Being the daughter of a deputy prime minister had its drawbacks, starting with all of the events she forced herself through.

Ramin took a piece of toast from the tray. Dipping it in the raspberry jam, he stuffed his mouth. He gave her a kiss on the forehead with a mouthful of bread, mumbling something about something, probably work related. He climbed the patio deck and disappeared behind the creaking screen door. She put the tray down, and he just left. He forgot what day it was.

By Hajji Firuz, I will have his nape.

She barely took a step back toward the house when something burst through the screen door. It was big, round, and furry, with yellow and black stripes. Two fuzzy antennae protruded from its head, and it wore a black mask and cape that was caught on the hinge of the door. Soraya could not stop from laughing. Her belly hurt and cramped as she placed her hands around her naval, afraid the baby would squeeze out from mirth.

"What is *that?*" Soraya was barely able to get the words out through her laughter.

"I'm Nikoo, the honey bee. Now help me out of here," gasped Ramin, unable to resist laughing himself.

"Wait, I can barely walk from the cramp," said Soraya as Ramin broke free of the hinge with a tug; the weight of the suit and sudden freedom sent him sprawling, stomach-first, onto the patio deck.

"Ramin!"

Soraya hobbled to her husband, still holding on to her belly, as he clumsily got up to his hands and knees.

"Are you okay?" Ramin asked, still in his compromising position.

"I'm fine," said Soraya, still in shock and unable to stop her laughter even through the growing cramp in her belly.

"I'm Nikoo, the honey bee, buzzing in to give you a treat for our anniversary. Happy Anniversary," said Ramin in a defeated tone.

Soraya stopped laughing, mirth replaced with sudden compassion. "Not satisfied with my heart, you must too take my liver. *Jigar-am.*"

"*Allahu akbar,*" said Ramin, with a satisfied smile.

"I will pray to Allah to take away your craziness," giggled Soraya.

"You are my craziness."

"I have no words." Soraya could feel an impossibly large smile on her face.

"How about 'I love you'?" asked Ramin.

They were snapped from their interlude by three short bursts of a car horn. Kazem was outside. Ramin was late for work.

IV

INTO THE DEEP

Icy winds whipped across the water's surface, as the tugboat struggled to keep from joining its former payload, now long gone beneath the waves. Bushov stood white-knuckled at the helm, while his crew reeled in the hawser line from the black waters beyond the gunwale.

"If it tangles in the rotors—"

"Just pull!" shouted Bushov.

The tugboat dipped beneath the spume, emerging out the other side, her hull rolling up the side of the next wave as the gunwale behind Bushov disappeared again beneath black waters.

"Dig in," roared the boatswain, as the tugboat went vertical.

The wind took beet and cabbage borsch fresh from someone's belly, as salt sprayed over them and the bow cleared the crest, the gunwale emerging from the dark sea. The *Europa* rode the storm from white crest to trough, while somewhere between Bear Island and Novaya Zemlya, the submarine lurked beneath the surface like a sea monster.

The electronic gauges and lights of the control stations monitored the Typhoon's main systems. The control room wasn't as Dmitri remembered. Its configuration was still the same. But tonight, nothing was as he remembered. It was supposed to be a new beginning for him and his crew. At least, that's what Dmitri wanted to believe.

The navigational and weapons control sections were to either side of his chair, behind the massive, hydraulic-powered periscope reserved for the Officer of the Deck—in this case, the captain. During a dive, the control room was usually abuzz with activity, but with barely a crew to man a shift, the silence was thick. Orders were executed without the slightest turn of focus. Even in the vast space of the control room, the tension made it claustrophobic.

Dmitri exhaled slowly to keep from suffocating. All systems had to work in perfect harmony to maintain the steel bubble and keep its limited crew safe from the enormous power of the surrounding sea. Like an airplane during takeoff and landing, the dive was when the boat was most vulnerable. They leveled off at sixty meters, about two hundred feet.

The bright white overhead lights and yellow paint of the control room were of deliberate design, the opposite of the cold, dark depths of this stormy water. The bright colors were to keep the crew and her officers alert and awake during long hours of stressful boredom that would often follow. There was always something to drill, a duty to attend, a task to complete. But exhaustion and the repetitive nature of their work led to dumb mistakes. The lights and colors had been a subtle psychological consideration by the designers of this boat. It was the simplest and cheapest of design points but one of the most effective.

Dmitri stared ahead at the helm and planesmen as they leveled the boat to the ordered bearing and depth. Typhoons were the largest submarines, and perhaps the most complex ever built, and with this crew it would make for a cavernously lonely voyage.

Dressed in the standard blue operational uniform of the Russian Navy, Boris Yassanov entered the control room, sweating from the work in the engine room two decks below. The *Simbirsk* had been laid up for over five years, and Boris had been her constant companion. He knew her better than anyone, even Dmitri.

"Good morning, Captain."

"Good morning, Boris. You're an old and welcome face, my friend. It's good to have you aboard," said Dmitri, remembering other places and times with the old seafarer.

"Thank you, sir. It's good to feel useful again."

They all came from the world of the forgotten, left to die like the hulks rusting on the dry-dock pylons and in the contaminated waters of the naval bases they once so proudly served. It wasn't a wonder, when asked, Boris gladly returned to service.

"Your report?"

"Control rods lowered and locked. Core reactivity within desired parameters. Both reactors are driving 600 bars through the primary circuits, and coolant flow is at twenty-five hundred. Inlet and outlet temperatures are within specification. She's running smooth for now, Captain."

"Thank you, Boris," said Dmitri, a weight lifting, if only for the moment, from his shoulders.

Of the things he most feared, fire and reactor containment were his priorities. With the *Simbirsk's* five years at the shipyard and so much corrosion to her systems, Dmitri knew the risk in taking this machine back out to sea. Only Boris could fix her, make her right again. As ambitious as the games played by the politicians behind the scenes, so too were his desires to once again captain this great vessel.

"Very well. Run a diagnostic of the turbo and diesel generators. I need to make sure the electrical systems are also in as good a shape. Then take a break. We'll be doing extensive fire drills and you need to sleep."

"Yes, sir," said Boris.

Misha Andreev, the executive officer of the boat, entered through the port door from the sonar room. Dmitri suspected what might have driven Misha here; reasons very different to his own. The same means to two very different ends made Dmitri wary of his old friend.

"We got her out from under their noses," said Misha, taking his position beside Dmitri at the plotting table.

"Yes, quiet as a mouse. Someone's always watching, though, Misha. Always watching," said Dmitri, gazing past the charts of the Barents laid out on the table. His own doubts cast their pall unto the intent of Misha's words. Misha was fishing for information, a hint perhaps at their destination when Dmitri wasn't at liberty to say. He didn't like to be baited, especially by an old friend. "You have the first watch."

"Aye, sir."

"Take us to heading two-one-zero, depth two-zero-zero meters, gradual descent beneath the thermal layer. Ahead two-thirds. Clear baffles at intermittent intervals: 29, 46, and 38 minutes. We need to make sure we weren't picked up by any NATO fast attacks. How many days' rations were you able to secure?" asked Dmitri, calculating.

"Thirty-one, and a kilogram of beluga with plenty of Stoli to pass the voyage," said Misha. A waft from somewhere in memory of the caviar's salty texture clawed at Dmitri's nose and taste buds.

"We will have to find the right moment to celebrate, then," Dmitri said, drawing his mind far from the salty temptation and any thought of celebration. The release of ballast and the rising water pressure during a dive, even in a gradual descent, would produce the most recognizable sounds to any experienced sonar man sitting somewhere off the Polyarny inlet.

"If we can keep clear of contact, we can maybe glide past the old underwater surveillance net and break away into the North Atlantic." He plotted the course across the chart straight for the Reykjanes Ridge, the mid-Atlantic, deep-sea mountain range where the edges of the North American and Eurasian tectonic plates came together.

They set the Typhoon to swim through the longest mountain range in the world, something both Russian and American commanders did plenty of during their Cold War games of hide and seek. Dmitri would have an advantage once inside the ridge, but only if NATO didn't know he was out here first.

"Assemble the officers for a briefing in the wardroom at 0800."

"The Atlantic is a big place, Captain."

"A cold place, Misha. I'm headed to the sauna for a bit, and then to a few hours' sleep. Enjoy first watch. You have the conn."

Dmitri hoped the insinuation of his own hit the mark.

"Aye, Captain," said Misha, as he watched Dmitri disappear past the bulkhead.

Dmitri felt the angle of the Typhoon's dive beneath his feet as he descended into her belly. Closing the door behind him, he eyed the contents of his stateroom. Everything about the Typhoon-class was larger than usual for a submarine. The captain's stateroom befitted a luxury apartment in Russia—at least, one a submariner could afford. The walls were of birch paneling. At the back were glass-encased shelves for the mementos from his many ports of call, among them Turkish bath salts and a box of Cuban Habaneros, saved for a special occasion or a relaxing time in his private sauna.

He moved briskly to the captain's command center in a nook next to his work station. From there, Dmitri could interface with all of the boat's vital systems: the Simfoniya and Tobol navigation complexes, Molniya communication system, Skat sonar system, and Omnibus combat information system. There wasn't anything Dmitri couldn't know about his boat whenever he wanted. Quick access to information meant the difference between life and death beneath the waves.

Dmitri pressed one of the panels above the alcove that housed the information systems display and the inter-ship communication system. The panel gave way with a click and he pulled it aside, revealing a small safe built into the wall. He lifted the plastic cover over the notch in the door, placing his right thumb into the slot. A slight twitch of his right eye was the only hint he gave that a needle pricked his skin. A green laser shot out from a slit at the top, scanning from the top down and side to side, followed by a second beam across both his eyes. The biometric facial recognition, retinal scan, fingerprint validation, and blood composition check were complete. The locking mechanism released; it granted access to Dmitri Borei alone. Anyone else, and the boat would have already been well on its way to a watery grave.

Dmitri pulled back the door, drawing a touchscreen tablet from the safe. He pressed the button at the bottom of the pad, and the system powered up, the port on the upper right again scanning a green light across his face. The system initiated a pre-programmed proximity scan for any other humans within the confines of the stateroom. Dmitri pulled a thumb drive from his coat pocket and inserted it into the USB port on the side of the tablet. When prompted, he input the sixteen-digit password. His finger hung over the last key for a moment, remembering Viktor's warning.

You'll have one try. Don't get the password wrong.

That was his only admonition. Viktor didn't elaborate as to the consequences. Dmitri took a deep breath and tapped the final key. The system screen went black. The seconds felt like hours; beads of sweat formed on his forehead. Something was wrong with the boat's environmentals.

A navigational chart appeared on the screen, and Dmitri released his breath. He sat down to relieve his knees. A list of waypoints scrolled on the left as the chart set the plot. He followed the lines and coordinates south, clear across the Atlantic, around the Cape of Good Hope to a tiny speck, deep in the Southern Ocean. His orders were the Heard and McDonald Islands, a barren chain of Antarctic wasteland.

What could Viktor want there?

He sat back in his chair as the touch pad screen went blank, his mind already racing.

Karl and his three guests made their way down the five flights of stairs to the third floor. The stairs were his morning exercise and the coffee with lemon his usual kick-starter to the day. Today he was going to need more than a little kick-starter. He could feel the pressure rising through his head, throbbing at his neck.

"Good morning, sir."

"Good morning," said Karl as they strode past two armed special operations officers in their black paramilitary uniforms. They approached the inch-thick, bomb-proof double glass doors at the end of the hallway. He passed his blue striped badge across the card reader, a beep and green light granting him access. The four men passed silently beneath the three seals of the Central Security Service. The second set of double glass doors opened up to the National Security Operations Center.

Large screens covered the walls, displaying a series of maps and link charts used by the various teams assigned to their respective specialties. The NSOC was constantly processing millions of data points, and the teams always had something to work on, each a small piece to the vast overall intelligence puzzle. But of all things in the Center, it was the message board that tickled Karl the most. The motto "Walk the walk and don't talk! Silence is a virtue," was posted in bold letters right across the top.

They cut quickly past the crescent-shaped tables and the cubicles toward the conference room where Katherine Brandt waited for them.

Karl first noticed Katherine as a young analyst at Air Force Cyber Command just out of basic training. She was nubile, no nonsense, and brilliant. With a Master's degree in mathematics out of Virginia Tech, she was ideal for his Central Security Service team. He called in a favor from an old friend at US Strategic Command and got Katherine an interview in his group. That's all it took. Karl got her transferred to NSA soon after that. But those were the simple days when emotion didn't cloud judgment. She'd worked with him for over five years and a lot had changed since then. She was his liaison to the DTRA, the Defense Threat Reduction Agency, and he knew she was already impatient with him this morning.

"Time moving a bit fast for you this morning, sir? Fresh coffee in the pot; last night's brew," said Katherine.

Karl could feel his systolic pressure rising in his neck again and not just because of her subject-matter specialty or her snide remark. His eyes torturously followed the contours of her wine-colored suit as she stood to greet the new arrivals. Her black hair was pulled back in a tight bun and she wore black-framed glasses. She had high cheekbones and a pale, lightly-freckled complexion. Karl's wife only met Katherine once; hated her from the get-go. It was Karl's little secret that he requested her assignment. If his wife ever found out, it would cost him. All four men stood a little straighter, held themselves a bit more crisply this morning. Karl noticed that even the slightly overfed Brian tried to give his best militaristic air.

They're trying to impress her! The dimwits figured she preferred a man in uniform. *She won't even look at a guy with less than Q clearance.*

"Good morning, Miss Brandt." Karl always kept his words brief with her. The less he spoke, the better. Anyone else would have thought he did not like her, but he and Katherine knew better.

She wasted no time getting to the meat of the matter as they each took a seat around the conference table. The National Security Agency Seal disappeared from the screen and was replaced by a series of vessel schematics Karl had never seen.

Katherine removed a document from the file folder at her side with an ENDSEAL and TALENT KEYHOLE classification control stamped across its header, representing its highly classified source of signals intelligence. She slid it across the table to Karl.

"Project 941—the Typhoon-class ballistic missile submarine, NATO designation," said Katherine, turning their attention to the images on the screen. "Carries twenty R-39 submarine-launched ballistic missiles, housing up to ten warheads, one hundred kilotons each—about eight times the blast payload at Hiroshima. The largest submarines ever built, they were too expensive to maintain after the demise of the Soviet Bloc. Six were built, a seventh never finished. Of the six, five were subsequently decommissioned and laid up at the shipyards in Murmansk Oblast. The missile systems to these boats had to be completely removed before they could be considered scrapped."

"And now these missiles are sitting aboard a freighter in a Chinese naval yard, headed God only knows where," interjected Karl, wanting to get to the obvious crux of the matter.

"We've seen components siphoned from Russian shipyards and sold onto open markets plenty before, but nothing like this," said Katherine.

"So this ain't no toilet seats," said Karl.

"No, sir. Intelligence suggests these are fully functional missiles — with their warheads," responded Katherine.

"Going where? Who's the buyer?" asked Karl.

Karl had to be careful not to jump to conclusions, not let his imagination run away from him. He remembered the name of that freighter from the night of the Peter Cole incident all those years ago, and he'd rather just not think on it. Better to convince himself there was no such thing as a Syndycate. There never had been.

Katherine shifted the image on the screen to an infrared photograph of a young woman. Tall, athletic, long dark hair pulled back much like Katherine's, with almond eyes and a slender sharp nose.

"Her name is Jiang Liu. These images of her with this man were captured last night at Hainan. He has obvious ties to the military, greeting Liu in plain sight. We're still working on establishing his identity."

Katherine took a moment for a sip of water, placing the bottle back on the table. Robert couldn't take his eyes off the mouth of that bottle with Katherine's lipstick smeared around it. Karl snorted.

This one really was an idiot driven by his gonads.

Karl was pleased when she gave Robert a smile that crushed him into his seat and continued with her report.

"Jiang Liu is the daughter of Dian Lun Chung, one of the purported Dragon Heads, or leaders of the 14K Triad. Originally an offshoot of the Nationalist Party, the 14K established themselves in Hong Kong by competing for supremacy in the black markets of Southeast Asia. Chinese state security has been cracking down on them for years, with a recent string of highly publicized successes. Under the leadership of Dian Lun, the group became one of the premier heroin and opium networks in the region, smuggling across Afghanistan into Iran. As big as 14K is, Langley has had a hard time recruiting assets in the organization—hence our information on him is limited. But this is the first time we link the 14K to this type of smuggling. Jiang Liu is ambitious, vicious, and extremely intelligent. She can be as subtle and precise or as merciless and ruthless as need be. They are going to make sure this shipment reaches its destination," said Katherine.

Karl could have sworn Katherine said that with a tinge of admiration.

"If she's so subtle and precise why appear so openly at a naval base where they know we're watching?" asked Robert.

"They want us to know. They want us to know what's in those crates," said Karl.

She really was beautiful.

Karl needed to be careful of his thoughts. The timbre of her voice made him think of things, unbecoming things of a married man. Things more perilous than just carnal desires. He suddenly needed air, badly. He stood. "If you'll excuse me, I need to get ready for a very long day."

"Sir," said the other four, as they rose quickly from their chairs.

Karl bolted for the door, taking one last look back at Katherine. The issue of the R-39s was decidedly the lesser problem.

V

ARCHETYPE

Easygoing was always his style, Richard liked to say. Backpack slung over a shoulder, dressed in denim, loafers, and a button-down, gray-checkered shirt, Richard looked more like a student than an adjunct professor. The lavender-striped tie from the morning was long gone. He liked dressing young, with the added touch of a nice tie. It was his bridge between the student and professional. He still passed for one of them, anyway, so why not look the part.

Richard quickly descended the well-worn steps of Healy Hall, making his way across the lawn, past the blooming cherry blossoms gifted from Japan in 1912. They were a special endowment from the mayor of Tokyo to replace their previous gift of two-thousand trees afflicted with disease and burned two years earlier. Such a beautiful, but ill-fated gift from the Japanese; perhaps it was a foreshadowing of things to come years later, mused Richard.

He should have let those kids out of class earlier, he thought, his musings turning to the day's agenda, stepping onto one of Georgetown's many side streets. His lecture on the Iranians and their revolution could have waited. He was late to meet Guillermo. Richard had gone to school with Guillermo, studied with him in his early days at Georgetown in the very rooms of Healy Hall. He found in him a source of great wit and exceptional intelligence. They were both Guija. Other than Anja, Guillermo was the only one Richard had met since the War. Theirs was a secret unspoken between them. They behaved no less human than anyone else, and that meant denial of any and everything that would make them anything other than that. So their conversations focused around the one thing both had in common, a cause for much discussion and more often debate: a burning passion— an obsession—for incredible art. It made them great friends.

Richard made his way out the South Gatehouse, straight onto O Street, when a familiar face caught his attention coming out one of the side alleys between a row of Federal-style homes.

"Hey, Freeman!" He stopped the exuberant youth in his tracks. Richard quickly caught up to the young man in his Hoya jersey.

"I like the colors, Freeman. You might get lucky at Buffalo Billiards with that bulldog face paint. Melanie Ann will never recognize you."

"You throwing shade at me, Mr. Robles? I can't even."

"Enjoy your day off, Mikey, and be ready for your exam next week."

"Not right, not right," said Mike, picking up and disappearing down the street as a cheer erupted from one of the many homes lining O Street.

Richard stopped at the corner of O Street and 35th and looked up at the sign over his head. The brown and yellow circular emblem of Saxby's Coffee, with the steaming coffee cup atop the name, hung over the wood-framed doorway. A young, dark-skinned man in a preppy dress shirt and slacks sat upright by the window with a steaming cup of coffee and a copy of the *Washington Post* on the table.

Guillermo tapped his watch with his forefinger as he stared at Richard through the window. His pursed lips and raised eyebrows evinced his sentiment. It was now twenty past and Richard just stood outside chatting away with that young boy in a man's body. But he was cute, that young man was. *He was very cute!* Still, no matter how cute, Guillermo hated to wait.

The nerve of him.

Guillermo rapped on the windowpane and showed him his wrist again, tapping with forefinger on his thick, leather-banded watch. Guillermo loved all things beautiful, and his watch was as much a work of art as the mocha-swirl latte on his table, or the face-painted young man that so consumed Richard's attention — and his, as a matter of fact. At least the kid was handsome.

Enough of this.

Guillermo threw a half-open pack of Splenda on the table when Richard finally waltzed through the door.

"It is twenty-three past," said Guillermo, sitting rigidly upright.

"Come on, Willie. Relax. It's a wonderful day to be alive. Clear blue skies, cherry blossoms, March Madness, and me! Can't ask for more," said Richard, with his flashy mischievous smile.

"You're not all that, Ritchie. That young man you were talking to, him maybe, but you? No, sweetheart, your days are long past," said Guillermo, with an air of satisfaction that he could release his frustrations on good old Ritchie.

"It's nice to see you too," said Richard settling into the chair opposite Guillermo.

"Don't mention it. You know I always look forward to our rendezvous."

"I wouldn't call them that," Richard corrected him rather quickly.

"Unfortunate, of course, for you. You don't know what you're missing." Guillermo returned Richard's mischievous smile.

"And I don't plan to find out."

"Your loss. You can't blame a boy for trying." Guillermo straightened himself in his chair, if one could do so any more, and brought the steaming cup to his nostrils to take in the aroma. "I love the smell of fresh coffee, tasting life with all your senses. The simple pleasure of a fresh brewed cup. Nothing like it."

"I guess not," answered Richard, sitting back in his chair and folding his hands before him. Guillermo eyed the carefully layered bandage over Richard's right hand. Richard's profession called for detailed use of that hand, and no small wound would need that much dressing.

"What's with the hand?" asked Guillermo, as he blew gently over the steaming coffee cup.

"Wood shop."

"Wood shop?" Guillermo's eyebrows lifted as he stopped blowing over his coffee.

"Yeah, wood shop," said Richard, sounding a bit defensive.

Taking a sip, Guillermo placed the coffee back on the table. "Our arrangement depends on the proper use of those hands. Actually, no, let me not. I'd really rather not know, really."

The métier of an art fence brought with it certain precautions, one of them being limited contact between the fence, who brought the client, and the thief, who brought the art. Richard was the thief, Guillermo the fence. Theirs was a friendship shrouded in secrecy, beyond just the question of *what* they both were, much to Richard's regret. Richard took care to share only what was needed, for both their sakes. He would not speak of what he'd done that night in Room XVI of the Pinacoteca, just as he dared not allude to the fact that he knew exactly who their client was. It was best they both played their game, that his feigned ignorance remain so, at least for now.

"Now, for a more entertaining subject. How does she look?" Guillermo worked hard not to let his voice crack through his whispered words.

"As beautiful as the day the last touch of oil dried on her canvas. Only the crackle would remind you of the passage of time."

"So you did it, you son of a bitch."

"You thought I would fail?" asked Richard, surprised for once.

"Strolling into the Vatican and walking out with a canvas three times your size doesn't have high odds for success."

"Yet, here we are. A bit worse for wear, but nothing a small Band-Aid can't fix," said Richard, lifting his bandaged hand to eye level.

"I would think you got that at home. Anja not wanting to give you any?"

"So crass for a PhD, and so curious for an otherwise reserved and careful young man," smirked Richard.

"Yes, let's let pheromones lie and return to the more immediate subject at hand," said Guillermo, with a sly smile of his own that made Richard slide a tad in his chair.

"Indeed, I have the piece ready to deliver, as I'm sure your client is ready to receive it," said Richard.

Guillermo carefully sipped his mocha. "I've heard no news out of the Vatican or otherwise as to its theft."

"When have you ever known me to leave a mark?" asked Richard.

"Of course. Still, I must inspect the work for myself. Standard protocol," continued Guillermo, slowly placing the cup back on the table.

"It's important for your client to know the original is hanging on his wall and not at the Pinacoteca. I fully understand."

"When can this be arranged?" asked Guillermo.

"When you present final payment, as per our agreement," said Richard, his tone suddenly dry to match the aridness of Guillermo's.

"I see it first. If satisfied, my client will wire the funds."

"Fourteen million and you can inspect the work all you like."

"We agreed to ten," said Guillermo, his lips pursing angrily at the mention of the higher sum.

"That was before you questioned my integrity. Besides, getting her took a bit more expense than anticipated, and I work for a profit."

"I cannot go back and now change the terms of the agreement," retorted Guillermo.

"Consider it a tip for good service, like you'd tip a waiter at your favorite restaurant for your favorite meal."

"Wow, you really are an asshole—but you know that."

"Yes, and I expect a little extra paper to wipe me clean," Richard said.

"You're such a dick, that's actually a little funny, fucker. Just a little," said Guillermo, stifling a smile.

"It's called negotiating your salary. Speaking of which, how's the job search going?" asked Richard.

"You're looking at the new curatorial assistant to the National Gallery of Art," said Guillermo, with less than joy in his tone.

"Congratulations, get a little money in your pocket," said Richard, as the barista placed a coffee on their table, Richard's usual.

"Money doesn't grow on trees. Just like you want your money first, I want my cut. What did you call it, negotiating your salary?" asked Guillermo, pleased with himself as his palms moistened with sweat.

"It's going to look nice hanging on your client's wall again," said Richard.

"You think you'd actually catch me with that, get me to reveal who it is?" asked Guillermo.

"I already did," Richard said with a reassuring smile.

"Then, if it makes you happy, yes, they're looking forward to it, asshole."

Guillermo gave Richard a wink over the rim of his coffee cup. Richard really hated it when he did that.

***

Katherine waited for Karl to return. She and the rest of the group ran through the scenarios, but Karl wasn't coming back, and she'd waited long enough. She had to get back to work, put together the report for the president's Daily Brief. The Brief was a top secret document delivered nearly every day to the president and a select few of his staff, with intelligence and

98

analysis from across all sixteen agencies on the latest international developments—and this would make that list.

With the exception of Brian, she hadn't met the two others with them in that conference room before. But that wasn't surprising around here. She seldom worked with the same person twice, except for Brian and Karl, of course. She found the younger one with the glasses amusing—Jonathan was his name, she recalled—and that naval commander, well, he was just typical of his type. She thought it hilarious reading men's minds.

Such base creatures, so easy to wrap around a finger. It was unwinding them that sometimes proved difficult. So why still think about him, the one named Robert?

She strode past the agency emblem toward her office, her soles echoing down the corridor to the rhythm of her step, when a near-exhausted bellow caught her attention.

"Katherine!"

She turned around and saw Karl huffing his way down the hall.

"Hurry up, Karl."

"Trust me, I can't run any faster, even if I wanted to," gasped Karl, as he swallowed a breath and the blood rushed from his red face.

"Might be a good idea to hit the gym," said Katherine with a knowing smile.

"You sure know how to make a guy feel confident."

She loved Karl like a father, and she knew it killed him.

He went on. "I got your report on the contents of the *Amplify*."

"The suspected contents," corrected Katherine.

"Yes, right. Thanks for getting it to me," said Karl, finally catching his breath.

"You didn't need to run me down for that," Katherine said with a compassionate smile. "But you're welcome, Karl."

"I have to brief the president and the Security Council on Monday. Might be good for you to join this one," he said.

It was the first she'd been asked to join that meeting in her time at NSA. If he wanted to tempt her, that was one way to do it.

"I can join you, if you'd like, but you have everything in that report. No need for me to really be there," said Katherine. She knew better than to give in so easily to the sweetness of what he offered.

Karl blocked traffic in the middle of the hall. "It's a good step for your career that the guys get to know you."

For an instant Karl seemed to almost regret saying those words. But once again he was his usual subdued self, burying the pang of jealousy deep down where she would not see. *So easy to wrap around a finger. Just wasn't fair.*

"Thank you, Karl." She embraced him with a smile. Karl gave in with one of his own.

"See you Monday then," said Katherine.

"Wait, one more thing before you go." Karl beckoned her away from the hall and unwanted ears into a small nearby conference room.

"Do you have any new updates on Andrei Birkin?" he asked.

"No positive ID on his new contact yet," said Katherine, speaking almost in a whisper. Before this whole rigmarole at Hainan, Karl asked she trace the whereabouts and activities of the new SVR director and any contacts made out of the Russian embassy, one of her already too-numerous tasks. It was an unusual request for her, outside her area of expertise, but not the first time Karl had given her an unacknowledged assignment of this type, one that only the two of them knew about.

"He's gone off the grid since their rendezvous at the coffee shop. Profiling suggests his contact was either Afghan or Iranian, probably military or like background. Behavior suggests intelligence service training, Islamic Republic or Russian. Our inclination is Iranian. We know he and Andrei exchanged something, since they both walked out with identical briefcases. He arrived through London Heathrow on a British passport under the name of Joseph Denham. But we got nothing from Interpol. Nothing came up in X-Keyscore or Boundless Informant, either. After their meeting, his contact paid a visit to the National Gallery to take in some art. He never left the museum."

"You mean our guys never saw him leave," said Karl.

"I guess you can call it that."

"Any speculation what might be in that briefcase?"

"I don't speculate," said Katherine.

"Of course not. Forget I asked. Just keep me posted on Birkin and I'll see you at the briefing."

"Yes, sir," said Katherine.

"Oh, and one more thing," said Karl, stopping her again before she left. "You'll do great."

Katherine gave him a big smile. For once, he'd shown her his gentle side.

"We both will," she said, returning the gratitude.

Karl remained until she disappeared out of sight. There were things he hadn't told her. Things no one knew. But his suspicions once again bubbled to the surface. That man in that coffee shop that day, his name was Vadim, and he was more than just an operative. Karl didn't need any special access program to figure that out.

It was who Vadim was tied to that scared Karl. No one at NSA knew of Viktor Kletnov yet. No one knew of the Syndycate. But Karl knew. Peter Cole existed because of Viktor. Karl learned quickly not just *who* Viktor was, but also *what* he was.

The mention of the incident with those Bladerunner boats gave it away. That freighter in their report, the *Amplify*, it was Viktor's. He tried hard not to think of that night, not to think of Peter Cole. But the memories kept creeping back in: the things they'd done, things he could not forget.

Karl shoved aside the guilt, and like a tower of iron will, he would do again what he must for his family, for countless families of enemy and friend alike. But if he felt so brave, then why the tumult in his belly? Because death would have been a mercy to Karl if any discovered the pact he made with the monster he knew as Viktor Kletnov. He returned to his office lost to his own thoughts. He wondered just how much he could trust Katherine — and how much he could trust himself with her.

***

"You are a mess." Kazem Shir-Del pulled up along a Ramin who was worse for wear, stirring his morning cup of cherry blossom tea on the tabletop counter.

"Good morning to you, too," responded Ramin, and took a careful sip from the steaming cup.

Kazem Shir-Del was the best friend Ramin never had while growing up. Always in his brother's shadow and having to provide at home after they lost their father, Ramin never found time for friends. He was a loner, a troublemaker, an outcast for being perhaps too smart. Until a particular day in a lecture hall of Tehran University, Ramin met Kazem and somehow this oddball pair clicked. A rare trust ensued. Their friendship became like that of brothers. While Ramin's older brother took a different path, he and Kazem dedicated themselves to their passion and their homes. Kazem was already on his second baby while Ramin his first, both working for a nuclear program few others knew of on campus. Ramin appreciated Kazem's commiseration this morning.

"You had quite a night last night," said Kazem.

"I did not expect Soraya to do the Haj Naranji," answered Ramin.

"You are lucky to have such a wonderful wife. She was the life of the party," said Kazem.

"Exactly. Everyone paid more attention to her dance than to President Amir."

"How could we not? Hers was the most beautiful pregnant performance of a Haj Naranji I have ever seen," Kazem said.

"How about we move on to a more boring subject like the test we have scheduled for today?"

"I was hoping you'd forgotten about that," said Kazem.

"Aren't you excited about seeing the results?"

"After the last three attempts, I'm a bit less optimistic."

"We've applied the changes to the rotors' oscillation frequencies. If we can sustain a 480 velocity without shattering the thing, I'd say we'll have a new type of centrifuge, thanks to our work," said Ramin.

"Until the Israelis come up with another little virus to make that one spin out of control too."

"Why do you always have to be so pessimistic?"

"I didn't say anything about either of us being next on their hit list, now did I? I don't want us to be six or seven. But if it's got to be one of us, I hope it's you first," said Kazem, with his usual morbid sense of humor.

Ramin remembered each of the previous five on that list well, the researchers the Israelis had murdered before them. He remembered the first most of all, his teacher and mentor Masoud Mohammadi. The old physicist saw in him a gift, a kindness Ramin didn't see in himself.

Without despair there can be no hope. Without darkness there can be no light.

Those were his last words to the young man. The next morning, a motorcycle bomb took Masoud's life just outside his home as he was leaving for the university. That memory welled only vengeance in the pit of Ramin's stomach, searing his heart with its black flame and the great shame of hatred. Ramin woke many a morning to the nightmares and the cold sweats, with Soraya's round belly resting peacefully beside him, wondering if this would be the day when he would be next on that list. He could never let her catch a glimpse of the terror that unsettled his soul. But it was there, the whispered laughter of his murderers waiting for him in the shadows.

Instead he remained steadfast to his life's work and forced the pain of death from his mind. Indulging it was only weakness. What those above him did with his invention was not for him to decide. Ramin repeated these mantras, whispered them to himself whenever he felt the darkness coming, when no one else was listening. He convinced himself for Soraya, for their unborn daughter.

And yet, they were there, the secrets, ones Kazem knew nothing of, ones beyond even Soraya. Like with so many things, he did not remember their place or their time, only their memory among the many voices in his head not his own, driving his mind slowly to madness.

Easier for the good in men to fall to darkness than for man himself to come forth to the light.

"Ramin," said Kazem, as he snapped his fingers in front of his friend's eyes. "Are you okay? You zoned out there for a good minute right when I said—"

"I know what you said," interjected Ramin, stopping Kazem in his tracks.

"I'm sorry I brought it up." Kazem leaned away from Ramin, with a wry expression at having been snapped at.

"As Gernot Zippe once said regarding the centrifuge, 'with a kitchen knife you can peel a potato or kill your neighbor.' I like French fries."

"That would be very American of you," said Kazem, smiling at his old friend and his attempt at a joke. "You know, you make for a great scientist, but a lousy stand-up comic."

Kazem followed Ramin out of the cafeteria. Ramin prayed this day would bring them success, for both their sakes.

***

Zhen Xin Liang never understood why only he saw the beauty in this painting. The massive black canvas towered over him as he stared at the image. He heard the narrative a hundred times from the art consultant who sold him the piece, but the image stirred in him something words could never express. Whatever that art consultant had called it, it didn't matter. It was majestic.

Zhen Xin Liang stood on the precipice of greatness. In a mere six months he would be preparing to take on the role of President and General Secretary to the Central Committee. His lifelong ambition, his vision of a unified China, one of economic prosperity and global strength, was at hand. He was to lead the sixth generation since the days of Chairman Mao and the Cultural Revolution. The thought could unnerve any man.

It had taken the painter four years to complete this piece, and just as the artist had carefully chosen his palette, Zhen Xin, too, carefully maneuvered through the political vetting and gamesmanship that came with holding office. As China moved to a market economy, it did so under the quiet rule of an iron fist and the eye of a watchful guardian.

Zhen Xin had been born into an agricultural family in Sichuan Province, at the outskirts of Chengdu proper, during the time of Mao. His father became a leading revolutionary among the first generation of the Communist Party and Zhen Xin swiftly followed in his wake, joining the Communist Youth League as a boy.

He quickly distinguished himself as a leading voice of the youth league faction, the Tuanpai. Those were the early days, when he had thoughts of a great new order and the vision of the socialist ideal, returned bittersweetly to him. They were good times, his days as party secretary in Fujian Province. He gazed at the canvas, lost in memories of what seemed a lifetime ago.

"What is it you find in that thing?"

Zhen Xin spun around, startled from his reverie by a soft and welcomingly familiar voice. Shi Ren Ming approached with their grandson in tow. Wearing a red silk dress with gray pearl earrings and necklace, she was a study of elegance and grace, with her porcelain skin, dark eyes and lashes, and long black hair with a touch of a fine gray streak. He smiled, remembering the day they met in Fujian for the first time. From that day, Shi Ren Ming had been the love of his life.

"You look at that thing like you looked at me when we first met," she said, with an air of amused jealousy. "There's a fish head coming out from the woman's, well, between her legs, right up there. It makes me concerned for you. And what is that in each hand?"

"A bird and a skull, probably a fish or a sharp-toothed horse," he answered, knowing where the conversation was going.

"And the dolls thrown on the tapestry below her?" she asked, continuing her set up.

"Those are her children," sighed Zhen Xin, getting ready to go through the story again.

"Children born of those fish head teeth! She has no head, with a decaying baby, and an armless Christian God on her chest. Zhen Xin, it is—it's grotesque, it's shocking."

"It is shockingly brilliant," he answered, with a patient and warm smile, one he only reserved for his wife.

"Is this what the Americans call 'contemporary art'?" asked Shi Ren.

"You do not mask your disdain well," said Zhen Xin, as he softly took his wife's hand.

"I have the luxury of not being a politician."

"But you are a politician's — and soon-to-be president's — wife."

The little boy suddenly broke free of his grandmother's hand and ran straight at the painting, but another hand reached out, catching the little guy by the shoulder and scooping him up.

"You haven't lost your reflexes," noted Shi Ren, smiling at her husband.

"Or my strength." Zhen Xin's voice strained as he gently put his grandson back down.

A new energy, out of place, suddenly entered the room.

"Who's the artist of this dramatic masterpiece?" asked the new arrival, in a New Englander accent.

Zhen Xin recognized the man — and the accent — from personal experience. He'd spent time in Massachusetts during the early nineties as part of a trade delegation. Boston was where he first gained his appetite for Western art, at the Isabella Stewart Gardner Museum.

"It's a piece by American artist Charles Pfahl."

"Well, how about that? An American painting, here of all places. The world is becoming a smaller and smaller place," said Ambassador William Boyd.

Zhen Xin graciously extended the American his hand. "Yes, Mr. Boyd. A world that brings our differences together. And in our differences, lie our strengths."

He turned to his wife with only a look. She took their grandson by the hand and politely withdrew, leaving the two men to their affairs. Zhen Xin hoped the American did not mistake her politeness for weakness. There was only one person stronger than Zhen Xin, and she had just left the room.

***

At the far ends of the picture hall, the security personnel stood at attention in their formal green overcoats, with ceremonial — but still lethal — carbine rifles at their sides. Objects of priceless ancient art filled the gallery: jade sculptures, intricate porcelain vases, and bronze statues, along with inked scrolls and paintings of Chinese life spanning the twelve dynasties lined the Great Hall.

Cao Qing watched his ward from the far entrance with the eyes of a hawk. He was the head of the Central Security Bureau's Unit 8341, a special operations group trained in personnel and facilities protection for all of China's senior government, party, and military officials. This evening he was personally charged with Zhen Xin's wellbeing. Anyone and everyone was a potential threat, and in the grand game playing itself out this evening, Vice President Xin's wellbeing was his wellbeing. Cao Qing's life depended on it.

So far the evening had gone according to plan. Cao Qing did his rounds. His first and fifth groups were positioned throughout the building as uniformed guards, waiters, door men, a gardener, and even a cook. Several of the guests themselves, mingling in the reception area and great dining hall, worked directly under his command. The security detail for this event was tight. Every year, delegates and political parties from all across China convened in what was known as the Two Meetings.

Journalists, foreign dignitaries, and other notables gathered, too, to drive their own agendas, political and otherwise. This year was especially hectic given the imminent change in power and the expected ascension of Zhen Xin to the position of Paramount Leader.

Cao Qing had been especially thorough in preparing for this year's gathering at the Diaoyutai Guest House, an imperial resort constructed by Emperor Qianlong during the latter half of the eighteenth century. The bright reds, blues, and yellows of the many pagodas, the jade walkways along Yuyuan Lake and through the gardens, the goldfish at the edge of tranquil waters, the lush greenery with their weeping willows and peach blossoms made for paradise on earth for the Emperors and all those who would follow after their fall. But Cao Qing was uneasy this evening as he stood on the small stone bridge overlooking the placid scenery.

"Sir, we are measuring unauthorized signal traffic from inside the perimeter," said a voice over his hidden earpiece.

The frequency was set for communication between him and the signals intelligence team, hidden away in one of the many rooms of the palace, assigned to support the security detail.

"Specify," ordered Cao Qing into the tiny transmitter attached to the base of his throat.

"An encrypted communication protocol on a high frequency band at randomly spaced intervals. Both source and target are within the perimeter."

"Can you triangulate?" he asked, as he looked across the lake to the trees beyond.

There was nothing but the rustling wind and the trickling of falling water.

"They are within fifty meters of each other."

"Where?"

"The picture gallery."

Cao Qing hadn't waited for the response to start running. His feet barely touched the stone as his mind demanded he move faster than his legs could take him.

Upon sight of the picture gallery doors he slowed to a brisk walk, palpating the forty caliber compact pistol nestled beneath his breast coat pocket. It was still snug and a quick draw away.

Cao Qing stepped through the door, exhaling slowly. He must project the calm of a leisurely stroll, not the urgency of a sprint across the grounds. He scanned the roomful of guests, his heart still pounded violently in his chest.

Party officials, committee directors, politburo members, and their wives all moved in an almost choreographed dance, greeting each other and their foreign guests. The delegates and dignitaries from the eleven states that made up the Association of Southeast Asian Nations engaged in lively chatter, as others laughed at what were probably stilted jokes. The wives spoke with their foreign counterparts, some in Chinese, most in broken—but polite—English. They feigned interest in the stale conversation as wine and champagne warmed in their glasses. The servers filled glasses and offered trays of dumplings, rolls, and other delicacies for the attendees to savor.

The threat could come from anywhere: a poisoned dish, a carefully placed blade, a bullet, or even a bomb. Cao Qing watched, noting his agents in the room, both servers and guests alike. He made a mental note of each guest and staff member, looking with singular focus for one who might stand out. Zhen Xin stood with his wife and politely spoke with the American ambassador by the towering black canvas at the far end of the gallery.

Cao Qing approached the vice president, scanning the crowd for threats. The innocent rosy cheeks of a young girl in the green and yellow silks of the Guest House serving staff caught his attention. She stared at him between the crowd, her gaze steady and unwavering, as she extended her guest a sample of the steamed dumplings.

"The shrimp and pork are exceptionally tasty," she said, her eyes never leaving Cao Qing's. He headed right at her.

Young girls don't do that.

He barely finished his thought when blades met his flesh. A palm-sized black disc sliced into his chest, shredding shirt, tie, and jacket. The second caught his left shoulder, its stainless-steel edges burying themselves halfway into his deltoid, slicing muscle clean of bone. The impact of both knocked him to the floor, where he lay in an already forming pool of blood. Lucky for him, he was wearing an armored vest. Unlucky for him, it didn't cover past his chest.

Voices screamed, plates shattered, and ancient sculptures and vases, priceless works of art, toppled over. The pandemonium shot out in every direction as those closest realized what happened. Cao Qing writhed on the floor as across the gallery, Zhen Xin sprawled over his wife and grandson. In the crowd's blind effort toward the doors, they indiscriminately trampled over Cao Qing's supine body with the soles of their fine leather shoes. Cao Qing trembled, the blood and pain leaving his body. The waitress knelt beside him as his fading eyes caught sight of the weapon beneath her sleeve. Cao Qing remembered it well from his days in the jungles of Vietnam—and the man he hoped to forget.

"Viktor sends his regards," said the young girl, as the narrow handspike perforated the jugular notch in his throat.

Back across the room, amid mayhem and panic, Zhen Xin set to sole purpose—his wife and grandson. "Get up," he ordered, dragging her and the boy to their feet. "To the door!" Shi Ren grabbed onto his arm to pull him with her.

"Leave," he commanded, as he tore her hand from his jacket when a waiter, pistol in hand, took hold of his shoulder. Instinct and desperation took over; Zhen Xin seized a collar and sleeve. Twisting body and hips into *uchi mata*, he launched the waiter over his shoulder into the hardwood floor beneath. Zhen Xin crushed into his chest with a cross-body *kesa gatame*, but the waiter continued with the momentum, rolling Zhen Xin over him and onto his back. Back on top, the waiter buried a knee into belly, and clinched an arm bar lock, holding the pistol to Zhen Xin's temple.

"Stay down, sir," gasped the waiter, securing him in place as a tall, slender woman in a long black evening dress calmly crossed the room amid the chaos, her heels crushing shards of broken glass. A sudden heavy thump and splatter followed and the waiter released his grip. The man slumped over Zhen Xin, a five-bladed disk protruding from his head. Zhen Xin pushed the dead waiter off his body as the woman stood over him. Her sparkling dress and gentle smile were the last things he saw before his consciousness greeted only darkness.

VI

BY WAY OF DECEPTION

Rolling gray clouds blanketed the skies as salty winds whipped in from across the fjord. The battered tugboat cut across the white crests, puttering its way in, as the two deck hands scurried from bow to stern, preparing the lines for arrival.

From across the docks, the lone man in a hooded gray sweater watched the tugboat struggling to moor at the pier. The morning was cold and wet, the overcast skies dark and heavy with rain. But the man with the unblinking crystal-gray eyes and a scar over his right brow cared little for his surroundings. He focused on the new arrival and waited with hands in his pockets beneath his hooded, olive-drab windbreaker. With matching pants and dirty work boots, he passed for any one of the civilian or military personnel working at Malaya Lopatka, the sealed-off naval base at the entrance to Zapadnaya Litsa.

The man made his way up the pier, past the rust-streaked row of dilapidated tugboats and trawlers. A seaman was sliding the looped end of the thick braided rope through the eye of a cleat when he noticed the man in the hoodie approach. He whipped the line with expert skill onto the large anvil-shaped mooring cleat at the edge of the pier. With a snap of his wrist, he wrapped the thick cord hooked around the left, then the right horn, cinching the line firmly, tying the bow of the tugboat into place.

"*Da?*" asked the seaman, face pale and drawn from the overnight storm, as the hooded man came to a stop at the edge of the pier.

"May I help you?" he asked, this time quietly gripping a wrench lying atop the counter just inside the cabin.

"Bushov," said the man in an impassive, deep voice.

"What is your business?" asked the boatswain. A second young man of similar blond hair, athletic build, and handsome face blocked the door into the cabin. The twins stood in his way.

"Step back," said a gruff voice from inside.

Bushov ducked out of the cabin, his haggard face covered in black and gray stubble, his tattered coat and pants caked in dry salt. He'd endured more than a tempest the night prior. Reeking of alcohol, he parted the two young men.

"What do you want?" asked Bushov, soberly addressing their arrival.

It hadn't taken but a glimpse for Bushov. The strange man's bearing revealed who he was and why he was here. Bushov led him through the cabin, past the counter strewn with nautical charts and a coffee pot that piped a fresh black brew.

The large round compass above the tugboat's helm pointed wildly in every direction: north, south, west, east and back to north. The effects of the radiation from the Andreeva Naval Yard, where all the spent nuclear fuel was housed, could be felt even this far away. Alcohol poisoning didn't kill in these parts, radiation did.

Past the bronze-plated ship's wheel and engine-order telegraph, a small oak door led into the tugboat's galley below. A chill crept down Bushov's spine as he pushed the heavy door forward. His instinct knew better than to give this man his back. But his heart knew it wouldn't make much difference. Either way, he would be dead in an instant if the stranger felt so inclined. The reason the stranger was here lay draped on the table below deck. It wasn't every day they fished a cadaver from the sea.

"Leave us," rasped the hooded man, not giving Bushov a second glance, his eyes dead set on the cadaver.

The captain shut the door behind him as quickly as the hinges would allow.

"Boys, just keep doing what you're doing and don't ask questions," Bushov bellowed as he climbed the last of the steps leading back from the galley. He paced the wheelhouse, wild-eyed with Scotch in hand. He promised the twins' mother he'd take care of them. That was a long time ago. They were now barely in their twenties and had lived their entire lives navigating the Barents. Working a tugboat wasn't for the weak of stomach or faint of heart, especially when pulling cadavers from the sea, ones with their chests blown open.

Bushov glowered at them through the glass. The cadaver—and now this stranger beneath their feet— only made him angrier, angrier that he couldn't gather up the courage and urge them to run. Bushov watched the twins get back to their duties as he got back to wringing his hands while muttering and pacing.

Meanwhile, below deck, the stranger pulled his hood back to reveal a sharp, hooked nose, a stern mouth, and a bald head with the high-ridged brow and dark skin of Russia's Caucuses. The stranger fixed his stare on the figure atop the table and used a gloved hand to tear back the wet black plastic. Vadim's blue-lipped face stared back at him.

The rhythmic footfalls above deck did little to disrupt the stranger's focus. He felt along the contours of the softball-sized exit wound out the cadaver's spine as he gently rolled the body back onto the table. Threading thumb and forefinger through a fold of his salt-caked vest, he plucked a black capsule from the dead man's pocket. Pulling back the lid, he inspected the device beneath the lamplight. The USB port was dry. The base of the memory stick seemed intact. He inserted it into a handheld decoder, and the content directory quickly appeared on the screen. Everything was there. He disabled the device and placed the memory stick in his side pocket. He removed a second cylindrical device from his jacket, pressing a button on it until the black face atop the cylinder came to life. A timer set at ninety seconds began to count down. He slipped the device through the entry wound in his chest and, with his gloved hand, closed Vadim's eyes.

No one gives the dead their due respect anymore.

He covered the body and climbed the few steps back out the galley.

"What are your orders?" asked Bushov when the stranger returned.

"Have a good day," said the stranger, as he replaced the hood over his head and walked out.

Stepping swiftly onto the pier, he walked back the way he came, as Bushov and the two brothers watched. Bushov rushed into the galley and pulled back the black tarp. The dead face stared at him as a blinking red light in his chest counted down: 5, 4, 3...

118

"Boys!" cried Bushov. But the brothers could not hear his call any more than the hooded man could.

A ball of flame ripped through the cadaver and into Bushov before he could give his final order. The wooden deck plates shredded as the tugboat's innards blew apart beneath their feet. Shards of shrapnel, bone, and twisted metal lifted out of the water, as the ball of flame and a black mushroom cloud shot into the air. The compression wave blasted past Anton Arlovsky as he coolly reached the end of the dock never looking back; his crystal-gray eyes beneath their cowl stayed dead set on the path ahead. He turned the corner as the smoldering, twisted remains of the tugboat crashed back into the water and sank to the bottom.

***

The aseptic white tiles and stainless-steel work stations glared beneath the bright halogen lights. An ashen face, eyes swollen shut, hung over the edge of the examination table. The pathologist pulled away the white evidence sheet, revealing two distorted, rubbery breasts. He placed a steel grossing knife at the top of the cadaver's right shoulder, as his attention turned for a moment to the reflection in the one-way mirror. The dead woman's upside-down swollen face patiently waited for her procedure. The young woman in a surgical mask and cap standing opposite the pathologist stared at the blade. Her left eye gave a slight twitch as the incising sound of steel cutting through flesh and bone filled the silence.

From behind the mirror, Saifa Moudan watched the procedure. Her focus lay entirely on the girl, noting every move, every reaction. The slight twitch of the left eye had not gone unnoticed. For what it was worth, her own reaction to that first cut had been much worse. The pathologist opened the chest cavity, drawing in his observer for a closer look. Saifa did not need to listen to the question and answer session on the other side of the glass. She watched for behavior. Saifa was Mossad, an instructor at the *midrasha*, the training center for female operatives. A select few were chosen each year for further training in the Naqab Desert to serve as the agency's assassins.

Much like this young girl, Saifa had been brought into Mossad at an early age. By twenty, she had been recruited into the service after her station in the Golan Heights with the YAMAG unit of the Israeli Border Police.

She became only the second woman to receive the Distinguished Service Medal for bravery, pulling her medic and squad leader from under harrowing AK-47 fire after a car bomb had gone off beside them while on patrol in the streets of Al Ghajar village.

After the incident, she was quietly approached by Mossad's Deputy Director of Operational Planning about her future and what it could mean to her and Israel. With eagerness of youth, Saifa quickly found herself immersed in a world she'd only known before in her favorite spy thrillers. A second-generation Persian Jew, she spoke flawless Hebrew, Farsi, and near-perfect Arabic with a touch of an Iraqi accent. Off the charts on her aptitude tests, she was fast-tracked at the *midrasha,* learning all of the trade secrets that came with living the life of a *katsa*, an intelligence field operative. She was then sent off deep into the Naqab Desert to learn the art of death, much like the prospective young *bat leveyha* on the other side of the glass this morning.

Saifa watched the pathologist cut around the back of the head with a fine scalpel and stifled a grin. The young girl wanted to gag. But she held her composure. *Good for her.* The girl's stoic face gave away what was about to happen next. The pathologist pulled the hair and scalp away from the bone. A sticky red and white orb glistened beneath the overhead halogens. Saifa turned away. She'd seen enough. She heard the high-pitched whine of the circular saw start up, shutting the door behind her as the pitch suddenly deepened. The saw's steel teeth bit into something. She didn't wait for the pop of the cranium coming undone. After all, the young girl was the trainee, not her.

Saifa never tried to attract attention. In her line of work, blending into a crowd was a blessing. Yet when she needed it, she had a sultry sway to her walk with her golden-brown, toned legs. She had a sharp nose, piercing black eyes, thick curly hair, and a gaze that could hold the most powerful men steady.

She noticed the ogling of the passing doctors even when she did her best not to attract attention. She was always amused by men's reactions, especially the pathologists in this place. Their wives didn't let them get out much. That or the only pretty girls they ever saw were, for the most part, dead.

The buzzing at her hip pulled her away from her whimsical thought for the day and from how she would grade the young girl. Saifa could think about many things at once, but the caller on the screen focused all her attentions. Mossad's Deputy Director did not call her every day. In fact, he would avoid talking to her altogether, given the choice.

"Yes," she answered, placing the phone to her ear.

She stopped in mid-stride as she listened to the words coming across the line. She stared ahead as if her consciousness had been suddenly transported to another place, another time.

***

Teymour glanced back down the alley as the key slid into the groove. It was a force of habit to always look back. He could never know when he was being followed. The bolt slid back, and he slipped through, locking the door again behind him with a heavy thud.

He climbed the steps. The wood creaked beneath his feet. Short of breath and with droplets rolling off his forehead, he reached the tarnished door at the top. The stale air and stench of putrid water gave way to a spring breeze and the smells of foodstuff from the bazaar below. A hodgepodge of meats, spices, flowers, and human sweat wafted through the open window into the small room Teymour Anjani called home. A half-eaten plate of *biryani*, minced mutton and rice, sat next to the keyboard in front of three displays too large for the small writing table against the far wall. A single mattress atop a hand woven Tabrizian rug, stacked with embroidered sheets and pillows strewn about, took up most of the tiny space. Posters of old American spy thrillers and action heroes lined the walls. The clamor of the bustling bazaar below filled Teymour's ears as he threw himself down in front of the computer screens.

His fingers danced across the keyboard as the peddlers wheeled and dealed along the narrow and shady corridors beneath his feet. His cryptic commands made their way across the cyber network and, like a spider's web, radiated out from his little room situated just above Tehran's Great Bazaar, the largest open-air market in the world, where anything could be bought and sold for the right price.

Teymour had been recruited into the Revolutionary Guard's Cyber Army. He played his part in the recent Comodo and DigiNotar attacks. But his ambitions were far more than what the Guard and the Ashiyane, the Iranian Cyber Army, could offer. In his small circle, suspicions of intent were all it would take to end his career—and maybe his life. Teymour stayed away from the others in the Ashiyane. Survival depended on having as few friends as possible.

He typed feverishly into his computer. He whisked through the digital back alleys and side streets of the target neural network. Teymour stared rapaciously into his computer. He forgot to eat and there was no time for sleep. The rush of sustained adrenaline made time constrict and his mind dilate. The port scans yielded the back doors he'd set into the target systems. A month in, and their security still hadn't discovered him. Cracking Beijing's e-mail servers produced its tidbits. He infiltrated the select targets with the messages he'd been given. He knew not to ask questions. Knowing too much was dangerous. But it also came with its advantages, so he made sure to keep a copy of all he'd done. He might need it for a rainy day.

He was always curious who his targets were, and this one, Viktor Kletnov, was of a particularly dark and mythical nature. The more Teymour did this sort of stuff, the more he looked over his shoulder. He trace-routed the message from Beijing's servers back to their originating location – the Kandinsky Group. Their servers lay behind a heavily armed intrusion-prevention system. It took him weeks of scripting before he managed to bypass their defenses into one of their hundreds of data directory servers. Their offices in Beijing were a treasure trove. Times like these called for the most restraint. Take only what was needed. The less the greed, the less he would have to mask his trace later.

He found the MAC address he'd been given. The malware key-logged exactly what he wanted, and with the snooped credentials, Teymour took over the terminal. Curious hunger raced into his gonads as a file directory folder yielded a document that filled the screen. At the top of the document were a crescent and thirteen stars; at its bottom were a crown and two lions.

Names Teymour did not recognize filled the page, referencing something called the Syndycate. The document detailed the assassination attempt on Zhen Xin Liang and what looked like Viktor Kletnov's and this Syndycate's involvement. The document was rich with detail Teymour would just as soon rather not know.

The sounds of the bazaar again filled his ears, as did greed fill his brain. His client paid him with Bitcoin, and she would pay plenty for this information. Teymour sat back and took in a deep breath of the morning's freshness. Yes, indeed, she would be pleased. She would be very pleased.

VII

THE GATHERING STORM

"Excuse me, but again, Secretary Bradford, can you please answer the question?" repeated Senator Michaels from her perch high above him in the center of the chamber.

"I'm sorry, Madam Chair, could you please repeat it? I was still trying to process the last one."

"Trying to keep your stories straight, Mr. Secretary?" came the outburst from one of the twelve senators seated around the podium. All glared down at David with varying degrees of envy and hate. Among the roomful of journalists and assistants sat James Fenway, taking careful notes.

"It's just the stench in this chamber, senator," said David.

"Let's recap from the top," Senator Michaels said in a soothing tone, completely ignoring his commentary.

It had been a long morning for David, who was still getting over the jet lag of his extended travels, both those on and off his published itinerary. The Senate Committee on Foreign Relations was out to know the truth about this so-called agreement he brought back with him, and by God, they were going to get it. The frustrations he must endure to preserve the secrecy of the Syndycate were, at times, vexing, to say the least. The crusade of fabricated facts this morning impressed even him. The theatrics made for a fun time, if anything. Humans were such fallible creatures, so shallow, so thin skinned, so easy to manipulate. It really wasn't a fair fight.

"You talk about these extended timeframes—what do you call them?" asked Senator Michaels.

She wasn't half-bad looking, actually. The vitriol gave her a certain *je ne sais quoi* that he would have otherwise thought insane if not for his borderline exhaustion.

"Eight to twenty-five years," affirmed David.

"Right, eight to twenty-five years of inspections, not built on trust but verifiability, you say."

"Yes, ma'am."

"But inspectors from countries that don't have diplomatic relations with the Islamic Republic are excluded from said inspections. That's America and Canada, last I checked."

"International Atomic Energy Agency inspectors have all been trained by us. They have the very same interests and face the very same risks we do should the Iranians fail to comply."

"That is weak, Mr. Secretary. We're putting our fate, America's best interest, in the hands of foreign nationals, allies or not."

"It's an international accord, our partners as important in the process as we are."

"So says its chief negotiator. Take on all the accolades while distributing the risk and the shit. Maybe that's the smell you mentioned, Mr. Secretary."

"Among others, Madam Chair," said David.

"What this reads as to us is an agreement where you leave the Iranians to produce any type of nuclear device, peaceful or otherwise, at the conclusion of these timelines."

"Twenty-five years, Madam Chair."

"Have you looked in the mirror lately, David?" retorted the senator, catching the room off guard. David wasn't sure if it was the question or the use of his first name. "You're three times that age. Look at you. You're older than dirt."

"For once, Madam Chair is right. I am older than dirt." She had no idea how right she really was.

"Twenty-five years is nothing. Goes by like that," she said, snapping her fingers with her best angry glare.

David wondered what it was about her. He found her countenance, contorted with the violence of her own personality, and that wild look in her eye appealing. He really did.

"They'll have their weapons and we'll have no leverage to negotiate. You might actually still be around to see it," mused the senator.

"Madam Chair—"

"No, you wait. I'm not done. You cite the Nuclear Non-Proliferation Treaty as the mechanism, the catch-all safety net, that's going to keep the Iranians compliant with the international community. You so conveniently forget how we once said the same thing about North Korea, and look at what they did. Does your senescence preclude that memory?"

"No, Madam Chair. It does not. But—"

"I'm still not done."

David couldn't get a word in edgewise. Giving James a glance, he grabbed at his water bottle and sat back for a long one.

"Throughout the course of this deal—I mean, it just boggles my mind—you extend the Iranians access to conventional weapons markets, lifting ballistic missile restrictions after the first five years. The first five years!"

David had never known the senator to raise her voice like that. It was so much fun.

"One hundred billion in remunerations to start out, though your colleagues here with you today would argue it's much less. By the way, does that include the $1.7 billion paid to Tehran in foreign currencies so we could not trace it? Or should we conveniently just overlook that?"

David took a big gulp of the water bottle, finishing what was left. "The hundred billion was their money."

Senator Michaels raised her finger at David, stopping him with his mouth wide open. "You do all this while not providing this Congress access to any of the additional side agreements made between the Atomic Energy Agency and Iran—to which you claim ignorance. You know nothing about them, so you say. You're the chief negotiator, for goodness' sake. An embarrassment!"

"That hurts my feelings." David spoke with such sincerity that it only made Senator Michaels angrier, if that were possible.

"You have the delusional gall to tell us, to tell the American people with an absolute straight face, that this is a good deal. Where did you get the talent, Mr. Bradford, for such chicanery?"

"I was born with it, Madam Chair. Madam Chair, you mince words to cast our negotiations in a light unfavorable to America's interest."

"Mr. Secretary, I do not mince my words. You could have negotiated a much stronger position. Not twenty-five years on uranium enrichment, but one hundred. Conventional arms embargo relief, but only with a permanent exclusion of a ballistic missile program. Access by Americans to all sites, military and otherwise, and no wait periods on inspections, just to name a few."

"Madam Chair, what you're implying is that we were the only ones in the room, negotiating with ourselves, in a utopian fantasy land where we got every single one of our wishes in exchange for whatever it was we wanted to give them, not what they in turn demanded for themselves. It's called a negotiation, Madam Chair. We each give to get, to come away with an agreement that we could both live with and we've done that here. We stop them from getting a bomb; they get what they wanted, sanctions relief."

"You are right, they got what they wanted. Their bomb, fifteen or twenty-five years from now. It doesn't matter. They will have it."

"Well, ma'am. Without this accord, fifteen or twenty-five years from now starts tomorrow. Would you rather have that?"

"In the hopes of a better deal, I would."

"There will be no better deal. If we reject this, our allies will not walk away from Iran. They will walk away from us."

"Because you and your boss put us in that position, Mr. Secretary. And now you try to intimidate us with your new draconian narrative: without this agreement there can only be war, you say. This Senate does not believe that, Mr. Bradford. What we do believe is that there are perhaps other agendas at work here we cannot fully see yet. But we will, Mr. Secretary. We absolutely will!"

"You hypothesize alongside the very best of conspiracy theorists, Madam Chair. Makes for great television. Your calling should have been Hollywood and not the Senate floor."

"We shall see, Mr. Secretary. We shall see."

***

The antacid tablets had long since worn off. Since his latest briefing with Brian Reese, his ops chief at the NSOC, he felt as if he'd been doubled over with a sledge hammer. Karl had the foul taste of a sure-to-be-terrible morning rolling around in his mouth, and it wasn't his wife's burnt toast. He hated finding out about things on TV that he should have already known about and while eating a plate of burnt toast, no less. His job was to know what was going to happen before it happened, to stop it from ever happening in the first place. That was what he always told his wife when he was pissed about something he couldn't talk about.

State Department officials on overseas assignments like the one Ambassador William Boyd had been on last night in Beijing was one of the more sensitive areas for Karl, one he always wanted to make sure was always well handled. This morning it looked like somebody on his watch dropped the ball. Luckily, the ambassador had escaped with his life, and no one was claiming responsibility yet. That made it only more difficult for Karl, the man who was supposed to always be in the know. After 9/11, a lot of finger-pointing went the way of the agency directors and not undeservedly so. The thought of an earful from a less-than-competent boss and his own expectations didn't make the prospect of coming in to work on a Saturday morning any brighter.

Karl was caught in the middle of the 295's early morning, parking-lot traffic jam, very unusual for a Saturday, when a call from Katherine came in. He replayed the day's prior report over and over again in his mind, both for the content and who had delivered it. Monday's briefing had urgently been moved to this morning. Karl's invitation to the briefing still stood.

He had every intention of having Katherine there. Even on a bad day, she had a way of easing his mind, at least when he gave in to the idea he'd never get more than an affectionate smile or friendly tap on the shoulder. But soon enough, he was pissed again, fighting with himself and she the reason for it. How he hated the torture.

The call came in so early in the morning and right on cue with his thoughts of her. Karl loved the synchronicity: right when he was thinking of her, she called. He needed to quit this thinking, these dumb romantic ideas. He was very married and not a pubescent schoolboy.

"Karl here."

"Where are you? We need to talk." She hadn't even slowed down to greet him. But he did like the urgency in her voice, made him feel important to her.

"On the 295, it's a parking lot this morning. But I'll be there on time." Karl glanced at the dashboard clock. *Barely.*

"We need to speak privately — before the briefing."

He hoped it was for something that had nothing to do with work, but he struck the thought. There went his masochist mind again. "Why? What's up?"

"I need to see you. Step on it." Clipped and abrupt, she was gone. But he didn't care. How he loved the sweetness of her words.

Stop it! Karl sighed. He needed to cease and desist from this dangerous line of thinking.

***

"*As-salam alaikum.*"

"*Wa alaikum as-salam,*" said Prince Bin Hasan, extending his hand toward the American who greeted him at the door just inside the circular office. The prince bowed ever so slightly, appreciative that this president at least knew how to stand well on etiquette and could get the names of his royal family right.

Following the prince was a second guest, the Israeli ambassador. He was much shorter, less stocky around the chest and belly, and had decidedly lighter skin. He wore a gray suit that matched his peppery silver hair and a red tie—in contrast to the royal prince's tailored beige cashmere shirt and pants.

"*Shalom aleichem,*" said both gentlemen, greeting the ambassador at the door, the prince with an accent of disdain, and the president, well, with just an accent.

"*Aleichem shalom,*" responded Moshe Eban. He was not new to this sort of affair.

With the custom and decorum of a practiced hand, the White House staff guided the prince and the ambassador to their respective places, each of them accompanied by a guest of their own. Their cohorts were decidedly younger, with similar dark complexions and wary gazes. They stood relaxed, with an air of controlled danger. Saudi and Israeli delegations had met many times and this meeting, though impromptu, was expected. On this occasion they had common ground, but still they eyed each other with equal suspicion and contempt.

Their host stood tall in the center of the room; perhaps only one in his place had ever stood taller. He was fit and handsome, with a youthful complexion that belied his age and a warm smile that was both inviting and disarming. Irving McNeal was serving his third year of his first term and already working steadfastly on his reelection campaign, and he needed the support of these two men on this critical issue. He was President McNeal, the forty-third president, and this was his Oval Office.

"Thank you both for coming so late and on such short notice. You remember Alan Gerstner," said McNeal, dispensing with pleasantries, as his defense secretary took his place alongside him. McNeal offered their guests a place at one of the couches center of the room.

Ambassador Eban was the first to sit. He cared little for decorum and even less for the Saudis. President McNeal quietly waited for the Saudi prince to be seated while he bit his tongue at the Israeli ambassador.

Ronen Peretz stood close behind the ambassador. He was the Mossad Intelligence Director in charge of the spy agency's worldwide operations. He flew in from Tel Aviv just for this visit. Prime Minister Ben-Gideon had requested he attend to this personally. The prime minister did not want just anyone at this meeting. Ronen took a brief glance down to the minute hand of his watch. He was set on the first flight back to Tel Aviv at the conclusion of this affair.

Ahmad Al Awari casually glanced at Ronen with more than a passing interest. He was with the Saudi intelligence services, and he knew of Ronen well. They had greeted each other in the reception area moments before with mutual respect. Ronen was known among their circles for what he'd done with their *kidon*. He was rumored to be the most accomplished of them all and the one responsible for Arafat's demise. Al Awari would have loved the chance to kill him.

They all took their place once Prince Bin Hassan found his spot, as the Secret Service detail sealed the doors behind them.

President McNeal cleared his throat. "Thank you all again for joining us."

"King Faisal thanks you for consulting him on your agreement with the Persians, and I too thank you for your consideration, Mr. President. But let's dispense with the pleasantries, shall we? It is no secret that your policies and actions in our region have left our family exposed to threats within and beyond the borders of our kingdom."

"Prince Hassan, we shared with you our intelligence on Iran throughout the entire process leading up to this agreement. We both know that this agreement curbs Iran's push for the bomb and keeps you strongest with all of our agreements fully in place."

"We all know the Iranians already have nuclear weapons. Have had them for a long time," said Ambassador Eban.

"As do you, Moshe, possess a vast nuclear arsenal in the Naqab Desert," said Prince Bin Hassan, turning to his counterpart.

"As do we both, prince. But that's not what we're here to discuss," said the ambassador.

"No, you are right. This agreement is about the wealth of nations and American interests," said Prince Bin Hassan, with a cynical smile meant for McNeal.

McNeal returned a smile of his own. "As well as yours. We've worked this deal with the best interest of peace and stability for your house and the region. You both are our greatest allies in the Middle East. This agreement in no way changes that."

"Our question is whether serving as America's greatest ally in our homelands still carries with it the benefit it once did," Ambassador Eban remarked dryly.

"It would for you, ambassador. I'm certain our support in the UN for your claims on the Leviathan gas fields would offset any claims Lebanon might have on those deposits," said McNeal, teasing his support for the Israelis on the new natural gas find.

"Your support is appreciated, but our claims are more than secure. This isn't about natural gas. It's about the continued existence of Israel and peace for all of the Middle East," said the ambassador, with a tone bordering on the confrontational.

"It's as much about your existence as it is about economics. I'm certain Prime Minister Ben-Gideon would agree," said McNeal, his sentiment met with icy stares.

"Anti-Semitic attacks and support for Hezbollah at our borders will only be emboldened by this deal. In the last year the Persians have only further pressed their advantage in Iraq and Yemen against Sunni and

Jewish people. This is more than just economics Mr. President. Much more..."

"Ambassador Eban, we know the rhetoric out of Tehran to be just that. Iran has the second-largest Jewish population in the region behind Israel. They even have a seat in parliament. They can travel to and from Israel, as can Iranians from your country, and they enjoy many of the same rights as Shiites. Compared to the racism in my own country, the Jews in Iran live a gifted life."

The door opened and one of the Secret Service agents stepped into the room. He gestured, and Alan Gerstner quickly rose from his place, briskly making his way to the door. They briefly exchanged hushed words, and Gerstner turned to the president.

"Sir, sincerest apologies, but I've been requested to step away on a matter."

"It's quite alright, Alan. I will brief with you this afternoon. Thank you," said McNeal.

"Thank you, Mr. President. Prince Bin Hassan, ambassador, if you'll excuse me," said Alan with a reverent nod as he stepped out the door, shutting it behind him.

Ronen and Ahmad watched very closely. The nature of their worlds made them question every motive, every action. What could be so important that would pull a defense secretary away from a meeting like this?

Bin Hassan broke the silence. "I applaud you on your impassioned plea, Mr. President, but I'm afraid our house has carefully reviewed your Persian plan and we do not see its virtues. We've decided that at this time, a revaluation of our currency-to-oil agreements with you may be warranted. We believe it is in the best long-term interest of the kingdom and OPEC to open the sale of our energy resources to multiple currencies. That would be particularly helpful to the Chinese and Russians. Your dollar would no longer be needed as our reserve currency. You should perhaps look at it this way, Mr. President. You'll be able to greatly increase your exports and pay down your impressive deficit. But I'm not certain exactly what it is you'll export."

"Maybe export enough oil to run your price into the ground," said McNeal, less than amused at this point.

"Maybe export another war," interjected the ambassador.

"What is it that you really want, Bin Hassan, for your support on this deal?"

The silence was long and drawn between the three men. Ronen and Ahmad watched like flies on a wall. The air was heavy and dry, as much as McNeal's question was emotionless and matter of fact.

"We want exclusive rights as the sole crude oil producer, refiner, and provider to your Trans Pacific Partnership treaty. We want access to your MOAB weapons technology and your most advanced missile defense systems, including the Aegis array. We also want to refresh our obsolete missiles with your latest Patriot battery defense system. We believe six thousand missiles should suffice. Oh, and we want you to curb the output of your shale gas reserves by half for equal to the maximum term of your Iran agreement, twenty-five years."

Ambassador Eban chimed in with a steadfast poker face. "These terms are as much for Saudi Arabia as they are for Israel, with exclusivity rights regarding the sale of our natural gas reserves to the sixteen countries in your TPP treaty."

McNeal stifled a laugh as the last of the ambassador's words rolled off his tongue. "Please forgive my rudeness gentlemen. The conversation suddenly turned amusing."

"We're glad to hear that, because for a long time the joke has been you, but even that has grown boring. If you want our support with the Persians, you'll meet our requests," said Bin Hassan.

"Thank you, gentlemen. That will be all."

The president watched them with a smile bordering on the maniacal. His guests waited with a sudden unease in their bellies. They sat in their places a moment longer than usual. Two Secret Service agents stood at the door at rigid attention, their focus squarely on the prince and the ambassador.

"Mr. President," said the two diplomats as they rose from their places, followed each by their own men. Ronen and Ahmad's attentions lingered on the president just a moment longer, confirming what they already knew of the man.

Irving McNeal was neither weak nor suffered fools. The door shut behind them, leaving Irving to gaze out the window at the oak tree that another president with a similar choice to make had planted some seventy years earlier. With the Persians, Eisenhower might have succumbed to the wrong side of history. Irving McNeal would not.

***

In one of 1600 Pennsylvania Ave's many hidden rooms, Karl sat at the main conference table, checking his watch every minute, on the minute. The White House Situation Room was a series of conference and meeting rooms originally built by the Kennedy administration after the Bay of Pigs failure. Since then it had served as an operations and communications center for the presidents and their top aides. Karl sat and waited as he had so many times before. He checked his watch again. Each time he looked, it was only to greater angst.

She said she had something important. Urged me to hurry. She should have been here already!

A bound copy of the National Intelligence Daily lay at the center of the table. A smiling but taciturn James Fenway sat opposite him; for the moment they were the only two in the room except for the duty officer at the door. Karl had a great distaste for Deputy Secretary Fenway. The fact that he had to stare at his smug face on a Saturday morning only served to heighten his dislike even more.

"I'm glad you made our meeting," said James. The lack of greeting reaffirmed their mutual disaffection.

Karl had met James at one of the White House galas he seldom attended shortly after Fenway's appointment as the head of the Executive Secretariat at the State Department. It had taken Karl all of thirty seconds to make up his mind about the man. "We will make great political allies," James had said upon meeting. At least each of them could smell bullshit.

"Any update on Ambassador Boyd's condition?" asked Karl, as the two men waited in the cold White House basement.

"He's already on a flight back to D.C."

"As usual, a response without answering the question."

"Fuck you, Karl. How are the wife and kids?" asked James disingenuously.

"I must say, I am impressed."

"Why's that?" James wore a genuine smile for a change.

"You've made a success of yourself being quite the asshole. Do you all make any coffee around here?" asked Karl.

What drove him perhaps the craziest was that James actually enjoyed their conversation, so he stopped it in its tracks. He looked to his watch again right when Secretary of State David Bradford entered through the main doors, followed by two other men wearing similar black suits with striped ties and little American flags pinned to their lapels.

"Good morning, Mr. Secretary," said Karl. He rose from his chair, James following suit.

Where was Katherine?!

"Good morning, gentlemen," said Defense Secretary Alan Gerstner, as he followed David around the far side of the table, the two taking up their usual spots near the center.

The third man approached Karl extending his hand.

"Ryan," acknowledged Karl, relieved to see his old friend.

"Good morning, Karl," said Ryan Douglas.

He was a big Texan with a bit of gray on his head, a square jaw, and broad shoulders and the current acting Director of National Intelligence. They'd been friends for a long time, going back to their days as flight officers during the Vietnam War. They worked well together whenever and wherever possible. Ryan oversaw the Intelligence community's sixteen branches, including the NSA. But Alan Gerstner, the

Secretary of Defense, a slight, rounded man with a large nose and thin bifocals, was still the boss.

"Gentlemen, before the president gets here, which won't be long, I'd like a brief on the who, the what, and the why, so we don't look as completely stupid—as we all ought to feel right about now," said Gerstner, as he looked at the two men opposite him at the table. The hot seat was nothing new for Karl. Without even a glance or a twitch, he broke into his prepackaged delivery of why they got caught with their pants down.

***

The girl in the blue turban caught Richard's gaze, just as she had so long ago in a memory from another time and place—a snowy and dark, bitter and gelid, gray and inhospitable place. Here, he was warm and cozy in the halls of the National Gallery, with Danny hoisted over his shoulders and Anja by his side, but his heart was as frozen as that inhospitable memory of so long ago. Something changed in Anja the night of the Pinacoteca. He tried to speak to her about what happened, about what he'd done, but she gave no hint, made no mention of anything.

Richard pushed the paranoia back into the recesses of his mind. But other memories surfaced, even older memories he wished he could forget. He stared at the painting under the spotlight, alone on the far wall. The secrets behind the eyes of the girl in the blue turban were far more than the thoughts she experienced those final days and nights Vermeer so lovingly painted her. Richard remembered those nights so vividly. He had been there.

For Guija, there was no barrier between the material and metaphysical. Richard could as easily move through time as navigate the imagination. He befriended the painter, burrowed into his mind. He violated him, plowed into him, taking what existed, warping, mutating the imagination into this material plane in the form of genius paintings, the *Ilythiium* trapped in the two-dimensional world of his canvases. Richard enslaved the creature, driving Vermeer himself to a frenzied madness. He let the thing eat away at the painter. He let Vermeer die.

A small price to pay.

Richard yearned to believe that lie. He purged the memories and feigned ignorance of the blame in Anja's eyes. He raised a finger to Danny's lips to keep him quiet as the three stared at the intimate canvas and the man who stood before it, his back to them.

"I never understood the obsession with the *Mona Lisa* when you have portraits like this." Richard's words echoed through the empty gallery as the man at the painting turned around sharply.

Richard stood with a big grin a few feet back, Danny still saddled over his shoulders. Richard knew this tactic required its subtleties, and personal distance stood out at the top of the list.

"May I help you?" asked the man, seeming startled by the approach of their family.

"Allow me," said Richard as he lowered Danny quickly to the ground. He carefully measured his step as he proffered his bandaged hand to the man. "It's an honor to meet you, Mr. Thorn."

"I'm sorry, but how do I know you?" The man was visibly concerned at the circumstances of the sudden meeting, but took the handshake.

"You don't," said Richard with a smile. "Danny, this is Edvard Thorn, the gentleman responsible for the restoration of this extraordinary painting."

"Do you work for the gallery?" asked Edvard, trying to right his confusion.

"We are friends of a friend," said Anja, taking Danny by the hand. She added in a soothing tone, "We wanted our boy to see Vermeer's great masterpiece, firsthand, before the crowds."

"Maybe I should call one of the museum's personnel," said Edvard with a politely nervous smile.

"That won't be necessary." Guillermo stood at the entrance to the special exhibit wing. "Richard, it's so nice of you to arrive two hours before we're open to the public," he added condescendingly.

"Thank you for having us over. This is a great experience for Danny." Richard looked down to his boy who just nodded quietly as he hugged his mom's leg.

"I take it you've met Edvard," said Guillermo in a more amenable tone as he approached the group.

"We were just getting acquainted," said Anja with a welcoming smile.

"I'm sorry, but I did not get your name." Edvard carefully kept himself between them and the painting.

"Richard Robles. A great fan of your work."

"I didn't know I had fans."

"It's not just anyone who can restore perfection."

"If you're referring to the *Pearl Earring*, it was a collaborative undertaking. But I accept the compliment nonetheless," said Edvard.

"I actually came to see this gentleman for a moment," Richard said, turning his attentions to

Guillermo. Guillermo, no doubt, knew the reason for the visit.

"Little Danny and I have never seen Vermeer's work. Could you give a tour?" Anja asked Edvard, still wearing her warm smile.

"Of course," conceded Edvard, with a slight bow of his head. They walked down the gallery away from the gathering storm between the two men.

Anja always got what she wanted.

"You must be kidding me, right? You must be kidding that you show up like this when we both know it's the first rule of business: no unnecessary contact, and nothing unannounced!" Guillermo looked over his shoulder with a twitchy tic to his right eye.

"Your client is dead."

"Come again?" asked Guillermo. The twitch stopped.

"Your client is dead. And fourteen million are sitting in my account."

"What do you mean, he's dead?"

"Netherlands police found the body of Christian Huygens in his home last night."

Guillermo steadied himself against a chair at the edge of the cafeteria terrace. A couple of servers were already preparing the buffet stand for the day's visitors. "I spoke with him yesterday afternoon. How'd you know it was Huygens?"

"Enough of the game, Willie. We've hidden behind polite banter and the pretense of ignorance long enough."

"I don't know what you're talking about."

"I invoked an orb of sanctuary the night I stole the Rembrandt," said Richard.

"Time dysplasia is forbidden! Never to speak of it, less do it. That was our oath!"

"What's done is done. To what effects we shall see," said Richard.

Guillermo sat in the chair, knees no longer able to hold him upright.

"I had no choice."

"No Richard, you always have a choice. You invoked an orb of sanctuary?! Why?!"

"That or be caught in the Vatican, at the mercy of the Syndycate."

"No, that's not how we play this game!"

"As I said, Willie. The game is up."

"The orb will act like a beacon, even now. It will awaken an awareness we cannot imagine. What we fled will come for us, like a moth to a flame. The Syndycate will know we still exist. They will hunt us down and tear us limb from limb." Guillermo spoke with the whispered panic of a terrible premonition.

"Does Anja know?" he asked.

"She said nothing since that night. It was as if I had channeled the power of an Armillary Sphere itself."

"Does she know?!" repeated Guillermo. Richard's response was silence.

"Armillary Sphere, orb of sanctuary, this can't be happening. I'm calling Huygens right now."

"No, you're not," said Richard matter-of-factly.

Guillermo scanned his phone for the latest news out of the Netherlands.

"There's nothing. Nothing on Huygens."

"Police have not released the information yet, pending initial investigation. No one would have known to target Huygens right as we're about to close our transaction for paintings no one should have known were stolen," said Richard rather calmly.

"The Syndycate," said Guillermo as the cafeteria manager walked by on her way into the kitchen.

Richard thought to mention the memory. He turned to the *Girl with the Pearl Earring* and gave her a long look. He saw the light and the color, the reflection, the expression in those eyes that had captivated so many. He thought to tell Guillermo, what he truly saw, what terrified him. *No more secrets.*

But his instinct, that voice deep inside, did not allow him. He needed a firm grip on his mind or he would lose much more. He would lose everything and everyone he ever loved.

"We need to secure the paintings and get off the grid," said Richard, walking right past Guillermo toward the little boy charging him from across the hall.

He scooped Danny up with a single arm, giving Guillermo a look and an easy smile. He gave Anja a kiss and a whisper as the three turned the corner, leaving Guillermo alone to ponder the shithole mess they'd sunk neck-deep into.

VIII

THE MONGOOSE & THE SERPENT

E ven Karl had heard enough. The Secretary of
Defense had come down on his longtime friend
Ryan as if he were responsible for the attack on
the ambassador and the Chinese Vice President
himself.

"Sir, we are gathering the facts!" retorted Karl, with
such anger that the room was taken aback by its
ferocity, leaving humiliation or retribution as the
defense secretary's only options.

"Perhaps we should hire a journalist or two, the
ones I keep seeing this morning. They seem to have a
better grasp of the situation than the lot of you," said
Alan, his neck bulging and face flush with anger.

Cabinet members were a funny bunch, career civil
servants and politicians. They had a streak of
something once useful in them, but now rotted away in
the ineptitude and toxic sludge of Washington politics.

"We have zero intelligence, no knowledge of the
group responsible for this attack. Nothing inside NSA
or CIA—or any other agency for that matter. Nothing
on these Zhu Quan Long, these Sovereign Tigers, as
the media is calling them. I wonder what exactly you
Ryan, and your doormat here do when you come to
work in the mornings," said Alan, without even the
courtesy of a look at Karl.

147

It was never good when your boss's boss called you a doormat.

Karl didn't care. His ire rose his blood pressure beyond any reason, and the smug faces of these incompetent asses only made it harder for him to think straight. If these sycophantic suckass politicians would let him do his job, perhaps Karl could give them some solid answers instead of sitting in this basement taking a reaming for no other reason than to save their political asses. He would love some one-on-one time with the Secretary of Defense. But instead he had to settle for this. Karl was glad for all of the times he didn't have to attend these meetings.

Where on God's green earth is Katherine?

He was looking at his watch when the far door opened and Katherine Brandt, as professionally dressed on a Saturday morning as on any day of the week, strode through the door. All attention turned to her as she pulled a chair up alongside Karl.

"Good morning, gentlemen," she said, placing her documentation and laptop on the table.

It didn't matter who was present, Katherine always took over the room.

"Glad you could make it," whispered Karl.

He gave Ryan a glance and that was enough. They'd worked together long enough to know each other's thoughts. All in the room suddenly stood at attention as the president entered, followed by his chief of staff, Edwin Birling.

"Good morning, Mr. President," said David, as the rest around the table welcomed him in turn.

"So what have you for me this morning?" asked President McNeal, with a copy of his Daily Brief in hand.

Now we'll see who has the last laugh.

Karl sat back in his chair. He was going to enjoy this almost as much as he enjoyed the torture of having Katherine this close.

***

Saifa had driven from the suburbs, from the pathology department, on into the city center. It was one of those drives she could hardly remember, because she was so engrossed in the memories of her past with this man. There was no need for him to call her now. There was no need for him to call her ever. She had made that very clear. She wished she could just ignore him. But she couldn't. One thing was sure, there would be plenty of pain to pass around this day for everyone.

She stopped the car at a corner of one of the many streets of downtown Tel Aviv. The streets were quieter than usual, especially for a Saturday evening. The sidewalks were empty except for a mother and child at the crosswalk of the far corner. The streetlight turned green as the woman scurried across, dragging the little girl to safety.

Saifa smiled bittersweetly. She woke up this morning with more agony than usual from her old injuries. The wounds, the scars, mocked her in the mirror—just as the man who put them there haunted her memories.

She turned off the street into a narrow side alleyway and parking lot, pulling up to her old space between two reinforced concrete pillars. She snatched the notebook from the passenger seat and caught a glimpse of her green iridescent eyes in the rearview mirror, eyes that had seen too much. She thought of the young woman back at the pathology center with those same green eyes.

Pass or fail.

Either mark, she wasn't doing the young woman any favors.

***

David had been listening and observing the tirade of questions and half-baked answers between the defense secretary and his staff for most of the morning. It had been barely seventy-two hours since the Syndycate's meeting in Rome, and here he was, back at it, with all the Washington theatrics.

"How are we supposed to handle the Chinese now that they are implicating the Taiwanese government?" asked Alan.

David didn't think the defense secretary's face could have gotten any redder. He could actually see an artery pulsing over the collar of his fat neck. This new development was not surprising. Nothing ever was. There was no such thing as coincidence. The Syndycate maneuvered for dominion, and the Chinese wanted their rightful place in the new order of things.

There were other enclaves like theirs that had their sights on a play for power, like a chess match many moves ahead of checkmate. This whole thing smelled of a false flag, a black propaganda operation, a ruse not of a nation state, but of select power-players intent to draw the Syndycate out into the open. Maybe even Syndycate members themselves, intent on their own ambitions. But David would never allow that, especially now. His time, his ascendance, was coming.

No one would stop what had been set in motion, no one.

"Any conclusions at this time would be premature," said Karl, drawing Alan Gerstner's focus away from Ryan.

"I'm curious as to your thinking, young lady," David said, speaking up for the first time. Everyone's attention turned to the young woman at the center of the room — not that everyone hadn't already noticed.

President McNeal sat back, so quiet that some in the room might have forgotten he was even there. Not David.

That's exactly what he wanted.

A silence followed David's question, one McNeal would only revel in more. The longer it lasted, the greater the stress. The greater the stress, the more truth came out — beautiful and grotesque truth alike.

"The response, along with the blame, has been too swift. Such direct action doesn't fall in line with what we know of the politically pragmatic Chinese," said Katherine, with a confidence beyond what another might have shown in her place.

Others might have been threatened, but to David, she was a curiosity and perhaps an opportunity. She didn't need to say much to capture men's imaginations in every sense of the word.

"They are too subtle and smart for such heavy-handedness. Unless they are playing to a more important card than Taiwan," she said.

"I'm sorry, I did not catch your name," said David.

"Katherine Brandt, DTRA liaison to NSA Central Security Services."

"Defense Threat Reduction Agency? Since when does DTRA make recommendations outside its area of expertise?" asked Defense Secretary Gerstner.

"I only make recommendations on what I know, sir."

"Then by all means, share with us what you know," said President McNeal, much to David's pleasure. Indeed, this young woman was an opportunity.

"At the direction of Mr. Downing, NSA had been analyzing transmissions from Beijing since before the incident last night. Analysts have confirmed at least one casualty in the attack; General Cao Qing, the head of the Central Security Bureau's Unit 8341, China's special protections team, akin to our Secret Service. He was the personal bodyguard to Vice President Zhen Xin Liang. As you know, Zhen Xin Liang survived the attack unharmed. The attackers, according to the same CSB reports, managed to evade capture. Two of our safe houses in Beijing were breached overnight, linking American support to what China is calling a failed assassination attempt."

"It's a set up," said David, as he studied Katherine Brandt's every gesture and expression, every word, every tell.

"An elaborate one. You may wonder, Secretary Gerstner, why an analyst for DTRA is presenting you these findings," said Katherine.

"Yes, I am."

"Seventy-two hours ago, NSA elements confirmed the presence of several high-ranking 14K Triad members at the Yulin Naval Base in Hainan. They were receiving a shipment of what we believe to be obsolete components smuggled out of a nuclear disposal center in Kamchatka—submarine-launched ballistic missile components, to be more specific. The leader of 14K is Dian Lung Chung. The man killed last night, Cao Qing, was Chung's brother and greatest supporter within the PLA.

"There is no such thing as coincidence," said President McNeal.

"I would agree with you, sir," said Katherine, giving her boss Karl a sideways look.

"Thank you, Ms. Brandt. That will be all."

"Yes, Mr. President."

She'd been excused when she least expected it. The president did not want whatever she knew released in the company of this group. That much was as obvious to David as it was Katherine.

Katherine glanced around the table, seeming claustrophobic in her own skin. "Good day, gentlemen." She gathered her things and left the way she came.

"Excuse me a moment." Karl stepped away from the table.

The young woman influenced Karl in more ways than just professionally, thought David, to his delight. David commiserated with Karl's simpleminded obsession with the young woman and noted its usefulness for when dealing with him at a later date. There was something different about her; something David had not seen in many generations.

Meanwhile, Karl strode past the Marine guards stationed at the entrance to the Situation Room, intent on her.

"Katherine!"

"Yes?" Her reply was curt and her stare did not waver.

"You said you needed to see me before the meeting. Not usual for you to be late." Her demeanor was defiant, an antagonism that bordered on the threatening. It was something Karl did not expect to feel from her.

"Was nothing at all, Karl. Nothing we didn't just cover in there," she said with an ease that belied what he was feeling.

"You did very well in there, by the way," he said, trying to penetrate the veil he suddenly felt between them.

"Thanks, Karl. I'll update you as soon as I've completed my assessments on what we have outstanding."

"I'll be on the lookout."

"I'm sure you will," said Katherine as she turned and left Karl with the shiver of a cold shoulder crawling down his spine.

Maybe it's just me. Maybe I'm reading into it too much. Yeah, it's just me.

But no matter how much he said it to himself, he couldn't shake the nauseous feeling that Katherine found what he hoped she would not find. Perhaps it was time she learned the truth about him and the Syndycate, about him and Viktor Kletnov. Karl went back into that meeting with that old taste of burnt toast in his mouth and his own foul mood.

***

The blood-orange rays shone through the floor-to-ceiling glass as the sun set over the Red Sea. Tel Aviv sprawled out in all directions. White buildings and red-tiled roofs, as far as the eye could see, basked in the setting sun. Cars, like ants, scurried along the streets far below, scintillating beneath the orange glow. Tel Aviv lay quiet and peaceful from this high up.

People from all walks of life went about for an evening meal or a family outing. Some were returning from a day at the beach, while others still strolled along the leafy streets of Rothschild Boulevard or along one of the many boardwalks by the sea. Saifa wanted to believe sometimes that, in some small way, those who did not know could enjoy peace because of the work they'd done, she and all her colleagues in arms. Though on most days, only the names on the Glilot memorial seemed to serve as consolation for their sacrifice.

She needed no reminder of the monsters that lurked throughout the lands of the Twelve Tribes: fatwas and jihads, murdering countless innocent Jews and Gentiles alike. The butchers had existed for centuries on both sides of the conflict and would long after she was gone. But on this Saturday afternoon, she pretended the scars were worth it, that peaceful people on both sides could enjoy an evening with loved ones — those who would be so fortunate.

"Being a deputy director has its privileges," said Ronen Peretz from the door.

"You get to sit up here atop your ivory tower, while the rest of us do the bleeding for you." She imagined herself upon the placid waters of the distant Red Sea, far enough away from him.

"We have all done our fair share of bleeding — no less than you, Saifa," said Ronen.

Saifa could see the exhaustion under his eyes. His years and all that travel were catching up to him.

"You called for me. What do you want?"

Ronen closed the door behind him. He went to his desk and placed a file folder inside the top drawer alongside the sleek, black curves of a P90 pistol. He closed the drawer, but not all the way.

Just open enough for quick access to its contents.

Saifa watched as he cautiously sat back in his chair. Ronen hadn't seen her in almost ten years, ever since the Peter Cole affair. She had remained below the radar, training her students, well-away from the Institute's barren corridors.

"It's nice to see you again," said Ronen.

"Let's be done with it. I have dinner plans," said Saifa coolly. Seeing Ronen again, she realized just how much the old wounds had healed. *Not one bit.* There would be no "picking up" where they left off.

***

The guards in their green overcoats and peaked caps stood at rigid attention on each side of Xinhua Gate, the main entrance to Zhongnanhai, the Sea Palaces, Beijing's seat of power.

The south gate opened slowly before the tinted black Mercedes sedan, as commandos in black combat fatigues, armed with CF-05 submachine guns, patrolled the compound's perimeter wall. Red and gold spherical lanterns hung above the gate beneath the five-star emblem of the Chinese Communist Party. The blue- and red-tiled roofs and balconies with gold-inlaid designs were usually a marvel to Zhen Xin. He was a man moved by visual stimulation, and the art of the ancient dynasties never got old. But this morning Zhen Xin took no notice. He was too absorbed with his own thoughts.

The black Mercedes rolled through the gate, turning past a terracotta wall inscribed in the calligraphy of Chairman Mao: "Serve the People."

The Mercedes followed the path along the tree-shaded perimeter road of the southern lake. The tranquil waters glistened through the trees beneath the rising sun. A flock of swans bathed by the shore, oblivious to the world around them and the troubles of man.

For a moment Zhen Xin almost forgot he wasn't alone. The two other men, both less than half his age, fit and disciplined with cropped hair, sat to each side of him in stony silence, their faces expressionless, their eyes hidden behind black shades. They were his new detail.

The Central Security Bureau wasn't taking any chances. Zhen Xin had been separated from his wife and family as a precaution. They'd been moved to an undisclosed location, unknown even to him. The thought did not sit well with him, and he would address it with the interim director of security. But first, the General Secretary awaited him.

***

Saifa was not well. She gazed out the acrylic window, toward the orange sun, now nearly faded over the city and distant desert. She prayed he'd be gone when she turned around. But Ronen was still there. He stayed at his desk, at arm's length of the P90 pistol.

If he needed it, he might be dead before he could draw it from its resting place.

Saifa could have killed him in a single motion and he knew it. The old wounds still festered deep within her. They would never heal. He would not receive her forgiveness. He would instead suffer the agony of what had been done to her—what he had done to her.

Ronen showed her an image of the bald man with dark skin and crystal-gray eyes.

Anton Arlovsky.

She rose from her chair with the phantom taste of blood in her mouth. The next thing she knew, she stood again looking over the crepuscule of the city she so loved, the home she'd all her life protected. The memories, so terrible, burned in her head. Saifa could see the scar over Anton's right eye, the one she had placed there.

Ronen broke the long silence. "The image was taken in Murmansk. Our operative was shadowing an Iranian intelligence asset, a deep operations mole within Russia, tied to the Kremlin and key oligarchs within Russia's oil and gas industries. He was one of Iran's most reliable intelligence sources and an occasional one for us, for the right price. He provided us some information before we lost contact. Before Anton caught up with him."

Ronen had denied the pain he inflicted on both of them far too long. Saifa turned to him with a feeling in her belly not of butterflies in her stomach, but hornets. The rancor at his betrayal still burned after all the years.

"You brought me here for Anton Arlovsky? After what you let him do to me?"

"This is our chance, Saifa, to make things right."

"There is no right, Ronen! There is only what was done."

"I need someone I can trust."

"Trust? Ten years and suddenly you think I can trust you again? You are no one to speak of trust," Saifa said, already planning what she was going to do to Ronen.

"No one knew Anton better than you." Hard-faced, Saifa gazed out again at the scintillating movement of the traffic through the winding streets of the city below. The purple hue of the distant skyline and orange glow of the setting sun could not soothe her turbid thoughts.

"You speak of trust. I once needed the same of you," she said, refusing to turn her stare from the sinking sun beyond the horizon. She was losing control of her thoughts. "This is why we never worked, Ronen."

"I can't order you. I won't force you. I can only ask you."

Ronen rose from his chair and stepped away from his desk, finally coming toward her.

Please, Ronen, don't. As if sensing the danger, he stopped. Relief washed over her. She was terrified of herself, of what she would do to him if he only came a step closer.

"I can't right my wrongs. I can't change what happened. I tried to reach out to you, but got only silence in return. I was never good at apologies," he said.

"Apologies don't change anything, Ronen. They never do. Only actions, and yours prove you're still the same," said Saifa.

"I will beg, writhe, and grovel on this floor if I have to."

"I'm waiting," said Saifa.

159

"I'm asking you… please."

The "please" finally brought a smile to her face.

"I think that's about as close as you'll ever get to begging, writhing, or groveling," she said, and walked, right past him, matter-of-factly, to the door.

"Will you help me?" asked Ronen.

Her answer was silence.

IX

THE LION & THE DRAGON

Chun Lai had been with the Ministry of State Security for a long time, longer than most could remember. Those were good times, those early days. The Ministry was an isolated place that few knew and fewer still spoke about, a place where colleagues often found themselves worn beyond their years and finished before their time. But this morning Chun Lai felt like a young man again, fresh on a first assignment. He was deputy director in charge of domestic counter-espionage with the Ministry, the number two in line of power within the agency, and the happenstance of the dead man before him was very much his problem.

He studied every pore, every facial muscle frozen in the terror of their final moment. The victim must have known terrible pain. He looked over the carnage with the same indifference he did most things. His face was narrow and pallid. His suit hung loose over his boney frame. He moved with absolute precision.

Cao Qing's body lay in a red cake of dried blood. Chun Lai studied the mangled flesh between the dead man's jaw and collarbones. A partially severed vertebrae in the back of the neck was all that remained between torso and head. The force had been brutal and swift. Eyewitness accounts and the security video of the attacker had shown a young girl, slight of stature.

161

Not nearly the type who could cause such damage to the human body.

One of the weapons had been left behind protruding from Cao Qing's shoulder. Chun Lai had never seen the design before. It looked like a palm-sized disc of black, steel-edged scimitars with a curious inscription etched in white into its center. With a light brush of his gloved fingertips, he removed a shred of torn cloth to reveal what looked like a scripted language.

On one side of the disk the script formed an image of two legs and a tail. On the other side was another scribed design of what looked like a winged creature. But he couldn't decipher any of the text.

The assassins were sadistic, purposeful in their viciousness. The puzzle that was a crime scene always started with a motive. Even if wrapped in threads of deception and fallacy to mislead and obfuscate, the motive was always simple. Chun Lai wondered as to the simple motive behind this one, behind the murder of the head of the CSB.

He draped the white sheet back over the corpse with purpose and care, looking about with a bespectacled stare at every item strewn across the reception room floor as the black painting of a headless mannequin towered behind him. The dolls at the bottom of the canvas stared down at him with the secrets of what they witnessed and would never reveal.

Three days later, the palm-sized disc lay atop the General Secretary's desk. Secretary Jun Longwei read Chun Lai's report very carefully. Chun Lai was Jun Longwei's most trusted advisor and a childhood friend from their days on the streets of Chung Du.

The assailants had gained entrance to the Diaoyutai Guest House without leaving a trace. Cameras had not picked up their movements until detected by the signals intelligence team assigned to the protection detail. The attack had been swift and surgical even amid the chaos recorded by the cameras in the main hall. They had used only bladed weapons and left two dead. The attackers had a clear opportunity at the one next in line as General Secretary, and yet they did not take it. Chun Lai wasn't certain which motive was more important: the killing of Cao Qing or the sparing of Zhen Xin Liang. He forced the burning sensation in his throat back into his stomach as the double doors at the far end of the hall opened and Zhen Xin entered, flanked by his men in black.

***

It was difficult to breathe with her heart pounding out of her chest and the taste of ammonia in her mouth. Blood throbbed in her ears as Saifa ducked around the corner. She barely registered a figure in front of her before her reflexes kicked in and her hand suddenly gripped around a throat. A pudgy, red-bearded face and bulging eyes glared at her as she held the man against the tiled wall.

He had crossed her path at the wrong place and the wrong time. A little boy at his side shrieked as she quickly released the befuddled man. He grabbed the boy and stumbled out of the bathroom, disappearing into the crowd.

She drew a small metallic canister from her coat pocket as she peered into the empty bathroom. The black stall doors were closed except for the last in the row. Inside the far stall stood the briefcase.

Her hand barely rose in time to protect her face as a black shadow filled the mirrors over the sinks and slammed her into the wall urinal. Flushing water rushed down her nape and back. Gloved fists pounded on her head and clamped around her throat. Her knee found the attacker's inner loins, and her nails clawed the blurred face. She pulled in a desperate gasp of air.

The faint tinge of freshly cut grass filled her nostrils. The aerosol can in her right hand had fired its dose of fentanyl into the stranger's eyes and ear. She pushed herself out from the urinal and crumpled to the floor. Her vision blurred. Nauseated, she lifted her chest off the cold tile as sweat burst from her pores. She gripped a pant leg as the shadow staggered past her, the black overcoat crashing into the far wall. She stood and, pushing herself along the wall, reached the exit and fell into the crowd.

The throng of trench coats and suits buffeted her from side to side. Languid pale faces contorted and stretched with every footfall. The crowd pulsated and hissed. She swooned through a distorted sea of black, thrusting and clawing her way, the smell of ammonia again filling her nostrils. A steely hand suddenly gripped her. His sharp crystal-gray eyes cut into her as she parried and struck, but her consciousness was slipping. The fentanyl had unintended effects. Steel flashed in the crowd as crimson blood shot over the stainless blade.

Saifa's memory vanished with the splash of cold water across her face. She stood in front of her mirror, doubled over the sink. She shut the valve. Her abdomen was flat and smooth now, but the pain of that serrated blade still panged deep inside her. The scar from that day was permanently tattooed across her stomach. She never forgot those eyes beneath the bald brow of that creature, more animal than man, the one known as Anton Arlovsky.

Toweling off her wet hair, she walked over to where the laptop lay open on the table. Ronen's words played themselves in her mind over and over. Anton had been waiting for her that day. Ronen gave the Hashishin her identity. He had risked her life to lure them out, and because of him, that thing's blade found her stomach. Her body survived the blade, but her heart not the betrayal.

She had loved Ronen above all else and for him to do that to her, for him to abandon her to those creatures, was his own death sentence. He would know her pain. She would exact her vengeance, and his soul would bear that price, and then his body.

But that was over ten years ago. She would have thought that maybe by now she would have forgotten, let go. But the scorn in her heart lingered, as did the memories of what happened to her. How could he have been so foolish, and she ever more the fool for still loving him?

She stared at the images, the ones this Vadim Iravani, this supposed operative with ties to Iranian intelligence, had provided. She worked with the Iranians once upon a time on cooperative arrangements that furthered both countries' agendas. But that was a long time ago. Perhaps when her heart first became a basilisk stone.

She glanced through the image files; a Typhoon submarine stretched across her screen. She suddenly pulled up another picture, of a young man, one who had nothing to do with this Vadim. One from her time working with the Iranians. One from the time she met Anton last. She stared at the face of the young scientist, the one who held her secret. He possessed what she had fought for. In his hands rested that briefcase, the very one Anton had eviscerated her for, the very one for which Ronen had betrayed her.

She wondered if he knew what he held in his hands. If she could not kill Anton Arlovsky, she would take the scientist, Ramin Ramjani. But she had been recalled to Tel Aviv, and he escaped his fate at her hands. But that was all a long time ago.

Saifa closed the laptop with a heavy thud and paced to the window. She considered Ronen's offer from today as she turned off the lamplight. Perhaps this was her chance—but not the way Ronen envisioned it. That last part was for her to decide. Saifa pondered her choice with the certainty of knowing she would get no sleep this night.

***

"Magnificent," said Amir, as he eyed the spinning cylinder inside the transparent titanium casing amid the bevy of scientists in white lab coats at the University of Tehran's nuclear research facility.

President Amir Haghigi was of slight build and stature with a neatly cropped gray beard and a presence that filled the room. His dark eyes narrowed with, as Ramin would always say, *a tad bit of madness* at the thing that lay behind the transparent casing. Amir believed himself of great ability, the destined leader of the Persian people, forged from Allah himself. He was the Mahdi, the bringer of peace, who would lead the Persian people beyond the Day of Judgment.

Ramin didn't know whether to laugh or fear the man's self-adulation. He and Kazem exchanged glances, echoing in their looks the many conversations they'd shared about the man. Their greatest curiosity was what Grand Ayatollah Khatami truly might have thought of Amir, each dying to know the words those two exchanged behind closed doors. One egomaniac balancing the impositions of the other. Somehow they made it work, for now. Such laughter at their expense kept conversation away from the darker truth in Ramin's heart, one Ramin prayed Kazem would never notice, one Ramin would forever deny even from himself. He took care to not stray his fidgety hands too far from his lab coat pockets and focused on keeping cool composure this morning. Ramin wondered how long before one of them would notice, before they started asking questions.

"This model centrifuge has the most perfectly balanced rotor ever built," Ramin said.

"Of course it would. I personally chose you to lead the project. How could I expect any less? As if I had created it myself," said Amir admiringly before the glass-encased centrifuge.

"Everything from the bellows to the extraction system has been upgraded to handle the efficiency of this new rotor. The tensile strength and density of this system will help the IR-10 produce five times more hexafluoride than even our IR-8s," added Kazem as he stood back to allow the president to bask in his moment.

"Yes, yes," was all Amir could say. Ramin gave Kazem a sideways glance. He needed to teach him not to get so detailed with *stuff* no one else but them would care about. The last thing they wanted was to make Amir feel less than genius — though that would take some serious doing. Amir gave Ramin a deeply satisfied smile.

"You should be proud to have created such a marvel. If I'd only produced so much at twice your age."

Ramin's eyes almost popped out their sockets. He had no idea Amir was capable of any humility. He might have taken it as genuine except for the nagging feeling Amir was more content with his politics than with the science of it all. If Ramin were ever lucky enough to become his shadow, that would be a grand achievement for the young man. That was probably how Amir really saw it.

"Because of you, our home will be a safer place for our children. This technology will spur even more advancement in energy efficiency, medicine, and defense. You have my personal gratitude and respect. *Tashakor mikonam*," said Amir.

"*Daste shoma dard nakone*," said Ramin. *May your hand not hurt.*

"This was a collaborative effort of love and dedication. I cannot take credit alone. The true credit goes to Dr. Kazem Shir-Del and his team, whose designs and tireless effort made this moment possible," he said, beckoning Kazem to the forefront.

"Well said, young man. You are right. I would be remiss not to acknowledge the true heroes of the Republic," said Amir, bowing his head before Kazem with hand over his heart.

"You honor me," said Kazem, returning the bow.

Amir righted himself, turning away from the humming cylinder. It was quite obvious where his preferences lay.

"All of you honor me and your Ayatollah," said Amir, never drawing his eyes from Ramin.

Ramin averted his gaze. His fists plunged deeper into his lab coat pockets so that none would see his hands shake. He did not know why the sudden terror. Perhaps Amir would see right through him, see his weakness — perhaps see the love he had in his heart for Soraya. Perhaps he would see what he dared not even whisper to her, the thing crawling inside him and the thoughts that it bred. Ramin glanced up at Amir. His smile filled him with dread. *He knew his secret. He had to.*

Amir leaned in close but said not a word, giving Ramin only a handshake and a kiss. He went to each man in turn, giving them a handshake and a kiss just the same, coming last to Kazem. He seemed to search for something in the young man, holding the handshake an uneasy moment longer than the others.

"The Republic owes you each a debt of service for what you achieved here today, and I will see it so. *Tashakor mikonam.*" said Amir turning his attentions back to the others, his eyes stopping again on Ramin. His guard detail appeared as if from inside the walls, closing rank and file around, guiding him out the way he'd come. And just like that, Amir was gone.

***

The streets of Beijing buzzed with whispered panic, while news flooded cyberspace and filled the airwaves with press conferences and conspiracy theories.

Governments the world over moved to publicly condemn the attack on Zhen Xin Liang, while others more than tolerated the news behind closed doors.

The whereabouts of the vice president were unknown and even less known was who might be responsible. Analysts conferred and bickered about what this might mean for the region and Sino-Western relations, while, somewhere on the grounds of Zhongnanhai, Zhen Xin sat in silence across from the General Secretary, China's paramount leader, Jun Longwei.

"Good fishing in muddy waters," said the elder statesman in his raspy voice.

Jun Longwei was gnarled with age and had a slight hunch to his back, but he still had youthful, clear eyes. The Great Hall stood silent beneath the towering walls and decorated ceilings of the ancient tradition. Endless bookcases lined the hall, their shelves containing the knowledge of the ancient world. In the center of the hall the two men sat across from each other at a plain desk, each in a high-backed chair.

Zhen Xin stared at the bladed disk that lay flat on the desk.

The bringer of peace and the army of the Jinn. From the mount of Alamut the will of Allah be served. Death giveth life so peace may reign over all men.

The translation had its origin in an ancient Avestan script once used in third-century Persia. The language of Zoroaster had been extinct for over fifteen centuries, but locked in its scripts were the ancient spirits of Asha and Druj. *Truth and deceit.*

The teachings of old whispered somewhere in the collective consciousness of the human mind, and in them were the seeds of good and evil that drove the

170

world even today. Seeing the ancient weapon that killed Cao Qing sent a chill down Zhen Xin's spine.

"My time is short, Zhen Xin. Soon it will be you who leads us," said Jun Longwei. Jun pushed the bladed disk toward his visitor. "This should frighten you."

"They could have killed me easily, yet they did not."

"If one could only wield youth and wisdom in the same hand," said Jun, searching for something in Zhen Xin's expression. "Time is a blade that incises wisdom at the price of vitality. A single lifetime is not enough. Imagine what you would become if time were not such, were not so cruel."

Jun rose slowly from his high-backed chair. A tiger and dragon ran up along its sides, facing each other in mortal combat. In the middle was the sacred pearl of wisdom.

"We are an ancient people, as are those who meant to snuff out your life," said Jun, adjusting his bifocals slowly and walking toward one of the endless bookshelves away from the light. Zhen Xin stole a glance at Chun Lai, who watched them patiently from where he stood, taking note of every nuance that made up the dance of these two men.

"We have struggled against many enemies over the centuries: the Japanese, the British, even the Romans. They birthed empires that grew strong at the cost of our flesh, served their vices from our toil, but in time they too withered, and flesh turned to bone, and bone to dust. My time has passed. But yours is now," Jun said with a pained grin, as he returned to the table with an old tome in a steady hand.

"The time has come to challenge the Lion, a beast with many heads. Your strength must be in your wisdom." Jun opened the tome, laying it on the table before Zhen Xin. "And wisdom is victory without war."

The original ancient *I Ching* manuscript lay on the table before Zhen Xin.

"Our people's destiny rests with you."

***

The day had been a long one. The test of the new centrifuge and Amir's visit made for much ado and more exhaustion. But all, including Kazem, had finally gone home for the evening, leaving Ramin to his desperate addiction. He looked down both ends of the corridor. The nights were quiet in the halls of Tehran University. He pressed the handle and slipped past a heavy wood door, closing it slowly behind him with a dull click of the latch.

He flipped the switch and the soft lamplight in the corner of the room came to life. Stepping across the blue and white patterned rug, he approached a ceiling-high cabinet of heavy gray steel. He turned the dial right, left, and then right again, coming to a stop at XIII on the knob. He pulled the latch and the bolt slid smoothly out the housing.

The well-oiled hinges gave way without complaint. A lone briefcase lay expectantly on the shelf, waist high. Gripping both edges, he carefully extracted the leather case from the cabinet. His arms strained under the weight as he set it carefully onto his desk. Ramin sat before the black case, pausing as he always did before opening it. He ran his fingertips over the shredded edge, stained in the unmistakable brown of dried blood. He always wondered how that happened, who had been the unlucky one.

This was his secret, one neither Kazem nor Soraya could ever know. His remorse was for Soraya; his sorrow was their baby. But he refused the pain any audience. He cast it aside with pure unrepentance. But the voice still hissed within, begging him. *She will take everything from you. Betrayal is her only truth. The Ilythiium...*

"Stop!" Ramin gritted his teeth. He clenched his eyes shut and coiled his innards. He willed the echoing whispers to silence. Ramin unlocked the case as his thoughts honed to purpose. The voice spoke only of her betrayal, this thing called the *Ilythiium*; a sphere of bending light and pulsating darkness, a creature of headless torso and limbs with her desiccated baby. It beckoned from the darkness as whispers loudened and time ticked faster.

Ague shrieks pierced through his head, skewering through his chest into his belly. He unclasped the briefcase and in blind pain ripped open his sleeve. His hands groped the contents of the case and reflexively repeated their ritual.

He planted his arm on the table, tying off the elastic band around his bicep, and plunged a needle into the vein bulging from the bend in his elbow. The tube in the receptacle filled a carmine red.

When the vial could hold no more, he released the band round his arm and slipped the needle from his vein. He pressed the vial into the aperture of a centrifuge at the center of the case. It began to rotate. His brain was racing, crashing into the walls of his imagination trying to escape the voice, the torrent of pain inside his cranium. He watched with disgust and terror as plasma and serum began to separate. There it was— the thing he waited for began to move. The first tentacle appeared and a toothed orifice suctioned against the glass. He crushed the vial beneath a clenched fist, the glass perforating deep into his flesh. The disgust of the tentacled orifice squirming in his grasp was only outdone by the searing pain eating into his arm and the hatred for what he was becoming.

***

The morning was crisp with the cool breeze of the coming spring equinox. The sun shone through the high pines planted by his great grandfather, a time so long ago the little boy could not imagine. The Shemiran District along the gentle slopes of the Alborz Mountains had been home to his family for over four generations, going back to the days of Reza Shah. It was rumored the Jawadi family had held position among the ruling class of every era as far back as the Parthians, and some believed even further. But that didn't matter to the little boy who slinked along the bushes after something unseen. What did he care that he would one day rule over his house? Aref just wanted to catch the cat.

"Aref, come here," shouted Bousseh, standing at the door of their home.

"He is a menace," she muttered. She watched him with the peeved smile of a mother proud of her mischievous son. "Allah give me patience."

Aref darted around trees and beneath rose bushes, chasing the cat through his grandmother's vegetable garden.

"Aref, get out of there!"

He would not listen. All that mattered was that cat. He grabbed its tail.

"Mana's roses! Aref, get back here now," shrieked Bousseh.

His grandmother's rose garden. Romina would be furious, and Salil was nowhere to protect his grandson. They could do nothing but spoil that little boy, so they said. Bousseh would never hear the end of it if he ruined her hedges. Aref disappeared beyond the rosebushes, out of sight.

He won't sit for a week.

Bousseh descended the steps.

"Here, Mustafa," cooed Aref as he crouched, slowly inching toward the cat who watched with an exasperated whiskered face.

"I have your tail!" he shouted with glee as he lunged, the cat simply darting away again. Instead of a cat and its fluffy tail, his little hands grabbed on to a pair of shiny black boots.

Javeed Ali-Zadeh had a dark complexion and wavy hair, with a gray-streaked beard and deep-set dark eyes. He stood at the entrance to the garden looking down with a smile at the boy. Four other men dressed in the olive green drab of the Revolutionary Guard stood behind him, weapons in hand.

Aref crouched, frozen, at his feet as Bousseh came fuming around the bend.

"Aref!"

"Mommy!" cried Aref, as the men grabbed and hoisted her up. They carried her kicking and screaming toward the house.

He ran to the aid of his mother, but Javeed's iron fist clamped down on him. Aref shook and punched and bit down on the hand that held him. Javeed thrust him to the ground. The boy had a sharp bite. Blood trickled from his hand.

Two guards quickly subdued the child, as four more poured through the front gate.

"Take the boy."

"Touch a hair on his head, and your eyes will be food for the crows." Romina stood center of the rose garden path, a rosebush scissor hidden in the palm of her hand. Her two guards appeared from inside the house, pointing MP-5's at the assailants.

"Don't shoot," she said.

"They have no intention to," said Javeed, as he signaled them.

They slowly lowered their weapons, unable to look her in the eye. The guards avoided her stare as they bowed their heads, stepping away from Romina, handing their weapons over to the Revolutionary Guards.

"Every man has his price," Javeed said.

"Mine will be your blood."

He smirked. "Strong words for an old woman."

Two guards grabbed at Romina, and she thrust out her hand with its hidden weapon. She drove the scissor deep into one man's thigh. The butt of a rifle smashed across her cheek, crushing bone and lacerating her eye. She crumpled, semiconscious, to the floor. The other guard howled and writhed next to her with a giant scissor firmly fixed in the meat of his thigh.

The black boots came to rest beside her as Romina struggled to her elbows, spitting out blood onto the floor. The rubber sole came down on the back of her head, plastering her face onto the pool of blood forming around her.

Javeed stood over her as he took a last drag of his cigarette and flicked it away into the rosebush. Romina gasped and twitched in the blood mud beneath his boot as he crouched over her, releasing the drag slowly onto her mangled face.

"Your time has finally come," said Javeed, as Romina's world disappeared into darkness.

***

President Amir watched through the one-way glass as Romina slumped in a chair. She had lain there for what seemed like hours, her body tossed raggedly about, no consideration for bones that might break or joints that might tear. The dark gray walls of béton block stood morbid and cold around her contorted body.

Amir had much to consider. Salil Jawadi was a problem. He'd been a thorn in Amir's side since the early days. Salil never got over what they did to his son. It was the price of serving his Republic. He should have known and accepted that.

But something else, something new gnawed at Amir. The VAJA, the ministry of intelligence, warned him of betrayal among the army, of forces loyal to Jawadi. He had paid that no heed. The armies were loyal to the Ayatollah, loyal to the death. They would never betray him. But beliefs he once considered so absolute were now fissured in uncertainty and doubt. Salil had taken a new direction, a new interest. He'd brought Parvin Ramjani to his side, the brother of Ramin Ramjani, and no one neared Ramin.

If Salil knew of Ramin, he must have been on to the others, the Exohumans. But the more Amir stared at the beating on the other side of the window, the more he gazed at Romina's crushed body, the more he demurred and wondered if he had been much more naïve than he could ever imagine. How could he have not seen the signs? With Exohumans on his side there would be nothing to stop him. Salil would destroy them all.

But something else so simple occurred to him. *Salil was one of them.* But he could not be. Amir would have known years ago. There was no way Salil could have kept that secret from him for so long. Amir had eradicated their Syndycate in his country, his men inside the intelligence services responsible for four of them. Four deaths and he'd witnessed every single one, and every single one had given him the clues, the path to the next one until there were none left. Just like he broke them, so too would he break Romina.

Amir watched casually through the glass as he placed a pinch of chewing tobacco in his mouth. *Salil will come for her, and he will be waiting.* The tobacco leaves eased his nerves.

The halogen spotlights on the other side of the glass beamed down onto the broad-shouldered man with thick muscular arms and barrel chest. He stood over Romina in his green and black uniform as her head hung low. Her dripping wet hair hid the dark sheen of viscous coagulation over her beaten face. Javeed waved away the burly interrogator and washed his hands at the sink. The water flushed pink from the blood on his knuckles. A metallic rolling cart with all his tools stood nearby.

"This job requires a certain cleanliness," said Javeed as he closed the faucet, drying his hands with the stained towel. "Now, back to where we left off. Where is he?"

He picked up something from the tray, tossing the small towel over his shoulder. Her head hung motionless. He would have thought her dead except for the slight heave of her chest. She sobbed quietly.

"I admire your courage. But it will only cause you more pain. Don't do this to yourself," he said parting her hair, caressing her disfigured cheek. "Where is your husband?"

She forced her head to rise. Anguish stained down her cheeks from eyes swollen shut. Her lips quavered but her mouth held.

"Please speak."

"I lament the womb that produced such a vile pig."

A hand swung down onto her skull. The cracking of bone clapped across the room.

"Where is Salil Jawadi?!"

"*Lex talionis*," Romina raucously laughed.

Javeed had seen this before, the maniacal laughter of the tortured. It was the last phase just before they broke. He stared at her bloodied teeth and the drool down her swollen and probably broken jaw.

"Eye for an eye," said Javeed, repeating what Romina spat out laughing. "Very well then." With the pliers, he approached her face.

X

SALIL JAWADI

Jagged-edged, snowcapped mountains stretched as far as the eye could see into the deep blue sky of the North Caucasus. Evergreen forests, centuries-old oaks, birches, towering pines, and spruces spanned the foothills of the valley below. Salil Jawadi could see the ebb and flow of the rolling forests over the rounded hilltops and the morning dew scintillating under the cold sun.

The night-camouflaged RH-53 Sea Stallion helicopter weaved its way along the valley, a remnant of America's influence in this part of the world. Its wide-bodied flat bottom was the perfect design to transport heavy military equipment or an entire platoon of men. But on this day it was just Salil Jawadi and Parvin Ramjani on the flight through the mountain pass.

Salil drew in a deep breath as he gazed out the open passenger door. He could taste the pines as the cold morning bit his face with the wind in his graying hair. His mind reached out to Romina.

What life would be like, content to live in a world such as this.

Romina loved places like this. She dreamed of living in her own fairytale castle surrounded by green mountains, her own Neuschwanstein.

Four days since he left, and forty years since they were married, and he still felt a strange flutter in his stomach every time he thought of her.

It must have been her cooking.

His thoughts took a turn to memories of Daveed, his son, and that day at Khorramshahr during the Iran-Iraq War. It had been almost thirty-five years to the day since the battle, and the memories were as fresh in his heart this cold morning as the warm blood that rolled down his hands that fateful day, when he held his dying son in his arms.

Bitter memories fled with the fresh sweetness of his grandson. *Grandpapa, let's catch the cat*, he would say. *If only Daveed could see Aref now. He'd be so proud of his sister's son.*

Salil thought of them every day, especially on days like today, so beautiful, so grotesquely beautiful.

Parvin watched the old man with the pride a son might have for a father. He met Salil seven years earlier while studying Islamic law at Tehran University. Salil had been a guest speaker during a course on *Sharia* military doctrine and Parvin soon found an affinity with many of his ideals. He sought him out and discovered the old man to be as kind as he was just.

The helicopter banked hard and to the left in a controlled — if still belly-churning — turn. Parvin looked through the cockpit door and beyond to the distant structure of the approaching estate, with its sloping terracotta roofs and turreted walls. He felt the pang of uncertainty clench his churning belly.

Salil, on the other hand, didn't bother to look. He'd been here times before. He further sank into himself in these final moments. *I pray to thee for divine light and guidance. For our family, for our just cause.* Their vision would soon become reality.

The rumbling helicopter pitched forward, toward the sea of green below. Parvin caught a glimpse of the winding dirt road between the trees before he turned his head away, afraid to be sick. He'd never flown before. As the giant helicopter leveled out above the treetops, Salil stared out the side window at a picture of peace and tranquility. But Parvin could see that behind Salil's eyes there was a dark foreboding. The helicopter pitched nose forward in final approach.

***

"I got you! Come here, you." Viktor huffed and puffed, lunging after the little girl in the black and yellow pirate outfit. She giggled as Viktor's large hand squeezed her little round belly. She squirmed and laughed, wiggling free of his grasp.

Vanya was a terror. At six years old his little *solnyshko* had more energy than Medovi, the boxer puppy nipping at their heels. Viktor had discovered early on Vanya had a leaning more toward boy games than playing with any dolls. Cutting and chopping the air with her little plastic sword, squinting behind a black eye patch, she ran for the sixth time around the Venetian pool.

Viktor gave chase with bellied laughter around that pool, seizing every moment he could with his granddaughter. The thirteen men who made up the Syndycate each had a life uniquely their own, he reflected. They were clothed in power and wealth, accustomed to a life of secrets, secrets they kept from the rest of the world, secrets they kept from each other.

There was often more to fear from the Syndycate itself than the world it hid itself from. Each of the thirteen lived as any other human observer might expect—lives of joy and hardship, health and sickness, birth and death, just as any other creature of this world would—while among them each was tasked with a specific role to play in their grand scheme of dominance for their collective benefit.

But for Viktor, there was no greater joy than these simple moments with this little girl. If only his ambitions, his ego, would set him free, content to live a life as such. But they could not. The affliction that cursed every one of his kind skewered his own mind. His ravenous lust for power seized him as in his coat pocket he again clasped the cobalt-blue benitoite stone. He had grown weary of only serving to further the interest of this Syndycate within the circles of Russia's elite. He was more than just a servant to a Deputy Chair or a Convenor. Viktor knew much more than any in the Syndycate ever intended for him to know, ever intended for him to remember, and it was only time before he'd take what should always have been his in the first place. He would again possess the *Ilythiium*, and those who still remained of this Syndycate would bow to him, starting with David Bradford, or they would wither in ash.

He stood his ground as the little girl, now a swashbuckling buccaneer, came back into full view, charging around the bend and brandishing her sword.

"Yar, Pappy, your life was a merry but short one."

"Shorter still is the plank, yer matey," said Viktor, scooping Vanya up onto his shoulders as Medovi nipped at his ankles.

Vanya squealed with delight as Viktor walked her to the edge of the pool. He stood before the glistening water as two men in black suits and ties, wielding AKS-74 submachine guns, approached across the courtyard through the wrought-iron gate.

"Sir, the guests arrive."

Viktor put Vanya down onto the pool's edge as the little girl watched grandpa do what he always did, leave her when the fun was just getting started.

"Vanya, go inside."

"Pappy," squealed the little girl, her voice high-pitched with disappointment.

"The plank will be waiting."

"Will not!"

"Will too, now go," insisted Viktor.

Vanya moaned as she moped back into the house, Medovi hopping and yelping after her. Viktor watched her go with a tenderness reserved only for that little girl, as the helicopter echoed its final approach.

***

Dry pine needles kicked up off the black asphalt as the RH-53 Sea Stallion nosed up gently and descended onto the landing area, casting its shadow over the whole of the tarmac. Its six-bladed main rotor thumped with the force of a giant eagle flapping its wings above its nest, buffeting its fledglings below. The whining turbines spewed the smell of heated exhaust and spent fuel that Viktor had grown to love. He was a seasoned helicopter pilot himself, owning a large majority stake in the Toporol Wingworks Bureau, one of Russia's top designers of rotary-winged attack aircraft. Of the entire process, from inception to prototype flight, his favorite moment was the kerosene smell that always accompanied helicopters of this type.

Viktor stood silhouetted at the hangar door as the Sea Stallion, emblazoned at its tail section with the four crescents and sword of the Islamic Republic of Iran, touched down with expert precision onto the pavement. A second man, a head taller, approached from inside the hangar. With gold wreath and double-headed eagle on his black-visored hat and three-star insignia on his squared shoulders, Vice Admiral Anatoly Pietrov waited as Viktor commanded.

Poised for a moment at the helicopter door's edge, Salil gathered himself, taking in his surroundings. Armed guards stood at every corner of the tarmac, as ground crews busily ran about locking down the landing gear, already servicing the helicopter. At the far end of the tarmac, a small hangar stood where two men waited in the shadows.

Argyll, grant me wisdom, grant me strength.

Salil stepped down gracefully and approached the far structure, Parvin close behind him. Viktor smiled at seeing his old friend again. Everything had a regal air about him, especially his designer suits. He even wore them when the circumstances might call for something a bit more comfortable—like the rear seat of a helicopter cabin.

"*Khosh amadid*, old friend," said Viktor over the fading whine of the helicopter rotors as he stepped out from the shadows to greet Salil.

"*Mamnoon*, my friend. You honor me with my tongue."

"What little I remember," Viktor said.

"Don't worry, it's as terrible now as it ever was." Salil laughed, clamping his large hands onto Viktor's shoulders and kissing both his cheeks, as was customary between them.

"It's been a long time coming," said Salil.

"You haven't aged a day since the last we met," Viktor remarked, noting how the years had so deeply creased Salil's face. Viktor knew to stand on etiquette. The lie had long since gotten old and Viktor wondered just how much longer Salil would choose to live as one of them.

"You always know how to say the right thing."

"Fifty years of friendship goes a long way," said Viktor.

"It does." Salil turned to Parvin. "Allow me to introduce my adjutant, Parvin Ramjani."

"Welcome."

"Thank you, Mr. Kletnov. The honor is mine."

"Did you get him this way or are all you Persians that polite?"

"Some of us were born with class in our veins," said Salil.

Viktor smiled warmly at the barb. "Salil, this is Vice Admiral Anatoly Pietrov, Chief Inspector to the Ministry of Defense."

"Welcome, Mr. Jawadi."

"Thank you, admiral."

They shook hands, each a picture of cool poise. Only Parvin's face reflected the palpable tension.

"I can still remember a time when I was much like you, innocent to the world's ways. In time you will understand," said Viktor, placing a hand over the young man's shoulder.

"Come, let us relax over tea. We still await our last guest," added Viktor, as the guards approached almost on cue.

"After you, I insist," urged Salil.

"I appreciate the kindness, but I am not the guest of honor."

"Of course," conceded Salil, walking on ahead with Parvin as Viktor and the admiral lagged behind. *Let not expression betray intention*, Salil reminded himself as they crossed through the glass double doors into the house.

***

A sleek, black SUV rolled along the dirt road, as the early morning sunlight peered through the forest's upper canopy. The wet, orange dirt clung to the truck's run-flat tires as it made its way along the winding path. From the comfort of the back seat, James Fenway looked over the document in his hand as he reached for his coffee in the cup holder by his knees.

"Where'd you guys get this ride?" he asked, as he took a sip of his straight-up American coffee: black, no sugar, no cream.

"Compliments of Ambassador Brentworth, sir," said the guard in the front passenger's seat.

"Nice. Should have had me one of these in Iraq. The AC works."

He replaced his cup in the holder. Not even a ripple formed on its surface. The T-98 truck, with its B7 anti-tank armor capable of stopping a 7.62 high-velocity round, was as tough as it was comfy and quiet. He stared out the window at the passing trees as the road opened up to a large clearing. A perimeter gate and guardhouse quickly came into view.

Meanwhile, the space where Salil found himself was vast and lavish. The walls and ceilings were of rustic French stone. A central chandelier of fine iron hung high overhead, its candelabra lighting the tiled floor. The tiles' undulating shades of yellow gave the impression of flying high over a crystallized desert floor. A smoky-blue Greek key pattern bordered the whole of the space. At the center of the room, between the divans where the four men sat, was a small glass table. On it was a large leather-bound book.

Opposite Salil sat Viktor and Admiral Pietrov. To his left sat Parvin. The floor-to-ceiling bulletproof glass at the far end opened up to the mountainous forest he'd flown over moments before. Like a ship on a sea of green, Mount Elbrus towered in the distance. It was a perfect day.

"Overwhelming, isn't it?" said Viktor, as he watched Salil opposite him, his back to the window.

"The peaceful beauty of a savage wilderness," said Salil.

"The devourer and devoured alike, living in its delicate balance, one unable to survive without the other," said Viktor. Salil made note of the gentle reminder.

A young woman placed a tray onto the small table. Four steaming cups were perfectly positioned at each corner of the tray, with a dish of rye toast and a small stick of butter by the black porcelain teapot in the middle.

"Cherry blossom," said Viktor, as the serving girl gently raised the first saucer to Salil.

"Thank you," said Salil, smiling graciously at the girl who didn't meet his gaze.

He glanced about the room as he sipped his tea. He measured everything. His sights fell to the tome resting on the table, *Picasso's 'Guernica'* by Anthony Blunt.

"*Guernica* is one of my favorite works," noted Viktor, as he saw Salil scan the book cover.

"The wholesale slaughter of innocent women and children at the hands of bloodthirsty dispassionate men, as Sir Blunt so eloquently described," remarked Admiral Pietrov.

"But when is war not such?" asked Viktor with a cutting smile aimed at Salil.

"When such war stops the tyranny of men," replied Salil.

"Ah, the cruelties of war justified by the righteous tyrant. Freedom to one man is but tyranny to another, my friend. It is the solemn right of the victor over the vanquished to write his own version of the truth," said Viktor, staring fixedly at Salil while sipping his tea when the rap of someone knocking at the Arabian double doors echoed through the space.

Viktor raised his hand as the guard at the entrance pulled back the door and another in an identical black suit and tie with a weapon slung over his shoulder entered the room. The rhythmic clacking of his shoes jarred the silence.

"The American delegation has arrived."

"They are punctual," remarked Viktor, looking at the clock over the fireplace behind Salil. "Then again, I've never known the Americans to be late. Send him in."

The guard gave a curt bow and withdrew from the room.

"How is Romina?" asked Viktor, as the four men rose from their places.

"She is well, thank you. We just celebrated our fortieth anniversary."

189

"Forty years since the *Khastegāri*. How time flies," noted Viktor, as the memories of Salil's engagement celebration momentarily flooded his mind.

"How do you know about their Khastegāri?" asked Parvin, surprised.

"Easy, I introduced them."

"Don't believe everything you hear," said Salil, quick to set them straight.

James Fenway strode through the double doors. Short and thin, he made up for his stature in poise and demeanor. His black suit and light blue tie reeked of pompous American greed and hegemony.

"Welcome to my home, Mr. Fenway," said Viktor with a heavy Russian accent to counter James's cheery Vermont English, as he extended him a greeting. Viktor made certain his intentions were felt keenly in his handshake. He let its strength serve the American as warning. "I'm glad to see your journey a safe one."

"It was, thank you. I just spent a few days with President Shukurov at the Munich Conference, so it wasn't too bad a trip to make the hop over."

"And how is Yury?" asked Viktor with feigned surprise.

"He's doing well, I would imagine, considering his speech on America's monopolistic world dominance."

"A dominance that has served him quite well, considering he's become the wealthiest man in all of Europe along the way," noted Viktor, with envy buried in his voice.

"Something we all aspire to," Pietrov said, as he stepped forward to greet the American.

"Allow me, this is Admiral Anatoly Pietrov."

"Chief Inspector to the Ministry of Defense—pleasure to finally meet you," said James before the admiral could utter a word.

"Are you a gambler, Mr. Fenway?" asked Pietrov.

"I don't leave what I can control to games of chance."

"Not all things can be controlled," said Pietrov with an amused look.

"I will take that then as *your* opinion."

Salil watched the American from where he stood with disappointment. Once again the American did not surprise. James turned his attentions to Salil, proffering a kiss to each cheek, the admiral already forgotten. "Mr. Jawadi, the honor is mine."

"Welcome," said Salil, with a polite, guarded distance.

"I am here to serve the greater good of all our peoples," said James, bowing slightly in a gesture of respect.

Viktor sat back in his chair, sipping the hot tea and taking in the wonderful dynamic of political jousting at play. Viktor knew Salil. But this man, this James Fenway, he'd met only once, the night of the Vatican conclave. The only way to truly know a man was by his tells, and Viktor would find James's tells.

Vanya suddenly burst through one of the many doors leading from the reception room, swashbuckling and yapping with Medovi, the boxer puppy baying and prancing after her. She raced around the delegation and ran out the other door as fast as she could, with one of the guards sealing it behind her with much chagrin at the interruption.

"Mr. Fenway, do you have any miscreants to boast of?" asked Viktor of his guest.

"If you mean children, yes, I do. Two of them, both girls."

"That is one of the few things I admire about your society, Mr. Fenway," said Salil.

"What is that?" asked James, with a laugh that Viktor keenly picked up on.

"The opportunities you give your young women as you would your men. I hope for my daughter to one day have the same."

"That is something fully in your purview to make happen."

"Perhaps," said Salil, as he sipped his tea and carefully eyed the American. Salil set the tea back onto the tray. "What offer do you make in regard to our proposition?"

All eyes turned to James, now the center of attention around the coffee table.

"Funny you should ask. It's a figure of speech, meaning I was looking forward to the question," he clarified for the four deadpan faces. They gave neither word nor reaction and just stared at him for what seemed like a long silence.

"May I?" He placed the thin, black, metal case, still cuffed to his wrist, onto the table. "Most appropriate to expose this plan over a book written by one of the Cambridge Five."

"Fancy you should know that," commented Viktor.

"I always thought Anthony Blunt more an historian than a spy. I hope this hall is more secure than the Enigma intercepts he helped decipher."

"You needn't worry; besides, he didn't decipher anything—he merely passed it on. That was Alan Turing's work," noted Viktor.

"Six of one, half dozen of the other," said James.

"Never ascribe one person's achievement to another. It speaks to an uninformed, messy mind. But I digress," said Viktor.

"You do, indeed," said James, with a tranquil ferocity behind his words that Viktor did not expect. James pulled out a hermetically sealed pouch from inside the case and placed it atop the table. He punched the security code, releasing the handcuff.

Viktor needed see no further. He despised arrogance and stupidity above all else, and perspicacity was not something this American had. He was disappointed in David that he would keep such company, that he would bring them this.

"Your terms are there for you to read, Mr. Jawadi. Take your time. The day is young," said James, sitting back with an all-too-satisfied grin.

Viktor had already decided what he would do with the man.

***

Salil perused the document, his eyes devouring every word. It was what he'd come to expect of the Syndycate. The greed and lust for power that was the heart of the Syndycate lay scrawled across this abominable document. The selfishness that caused the War, the loathing in every single last one of them, still lingered as much in Salil as in Viktor across from him. Victor eyed Salil, groping along the edges of his mind, trying to find an opening into his thoughts. Salil had been made to forget their history and Viktor pried cautiously at what he might still remember — at what he might still know. But Salil gave no quarter. His mind was an empty slate. Not all things came to pass as the Syndycate or Viktor would have wished. Salil would never allow Viktor to know he remembered everything.

Centuries ago, Argylian scientists discovered a way for them to adapt to this inhospitable place. They discovered a blank slate in the genetic blueprint of the human race: noncoding strands of the human double helix that could fit their own genome, hidden away such that no one would ever find any trace of their alien DNA. Their entire being, their memories, everything they ever were, imprinted into man, a hybrid of both species. Everything that made them Argylian lay dormant in the human genome, while their memories, their awareness, remained active and present in these new vessels they called bodies. They learned to live, grow, and die, to be reborn again as one of them, a human, generation after generation, their essence buried within the human flesh they'd taken.

But that was not all. Just as their scientists mutated their very fibers into the corporeal form of human flesh, so too had they devised a way back. They were the fabled Rings of Reversion: thirteen rings, each uniquely forged for a single member of the Syndycate, each containing a unique hydrocarbon polymer, indigenous to their home world, modulated to activate the dormant chromosomes of their wearer, initiating the cellular mitosis and protein synthesis that would revert them to what they'd once been when they arrived on this world.

The rings were shown to them only once at their first conclave over a millennium ago and sealed in the deepest vaults of the Syndycate. They each swore an oath never to use them. The price of such was too heavy to bear. Argylians would not survive for long without the protection of their human flesh. This environment was a venom to their beings. The more they harnessed their innate powers, what made them Argylians, the faster this world would kill them.

But Salil could no longer abide by the principles of this Syndycate. Years he planned, waited for this moment. Salil had learned he was not the only one made to bend to the will of those who commanded the Syndycate. Their abuses extended to other species, once part of their societies, part of their home worlds, forced to flee their savage greed and butchery.

He found a Guija. Once a slave race to his own, the Guija were creatures of incredible guile and dexterity, able to morph and mutate the material plane in ways Argylians, even with all their technology, could only dream of. This Guija and others like her had survived centuries here. She was what he needed, and he was what she wanted. They each hated the Syndycate and each wanted their vengeance. They struck a bargain. She would facilitate that vengeance, and he would deliver it.

Anja Robles stole a ring for him from the vaults. In exchange for what he promised her, Salil finally held "his ring," locked in the amulet around his neck, and soon, once again, he would wear it. He would have his vengeance on the Syndycate. He would make this agreement serve his purpose, his purpose only.

"I will not sign this," said Salil, puncturing the silence. He rested the document again atop the briefcase on the table.

James leaned back in his chair. He knew to expect this, a knee-jerk reaction to a deal that, on paper, looks so terribly bad — because it was.

"Mr. Jawadi, the terms are more than fair."

"Arrogant American demands. Once again you appropriate what is not yours to take," said Salil, as he placed the pen down onto the document. "Your human brain cannot fathom what it is you ask of me." Viktor made note of what Salil said and the fine line he was fast approaching. But Salil refrained his impulse and modulated his intensity with a soothing smile. "My apologies, Mr. Fenway, but in countenance of your ignorance, I must politely refuse."

"You're asking us to dance with the devil, Mr. Jawadi. That comes at a price, one, I might add, that pays us both back handsomely. Besides, it's much less to ask for than what your very own Mossadeq offered during the Abadan debacle, which we had to, of course, politely refuse."

"You should take care where you tread. You may not find so sure a footing," responded Salil, his soothing smile, all but gone.

James looked around, as the four men stared at him in stark silence. "You do not walk away from the Syndycate. None of us do."

"Do not mistake David's wardship for safety. You are but a mere servant. Your life and death depend on but a single breath from my lips," Viktor said.

James stared at them, blood drawn and gaunt, forgetting to blink and even to breathe. He lifted the silver felt pen from the document and extended it, his hand trembling before Salil. Salil took measure of the young man. In all his fallible ambitions, he at least had one redeeming quality.

The young man has brass balls. At least he has that.

An ornately crafted hourglass cut of cherry wood stood atop the far bookshelf. Fine grains of powdered diamond flowed through its neck, neatly piling at the bottom. The day elongated as the sun passed its peak. The shadows began to play over the Dorado floor.

Salil said not a word as he pored over the document. The weight of the hours' long silence was crushing. Salil could see the sweat forming over James' brow. He watched James fight to stay calm, and the harder he worked, the more palpable was the panic. David had been very clear. He would be given his demands, or he would take them. The prospect of David's ire was enough to give every one of them in that room pause. But Salil looked beyond to consequences they could not fathom, consequences he would rain down upon them.

Salil held the platinum pen. Hand resting on the document, leaning forward with his weight pressing against the table, he stared at James. Salil was an old political cat and as the Syndycate had counted contingencies, so had he. He agreed to the group's terms, his the weaker position. The American would take back an executed accord just as planned.

The felt tip traced its black ink over the line. From right to left Salil punctuated his signature with a period. He always did.

"Allahu akbar," murmured Parvin, piercing the silence.

The other men in the room knew not to speak. Salil placed the pen back atop the document.

"Everything will be as we have discussed, as per the agreement," said James. The gaunt, pallid flesh of his face regained some of its flush pink and his voice some of its prior confidence. With quavering hand, he returned the document to the thin case, once again clasping the handcuff around his wrist.

"I wish I could stay for the celebratory cup of tea. But I have priorities to attend elsewhere." He was to his feet when the thick double doors opened up to the terracotta Arabian archways.

At the front of the house stood his armored vehicle with its sleek black contours, engine humming beneath the overhanging vines that wrapped through the driveway's pergola carport.

"Perhaps your daughter will be able to enjoy the same freedoms ours do someday," said James, extending Salil a strained, steady hand.

"Have a safe journey home, Mr. Fenway," said Salil. He did not rise. He did not take his hand.

"Of course," said James, withdrawing with a twitchy smile. He acknowledged the three other men and briskly strode out the front, sliding into the truck as one of the guards closed the door behind him. The four watched the truck disappear into the distance.

"Let's go for a walk," said Viktor to Salil.

***

The setting sun shone on the lush red and white flower petals as they strolled along the hedges that formed Viktor's rose garden. The young man followed their stroll several paces back, too far for any whisper the wind might carry his way. Viktor was amused with his curiosity, knowing Parvin would find only silence.

"If I were only afforded this luxury more often," mused Viktor, standing at one of the many hedges, scissors in hand. He pruned the leaves from a stem as he parted the bush, careful of the sharp thorns. "Where did all the years go, Salil?"

"I wish I could say."

198

Salil stood on the graveled path, hands in his pockets as he focused on a lone rosebud. "Perhaps it's a question for another time," said Viktor, with bitterness to his gaze that was gone as soon as it arrived.

Parvin watched the two men as the breeze brushed through the trees and swept over the hedges.

"Anger will not return to you what was lost," said Viktor.

"You of all would know what I've lost."

Viktor wondered how far to push Salil. It was a very careful thread he must weave. He pruned a stem, cupping the rosebud gently in his palm. Argylians were forbidden to mate with any species other than their own. It was a precept still held sacred among the Syndycate. And yet Salil had broken that oath and of it a son and daughter were born.

"If they had learned of your transgressions, you would have lost them all."

"Instead I sacrificed my son, in exchange for your silence," said Salil, too calmly for Viktor.

"Hybrid Exohumans have always been forbidden. None know that better than you."

"Are you not guilty of the same crimes, Viktor? What say you of your granddaughter? Is she not a hybrid as were my own?"

"I made sure her birth was free of this disease."

"That is what we have become, then, in your eyes. What are we all, if not mutants, we and humans alike? They are as foreign to this world as we are. They have no more claim over it than we do. Should we not share in it all the same, in peace?"

"Is that what you delude yourself to believe? You ask me for weapons. You prepare for war and yet you speak of equality among our kind. There is a certain madness to selective ignorance, Salil." The last words pierced Salil like a sharp needle and Viktor knew it.

"The Syndycate was created not to govern them, but to govern us. And there are those among us who have taken advantage of their power far too long," said Salil.

"And now it is our turn, of course," said Viktor with a cynical smile, forgetting his own admonition of how careful a thread to weave.

"David will stop at nothing, and neither will I."

"In the end, that will not matter," said Viktor, as he observed the dying bud in his hand, gently parting the petals with a finger.

"If our plans unfold as we have set them," responded Salil with a brazen stare.

"Parvin, could you give us a moment?" Viktor turned to the young man as he gently caressed the dying bud in his hand. Salil gave a conceding glance.

"Of course," said Parvin, bowing respectfully and proceeding back down the path the way they came.

"He reminds me of you so long ago," said Viktor.

Parvin patiently waited at the far side of the pool as Vanya and the puppy ran annoying circles around him. Viktor turned a longing gaze away from the innocent scene and continued their stroll. Around a bend, their path opened to a large windowless structure at the far end of the garden with steel-banded, oaken double doors at its face. Two winged manticores of sandstone marble stood guard beneath the arched entrance embedded with the five-pointed crown and keystone of Delft.

They followed the rose garden path as Salil focused on the borders of the arched entrance, discerning the intricate Avestan Sanskrit carved into the stone. The manticores watched; their eyes eerily followed him. A chill traveled down his spine at the sight of the perfectly sculpted creatures.

"The burden you will bear, you cannot imagine," said Viktor.

"It is time we finish this."

"Salil, you amuse me. You're so intelligent, yet still you believe in your own self righteousness. This world will long outlive us all, as will its inhabitants. Just as their problems will continue long after you and I are gone, so too will they find a way to solve them. Do not underestimate the likes of James Fenway, or the young man Parvin you so treasure. They are guileful and treacherous. It is a lesson the Syndycate learned long ago and one you should endeavor to remember," said Viktor, stopping at the doors to this strange building. The archway towered above them as he gently rubbed the last of the rose petals between his fingers.

"What of the weapon, Viktor?"

The petals fell from between Viktor's fingers, settling onto the floor. He turned his gaze from the falling petals and stared into Salil's heartless eyes. The heavy oaken doors creaked open to the rush of cold air as shafts of evening light pierced the pitch black chamber. Viktor stepped forward, his footfalls cleaving into the tenebrous stillness. Like the mantle of a death shadow, darkness wrapped itself around him. Salil stood at the chamber's entrance beneath the rustle of the treetops and the gaze of the stone guardians to either side.

Orange and yellow haze in glass lamps came to life all along the walls, as a figure emanated slowly from the blackness, its outlines etched in the edges of the light. A dark bronze statue of an introspective man sitting in contemplative thought at the center dais towered above Viktor as the shadows melted away beneath the illuminating candelabra nestled in the chamber's vaulted ceiling.

Viktor stood in silent contemplation as more statues emerged from the darkness. Other bronzes surrounded the thinking man, each in their unique pose, their unique human condition. Staring at him from under one of the corner lamps, alone on the far wall, another man in a canvas with black top hat, red mustache, and pursed lips followed his step with an accusing eye.

"Frozen in his moment, he holds the power to shape his destiny with the stroke of a pen," said Viktor, as footfalls echoed Salil's approach. Viktor wondered how much Salil suspected of his own motives; how much he knew of the *Ilythiium* and the benitoite stone in his pocket.

They walked along the edges of the chamber as Salil took in the enigmatic art. He stopped in front of a violent tempest of howling wind and raging ocean. Like a hand, the white-crested ocean rose over the sailboat's bow, wrapping itself around her hull.

"You can almost hear the howling wind and taste the sea salt. Funny, isn't it, how the painter used a biblical scene to depict the futility of religion: the twelve apostles helpless to protect their own savior from the ocean's grip."

"I see a thirteenth," said Salil, as he neared the canvas, peering closely at what looked like a rough cut meticulously covered over with paint along the border of the canvas.

"Rembrandt inserted himself somehow into everything he did. He had a thing for self-portraits. Vanity, what can I say?"

"A most appropriate image, considering our own circle. What of the weapon, Viktor?"

"Patience, my friend."

"My patience runs thin." Salil smiled, a grin not meant to comfort.

"Come, let me show you."

They turned their attention to another painting of a similar style. It hung alone on the wall. Two high-backed, velvet-cushioned Spanish chairs stood at either corner.

"The prize of my collection," said Viktor reverently, as they stopped before the canvas.

A man with his back to the viewer, with what looked like a Spanish guitar in hand, sat before a harpsichord. A checkered floor and red chair bathed in a soft morning light completed the scene, as a young girl played the harpsichord while another sang a solemn hymn.

Viktor could see the music, a silent concerto of harmonious color, its melody overwhelming his visual senses. Salil approached the canvas. At its frame, as with the picture depicting the terrible storm, a rough cut was meticulously plastered over with paint, leaving an almost untraceable mark along its edges.

"It took me three years to restore both her and *The Storm*. The pigs had cut them away from their frames, without any regard. They met their due course," said Viktor, their howls of agony still fresh in his mind.

"I know this painting," Salil said, turning to Viktor with an arched eyebrow.

"You asked me about the weapon. I have a proposition for you. Johan Vermeer created paintings of magnificent beauty in his time, thirty-six of which are still extant. They are coming together in a single exhibit at the National Gallery in Washington, D.C. We each have our obsessions, Salil. This is mine. The paintings will be stolen, and there's one man who can do it. You will convince him to do it for me. This is my one condition. I deliver you your Typhoon. You deliver me this man. You deliver me Vermeer."

XI

THE THIEF & THE ASSASSIN

Richard eyed the pedestrian scooting across the street just as the light turned green. He'd be quick to be on his way, too, around these parts this time of night. He lightly pressed on the gas. The shiny alloy wheels and cool metallic paint reflected the overhead semaphore as the BMW turned the corner into the parking lot around the back of Fresh Fast Foods. The place was packed. The stench of fried rice assaulted his nostrils. Even at this late hour, the place still churned out its artery-clogging comfort food. Richard had left the vents open to the outside, but he made fast work of fixing the problem. He blasted the cold air inside the car as the surround sound came to life with the second movement of Brahms's first concerto.

Richard backed the BMW into an open garage behind the restaurant, the door panels descending as he rolled through. Inside was what looked like a body shop. A half-assembled car lay atop a hydraulic lift; hoses, mechanical arms, a tool cart, and an oil pan stood beneath the vehicle. Someone had recently been working here.

Richard got out and shut the door behind him with a muffled thump. He went to the vintage World War II "Uncle Sam Wants You" poster framed on the wall and unhooked it from its place. Imbedded in the bare wall behind it was a keypad.

He punched a code and pulled back the small handle, revealing a lead-encased niche lined in black felt. He placed his keys on a small hook inside and withdrew another key, and a Glock 26. Sealing the door once again, he replaced the vintage poster on the hook. Uncle Sam pointed his craggy finger right at him.

Pushy old man.

Richard walked through a storeroom lined with shelves of grungy oil filters, spark plugs, and engine hoses. He stopped at the far corner. Grabbing the edge of an empty shelf, he pulled back, revealing a second keypad similar to the first. He placed his right eye in front of a small lens above the dials as a red laser scanned over his iris. The tumblers somewhere inside gave way and the door pulled back to a hewn stone stairwell descending into darkness below.

His flashlight illuminated a narrow corridor barely high enough for Richard to walk through, lined with moss-covered colonial pavers. A light draft carried the musty smell of dank water and decay. Beneath the grounds of the cemetery at Mount Olivet were corridors and chambers, crypts long forgotten from when Washington was first drained and built. The abandoned maze sprawled out beyond the edges of the cemetery, underground tunnels and chambers that even Richard had yet to fully explore. He himself wasn't certain of all that lurked in this darkness below. He was a bit of a thanatomaniac. He had a thing for the dead.

He advanced carefully along the subterranean path, but the self-doubt he fought so hard to subdue again surged, the churning shame in his belly burning his throat. Palpitations raced and squeezed his chest; weakness rolled down his loins. Anja still had not mentioned a word of what happened the night of the Pinacoteca. He tried to broach the subject over late-night evenings and silent dinners, but he couldn't bring himself to admit he broke their cardinal vow to never forsake the other. Tampering with time brought with it grave consequences. Her silence could only mean a worse fate awaited him. Christian Huygens's death was only the beginning. He would face his demons. He would tell her this night.

He extinguished his flashlight, as the smell of candle wax filled his nostrils. When a soft light emerged around a bend at the end of the corridor, he drew his Glock. A glow flickered on the wall as he approached with a careful step of his soft-soled shoes. He peered around the corner, past a stone archway. At the far end was an alcove lit with burning wall sconces and candles. A soft blanket covered a crate reclining against the wall, alongside a silhouette of a person.

"Stop being so over dramatic and put away the gun," echoed a voice through the corridor. Anja appeared from the shadows cast by the flickering sconces behind her.

"You never know what you might find down here," said Richard with a sense of relief, holstering his pistol as he passed beneath the arch. He straightened out his back, glad for the open space.

"Just me in leather and a medieval torture rack. You would like that, wouldn't you?" Anja approached him with a devilish grin, planting a gentle kiss on his lips.

Talking to Anja was like honey to his ears; the way she made his heart race with excitement. But the purposeful concealment of what they both knew was like waiting for a sledge hammer to fall on his head with every word from her mouth.

"What's with bringing him here?" asked Anja turning to the far side of the chamber.

Guillermo sat blindfolded and pouting like a little boy alongside the crate.

"You know, I don't need this. I really don't. Your little shenanigans about our so-called dead client. I want my money. I want my cut."

Anja walked over and stripped the blindfold with an extra tug.

And a certain satisfaction, noted Richard with a grin.

"Why do you always do that? Wait, is this a crypt?" asked Guillermo, trying to get his bearing in this creepy place.

Richard took a hammer from a toolbox next to the crate and began to pry the nails from the edges of the wood.

"Richard, this is a crypt! This isn't funny. Your little story about Huygens, it's not funny. None of it, not funny, not funny," whined Guillermo, going on about his dilemma.

Richard pried the last of the nails and unclasped the lid of the box. He lifted and walked it aside, gently removing the blanket covering the dark canvas within. Guillermo couldn't take his eyes off the Christ nor any of the other characters. Caravaggio's *Entombment* towered over them as the candlelight danced softly along the chiaroscuro palette.

"I broke our vow. The night of the Pinacoteca. I did what we swore we never would," said Richard, breaking the excruciating silence.

"I know."

"Why didn't you say anything?"

"Why did you do it?" asked Anja with a smile that filled Richard's heart with only more regret.

"To save—to save myself." Richard swallowed his shame, hoping for solace where there was none.

"I was just as terrified of that answer as you are. You knew an orb of sanctuary would be a death sentence for us all, and you invoked it anyway."

Anja approached the second open crate behind them. Leaning against one of the Doric columns, another canvas lay beneath a white sheet. She gently tugged away at the fabric. The angry Samson glared at them with his one good eye. Richard stared at the image of that vitriolic moment, of a man blinded with the cold blade of a knife. The same cold blade that now cut out his own heart.

"We have the Armillary Sphere. With the three of us we can reset this timeline," said Richard.

"What of the other twelve, Richard? What of the *Ilythiium*?"

"The secret of the Vermeers will die with us."

"The *Ilythiium* was destroyed during the War. What does the *Ilythiium* have to do with Vermeer?" asked Guillermo.

"The *Ilythiium* was not destroyed. It was imprisoned," said Anja.

"How imprisoned?" asked Guillermo, incredulity cracking his voice.

"The physical world is no different from that of the imagination, at least to a Guija. You know that. Some

209

of us can enter those worlds, control those worlds more than others. That's what always fascinated me about painters. That some humans have the eye to glimpse into those worlds, to bring them to life on a canvas is a mystery and an obsession for me. For both of us, isn't it, Willie?"

"Richard, what does this have to do with the *Ilythiium*? Please don't tell me what I think it is you're going to tell me."

"I lured the *Ilythiium* away from Viktor into one of those very worlds with the help of a painter of many centuries ago, Johan Vermeer."

"Yep, he told me what I thought he was going to tell me."

"The *Ilythiium* was imprisoned inside a canvas, actually several canvases, all leading back to that imaginary plane. A series of two-dimensional gateways into a nine-dimensional universe. The perfect place to ensnare such a monster and the last place the Syndycate would ever bother to look."

"Until Christian Huygens."

"He was onto something. He suspected. But he was looking in all the wrong places. I made sure of that," said Richard.

"Richard, really? Do you know what you're even saying?! The *Ilythiium* is death, a monster escaped from a universe where only grotesque agony exists, where life is decay and pain, a forever awareness of the moment of death without the luxury of actually dying. Every one of our kind, every Guija, was consumed by that thing. She destroyed our entire species at the behest of the fucking Syndycate!"

"We must take the Vermeers back," said Richard.

"All of Vermeer's extant works will be in one place at one time," said Guillermo, terror cracking his voice.

"We steal them from the National Gallery."

"Oh no, I just got this job. We're doing no such thing," insisted Guillermo.

"It's the perfect opportunity for the Syndycate," said Anja.

"The perfect opportunity for us," urged Richard, wishing he could know what lay behind her eyes. He tried to reach her in ways only a Guija could when mated to another. But Anja denied him their greatest intimacy; she denied him her imagination. He could only guess at her thoughts. He wondered how humans could cope with this aloofness of the mind that Anja now punished him with. He reverted to the only thing left him, this limited human language.

"Time is awareness beyond our control, Anja. Perhaps the night of the Pinacoteca was a fate already set for us."

"Please do not place blame elsewhere. There is no synchronicity to this timeline, no déjà vu. We severed the Lemniscate Paradox. There is no such thing as coincidence."

"To think in absolutes when referring to time is arrogance bordering on the dangerous," said Richard.

"You know, I think maybe it's best you all continue this conversation without me," suggested Guillermo.

"You stay right there," Anja said, without any other option in her tone.

Richard looked to Anja, but she gave him only silence. "We steal the Vermeers, then. Before someone else does. There's no such thing as coincidence."

Giovanni Battista, Inspector General to the Holy See, picked at his shrimp fried rice but couldn't bring himself to finish it. The moist box in his hand and the stench of grease were more than he could handle.

I should have brought my own food.

He sealed the box and tossed it with the chopsticks into the white plastic bag they came in. He never understood how Americans could eat this shit so late at night. He heard the Italian food was pretty good in D.C., but he'd have to check it out when he wasn't working.

Giovanni stared at the takeout place across the street. One would think it was lunchtime, seeing how busy it was. But his thoughts shifted to more pleasant things, like how he hadn't lost his touch. If he needed to track someone or something down, he still had the chops to do it.

His Holiness had requested their services, and who was he to not abide by the pope's wishes. The Sicaari were devoutly loyal to Rome, and Giovanni was subject to His Holiness, and the Sicaari were subject to him. The Sicaari were known only to a handful in the Vatican, and as the rumor went, they were as dangerous to their prey as to the hand that fed them.

Long ago, two sects versed in the dark arts of discreet justice had emerged. In the Near East and the Iberian Peninsula, a new power pressed its agenda against the church. They had brought the Crusades to Europe's doorstep. Popes and kings were quietly dying in their chambers, on their beds, and at their tables. A new order of Nizari Assassins, the Hashishin under

Hasan i-Sabah, had declared their war. It was because of them that the Sicaari were born.

Formed from the ranks of the Order of the Blessed Virgin by Pope Gregory IX, those selected as Sicaari were sent out to eradicate the new threat. Death shadows quietly pressed their war of poison blades in close quarters, engaging in merciless encounters along back alleyways. When the Mongols invaded in the late thirteenth century and toppled Alamut, the seat of Hashishin power, almost all record of the Hashishin and the Sicaari having ever existed was destroyed.

At least, that was what Rome would have everyone believe. But Giovanni knew the truth. He lived through the bloodline and what their masters had done. Just as their Argylian masters had mutated the human genome so they might survive in this harsh environment; they, too, created the Sicaari. Giovanni was one of the first generation, the old guard. They were human and Argylian hybrids, spawned and incubated, made to serve as guardian assassins to their Argylian masters. They were bred unique to specific clans, love and loyalty for their masters encoded into their beings.

But in their ambition, the Syndycate made their creation too perfect. Among the Sicaari of old, certain ideas began to fester in the whispered words of a language they created, one the Argylians could never comprehend, one that had no basis in the hybrid tongue the Syndycate had developed to fit into the world of men. Monsters of cunning and intellect to rival the greatest Argylian minds, a few among the Sicaari, led by those whose name Giovanni still refused to pronounce, broke from their oaths and formed a new lineage. They turned against their brethren and gave rise to a new species never intended to walk this world. From these treasonous lechers the Hashishin were born, and the Second Schism descended upon them.

Their war pitted brother and sister against each other, against master, bringing the many species cohabiting this world — and the Syndycate itself — to the brink of extinction over a millennium ago. Remnants of that war still lingered today in the dark alleyways and bedchambers of modern society.

His Holiness had tasked Giovanni with finding Christian Huygens, and as they had done so long ago — the Sicaari would again serve in their masters' stead.

It didn't take Giovanni long to track down Huygens. He had much information to share, none of which saved him from a more painful death. Huygens did share something interesting before he died: information on the disappearance of Father Fleitas. A Hashishin had taken the priest in the night and with him the original *Fourth Secret of Fatima*. She had fled to Alexandria, to the quarries of the red granite, the origin of the Vatican obelisks, thirteen in all, one for each member of the Syndycate. Giovanni already had a Sicaari en route to Egypt to find this Hashishin and what might remain of the priest, to retrieve once again what was wrongfully taken. But even more interesting was what brought Giovanni here. It hadn't taken long for Giovanni to trace Huygens's plans through all his aliases and proxy accounts. What he failed to volunteer, his records divulged. It surprised Giovanni that the torture could not get more out of him. He wondered if Huygens knew what Giovanni had discovered at the Pinacoteca.

The paintings weren't what kept Giovanni awake at night. They were fakes. He would normally have been obsessed with how the thieves had done it. How could they replace one painting with another so exact that even with spectral analysis, it still looked authentic? But the blood, the blood he found that night. The lab had performed their tests again, and again, and again. This was no ordinary blood he found. Cardinal Scarlatti immediately sealed the results. Giovanni had noted a strange visit from a flustered Wilhelm Gottfried, usually ever collected. He stayed the next day, after the Syndycate had left, in a closed-door meeting with the cardinals and pathologists. No record of the meeting existed. Giovanni had been completely shut out. He lived what they whispered of behind their closed doors; the nausea of that night, the helplessness of losing control. An awareness bordering on madness, what the results called "the dysplasia of time," still haunted him. That blood belonged to the only species who could do that, a species long extinct. The blood belonged to a Guija.

To the Syndycate they were more valuable, more dangerous, more reviled than any Sicaari or Hashishin would ever be. They were rumored to alter the unseen fabric of time, and Giovanni particularly despised them for that. They were the only ones capable of handling the Armillary Spheres, the only ones capable of commanding the *Ilythiium*. The Guija had sided with the Hashishin during the war, and with the *Ilythiium* they nearly destroyed the Syndycate and all their kind. But the Guija were hunted and the *Ilythiium* banished; the Guija, every last one of them, eradicated over a millennium ago at the hands of the Sicaari.

That was the version of history Giovanni chose to believe. He served the Syndycate and service demanded loyalty of belief, unwavering belief even if that belief contradicted the face of memory. Belief warped memory and spawned hatred, and that one still survived, as Wilhelm had attested behind closed doors, was a blasphemy to all that the Syndycate now stood for. He had known of this Guija, Christian Huygens had. He had employed this creature to make a mockery of them, to steal the paintings from right under their noses. To what end, Giovanni had been tasked to find out. But unfortunately that was the one thing Huygens could not divulge fast enough. The Sicaari had been too efficient. They killed him too quickly.

Giovanni's head raced as he sat in front of the Chinese takeout place. It was incredible to think these creatures still existed. Perhaps this one wasn't the only one. Perhaps there were others. He was curious how a Guija could have survived for so long without the Syndycate knowing about it. Richard Robles was a fascinating quandary indeed.

***

Karl sat at his chair, staring at the serpentine flow of headlights and red taillights far below on the Baltimore-Washington Parkway. The day's congestion was picking up with the sunrise, the flow of traffic coming to its usual standstill. This clear morning, Karl's yellow coffee mug stood empty at his table alongside a pressboard file folder stamped with the classification and control "TOP SECRET HCS-O ORCON." It was his personal file, solely under his

216

control, his file on all his human intelligence assets, all their years of operation under his sole direction. But he paid that no heed. His attentions focused instead on the frustrations of Maryland traffic. Anything right now would be better than the images in those pages and the thoughts rolling through his head that gave him no respite.

Karl hadn't seen Katherine since their Saturday briefing. Not seeing her these last four days was more like the asphyxiating desperation of waterboarding than longing for someone. Katherine pursued his thoughts most moments of his waking day and more than on one occasion had invaded his sleep. She had become a controlled obsession, the likes of which he could share with no one. His wife had ignored the aloofness of the last days. Bizarre behavior was nothing new to their thirty-five-year marriage. But no coffee, that was a symptom Karl knew she would not ignore and a measly assassination attempt on some Chinese politician blamed on his government wasn't nearly enough to make Karl kick his coffee habit.

Karl had come by Katherine's cubicle and forwarded her reminders, even requested calendar updates for their meetings. But Katherine was a no-show. The day of their briefing, Katherine's first with the National Security Council, she was late. That was something she just wouldn't do. She valued her career above most else, and the way she treated him on her way out, the way he felt, nothing really surprised Karl anymore, except somehow that. It hurt him. It surprised him just how much it did. She hadn't been in the office since, and she hadn't made any of his meetings. But that didn't anger him. Instead, slithering up through his prostate, winding their way through his tripe like serpents, guilt and self-doubt bit into his belly, their poison flooding his brain. He loved her with a madness he could hardly admit to himself. He swiveled toward the door, clasping the file folder, slipping it into an ajar drawer as the rap at the door echoed in his head. He snuffed out any kindness that was left him.

"Come in."

Katherine entered, as poised as always in her white flannel shirt and gray dress suit. Tall and confident, she strode into his office and placed another file folder atop his desk, this one with the ENDSEAL classification control "TOP SECRET EL ECRU" stamped across its header.

"My assessment, for your review."

"Not even a greeting. You don't offer much by way of subtlety," said Karl, taking the file folder from the desk.

"You've been requesting my work product for the better part of four days. Didn't think you'd be satisfied until I brought it in to you in person."

"What has gotten into you since Saturday's meeting? You were late and now AWOL and unresponsive. Unacceptable. Most would be on their way out the door with that behavior."

"Maybe you should follow through with your threat, Karl. Then again, you're partial to more surreptitious methods."

"Enough of this, Katherine!"

"You lied to me."

"About what?"

"Exactly. So many lies, you're not sure which one I'm talking about. Why did you put me on the Birkin assignment? To know if your cover-up was good enough?"

Karl sat silent.

"You knew who Vadim Iravani was all along. You had direct contact with Birkin. You created the alias Jonathan Denham for him, provided it to the Russians. Is that what you used me for? If I couldn't find it, no one could?"

"Why such anger, Katherine? We've done nothing wrong," said Karl.

"You created the alias Jonathan Denham with my credentials, Karl! And I have no idea what for, other than Vadim Iravani is an intelligence asset working for the Iranians and the Israelis. He's a deep operations mole inside Russia, here in Washington with something in that briefcase that the Russian really wanted. Iravani is so shielded, I couldn't get any background on him, nothing, like a ghost. I only saw what you did because I pulled the files from the General Register Office in England. Actually, it was a sloppy job, didn't have much by way of public record, as if you'd done it in a hurry, as if you want me to find it, Karl. What you do, Karl, what games you play, I don't give a shit. But when you implicate me in your games, that's my problem, Karl. That's my problem!"

"Are you finished?" asked Karl.

"For the moment."

"Then leave."

Katherine stood confused, expecting something from Karl, anything except that.

"Should I have security escort you from my office?"

Katherine stepped back, unsure for an instant of her footing. Puzzlement gave her pause enough to breathe. The clearer her thoughts, the more despair crawled into her head. She reached for the door, stopping for a moment with a sickly squeeze enveloping around her throat. She longed to turn back to ask for an explanation, but instead just left the way she came.

Karl threw her folder onto his desk without bothering to open it. There wouldn't be anything in there he didn't already know. Instead he pulled the other from his side drawer. He opened the cover and stared at the faces of the men in that file. He'd pledged his loyalty to his country. He'd given his vow to his wife. But he served another master and he had come calling. He only met them once; the ones most knew as the deep state. The ones he knew as the Syndycate. Katherine was the right one. She was the one who must know. He stared at their faces as he turned to his computer screen and typed in his credentials. A couple of swift key strokes was all it took. He granted Katherine access to everything: everything he had on the Phoenix program, everything he'd ever done. Everything about Peter Cole and Viktor Kletnov. Everything he ever collected on the Syndycate.

***

Rain clouds hung in the far distance. It had been a long and rocky journey from Tel Aviv. Saifa hadn't slept any on the flight. But it was the turbulence in her heart that kept her wide awake. She chose to help Ronen after so many years of resentment and hate. She thought perhaps she'd find some solace, some vindication in all this. But there were two voices in her head, and only one of them she knew to be right. Her instinct demanded she not come, but her heart compelled otherwise. The last time that happened, she paid a steep price. This time there would be no way out—for any of them.

It was still early morning in D.C. by the time she arrived, with traffic just beginning to pick up on the George Washington Memorial Parkway as the cab made its way out of Reagan International. To her left stood the Pentagon as they rolled along the highway. It had been over fifteen years since Flight 77. For Saifa it felt like yesterday.

The *sayan* who had picked her up at the airport hadn't uttered a word. She knew what he was and he knew enough not to ask questions. *Sayanim* were Israel's contact network. They numbered in the thousands in cities throughout the world and helped Israel move operatives and resources, often gathering invaluable information. They were a vital component to their intelligence apparatus. It was critical they kept to the mantra "the less we know, the better," and the cab driver did just that. He kept his eyes on the road without so much as a glance back.

The cab turned onto Arlington Memorial Bridge and came around the rear of the Lincoln Memorial. She stared at the exterior marble walls of the Greek temple housing the effigy of the man. Lincoln had been a great man weighed by the burdens of terrible times. Then, as now, the world was governed by fear and hate, and it always would be. All it took was the right tool in the wrong hands and there was no measure to what damage could be done. Her enemies were just as likely to use airplanes as they would nuclear bombs—maybe both.

She'd followed the reports on that missing Malaysian Air jet, read about it on the flight over. Rumors circulated of a landing in Kazakhstan. Rumors circulated of Chechens. Rumors circulated of a terrible weapon. Meanwhile, the world searched the Indian Ocean, and governments went to any length to hide the truth. She did not blame them. That's why women like her existed: to stop those who would commit such madness.

The cab rolled up onto 23rd Street, past the Jefferson and Vietnam memorials. She remembered Glilot and the 603 names inscribed along its furrows and ridges.

"Intelligence was all about the mind."

She remembered the words of Meir Amit, the famed Mossad director, as they drove past the granite walls and bronze statues: *kidon* lived by the sword and died by it. No one knew that better than her.

The cab pulled up to the curb of one of the many Georgetown side streets. Saifa paid her fare and stepped out into a narrow side alleyway between two brownstones, beneath a wood awning into a back doorway. She pulled out her phone, clicking on one of the application icons. Her eyes darted down the alleyway as fat raindrops began to plop on the pavement. A city map spread across the small screen as a series of roaming dots appeared on the digital map.

No matches.

The face-recognition surveillance system set for the perimeter had turned up nothing. There were no shadows following her at least any known within coverage. She walked back out onto the sidewalk, sidestepping the small puddles from the rain that had come and gone. She approached another side alley along one of the smaller streets of the colonial neighborhood, unable shake the uneasy feeling of eyes watching her.

She briskly climbed a set of worn steps and punched the passcode she'd been given into a keypad. The lock clicked open as a buzzing sound welcomed her in. She pushed past the door, slipping through as it shut with a thud behind her. She found herself in a shadowed alcove of an interior courtyard.

"Welcome to *Keilah*," boomed the voice across the enclosed courtyard.

The Citadel.

Only Ronen would choose such a name for his safe house. He stood at the window, looking down at Saifa from his second-story perch.

"Thirteen hours. You must be tired," he said with a satisfied grin.

The embers of what pride might still live in her were doused in shame. She would never give him her reasons, but she had chosen. She had come for him.

One of the four doors facing the courtyard opened up, letting her in. The wood floor creaked under her weight as she stepped through the foyer. Coats hung to one side and a mirror stood to the other. She caught a glimpse of herself with her hair pulled up in a bun, wearing a gray shirt and black jeans. She unclipped the bun, shaking out her thick curls.

"I see you keep good company, Ronen," said a young man, as he appeared in the hallway.

He walked like a leopard, graceful on his feet. Saifa sensed the danger. He had the crystal-gray eyes, those same eyes of the man who had eviscerated her. They struck panic in her heart, but not any that someone else would notice. The more fear in her heart, the more stoic and steadfast—the more dangerous—she became. But, by God, he was handsome. With a light five o'clock shadow over a decidedly square jaw, muscled shoulders, and lean frame, he passed as the American ideal of a beautiful man. Hearing his slight touch of a Midwest accent, no one would have ever known he was Mossad.

"Steve," said the young man as he politely extended his hand to Saifa.

"Hello," was all she said, with an amused grin on her face to hide her terror. If he thought he was going to get in her pants, maybe he was right.

"I'm making some *kafe botz*. Would you like some?"

"Please," said Saifa.

"Make that three," said Ronen, like a groundhog between two peacocks.

"I'll take your bag."

"I can see my way, thank you," said Saifa, keeping her eyes on Steve a second longer than she should have.

Steve gracefully bowed out with a grin. Saifa wasn't about to expose this handsome young man to ten years of resentment over some light conversation and mud coffee with Ronen. She didn't need that mix swimming in her stomach.

***

Richard watched Anja standing by the fireplace. She stared at their family portrait atop the mantle. She wouldn't face him. He saw confusion and anger, how they boiled within her to the point of blindness. The chasm between him and Anja only grew wider by the day. The night of Mount Olivet she retreated deeper into her shell. Getting Guillermo to agree to the heist of the National Gallery was easy. Guillermo thought they were crazy. But Anja was again silent. *What was done, was done.* He couldn't take back the night of the Pinacoteca. He dared not even try. Playing with time never left but the direst consequences. He gave himself no other choice now. Their secret must be protected, and this was the only way. He would not stop until he earned Anja's forgiveness. *Two wrongs would make a right.*

"The floor plan to the National Gallery is straightforward, a large main corridor leading from the central dome. Guillermo confirmed—the exhibit will be off to the right in Rooms 24 and 25. Getting to the Vermeers unnoticed will be one thing, stealing them will be another. We will have to pry them off their frames and cold-pimp climb them back out that dome."

Danny burst into the living room and onto the couch.

"It's time for bed, honey," said Anja.

"Mom, can I stay up, ten more minutes, please?"

"Go. I promise, your video game will still be here tomorrow. Go to bed, sweetheart," she said, crouching before the little boy.

"Listen to your mom. I'll be there in a bit. Got a surprise for you," said Richard with a mischievous smile.

"A comic?!"

"Better!"

"What is it?!"

"The faster you go. The faster I'll be there. Now scoot."

Danny pattered back into his room, leaving the door open. That little boy had things in him, gifts no superhero in any of his greatest comics could ever touch. But fate would be a cruel master. It would give that little boy no quarter, and no matter how much Richard and Anja tried to protect him from that fate, it somehow always found its way back across his path. Danny would one day face those demons alone. But not this day. Rage curled in the pit of Richard's stomach, rage that they'd come somehow to this.

"That boy is everything."

"He is…" said Anja, rising to her feet.

"No matter what we do, Anja, we cannot shield him from what awaits him."

"You had a choice. You knew what it meant to invoke the orb. You knew what it meant to disrupt the flow of time. It was the perfect weave, Richard. Such sacrifice to create it, like the most beautiful, most perfect of canvases, and you did what we swore, what we gave an oath *never* to do. You did it."

"The Syndycate will never find us."

Anja spun and flung something at him. It was a dagger, a cold black blade. The dagger hung still in the air, its black blade zeroed on Richard. Her other hand cupped a sphere of lapis lazuli blue. It leapt from her palm, rippling through her, enveloping them both beneath a dome of echoing light, and images collaged around them in intersecting moments of events and time — an orb of sanctuary.

The blade was still bound to the flow of time outside the orb and seemed to come to a standstill. Anja sprung like a jaguar, her face morphing into smooth green and yellow flesh. Her iridescent saffron eyes with black slit irises glowered at Richard, as her hands, boned and scaled, struck with savage precision. He faded and parried, ducked and guarded, cutting the corner, shuffling right. The blade still hung suspended in air, Anja now in its path.

"What are you doing?!"

"You say the Syndycate will never find us? Nothing in this multiverse is without consequence, Richard."

She pressed the attack again with a speed Richard could not maintain. He clinched into her. Turning a hip, he flipped her into the air over his shoulder and onto the wood floor. The black blade approached ever closer, now behind Richard. She whipped her legs around, hooking her foot to his ankle, stumbling him backward, the blade at the nape of his neck.

"Stop this!"

She grabbed the legs of a side table, throwing it at him with demonic force. The sphere vanished around them, the table splintering into the wall as if ejected from a canon. Richard sidestepped as the blade buried itself in the far wall. It missed him by a hair as Anja's countenance returned to that of the fair skinned redhead Richard knew. He could not remember the last time either of them allowed their other half to take hold of this human flesh they inhabited.

"Mommy?" asked Danny, trembling at the edge of the living room.

"It's alright, Danny. Your dad and I were just having a conversation."

"I'll be there in a minute," gasped Richard, catching his breath. He gave his son the look. Danny retreated to his room, this time shutting the door behind him. He set the lock.

"Why did you do that, Anja?!"

"You're an intruder in my home, a threat to my son, to me."

"Is that what I really am to you?"

"You're not the Richard I knew, maybe you never were. But it's my fault, for believing all those years what my heart wanted to feel, and not what my eyes now see."

Richard went numb, deaf to all else but the sound of those words. His black slit, sudden saffron eyes narrowed in rage and shame. The Guija in him pushed aside the human traits of this body that felt as if it were imploding into nothingness.

You want to steal the Vermeers? Is that what you really want?" asked Anja.

"My want is for none of this to have ever happened. To go back and change the night of the Pinacoteca. To be what we once where, even if in your eyes, you might have thought that a lie. But that will mean I once again break my oath to you. And I won't do that—I can't do that—I refuse. Our only chance is the here and now, to put aside my mistakes, to trust once again."

Richard saw Anja's mind working behind those eyes, mulling and weighing, making decisions, but not letting him in to share them with.

"I will handle the security. I'll work Edvard Thorn. You handle Guillermo," she finally said with a decisiveness that gave Richard pause.

"I can do that."

"You're wondering if you can still trust me," she added with a gentle smile that caused more fear than solace.

"The thought crossed my mind."
She walked to the front door and grabbed her keys. "You have a son waiting for you. Everything I do is for him. Don't forget that."

Anja walked out the front door, leaving Richard to pick up the broken side table and what remained of his shattered heart.

***

Steve worked for Ronen, followed his orders, served his wishes. Ronen could have demanded Steve climb the Washington Monument and jump off its very spire, with nothing more than a bungee cord round his waist and the possibility of that strap snapping, and Steve would have done it. That was the level of command and control Ronen had built through training, through fear, into his *katsas*, and yet this morning, Ronen couldn't bring himself to even glance at him.

Steve swirled the steaming coffee cup as he plopped in his one lump of sugar. Ronen sat opposite him on the other side of the kitchen counter, burying his focus into the laptop screen in front of him.

"Not the first time you've worked together, seems like," said Steve, bringing the cup to his lips.

"Best you mind your own business," said Ronen, without even a glance. He was terrified of jumping out of his own skin and strangling the man.

"I'm surprised," continued Steve, flashing a charismatic grin.

The jealousy was suddenly very real for Ronen. "At?"

"I thought *kidon* worked in teams."

"We do," Saifa said as she appeared at the doorway to the kitchen. "But we handle ourselves best when we're on our own."

Steve gave her a saucer and teacup, and she a flirtatious smile back at him. The pressure in Ronen's chest rolled down the inside of his arm. He ground his teeth and clenched his hands to keep from springing from his skin at them both.

Instead, he turned the laptop on the counter around to them, afraid to say (or *do*) something he might regret. "Let's get down to business, shall we?"

Saifa was happy to see a little bit of pain in those eyes of his. The jealousy made her feel good in ways it shouldn't have. The joy of him feeling pain at her hands actually terrified her. She wasn't supposed to feel anything at all when it came to this man, not after all he'd done to her.

"A week ago, our signals intelligence team intercepted communications between the Russian embassy, here in Washington, and the Kandinsky Group. They're a natural gas and oil conglomerate, the largest in Russia," said Ronen, hiding his own turmoil in the dryness of the facts.

"Kandinsky—aren't they suspected of providing arms, weapons-grade uranium, and plutonium to Iran?" Saifa asked.

"Yes, on all counts. Kandinsky has major stakes in Toporol, the Russian aerospace holding company, and Vertoskval."

"The designers of the MI-25?" asked Steve.

"The export version of the Hind attack helicopters recently sent to Syria, stopped by the British off the coast of Scotland," said Ronen, clicking through to a familiar image of a bearded face and dark eyes. A memory tugged at the back of Saifa's mind like déjà vu, pulling at the very strands of her DNA.

"Viktor Kletnov is the chairman of their board. We consider him one of the most powerful men in Russia, just behind President Shukurov. But little is known of him to most others in the West; we believe his identity is suppressed by design. Last month we intercepted communications out of the Russian embassy directly with the Kandinsky Group. A diplomatic visa was granted to one of its representatives, Vadim Iravani. He's an Iranian intelligence asset who also works for us on occasion."

"The Iranian works for Kletnov?" asked Steve.

"He's a deep cover operative, perhaps known to Kletnov, perhaps working for him, definitely siphoning information back to us and Tehran."

"Where is this Vadim now?" asked Steve.

"Unknown. He was picked up by our *sayanim* here in D.C., meeting with Andrei Birkin, head of Russian intel. A week later, again, this time in Murmansk, near the Nerpichya naval base."

"In D.C. one week, and Murmansk the next? Why would Kletnov send this guy on such a strange itinerary, if in fact it was Kletnov?" asked Steve.

"We believe as a courier. He carried a briefcase, one that did not leave his side for an instant," said Ronen.

"Was it given to Birkin?" asked Saifa.

"No. He met with Birkin at a coffee shop on Thirteenth and F Street, had a brief conversation, and then made his way to the National Gallery, where we lost contact until his whereabouts were reacquired a week later."

"Okay, so why so much interest in this one Iranian operative?" asked Steve.

Ronen glanced at Saifa, who averted her eyes nearly as fast. *What was it he just saw?* There was something icy in her look, something she did not want him to see—something he recognized in the Saifa he knew a long time ago. Maybe some tenderness, or maybe some regret. Ronen was suddenly wary of his own person. Believing that Saifa would somehow fall in love with him again, that she actually never stopped loving him, was a delusion his reason knew could not be true. His fight wasn't with Viktor or this Vadim, it was with the dichotomy of loving her. He was terrified of letting go of what he feared most: finding joy and having someone else take it away from him, like Steve could so easily do now. Ronen used the facts to deflect his own madness.

"Vadim is an enigmatic source, providing us information on occasion—when it suited him and for the right price. We always went to him. But this time, he came to us. What you see here is a Russian Typhoon-class submarine," he said, shifting to a thermal image of an orange, red, and magenta shape.

"Vadim uploaded these images to one of our com satellites reserved for only the most sensitive transmissions. Our analysts authenticated the message and confirmed the spectral image as the TK-12, the *Simbirsk*. That submarine was supposedly decommissioned and scrapped for parts six years ago."

"An old rust bucket. So what? The Russians got plenty of those lying around," said Steve.

"Not ones commanded by this man," added Ronen, shifting to an infrared image of a man with the crooked nose of an old boxer and a captain's insignia on his uniform. That face struck a chord in Saifa, another old memory, this one of a night in Crimea.

"We suspect the *Simbirsk* to be functional again, commanded by this man, Dmitri Borei."

"Why would Vadim volunteer this information, unsolicited?" asked Saifa.

"We don't know. His handler has been unable to establish contact since that night. We believe something big is in the works, something Vadim wanted us to know about. We need both of you to establish contact with Birkin and get him to talk," said Ronen.

"Why both of us? As grateful as I am for Saifa, why a *kidon*?"

"In case you get in a little over your head," said Ronen.

"I'm sure you're just the kind of girl to keep me out of trouble," said Steve with a grin of pure joy that snapped something in Ronen.

"If you were only so lucky," said Saifa, with a grin of her own that was more warning than reassurance. Ronen pursed his lips and crushed his jealousy. Steve would learn to be careful of his words, and Saifa would again learn to respect him.

***

The crystal-gray eyes in the rearview mirror did not blink. They considered something in the distance, perhaps the conversations of earlier in the day. Ronen had made clear his intentions about the operation and his *kidon*. But they were still hiding things from him, things they had kept for themselves. That didn't bother him though. No one ever gave away the truth for free, not even this Vadim character they'd discussed. So Steve had taken his liberty, a foray of his own, a brief jaunt to get better acquainted with Andrei Birkin, the one Ronen had been so adamant about.

Steve sat motionless in front of an unremarkable building of concrete gray and wrought-iron black. If there was one thing good about America winning the Cold War, it was that rest of the world didn't have to deal with the tastes of old Soviet architects any longer. Everything about Russia had to be big, but they didn't need to make it so square.

The opening of those iron gates to the embassy was the reward for his long wait. A white Mercedes SUV rolled slowly past the perimeter wall, turning onto the pavement and whisking away down the tree-lined street. So it seemed he wasn't the only one interested in Andrei after all. The brunette in that driver's seat was a pleasant surprise to see. Katherine Brandt really was a beautiful woman. Interesting that the Agency's DTRA liaison would be paying the embassy a visit. One of the many perks of his trade was the women he met along the way. Having to kill them from time to time wasn't one of the more fun aspects of his business.

Steve remembered every one of them, every victim. They'd each taken a piece of him. He wondered if Saifa had seen it in his eyes, the empty shell of a man he had become. She was no less accomplished than he and more than wise to the realities of their worlds. He actually fancied the girl. After all, their shared history was more than she could yet imagine. It had been a long time since Steve thought he might have a conscience. He needed to move swiftly before guilt got in the way. Mossad still had its uses for him.

A second Mercedes, this time a black C-class, followed through the embassy gates, its windows tinted, its bumper decorated with diplomatic plates. Finally, the gentleman he wanted to meet. Andrei turned the corner and sped off after the white SUV in the direction of his Georgetown haunt. Steve gave it a moment and turned on his engine. He wasn't in any rush. He knew where Andrei was going. He shifted out of park and rolled onto the street after the black Mercedes. He was looking forward to getting to know Andrei Birkin.

XII

THE REYKJANES

The fetid air lay still and tepid over the room. Dmitri sat at the back of the officer's mess, hidden away from the world and the dangers that lurked in the blackness a thousand feet below the surface. The shelves and their books towered behind him as he held the silver coin between his fingers. He admired the proud forehead and chin on its face and the double-headed eagle on its back. Its mint year was 1825.

He pressed his forefinger over the ridge of the coin as he stood it on the birch table. A slight tarnish formed around the lettering along its rim. He slowly took his finger off the top. It stood perfectly in place.

The Typhoon had leveled off deep beneath the waves. The life of a submariner had always been a difficult one. Cramped quarters and the dangers of months at sea created camaraderie between men understood only by them. No matter where he came from, the submariner shared this common bond.

His crew had rigged the *Simbirsk* for silent running on their long journey. Thirty-nine men had joined him. They were barely enough to run a boat made for a crew of one-hundred-eighty.

The emptiness made for a lonely voyage and the workload for an exhausting one. Luckily for them, the work kept their minds off where they were going. To the men aboard, it was a military exercise, and they asked no questions. It was best, often, not to know. The creaking of rusty hinges lifted Dmitri's attentions from the coin. Misha Andreev approached in his clean, pressed, dark blue tunic. Misha was an elegant man even under the harshest of conditions.

"We have passed Iceland and the old detection net along the GIUK and leveled off over the Reykjanes at 400 meters, speed four knots. We are on course to the Charlie Gibbs, set to turn toward the Azores Triple Junction, as ordered, Captain."

"You are precise, Misha, thank you. Sit, join me for a while," said Dmitri, as he pulled a gold-filtered Sobraine Black Russian from the pack in his front pocket. "Smoke?"

"Trying to cut down," said Misha.

"You want something else to kill you, I take it."

"At least whatever does will come as a surprise."

"I'll need to remember that," said Dmitri, lighting the cigarette with his platinum butane lighter. He blew a puff of heavy smoke into the air. "Gives you something to look forward to, I guess."

"We've made no contacts other than the regular merchant traffic in and out of the Barents," said Misha, turning his attentions back to his duties.

"It's quiet out here."

"Yes, sir. How we like it."

"And cold, well, maybe not so cold," said Dmitri, taking in another drag, flicking the ash into the tray.

"Boris is working on the environmental system to make it a bit more comfortable for the men."

"I meant the sea."

"The sea is cold, but it contains the hottest blood of all. D.H. Lawrence, sir."

Dmitri couldn't help but smile. Misha was a trustworthy officer and a well-educated man.

"And how are the men?"

"They are good, Captain. The work is exhausting, but morale is high. It's good to serve aboard the *Simbirsk* again, under Captain Borei."

"Precise and complimentary, the characteristics of a highly successful career officer in the Russian Navy," said Dmitri with a grin.

"Thank you, Captain. They have helped on occasion. That is an interesting coin." Misha gestured at the piece standing on its rim atop the table.

"The scepter and crown, the double-headed eagle of the Russian Empire. It's an old Constantine ruble."

"The Czar Constantine?" asked Misha with surprise.

"The Czar who never was," said Dmitri as he slid the coin across the table. "They'd produced only eight of them at the Petersburg mint before Constantine rejected the throne."

"Maybe Constantine was the smart one," said Misha, as he studied the coin under the light. He handed the piece back to Dmitri. "It must be priceless."

"Definitely very expensive. Several were produced throughout the years to resemble the originals," said Dmitri.

"It's a fake?" asked Misha.

Dmitri smiled as he considered the question and put out the cigarette in the tray. "It's been in my family for generations, handed down father to son. It's good luck," said Dmitri, sidestepping the question.

"You might be holding a fortune."

"The human mind delights in grand conceptions."

"Sir?"

"A quote from *Twenty Thousand Leagues Under the Sea*. I must have read it a hundred times as a boy. 'Where I could hide away under the waves, where I would be free,'" quoted Dmitri, as he took in a breath to ease the memory.

"I joined the Navy thanks to *Moby Dick*."

"Now there's a story." Dmitri chuckled.

"'*I thought I would sail about a little, and see the watery part of the world,*'" they both recited in joyful unison.

"That Herman Melville was a master, a near-forgotten one at that. Can you believe, I read him on my first assignment? Black Sea Fleet, Junior Lieutenant, right out of Leninsky," said Dmitri, flipping the ruble between his fingers.

"The *Alrosa*," said Misha.

"Very good," said Dmitri, arching his eyebrows in surprise.

"I know a thing or two about you, Captain."

"That you do, my friend."

"But in all the years I've known you, you never mentioned your family," Misha said.

"Irina died giving birth to our daughter."

"My deepest condolences to you." Misha dipped his gaze. He knew just how much he'd overstepped his bounds.

"One need not wonder why some men are content to watch the world burn," said Dmitri with a smile that bore no joy.

"Aye, Captain. May they be wary of their pain and hate, lest they too befall Ahab's fate, sir."

"Indeed, Misha. Indeed…"

**

The pain of the morning after March Madness was real. Mike had stumbled out of the shower, with the aftermath of the night prior still reeking out his pores and breath. He had a vague recollection about some extra-strength sports bra snapping across his cheek and a sudden claustrophobic mass of flesh suffocating his face. Whatever that was last night could not have been Melanie Ann, just could not have been. The stench of regurgitated chips and wings still fresh on his shirt and the memory of what was never supposed to happen to him were too traumatic for his ego. The struggle was indeed real.

All in all, it wasn't a bad way to start the morning. Professor Robles would have been proud of the effort, at least. Mike couldn't even remember if the Hoyas had won. If his ragged looks were any indication, they dominated. He was exhausted but at least not for the wrong reasons. His mind had already blocked out most of the horrors of the night prior.

He made his way past the security checkpoint of the NMIC, the National Maritime Intelligence Center. It was a process he'd done countless times since he started his post-grad internship, part of his curriculum at Georgetown's naval engineering program. He strolled past the detector while his bag rolled through the scanner. He showed the guard his badge as he had three times a week for the past three months. Past the checkpoint, he made his way up the stairs with his vague recollections and the scent of whoever that was last night all over his neck. He definitely needed to take scrubbier showers.

He ambled down the hallway with backpack slung over his shoulder, stopping at one of the many nondescript doors. Sliding his card through the reader, he pushed the door open. Thoughts of Melanie Ann quickly vanished as he entered the cubicle area with its computer terminals lining the whole of the floor. He sighed with the weight of the world over his shoulders. This was no way to cure a hangover.

He ripped the little yellow sticky note from his terminal screen.

Record, classify, and catalog undersea vent activity, sector 946-B. Have fun!

"How thrilling." Mike dropped his bag and settled in for a long afternoon in a less-than-comfortable, worn-out chair.

***

Commander Chamberlain Phelps usually enjoyed the early morning bustle beneath the blue lights of the control room aboard the USS Miami. She was a fast-attack Los Angeles–class submarine on her return leg to New London after a three-month assignment patrolling the Barents, and the men were looking forward to some much needed shore time with family they hadn't seen or heard from in as many days.

The control room was tight but ergonomic and purpose-built, with easy access to the many stations that managed the boat. Commander Phelps stood this morning as dive officer of the watch in front of the Type 2 and Type 18 periscopes. His chief of the watch worked at the helm and plane stations to his left as other chiefs and quartermasters moved between fire-control and sonar, relaying information to the navigation supervisor at the plotting table behind him. The gradual tilt like a pendulum from port to starboard was the only hint of the tempest raging on the surface above.

Commander Phelps liked his coffee black. It was particularly strong this morning and tasted better than usual. He eyed his boatswain's mate suspiciously.

"Hey Washington, the coffee's pretty good this morning."

"Yes, sir. Extra-strong brew. They know how you like it, commander."

"Yeah, I bet."

Phelps thought twice about taking another taste. He wondered if Washington had taken a detour from the mess. The boatswain didn't flinch or crack a smile. He went about his duties straight-faced and detached from the conversation. A bit too detached. He was hiding something.

"Would you like to try the coffee this morning?"

"Already had some, sir. Thank you."

"Right," said Phelps, as he took another taste from his mug.

For what it was worth, the coffee was delicious.

The commander wasn't one to usually pull a double shift, but the lieutenant was sick in the infirmary; he didn't rightly know with what. Curious how the malady came up after the late-night captain's birthday in the mess. Phelps wondered how he let them sucker him with that sob story. He counted the minutes till he'd be back in his quarters and the comfort of his bed.

They equalized ballast tanks and leveled at their new depth as the navigator and plot supervisor worked behind him, between the consoles and tables, refining the passage plan to New London. Their job was to make sure the boat got where it was going without any sudden obstacles getting in their way. The GIUK gap between Greenland, Iceland, and the United Kingdom was well-surveyed, but at over 900 feet beneath the surface, anything was possible. He heard the stories of the *San Francisco* a few years earlier, and they were the kind of nightmare this officer of the watch didn't want to experience, let alone have on his record.

"Conn, sonar," came the familiar voice over the 1MC, as Phelps turned his attentions back to his coffee.

"Conn, aye," said Phelps into the handheld, taking a swig.

"Conn, we have a possible submerged contact, sierra zero five."

"Fuck." And he was looking forward to his bed. Phelps looked over the analog monitors feeding sonar contact information into the control room. "Where are you picking her up? We're not seeing shit here."

"The real thin line at the top of the waterfall in the ten-hertz range, see it?"

"Not really, but I'll take your word for it."

"It's there, and it's definitely man-made, twin screws. She's running slow and deep, beneath the thermal layer, probably less than five knots."

"Can you get a bearing?"

"That's a negative. Not getting any transients or other source levels. She's too far away, fading in and out."

"Do we have anyone else out here?" Phelps asked Washington.

"Far as I know sir, report was we're the only ones. Could be a NATO fast-attack."

"I'd bet she's a boomer, sir," came the voice over the 1MC.

"What makes you say that?" asked Phelps.

"Just a hunch. Besides, it'll gimme something exciting to do."

The last thing Phelps needed right now was the excitement of chasing some noise in the water with a tight-wound ping jockey hell-bent on some hunch.

"Sir, I recommend we deploy the thin line, speed one-third, for a better look."

"Conn, aye. Washington, deploy the towed array, bring speed to five knots, maintain depth and course."

Phelps stared down at his empty mug. He was going to need a lot more of this brew.

"Washington, order me another round of coffee, will ya, and regular this time."

"Aye, sir," said Washington as he took the cup—guiltily avoiding eye contact, it seemed to Phelps.

Phelps turned back to the sonar display and looked for that so-called thin line. "How do they find the needle in that shit?"

He picked up the growler phone and punched the dial.

"This is Phelps. Get me the cap'n."

***

Her voice whispered softly in his ear. Her soft touch gently caressed his shoulder. A chill went down his spine as her warm breath prickled the skin of his neck. He could feel her supple breasts heaving slowly behind him.

"Freeman, I'm going to count to two," said the gruff voice of Lieutenant Patricia Larson, the area supervisor of the oceanic topography section. The sharp pain of his ear being twisted startled him awake, and it wasn't Melanie nibbling on his lobe.

"Yes, ma'am," said Mike, as he righted himself abruptly and wiped the drool from his lips.

"Shut-eye helps you really focus on those sounds, right, Freeman?" said Larson. She was dressed in her Navy whites, with her hair picked up in her cap. She had a long neck and a generous mouth that gave way to a devilish grin.

"Absolutely, ma'am," said Mike, afraid to blush.

"At least you admit when you're caught red-handed; I like that."

"Thank you, ma'am."

"I'll look for your report on those hydrothermal vents in my inbox before you go. And try not to blush when I give you a shakedown. You're just a civvy, after all," she said, this time whispering gently in his ear.

The hairs stood on the back of his neck. She stood upright, giving a smile to Ganesh, the guy in the cubicle across the way who was staring at them, mouth agape.

"Man, she sure looks like a fun one," said Ganesh, watching her hips and long legs as she strutted down the line and turned past the corner out of sight.

Ganesh Bushir was a graduate petroleum engineering student at Georgetown and Mike's best friend since their freshman undergrad year. Ganesh was born in Baghpat, from the territory of Delhi, the land of tigers. But Ganesh was no tiger; he was more like a gentle little pussycat.

"God, I wish she'd give me a shakedown," Ganesh said.

"She doesn't like guys who smell like curry."

"Why do you have to be so racist?"

"I like curry. I just don't eat it twice a day, every day," said Mike as he took out a textbook from his bag.

"Nothing funner than studying Mideast geopolitics while listening to static from the bottom of the ocean, huh, Mikey? I'm so glad your Hoyas lost their little basketball game. I should have doubled up on your ass. Kept you in Professor Robles's class a few more semesters," said Ganesh, with a certain satisfaction.

"Man, you are one angry Hindu."

"Yeah, well you sound like one pretty pissed-off white guy. Everything's not so bad. Yeah, the Hoyas suck and you're getting no play. But look on the bright side: you're cataloging one of the largest underwater ecosystems in the world, devoid of sunlight, thousands of miles away and even more miles beneath the sea — cutting edge. That's hot."

"Listening to fucking static, in this cubicle, with your dumb, devoid-of-sunlight ass is not hot. Chillin' on the beaches of the Azores with Melanie Ann, that's hot. Now if you'll excuse me, I have a date with some hydrothermal displacements."

Mike put on the headset and propped the book up by the monitor. A crumpled ball of paper bounced on his head, falling into his lap.

"I was trying for a three into your wastepaper basket. I'm sorry, is that what cost the Hoyas the game last night? I shoot about as good as your point guard, sorry."

Mike's hand shot out toward Ganesh, his middle finger saying exactly what he thought of his comment. He buried himself in his midterm prep and in the steady sounds of the hydrophones thousands of miles away at the bottom of a cold and dark ocean.

XIII

ALPHA & OMEGA

"Every time, Daddy. Every time, you have to go. Let's play ball. Please?"

"Not right now, Danny. Daddy's got work to do."

His head hung low, and his cheeks twitched with sadness. Danny hugged the glove that was half the size of his body as he listened to the words he'd heard over and over. He pattered down the hall as fast as his little feet could take him, as the sensation of having drunk liquid coal poured down Richard's throat.

"Danny!"

He tossed and turned all night thinking about that little boy. He stared at Anja fast asleep beside him. He wanted so badly to wake her, to hear her whisper all would be alright, or feel a caress, just a touch. He reached out, but only recoiled. She laid next to him and still they couldn't be any farther apart.

"If you're not careful, you'll lose more than just the time on your watch," said Anja the next morning, as she walked into the bathroom and handed him his timepiece.

She'd seen the exchange of the night before and must have felt he needed a reminder of what was most important. He tried to talk to her, but before he could utter a word, she was gone. He went through the morning's routine of shower, shave, and a coffee as if the unravelling of his life simply wasn't happening.

Richard grappled with the loneliness, exchanging not a word the rest of the morning. He did his tie as he stared at the reproduction of *The Concert* in the mirror. Danny didn't come out of his room that morning until his mommy knocked on the door to take him to school.

"*Bye, Dad,*" was all he heard, and Danny was gone.

The grass beneath his soles was wet this morning from the rolling fog and low-hanging rain clouds . But more than just clouds hung heavy over Richard's thoughts. The police had continued their investigation of Christian Huygens's death, and his snooping of their files, as he suspected, had gone unfettered. Huygens's passing was ruled a suicide. But he and the police knew better. It was a targeted murder. He gained access to their electronic records and crime scene photos. He read the e-mails and heard the voice calls. They were going to cover it all up. Someone had called in a favor, and Christian Huygens wouldn't be missed anyway, so best not make a fuss about it.

While Dutch police focused on the use of a serrated garrote wire around the victim's throat that had cut through to the base of his skull, leaving the victim's face in a viscous pool of black blood, Richard took more interest in the other markings they'd found. Curves were carved into Huygens's back.

What was murky to police was clear to Richard. The cuts were no mere curves, but runes, the uncial forms of Omega from the Gothic script. It meant the end to Alpha's beginning. It was a mark used only by one group and placed on the body to send a message. He hadn't slept for the past two nights.

He had promised Anja. *The Syndycate would never find them.* But the murder proved him wrong. Christian

Huygens was the work of the Sicaari and that meant it was only a matter of time before the Syndycate would catch up with them. The night of the Pinacoteca had altered this timeline and she would blame him for it. He needed to plan, to think through all of this. *Alter the timeline yet again perhaps? But how?*

There was no telling what consequences such an attempt might bring. What other horrors might he awaken with such folly. Anja had to trust him again somehow. Maybe he could find a way, somehow protect them, somehow make it so that none of this ever happened; so that Anja might find in him again the man she once knew and loved. He wanted this more than anything else, for her and for Danny.

He cut quickly across the empty courtyard before the morning bustle of students and faculty. The rhythmic sound of his step and the cold wetness on his skin kept his mind fixed on the present as he ascended the well-worn steps to Healy Hall.

He stood in the corridor as he had a thousand times before, but the hallway was ominously silent. The street lamps faded over the courtyard as the morning seeped through the clouds outside. No one should have been here this early, not even him. He approached the first door ajar to his right and peered into his lecture hall.

If no one was supposed to be here, then who was the shrouded figure at the far corner of the room?

***

Gray storm clouds blanketed the sky over the old quarter, as a cleaning truck turned onto Pennsylvania Avenue below. David picked out a single chunk of ice from the bucket on a small round table as he stared out the floor-to-ceiling window. He released the tongs, the rectangular cube plopping into the empty glass.

He slowly removed the top from a finely crafted bottle at the table, the stopper of which was etched with an intricate pattern of leaves. He gripped its neck as he slowly poured its amber contents over the single cube, then placed the decanter back onto the table. He brought the glass to his nostrils, swirling its contents as a cloud slowly formed in the drink, and fog enveloped the pyramid peak of the Washington Monument.

David reclined into his plush, high-backed chair as he put his lips to the cool rim. The aromas of peat smoke and dried orange peel assaulted his senses. He hardly noticed the albino or James Fenway. They sat to his right and quietly looked out the window, no drinks in their hands. They made no move for the bottle. The rooftop lounge of the HW Hotel stood otherwise empty except for the khaki-clad waiter and the unmistakable black suits of the Diplomatic Security Services guarding the entrances to the indoor bar.

"I love the quiet feel of this place. I could sit here all day staring at the rain clouds," said David, as he slowly took his first sip.

"Macallan 64, sir?" asked James, as he smelled the aroma from where he sat.

The words "Macallan in Lalique" read along the edge of the glass.

"One of these recently sold at Sotheby's for what was it, $460,000?"

"I believe so, sir," said the albino. The scar over his left cheek was especially pronounced this morning.

"I didn't take you for a Scotch connoisseur," said James condescendingly.

"What else do you not take me for," sibilated the question in James' head. The albino stared at him with iridescent yellow eyes and grinned with yellow-stained fangs. Beneath waxed-paper-thin skin, green and red capillaries radiated out from a black, malignant scar on his cheek.

James seized the armchair and clenched to keep from losing control of his bladder.

"Stay focused on me, James," said David as he held the glass close to bask in the aroma. "Everything else is just a distraction."

The albino's face was again the unpleasant countenance James remembered, pale with jaundiced eyes and twisted, stained teeth, not the ghoulish creature he just witnessed.

Was just my imagination.

"Was it? Naïve little pup," again hissed the voice in his ears.

"Enough," boomed another voice within the confines of their minds. David glowered at the albino who shifted slightly in his chair daring not to meet his stare. Like a dog, the albino knew his place with his master. James glanced away but he could not hide the confusion of rage and panic in his thoughts. James wanted more than anything to be like one of them. He had the poise and polish for a Deputy Secretary of State, but what he wanted required a lot more than Ivy League smarts and political experience. For the moment, David saw only weakness, and James's loathing and fear of the albino only furthered his opinion.

"Salil signed the agreement," said David.

"Clothed in shame and regret even before he finished with the period at the end of his name,"

251

replied James, handing David the original from the thin black case at his feet.

"As I knew he would. While everyone yaps about the president's landmark foreign policy achievement, Salil Jawadi turns everything on its head. No price is too steep if it means a chance at retribution for what the clerics did to him and his son all those years ago in Khorramshahr," said David.

Khorramshahr was an old memory for David, but one he knew would some day serve him well. The Syndycate, from its earliest days, had been forbidden from ever bringing children into this world for fear of what such a birth might create. For centuries they held this precept, until certain of them chose to break with their oath. Salil was one among them. He fathered a son and daughter with a wife named Romina.

The Syndycate had no choice but to act. But David was temperate. He was just and fair. He granted Salil the benefit of due process. They quietly tested the children for the genetic markers hidden in the noncoding strands of their double helix. His daughter was innocent, untarnished. She was fully human. But the son was not so fortunate. He was tainted with their genome, spawned outside the control of their laboratories. Again David elected restraint and instead chose to study his growth. But with time, it became evident the young man was too dangerous for them. He exhibited mutations and abilities never seen by any of their kind, beyond that of even the Guija or Sicaari.

With no control over him, David made a choice. He, too, broke with their oath. He spared Salil. Instead Salil's son was murdered by the very hands of those who Salil held dearest so that blame would never find its way back to the Syndycate. Amir Haghigi, Salil's most trusted human, had murdered his son. The same Amir who was now the president of Iran. The circumstances couldn't have played any better into David's hand. Salil would do whatever it was David commanded for his chance at retribution.

"And his obligations as per the agreement?" asked David, refocusing from his reverie.

"Tankers already began shipping oil from both Bushehr and Bandar Abbas, the first of which will reach Eliat in three days. We're targeting a million barrels a day over the next ninety days to reach Ashkelon through the pipeline. The Vatican's Praetorium Bank has disbursed funds, while LVS Bank and BNC Internationale have quietly begun the purchase of the credit default swaps from the Central Bank of Iran. The first five hundred million were confirmed this morning with Wilhelm," said James.

"The funds have begun to move as expected," said David, as he watched the cloud swirl in his drink.

"We should see the first payment of 1.7 billion transferred from the Central Bank to LVS by the end of the month," said James.

"That should unwind Wilhelm's ass a little bit," said the albino.

"It'll only make him worse. Besides, who wants a banker who doesn't obsess over money?" asked David.

"We expect a collective profit of just over three hundred billion to be partitioned across the members, as agreed to in Rome," said James.

"The Chinese concern me," said David, as the fog enveloped what remained of the Washington Monument, leaving only a gray cotton blanket for a view.

"As they should, sir. The agreement with Jawadi gives Spancore a twenty percent stake in Petroran Oil, granting us control of both the Azadegan and Yadavaran oil fields. Neither is something the Chinese will easily give up, nor something Spancore's CEO, Nathanial Brandenburg will back away from. His support in the Syndycate was critical in Rome and we cannot afford to lose him now," said James, as David took another sip of his Macallan.

"Someone tried to assassinate Zhen Xin Liang, framing our involvement, on the heels of our Rome conclave. A conflict with the Chinese is exactly what the Syndycate does not need. Whoever devised the attack knows it," said David.

"The bigger issue is the NSA report out of Hainan—if Ben-Gideon learns of that report," said James.

"Mossad likely knows of it already," interrupted the albino, stopping James in mid-sentence.

"That report is only a small piece to a larger puzzle," said David, as he placed his glass onto the tabletop.

A betrayal lingered in the air. The members of the Syndycate each played their parts so well, it was sometimes easy to forget what they really were, even for David. He sat silent for a long time as James and the albino waited.

"Gentlemen, thank you for the company this morning," said David, as he returned the stopper to the decanter on the table.

He rose from his chair, the waiter and security detail moving like clockwork. David buttoned his jacket as the waiter retrieved the bottle and the guards waited by the door.

"Rome was only the beginning. But our preparations, however, may not be enough. More extreme measures will be needed," said David.

"We stand ready to serve," said the albino.

James bowed in silence and averted his gaze. David considered the young man. He considered prying one more time, but digging into the mind took its effort without any certainty to what he might find. James had still much to learn, and there was no better lesson than being thrown to the wolves.

"I have another assignment for you. I will call for you when ready." David thought he saw something in his eyes, a hint of what should not be there. If it was there, James hid it well. David abruptly departed with his security service at his side, leaving the two men to consider the foggy D.C. morning.

***

The spring day had been more like a gray Moscow winter morning. Andrei reversed the car into an open space along a side street of his residential Georgetown neighborhood. No matter how much he loved D.C., he felt nostalgia for home, especially on days like this one. He always looked back in the rear view mirror before he stepped out of the car. Lately he'd been in a state of heightened awareness. Ever since his encounter with Vadim, strange things had been happening. It felt similar to walking into a room and noticing that something had been moved out of place, but just not being able to tell what. Something wasn't right. The visit from Katherine Brandt only confirmed that.

A DTRA agent coming to visit the head of Russian intelligence wasn't so unusual. What Andrei had in his possession was. He didn't know Viktor's intentions and had learned early not to question. But he had a portable nuclear device on American soil, and an American investigator just paid him a visit. Viktor's explicit instructions had been for absolute secrecy, no formal reporting via any means, not even to his general director. Andrei had not heard from Viktor since receiving the device. It had been over a month, and he was out here on his own, waiting. He took his briefcase from the passenger seat as he exited the car. The smell of the coming rain filled the air. The damp breeze blanketed his skin as he walked the way he had every day on his jaunt home from the embassy.

Andrei would have noted just how pleasing Katherine was to look at, if not for the panic that seized his gonads. But she hadn't come about the nuke. She'd come to ask about something more troubling: the death of Admiral Nygev. The report from the FSB on Nygev's death had been conclusive. The admiral was poisoned with fifty sieverts of polonium, out of the shower head, over ten times the median lethal dose. A dead admiral with orders signed for a phantom Typhoon submarine. Katherine had come snooping around a very touchy subject. It was a most unusual way to go about gathering information on such a sensitive topic.

If she knew about Nygev, what else does she know?

Nygev had been exposed to more than double what had killed Louis Slotin during the Manhattan Project. Nygev had died in a few agonizing minutes that Andrei could only imagine must have felt like an eternity to the poor man. The radiation had basically melted him alive from the inside out. It had blistered the flesh off his face and holed out his stomach. The facility had been condemned and all personnel quietly evacuated.

Fifty sieverts of radiation at a Russian naval base wasn't something too terribly difficult to cover up when abandoned nuclear vessels were decaying on the dock. But when a Russian admiral was killed, it was sure to get attention from a very select group of people.

He turned around. He thought he heard something. Maybe it wasn't the American woman he should be worried about. There was nothing coincidental about these seemingly disconnected events.

The street was eerily empty, breeze blowing along the treetops, when the first droplet hit his skin.

No point in running. I won't get any less wet.

He climbed the steps to his brownstone home as the questions from Katherine Brandt ran through his mind. He loved her raven hair and sultry voice. With every question, her talons dug deeper into his chest, and she wouldn't let go.

He pressed his thumb against the fingerprint reader by the entrance as the bolt pulled back with a dry thud and the door creaked open. The wood floor complained beneath his step as the automatic lamp illuminated the living room. The door shut behind him, not a whisper in the house.

Andrei had spartan taste: the less, the better. He was a minimalist with a modern, square-edged preference in furniture. A Pratfall mahogany chair with black leather upholstery and a matching armchair sofa filled the living room. A copy of Francis Bacon's *Study of Pope Innocent X* hung on the far wall opposite the LED flat panel. A signed Spartak 2009 championship soccer ball stood atop the glass shelf attached to the wall.

Andrei was a huge football fan and a former player himself. He still fancied the game to keep in shape, playing with the guys from the Zaslon special forces detachment assigned to their embassy. The Spec Ops guys thought they were badasses until Andrei schooled them on the art of moving a ball.

Andrei looked over the space carefully. He stood stone-still, noting that everything had been left as it was. Paranoia was a daily habit for him. He placed his keys on the glass Noguchi coffee table, setting the briefcase on the sofa. The door to the study was open, the room beyond pitch black. With a fluid motion, he drew his Makarov from his side holster.

He gripped the soccer ball and pulled it from the shelf, as he took two silent steps back. Aiming the pistol into the darkness, he pitched the ball. It slowly rolled along the short corridor, the signatures blurring on its white leather face. It disappeared into the room, the darkness swallowing it.

The lights were supposed to always turn on, always!

***

"Hello, Richard. It's nice to see you again."

The shadow in the back of the room was a familiar voice, an unwelcome voice. There was no doubt left in Richard now. Christian Huygens was dead, and now Karl Downing was here. Any control he thought he still might have was gone. The Syndycate could be anywhere—they might already know his secret. A venomous loathing welled in Richard, fueled by the memories of this man from so long ago. But he steeled his nerve, and bent his rage to his will. He swore a promise to Anja, and he would not break it again.

258

"Unfortunately for you, I don't share your sentiment," said Richard, standing at the door to his classroom. "Hiding in the shadows, appearing here uninvited, is hazardous to your health, Karl."

He placed his briefcase on the desk. "We had an agreement: you never contact me."

"Sometimes life leaves us no choice. Promises must be broken," said Karl, sitting at the back corner by the window.

Those words clove deep into his belly, reminded him of Anja's blame, and what he wished he could take back.

"Enough of your flowery bullshit, Karl. I don't work for you anymore."

"Richard Robles never worked for me. Peter Cole did."

The blur barely registered as desks were strewn aside. In one hand, Richard had Karl's throat. In the other, his clenched fingers clawed at the Mideast Studies textbook.

"It's good to see you haven't lost your reflexes," gasped Karl through a constricted airway. A cold sweat formed over his face.

Karl slowly raised a pistol from one of his many hidden trench coat pockets. It pressed to purpose beneath Richard's chin. He gasped with a pained smile as his lips began to turn a shade blue. Richard released his grip. The air rushed back into Karl's lungs.

"That name is dead. My days with the SCS are long over, Karl."

"Something serious is moving in Iran. Something big and we think it's coming through the Chinese."

So Karl wasn't here for Huygens. At least it wasn't his angle for now. They both knew what Christian

Huygens was and the dangerous circles he kept. Richard wondered if Karl might know of the Vatican theft. For now, Karl spoke of the Chinese. Richard knew of them—of who was at play. He knew full well that it was better to stay away than involve himself with those circles.

"I don't know shit of the Chinese."

"The Zhen Xin Liang assassination attempt."

"Nope."

"You were always a bad liar," said Karl.

Karl was right. Richard had followed every bit of the Zhen Xin Liang affair.

"I suggest you leave. Now."

"There's a major shipment of nuclear weapons coming across the Golden Triangle, and Zhen Xin Liang is at its center. We suspect intended for Iran. R-39 missiles, with their payload. We estimate two hundred warheads, 100 megatons each. Enough to wipe out all of Europe and the Mideast."

"Those can only be launched from a Typhoon-class submarine. Without that, they're useless," said Richard.

"Not if they're being retrofitted for land use," said Karl.

"Karl, you have to leave."

"It's Viktor Kletnov," said Karl.

Richard's fate had spun out of control long before this moment. As a boy in the corridors of the Gardner Museum, the time he laid his eyes on that painting, the silent man with his back to him strumming his stringed instrument were but instants of solace and peace his little heart felt in those few seconds. Little did he know those paintings were but a window into another world he created long ago, a world he made himself forget.

The Syndycate and their humans would play any game for power at any cost, at the cost of the Guija, of his Anja, of his son. They had found them. They had come for him. He saw in Karl his own guilt, the ugly contortions of his own heart, and for that there could be no greater loathing. In the silence, one could hear a pin drop.

"I could turn to no one else for this," said Karl.

"Find someone else to play your game. Next time we meet; you won't be so fortunate."

Richard clung to his promise. He would never put Anja or Danny at risk again. He gathered his case and disappeared out the door the way he came and fled his desire to kill this man.

Karl watched through the window as Richard escaped the school grounds into the fog-covered Georgetown neighborhood. He pulled a picture from his side pocket. Anton Arlovsky stared back at him.

***

Andrei thrust his hand upward, fingers clawed at those eyes behind the balaclava mask. Andrei didn't have time to question his instinct. His hands moved, as they were trained to do. He twisted into an *ippon seoi nage*, a single-handed, over-the-shoulder throw.

The thing came down with a crash over the Noguchi coffee table, splintering glass across the bamboo floor. In a blur, the black shadow sprung from the ground, the shards covered in a film of red.

The shadow bled.

A muzzle flash filled the air. The smell of burnt gunpowder hit his nose. He could see the casing escape the chamber of his pistol. The shadow clamped onto the barrel jacket of the gun, tore it from his grip.

He blocked the roundhouse kick to his ribcage with his forearm and shin, as the floor beneath his feet left him. The equilibrium of midair suspension had a despairing quality to it. Andrei crashed into the wall. The glass shelf shattered on impact.

A shard of glass protruded from the muscle connecting his shoulder and neck. Blood was ruining his Thierry Mugler shirt. The eyes behind the balaclava mask, those crystal-gray eyes, stared at him like a stone statue. The briefcase lay undisturbed on the sofa behind him.

"Where are your friends when you need them most?" rasped the black shadow.

They circled each other, crushing glass beneath their feet. A palm strike to the chin and a spear hand to the throat: Andrei had found his mark. But the thing parried and evaded, waiting for an opportunity to strike. A sharp burn slashed Andrei's neck. His lungs could find no air. In a flash, his belly pressed into the glass on the bamboo floor. The creature was crushing his spine. He reached up behind him, his fingers clawing the mask. The shadow knelt above him. The steel garrote wrapped around his throat disappeared into the flesh beneath his skin.

"Please, no." Andrei mouthed the words as tears formed in his eyes.

"Just relax. You'll die faster," whispered the shadow sweetly, as Andrei's eyes began to roll into the back of his head.

The tears dripped on the floor as the wire slowly bit through. Blood violently spurted from his neck. The wire sliced the carotids. His hand clenched in a death grip, tearing into the assailant's mask. He released a violent shudder and thrust.

Andrei pushed both arms into the floor, lifting his stomach from the ground as, with a final violent tug, the wire sliced deeper. Andrei succumbed, collapsing beneath the enormous weight of the shadow. The last of life and body exited out all his orifices.

"There you go. That's a good boy," rasped the shadow from beneath the balaclava mask.

XIV

CONQUESTS & KINGDOMS

Chalk dust kicked up along an empty road that ran through one of the many grassy expanses of the Panjshir Valley. The snowcapped Hindu Kush loomed in the distance, as a lone vehicle approached the outskirts of Bagram. Once known as "Alexandria on the Caucasus," it was the gateway along the Silk Road between the Ancient Persian and Indian kingdoms. The bandits and thieves on horseback that once patrolled the stretch of road just north of Kabul where Azar Behnam found himself had been replaced by Taliban soldiers and roadside bombs.

Afghanistan had suffered centuries of conquests and kingdoms. The scars left were no less deep than those in the hearts of the Pashtun who inhabited her lands. Azar contemplated the jagged mountains across the plain from the back of his dust-covered, red Toyota Corolla. As serene as those mountains were, they were unforgiving and desolate. He had never thought of the world as a ruthless place. To do so would have meant he knew mercy.

Azar grew up as an orphan in the dirty streets of Zahedan, a child of the Sistan winds. Thrown to the streets and the wolves of men who came along the trade routes, he learned quickly that life depended on his cunning and the sharp edge of his blade, and faith was only as good as the bushel of grain, or the bag of opium it fetched.

His trust lay only in himself and the young man who sat next to him, Darhab Behnam. Young and slender, with a wiry frame and dark olive skin, Darhab gazed out at the snowcaps in the distance. A younger cousin of Azar, he had grown up in the province of Balochistan, on the harsh streets of Zabol, a dangerous Iranian-Afghan border checkpoint.

A hard life had brought them both to Zabol, and fate made them cohorts. Cousins became as brothers, hardened and galvanized against the blight and pestilence that was this hell on earth. Known for opium, petrol, and weapons, Zabol was the aperture into the Golden Crescent, a place where Sunni and Shiite lived together forever on the tip of a double-edged dagger, a world where each survived because of the other.

As teenagers they met a man, a cleric, who taught them the precepts of the Deobandi and the Pashtun way of life. He inspired and taught them, groomed them to be better men, to be warriors of God. Then, one day, the man they knew only as Mahmoud was gone. But they'd learned all they needed from him. They gathered their few belongings and left for the treacherous journey over land and sea to study at the Islamic University in Karachi, Pakistan. The Brotherhood had been born. They had returned home soldiers of Allah.

"Beautiful, isn't it?" said Darhab, as dust and wind bit into his parched lips through the open window.

Azar took in a deep breath of the morning air. Even with the dust, the air here had a fresher, moister taste. "Serene as an early morning on the Arabian sea. There in those mountains, the enemy lurks like a shark beneath placid waters. He will tear your heart out, if you let him."

"You're in a good mood this morning," quipped Darhab.

"I'm in a good mood every morning." Azar returned his sights to the distant snow.

Their vehicle made its way through the outskirts of Bagram. Homes with clay walls and flat roofs, like boxes under a baking sun, spanned out along dirt roads in every direction. Along the bazaar, merchants peddled their wares, from CDs, books, and toys to opium, guns, and IED starter kits.

Men in brown jackets and white *shalwar kameez*, *pakul* hats, and *Peshawari* sandals, the traditional Pashtun garb, busily made their way about with carts and baskets of breads, fruits, and maggot-infested meats.

Women wrapped from head to toe in bright-hued *hijabs* and *burqas* of flowing aqua blues, fiery reds, and greens, with jars on their heads and baskets propped between hand and hip, busily walked their well-worn paths to and from their day's activities. Children straggled along, sticks and rocks in hand. Street corner dogs scratched fleas and chased their own tails. For Azar and Darhab, these mud homes—and especially this weather—were paradise.

The car worked its way along the many bumps and crags of a sloping dirt path, as two old men with dark brown, wind-worn, wrinkled faces watched curiously. The car rolled to a stop in front of one of the many clay homes. This mud-brick abode was no different from the rest. Yellow and sun-bleached, it stood desolate. The square holes in the walls for windows were pitch black. The breeze smelled of horse manure and man sweat. But the scent was a bit off.

Azar sniffed at the air when the rest of his senses caught up with his nose. At each end of the dirt road he saw them. Nestled in alcoves, just a few homes down, the gunmen blended almost perfectly with the sun-bleached clay surrounding them. Their black eyes scorched into Azar's back as he stepped out of the car, followed by Darhab. He looked down the street. More of them slowly appeared in the nooks and crannies along the whole of this not-so-busy street.

"We're here," said Azar, already planning his escape route as Darhab pulled out a smoke.

"Put that away," Azar said, his attention steadfast on the shawled gunmen waiting in the shadows. This was no ordinary meeting. He should have listened to his instinct and never come.

"Let's go," he said, as he made his way to the door.

Darhab muttered an insult under his breath, something about strangling someone for not letting him smoke, as he placed his cigarette back in its pack, all the while following never more than two steps behind.

Azar pushed aside the beaded curtain as he ducked in under the low-hanging doorway. Five men sat around a red and white Tabrizian rug, its edges yellowed from dirt and wear. Cups of morning tea and a small plate of naan sat atop the carpet. None of the men looked like they belonged there. Nearest to Azar sat a man with his back to the door, a brown sash draped over his broad shoulders. A gray streak ran through the curling dark hair over his collar. The man gently sipped his tea, paying no attention to the new arrival. He did not even bother to turn toward them.

To his immediate left was a Chinese gentleman. He studied Azar carefully through narrow black eyes. His hair was as jet black and neat as his perfectly pressed suit. Dian Lun Chung looked like he could jump from his place and rip Azar's throat out in a single gesture.

He must be dying of heat in that thing.

Even in a mud-brick house, it was as hot as a furnace beneath the Afghan sun. Azar couldn't understand what comfort anyone saw in wearing a suit anyway, a Western sartorial habit that had no place here. Opposite Dian Lun Chung were the two blond Americans. They were the ones Azar had been scheduled to rendezvous with. He demanded full payment and the identities of his Western contacts from his Mossad handlers before he agreed to meet. Bitter enemies met at the table for a common cause, each with their own advantage to gain.

The next man needed no introduction, not to Azar at least. A brown-skinned man with a thin mustache and wiry frame sat cross-legged between the Americans and the Chinese. Lieutenant Colonel Farhan Abad was from deep within the SS Directorate. Unknown to the usual intelligence circles, even within Pakistani intelligence, he had managed a vast network of informants and operatives for years, with barely a trace of his existence. The saw-scaled viper that was Abad had emerged from the shadows.

Azar could hear the sound of sizzling water on a hot pan somewhere in the next room. The shawled gunmen men outside now seemed like child's play. The dark-haired man with the brown sash and broad shoulders slowly turned around. Salil Jawadi stared at the two young men with his warm, embracing smile.

"We've been waiting for you."

The beads on the flat-panel windows refracted the glow of the overhead lamp inside the wheelhouse. The ventilator puttered overtime to keep the cabin cool and dry. The ocean was a sheet of glass this night. The moon above shone full and bright. The cottony clouds caught the light and hung lazily overhead as the *Amplify* slowly cut across the water.

Jiang Liu stared out over the glistening calm. The captain and crew coolly worked their instruments, one eye on the task, the other on her. They hadn't seen a woman in weeks and one like Jiang Liu, maybe never. She paid no heed to their mindless stares.

The crackle of a distress call over the horn broke the calm. A trolley was taking on water and listing. Those were the last words the captain heard before the static overtook the desperate message. He turned to his most welcome guest, happy for an opportunity to talk. But she was nowhere to be found. The rusty bulkhead door at the back of the wheelhouse hung ajar.

Somewhere else over those calm waters, Ho Than Minh marveled, never having seen such a beautiful moonlit ocean. His boots could almost touch the surface as he sat with his legs out the edge of their bird. This American helicopter hummed smoothly without the slightest bump or rattle. The blades were near silent, no thud, only the whine of the turbines and the wind over his ears. The taste of salt filled his mouth with a slight tinge of stomach acid. He was a seasoned member of Dac Cong, the Special Operations Group of the Navy of the Republic of Vietnam. But working with the Americans was a first.

He was a generation removed from the war, but he knew all the stories, all the sacrifices. He didn't blame anyone. He'd grown up with conflict as a part of life. The Americans were yesterday's enemy, and perhaps again tomorrow's. Right now he focused on today's.

"Sixty seconds," came the voice from the cockpit.

His lieutenant gave the signal. Ho Than unclipped the safety release and slid the fast rope insertion bar into position, checking that the pin was in place just like countless times in training. The helicopter lifted away from the water as his stomach came up from under him. He gave the rope a tug as the rotor blades pitched forward. His leather gloves were already burning along the line, halfway down before the rope even touched the deck.

"Secure the perimeter," came the command, as his feet hit the ground.

Ho Than moved with his AKS-74U rifle sighted ahead, the night a sharp green through his lenses. He crouched forward, fanning for a target. The last of the eight-man team reached their positions as the birds were already turning away, dipping below the deck, vanishing into the night. They couldn't have asked for a more textbook insertion. Not a sign or sound of resistance met them.

"Take point," came the voice of the lieutenant over the headset.

That was his specialty. Ho Than moved along the expected path. He'd studied the schematics of the vessel until he could sketch them in his sleep. He moved ahead with the uneasy taste of stomach acid stronger than ever in his mouth.

***

"Sir, strike team in position."

"Bring our range to one thousand, maintain depth fifty meters."

"Aye, Captain."

Captain Jeff Stolle had started as an ensign aboard the *Tunny*, an old Sturgeon-class submarine, later serving on an Ohio with a series of shore-side assignments with both the Atlantic and Pacific fleets, finally earning his first command as captain of the Los Angeles–class submarine *Florida*, and in all that time, this was a first. This wouldn't have been any more unusual than morning chow on the mess deck if not for the mission detail.

On patrol in the South China Sea, the *Florida* had been ordered to DEFCON 4 and directed here by 7th Fleet Command. Captain Stolle didn't know what the reason was except that the Chinese were at it again, bent out of shape over Taiwan or some other piece of rock they were laying claim to in the South China Sea.

The *Florida* had rendezvoused with a Vietnamese patrol boat on those same orders from fleet command and picked up Jonathan Fraker with CIA Special Collection Services and Thien Hoc Lo, a Vietnamese national and naval officer. Their orders at first had been simple: locate and track the cargo vessel known as the *Amplify*, and brief their two guests as to the ship's location and bearing.

Captain Stolle was curious as to why the fuss over this one cargo ship, but none of his guests would give any answers, and he knew better than to ask. They waited in deep waters for two days just outside the internationally recognized twelve-mile territorial limits. But try telling the Chinese these weren't their waters. Naval activity out of Yulin had been hectic. Yesterday, two Sovremeny-class destroyers sailed northeast from Yulin, and the patrol frequency of their Type 022 missile boats, the stealth boats used to protect littoral waters, had dramatically increased.

Captain Stolle had made sure his ping jockeys, the sonar men, were sharp and rested. If there was another attack sub in these waters, he needed to know about it first.

Couldn't we just solve our problems over a ping pong death match or something?

It was hot as shit tonight in the control room. He looked like he'd stepped out of a dive chamber in his khakis. Lucky for him, he wasn't the only one sweating it. No one really bothered to notice the sweat or the smell. He watched the surface puke, this Jonathan Fraker character, and Hoc Lo as the reports came back over the VHF radio. They brought a VHF transceiver with them and set it on the Type 18 periscope as its antenna. VHF could travel far and with minimal output, a good thing for these types of operations. They didn't want anyone knowing they were there. Stolle didn't have anything against the Vietnamese, but he sure as shit didn't understand what the hell they were saying, and he didn't like it. He got a translation, broken at best, and after the fact. He and his crew were now bound to the orders of the surface puke commanding the operation.

"Fuckin' soup sandwich, if you ask me," muttered Stolle under his breath.

Back across the Pacific, and on the opposite coast, the sun burned bright in the clear blue Washington, D.C., sky. But Robert Madison and Brian Reese didn't care. They were locked deep inside the special operations center at the Naval Research Facility. It could have been the dead of night if they were measuring by how exhausted they felt.

"We're picking up our target, sir. The *Florida* is in. One-five-zero-zero meters and closing," said Robert. Before them on the tri-panel screen was the operational picture for all the forces in the South China Sea. Task Force 70 was in position right where it was supposed to be, ringed by vessels of the Chinese Navy's Fourth Fleet, with additional resources approaching out of Yulin.

The president and his staff had negotiated the tense standoff between the PLA Navy and the 7th Fleet since the Zhen Xin Liang incident and all the news outlets were busily covering the round the clock developments off Taiwan's coast. The markets were tanking, investors selling off on fears of conflict, with oil prices skyrocketing. At every turn there was coverage of the assassination attempt and the so-called American cover-up. But the two men inside the command center had other concerns. Theirs were the little blue and red dots a few hundred kilometers south of where the world was watching, the outer rim of the South China Sea.

"We have less than an hour remaining of airtime," said Brian, as he checked the status of the TacSat-4 reconnaissance satellite.

"More than enough to get what we need," said Robert, confident in his own success.

"Fraker, status?" asked Madison.

"Strike team is moving through the ship now. Zero contact. So far the ship is clear— too clear, sir," replied Jonathan through the VHF transceiver.

This was an unacknowledged special access program to retrieve intelligence on the contents of the crates aboard the *Amplify*. Conceived by Robert and supported by Karl, it was approved by Ryan Douglas, the Director of National Intelligence. No one knew about it, not even the president.

If they fucked up...

Robert struck the thought from his head. There was no room for thinking about that now.

"This is starting to smell like we stepped in a pile of mushy dog shit," said Brian.

"This is a Vietnamese-run operation," Robert said.

"Good to know. Maybe Ho Chi Min City will be our next posting."

"I heard great things about the place. They still love Americans there."

"Strike team has breached the main cargo hold. Proceeding to target," came the message over the VHF.

"There's no way those crates would be undefended," said Robert.

"For some reason I'm not getting any response from the satellite," said Brian with sudden dismay.

"What do you mean?"

"The controls are frozen."

"Try to restart the interface on the backup partition," said Robert.

"The system is downloading, except I didn't issue the command. I still can't access control!"

"Can you shut it down?"

"Negative," said Brian, panic painted across his face.

"*Florida*, do you copy, over? Jonathan, do you copy, over? Jonathan?!"

All they heard was silence and static over the comm.

***

Ho Than crouched with his back against a crate somewhere in the maze of corridors between boxes and shipping containers deep in the belly of the *Amplify*. He adjusted the small mirror mounted on the rail of his rifle and propped the weapon around the corner edge. There was no one in the reflection. Still no resistance.

Clear.

The cargo vessel had been like a ghost ship, and nothing was more terrifying than feeling you're being watched, not knowing where or when the enemy would strike. Ho Than spun around the corner quickly, careful to stay low and against the crate. He raised his fist, dropping to one knee, the signal to hold for the rest of the team. He waited. His heart pounded out his ears. For the first time, he could feel the sweat drenching his bodysuit. It was searing hot, suited up in here in full kit. He looked at the spectrometer strapped to his forearm. The green detection graph on the LCD had jumped with every step he took closer to the box at the far end of this passageway between the containers. Low-level gamma emissions were coming from that crate. They were the type of results one could expect from the deteriorated casing of a nuclear warhead.

"Sir, I think we've located the package," whispered Ho Than.

"Regroup to extraction point omega," came the order over his headset.

Ho Than, for a moment, didn't understand the command.

"Say again, Fox One. I repeat, we have possible package. Requesting permission to proceed."

A muffled whine rose from the crate. He took a step closer and the spectrometer again jumped. What sounded like a buzz saw grew louder with every breath.

"Solid copy on the package. Repeat, pull back to extraction point one. Fox Two, do you copy, over?"

"Than, let's go," whispered one of the Dac Cong commandos who had been covering his six, his rear.

"Hold your position," ordered Than, as the two men behind him scanned down both ends of the passageway.

"Fox Two, what is your status, over?"

"Fox One, pulling back, copy," said Ho Than.

He pulled a pry bar from his kit, the perfect tool for ripping open a crate. He lodged the flat edge between the lip and the casing, pushing the rod forward as the nails gave way easily to the force. He set the pry bar on the grated floor and, wrapping gloved hands around its edge, he ripped the lid the rest of the way from the box.

In the bilious green of their night vision lenses, they could see the massive crate was empty except for two long tubes placed dead center, sitting atop two metal holders. The near end was a perfect cone, and on the other, small propellers whined plaintively from the lack of water around them. Ho Than recognized what they were right away, but it was too late for them.

"Fox Two, status?"

A massive compression wave ripped the upper deck in half. A ball of roaring flame shot into the clear night sky, illuminating the glassy waters for miles around.

Jiang Liu watched the distant orange glow dance off the clouds. She stood on the bow of the Houbei missile boat as the warm breeze caressed her face. She neither smiled nor uttered a word as the *Amplify* listed to starboard and the orange-red dragon fire slowly extinguished from the night sky, leaving the ocean once again peaceful and still.

XV

A DISH BEST SERVED COLD

The coffee was like burnt tar this morning. The only thing worse for Karl was the sight of Robert Madison sitting in front of his desk.

"We need some tax dollars for a new coffee maker," said Karl.

Karl had learned how to get a good night's sleep, especially the night before a major operation. Experience had already taught him he could easily go the next few nights without any.

"Do you know what an unacknowledged special access program means?" asked Karl, as he sat at the edge of his desk with his most condescending, fatherly smile.

"No one knows about it, sir."

"And how do we know that no one knows about it, Robert? When I don't hear about it first thing in the morning on CNN, and I don't get to explain to the president why the fuck we were in the middle of an op involving the Chinese without him knowing, in the middle of all this brouhaha, no less! That's when I know that no one knows about it!"

"Sir, if you read my report..."

"Are you questioning me, Mr. Madison? Do you think I'm that fucking lazy that I didn't read the shit you wrote? Our satellite system was hacked by

Chinese PLA, Unit 61398. Preliminary reports out of Beijing have identified the signatures of two MK48 torpedoes that struck the *Amplify*," said Karl, reciting Robert's report verbatim.

"No torpedoes were fired."

"How do I know that? How do I assure the president of that? The Navy conveniently reported the presence of the *Florida* in *their* waters, which we, of course, now deny. How do I explain that one to the president?"

"The Vietnamese are taking responsibility."

"Don't give me that shit. That's good for the press, but not for me. That means we owe someone in Hanoi. And if you know me, I don't like to owe anyone anything, especially Hanoi," said Karl.

"We were able to recover the satellite before the Chinese were able to gather any information from its sensors. We did get one piece of valuable information that I think you should see. I left it out of the report," said Robert, as he placed a manila folder onto Karl's desk.

"What the fuck is this?"

"The satellite picked up two vessels moving away from the incident during the engagement. Two Chinese Houbei stealth boats. They disappeared off the Vietnamese coast, entering the Thuận An estuary into the Perfume River. Our guess is they stopped somewhere between there and Huế. They're large enough to carry the cargo we were looking for, if carefully placed. I might ask around quietly about what Chinese patrol boats were doing on the Perfume River."

"You're not asking shit! You hear me? Not shit. Not anything," said Karl, once again with his fatherly smile.

Robert felt the quaking in his nuts. He was going to suffer terribly — terribly for this, indeed.

***

Katherine had received the preliminary after-action report on the *Amplify* at the same time Karl got it. She hadn't slept since. Then again, she hadn't slept much since the morning of Karl's office. She'd taken to drinking the tar that Karl called coffee, poring through the avalanche of data that had come down on her head as soon as she walked out that door. Her email had over a hundred privileged-access-granted notifications waiting in her inbox, all SCI files she had no idea ever existed.

The sixteen agencies all worked with top secret security clearances and sub-clearances of Sensitive Compartmented Information, as they so eloquently termed it: information access granted only on a need-to-know basis. The vastness of the data in the clandestine world of SCI, both the acknowledged and unacknowledged kind, was so great that no one could really grasp the trove of secrets that existed in the deepest vaults of America's intelligence community. The more Katherine learned, the more laughable were the claims of these recent 'whistleblowers,' as the public liked to call them. What they exposed was just the tip of a ginormous iceberg.

Katherine was still struggling to come to terms with it all. She had wrestled with the shame of Karl's betrayal since the night before their meeting, her first meeting with the National Security Council. She had so vigorously prepared for that meeting, wanting to impress the big bosses, but even more so Karl. There could be no better way than making him shine at that meeting with her presentation. He had done so much for her, and she'd been so hard on him, knowing his feelings for her. She wanted to, she needed to give back, as might a daughter for her father. Until she discovered this. He had used her, used her to gain this Vadim Iravani a new identity, effect him access into this country. He then used her to validate and cover his own tracks with her investigation. If they were discovered, there would be no way she could counter the claims. She had granted entry to a foreign national intelligence asset through falsified documentation, independent of any authorization or oversight. All evidence proved she had done it, and she had done it rogue.

She stood at the office door to the head of the Directorate for Security and Counterintelligence. She had been violated and worse, made to look the violator by the one person she most trusted. All she could think was to pour the Q Group down Karl's throat and expose everything he might have ever done, no matter her consequences. But she didn't. She instead went back to her desk and bawled from the rage, from the incredible rage. She could either let it overwhelm her or do something about it. So she began to click on each privileged-access link. She decided to dig and see what this was, what all this was Karl Downing had granted her.

Her head whirled and swam with every read-through of the reports on her screen. Her eyes were burning from lack of sleep, exhausted from disbelief, and countless hours of staring at the bright laptop screen. Katherine couldn't believe that such could exist, even within NSA. She cross-referenced the name in the header of this document—The Phoenix Program—with all of the agency databases, finding the name associated with an assassination program during the Vietnam War led by the CIA's Special Activities Division meant to kill members of the Viet Cong. But that had nothing to do with this, or so it seemed.

This thing described a eugenics program testing a genome sequence the OSS, the Office of Strategic Services, had found in records and lab samples that should have never existed.

Katherine suddenly recalled one late afternoon during her second year at Virginia Tech. Her professor lectured on the mathematics of the human double helix and its discovery at Cambridge University in 1953. But that version of history was somehow wrong. The professor forgot to mention that the original copy of the famous Photograph 51 used for the design of the double helix lay locked away in an archive vault of the OSS. It had been part of the hoard smuggled from the Nazi Chancellery at the end of the War.

Kathrine had a hard time believing anything at this point, that professor, or this report. But her heart knew what she was reading contained an ominous truth. Nazi chemists and molecular biologists had somehow mapped and sequenced the human genome to a level of detail beyond anything instruments of the time should have been able to produce. They laid out the complete nucleotide sequencing describing eighty percent of the human genome as what they called noncoding, like a blank slate coiled inside the double helix. The Nazis used an adenovirus vector, an icosahedral virus, to introduce into their human hosts an unknown genome sequence beyond anything their limited capabilities could recreate, what their records called the "Exohuman blueprint." The virus invoked a process they described as mutagenesis, inciting RNA to form proteins that modified the physical and mental characteristics of their hosts, genotype and phenotype mutations.

Dread like molten lead sank through her stomach, rolling down past her knees. They murdered thousands with their failed experiments in their quest for what they called their *Übermensch*, their superhuman.

The OSS had apparently found all this after the War and the CIA continued the program, guarding these Exohuman genome samples they'd recovered, enhancing their methods, testing on animal and human hosts. The outcomes were horrific, recorded in the minutest, most abominable of details. They continued for years with a succession of short-lived program directors until a name was finally appointed some twenty-five years ago, a name Katherine knew well: Karl Downing.

Under Karl, the program flourished. They increased their human testing to diabolical results, immeasurable human suffering. There was one subject among them, one host that reacted in ways Katherine could not fathom even reading the descriptions on the page: telekinesis, telepathy, transmogrification, spectral vision, dermal respiration, regeneration, feats of strength, stamina, enhanced fine-motor skills, immeasurable intelligence aptitude results across countless areas of human expertise. The name of that host was Peter Cole. What he endured, what Karl had done to him, the words on these pages could not fully convey. What he became, Karl Downing controlled— until he was killed at their whim during an unacknowledged operation on the beaches of Crimea.

Karl had honed and directed this Peter Cole under the orders of another man: Viktor Kletnov, an obscure figure in the Russian business world. He was the chairman of the Kandinsky Group, a natural gas and oil conglomerate and the fourth-largest company in the world.

How had she never heard of this man?

She cross-referenced him with the Russian embassy and uncovered recent communications with the Kandinsky Group in Washington. Vadim Iravani was with the Kandinsky Group and Karl had framed her in all this.

What relationship did Karl Downing have with this Viktor Kletnov? How could any of this even be real?

The reports replayed themselves again and again in her head as she entered her office this morning, placing her coat on the hanger by the door. She had a thing about being organized and clean, aseptic almost, and everything was just as she left it, except for the package atop her desk.

She walked over carefully. It was wrapped in brown waxed paper, crinkled at the edges, and lassoed with a thin, ropelike tether. Great care had been taken, like a gift from a specialty boutique in Georgetown. A small card, partially opened, lay atop, the trailing ink of the last letter visible to her eye. She pulled back the flap.

Katherine Brandt, alles Liebe.

Crypto City was supposed to be one of the most secure places on the planet. Nobody got in or out of her office without her knowledge, not even Karl. She could call security to inspect the package; it could be a bomb or worse. But her better sense did not prevail. If somebody wanted her dead, she hoped they'd figure out a more interesting way to do it.

With a quick snatch of the scissors, she snipped the lasso and with the edge of the blade, cut away the wrapping. She doubted whoever placed this here had left any fingerprints, but she would check later with forensics anyway. The waxed paper revealed a plain white box beneath. At arm's length, and with the sharp end of the scissors, she slowly lifted the lid. The top gave way without resistance. She held her breath and averted her face, as if it would make any difference. Inside was a manila envelope. A set of hand and finger prints, in what looked like dried brown blood, were smeared across the face of the envelope. A chill ran through her spine. A tremor ran down her inner thigh.

She picked up the envelope at each corner and slowly tipped the open end down. A notebook with a black plastic binding slid onto the calendar on her desk. With the end of the scissors she flipped open the black cover. A typewritten page in Cyrillic stared at her, dated at the top January 17, 2016.

The name below the date was Admiral Vasily Nygev, and what followed was his full autopsy report. The document was part of a Russian intelligence dossier on the Kandinsky Group directed to the attention of Andrei Birkin and never intended for Katherine. The blood on the folder hinted to a similar fate as that of Nygev's.

I just saw him a week ago, and now this!

She thought to call Andrei, but dread seized her throat and held her hand.

The blood may be anyone's, even his.

They were feeding her with information while intimidating her, exposing her while reigning her in. She was suffocating. The tentacles wrapping around her reached far deeper and far wider than she could imagine, even within the walls of NSA. She was alone and terrified. She wanted no part of this. But it was too late for that sentiment. Against every instinct, she could think of no one else to turn to; she could turn to no one else except Karl Downing.

***

Andrei had not followed his usual routine this morning. Saifa had made it a game to time his three-mile runs. The last, at just a hair over nineteen minutes, was really not bad at all. He always had his coffee, then took a brisk shower, and then promenaded himself naked across the house (which she had caught a glimpse of — or two).

The man was well put together, in every respect, and he definitely deserved plenty of respect. He was always out of the house with at least forty minutes to get to the embassy. But today there was nothing, no usual routine, no nothing.

The wire taps picked up two calls to his cell from a number at the embassy. They went straight to voicemail, and he'd placed no calls since yesterday. There wasn't any traffic over the network, no logins, no e-mail. His car was still parked along the street where Saifa had last seen him. She had watched him arrive the day before and, according to Steve, he hadn't left.

"It could be anything. The guy might just be sick in bed for all we know," said Steve, as he watched for activity along the street.

"The sensors would have detected movement in the house," said Saifa dryly.

"Maybe their security services discovered our gear."

"Signals intelligence confirmed everything is working as it should."

"Doesn't mean anything. Just left it undisturbed till one of us shows up," said Steve.

"We're about to find out."

"Are you kidding me? We go anywhere near that place, and we'll have every cop south of Van Ness here in ten minutes," retorted Steve.

"I only need five," Saifa said. She was on the sidewalk before Steve could get out another sentence.

He gripped Saifa by the arm, stopping her cold on the sidewalk. "We work as a team. Cowboys in this business end up dead."

"I never said you could touch me. Let go of my arm," said Saifa, with a straight face that bordered on hatred.

"Who am I to impose on you," asked Steve, letting go of his grip with a sudden charming docility that Saifa wouldn't have expected from him. She cataloged that for later and walked right up to the house as if visiting a neighbor. She punched the code and pressed her thumb onto the fingerprint reader by the door. The system demurred a long moment, and then the lock snapped dryly. She turned the handle and the hinges gave way. Signals intelligence phished the door code, and the print was on a latex glove they fashioned using a sample they'd lifted with the help of a *sayan* at the embassy. Saifa was in the house.

She held her pistol close to her side as she stepped through the corridor into a vacuum of silence. Her heart raced and her finger pressed hard on the side of the small barrel. Her palm was pure sweat around the grip, but her hand was steady. She raised the pistol in front of her, nearing the entrance into what looked like a living room.

Steve came up beside her, eyes darting in every direction with so many rooms for someone to lie in wait. The smell confirmed what she feared. She couldn't get any closer to Andrei without stepping in a pool of coagulated blood.

A crushed glass table and broken shelves had spread shards in every direction from some terrible impacts. The handles of a garrote wire lay atop his back. The wire had dug deep, way deep.

"We need to get the fuck out of here," Steve said.

Saifa didn't utter a word, but instead climbed the steps up to the second floor. If anyone else had been there, they'd already be dead. Steve stood at the base of the stairs by the entrance, his weapon trained on the second floor. A little black cat slipped away from the edge of the landing. Steve slowly moved up the stairs as Saifa eyed every item, every surface of a room as might a detective doing an initial walk-through examination of a crime scene without the luxury of time on her side.

The second floor was a series of narrow rooms with high ceilings. Andrei had been a neat freak. Everything was picked up, without a strand of dust. The dark red, cherry wood floor shone with quality and cleanliness. Everything was meticulously placed, as if set and untouched by human hands. The white linens were of the highest quality and the house was furnished in spare designer furniture. The clean corners and minimalist detail reminded Saifa of a modern home magazine spread. But whoever had killed Andrei hadn't been interested in thieving the place.

The air conditioning started up with a low buzz. The breeze and the smell of blood hit her face when her eye caught a business card lying on the nightstand.

Michael Hearst, Director, the National Gallery.

"Saifa," called Steve from one of the other rooms, as she slid the card into her pocket.

She moved swiftly to Steve, who stood by the edge of the second-floor window, looking out over the back yard.

"We have to leave right now."

Two men in black combat fatigues with white-, blue-, and red-striped insignias over their left shoulders moved across the back lawn, their weapons trained on the house.

***

"Thank you, everyone," said President McNeal, stepping away from the White House podium, ducking from the stage and the cameras.

"Have you spoken with Vice President Liang of the attack?" shouted one of two dozen reporters cramming the White House press room.

"Those will be all the questions for now," said Press Secretary Gifford, as he took the podium in place of the president. "Thank you."

He gave the signal as the men in black quickly took their positions at the exits and began to usher out the media. Back in the halls of the West Wing, President McNeal made his way toward the Oval Office flanked by two of his Service detail, as Edwin Birling, his chief of staff, handed him the preliminary after-action report. His Daily Brief was about twice the normal thickness.

The stupid shit people do.

McNeal took a moment to breathe.

"Sir, are you alright?" asked one of the agents.

"I'm fine. Just need a minute."

He stared at a portrait in the hallway of Abraham Lincoln and wondered if the stresses were as apparent on him as on good old Abe. Only someone who'd sat in this office could know the presidency was the least enviable of all positions. He turned away, only to see the deadpan face of David Bradford staring at him in return.

"Good morning, Irving."

"You know, I never suffered your contemptuous, snide remarks much."

"Thank you, Mr. President."

"Who on God's earth authorized this operation?" asked McNeal, in an outburst that turned heads in the hallway and adjacent rooms.

"I would ask Ryan Douglas. He's waiting for you in the briefing room, Mr. President."

"I don't need to tell you what a war with the Chinese would mean for us," said McNeal in much calmer tones.

"Whoever authorized this operation is just part of a puzzle crafted to fulfill some larger political goal — that in time will become clear. We either discern it for ourselves, or let whoever's behind it do it for us. If we allow the latter, it will be we who pay the steepest price."

McNeal could never get over how David talked to him, as if speaking to a child. He questioned why he ever allowed himself to be influenced into appointing him as Secretary of State. A change was coming, and both men knew it. McNeal decided perhaps it was best he waited to ask for David's resignation, at least for the time being, until all this blew over.

"I need you to go to Beijing. Find us a diplomatic solution that makes those plans clear. Neither of us can afford a conflict with the Chinese, not now," urged McNeal.

"I will have my staff see to it right away."

McNeal fidgeted, flipping through the Daily Brief. "Don't worry, that's already taken care of for you. Now if you'll excuse me I have to go deal with Mr. Douglas."

David watched the smug imbecile walk away. The president cared only about his new deal with the Chinese and the donors who would fill his coffers with cash and their many thanks during his reelection. *Five more years!* McNeal had confided to him his support for the next presidential nomination. But David would have to wait his turn patiently; McNeal had one more term to go. In the meantime, David would have to walk a fine line till then. He knew McNeal's support was all a lie. Neither could mask their abhorrence for the other. As political as each were, they were anything but with each other.

A lot was going to happen to Mr. President over the next five years. David took a bit of solace in that fact.

If that were all he felt, it would have been just another day for David. But the gut-twisting and wrenching agony in his bowels was something more. Something more contorted his face. David reached into a pocket and clasped the cold, burning object, pulsating relief into his loins and belly. He opened his palm to view a ring of reversion, thick and gray, inscribed with a script legible to no one, a ring wearable by no one except him. He yearned desperately to place it on his finger, to embrace the power so wrongly taken from him so long ago. But he stopped. He could not. The time had not yet come. But soon—soon the Syndycate would align to his wishes, as they should have long ago. Soon they all would get what was coming to them.

***

"That's not the way we work," said Steve, spewing vitriol as he threw down his gear and placed his pistol smack center of the kitchen counter. "You put us both at grave risk!"

Saifa sat calmly with Ronen opposite her at the other end of the bar. "We had to move before the police arrived," she said, lighting a cigarette.

"For what, to find out he was already dead? What else did we get out of waltzing into a crime scene besides almost getting our heads taken off by the Russians?"

"We know he didn't slip on a fucking banana peel," said Saifa, with a puff of smoke.

"Is that supposed to be fucking funny?" asked Steve.

Ronen watched with an amused smile. He was probably glad to see it wasn't him pulling his hair out

292

this time. But Saifa wasn't listening. Her mind was someplace else.

"Where were you yesterday afternoon?" she asked suddenly of Steve.

"What do you mean where was I?"

"Where were you from about six to eight?"

"Where I was supposed to be, at the end of the street watching for movement in and out of the house. Are you trying to get at something with your line of questioning?"

"Just asking," said Saifa unable to shake the lingering memories every time she looked into Steve's crystal-gray eyes. She'd seen that kind of work one other time. She struck wild thoughts from her head, instead turning her attention again to Ronen and his motives.

"A *Hashishin*," she said, taking the ashtray from Ronen.

"A what?" asked Steve, with clear and unbridled frustration.

"The thing that did this to him was a Hashishin," said Saifa, fixed on Ronen.

"You mean like the ancient Persian assassins?" asked Steve.

"Something like that," she said, exhaling a long drag.

"A Hashishin killed our boy back there," said Steve, mulling it over in what looked like deep thought when it finally hit him. "Right. Must be the hash in that cigarette of yours. Mind if I take a hit?"

She so wanted to smack him that she actually laughed.

"That has got to be the most ridiculous bullshit I have ever heard. I mean, seriously, is this what you teach your *kidon* at Henzelia?" asked Steve, pouring himself his third Turkish coffee.

"The cut was smooth, clean through the neck. Something only a skilled hand could manage," said Saifa.

"Is that the sort of thing that creams your jeans?"

Saifa exhaled a drag and extinguished the cigarette. She watched how her smile only riled him more. She swore Steve would start twitching and writhing as he went for a fourth Turkish coffee.

"So we blow our cover with nothing to come of it except for some ancient assassin bullshit. Our faces for sure pencil-sketched on the evening news, or worse, photos, or heck, videos of us waltzing into Birkin's home. Will be even better when the Russians realize two Mossad were at the scene, and their guy dead as a doornail. Gonna sit real well in Tel Aviv, and best of all we'll have a Zaslon hit squad up our asses."

"If you'll excuse me," said Saifa, crushing the last of the embers in the tray.

"Where do you think you're going?" asked Steve in a rather authoritative tone.

"A stroll for a bit, to alleviate myself of your breath. If it's alright with you." Saifa smiled ingratiatingly.

Ronen watched as she strutted her way across the living room and out the door without another word.

"Mighty fine coffee if you ask me," said Ronen, lifting his saucer to Steve and taking a sip.

***

"The thieves made their way to the Rembrandt first…"

The man in the black suit stood in front of the small group. He directed their attention to the image on the wall. Before him sat an audience of about ten, listening to a presentation on a subject Saifa knew little about.

Saifa had left the safe house needing to get away from them all. Her heart again filled with the mistrust and doubt she always had of Ronen's intentions. But her neurosis went now further than just Ronen's intentions. She was wary of them all, even Steve. Those crystal-gray eyes looked at her as might a wolf. The more she watched him, the more they became those eyes from that night in Crimea, those eyes from her nightmares. Those same eyes she knew to belong to Anton Arlovsky.

Ronen had lured her here with a purpose for which she should have never come. The murder was the work of Anton. She'd seen enough death at his hands to know. Precise and violent, she could do the same. She was numb to this sort of thing, having seen it, having done it herself so many times before. But Anton Arlovsky was a terrible nightmare, and the same terror that once so debilitated her, gripped her again. She pulled out the business card she found on the victim's nightstand. She guessed any contact Andrei may have had with the owner of the card, this Michael Hearst, would have been recent. She quickly found his photo and bio on the National Gallery's web site. The museum was worth a visit.

There was a presentation—"by invitation only," said the guard—when Saifa arrived. But it didn't take long for him to add her to the list of esteemed guests. The perfume of her skin cast its spell on the old man. He wrote her name on an index card and handed her a temporary badge.

"Up the stairs, down the hall, and to the right," he said, as she gave him a grateful smile.

It probably made his evening. She climbed the stairs, certain he'd memorize her every step.

From the back of the room, she glanced carefully over the audience. The speaker welcomed the members and select guests to the special presentation for the upcoming Vermeer exhibit. She knew the name to be that of an old Dutch painter, but not much more on the man or his work.

At the back of the hall stood a young man, dark-skinned with a wild head of curly hair. He looked familiar, perhaps Aramean or Druze — then again, like any of half a dozen Middle Eastern ethnicities. Someone else stood beside him, but she couldn't make out the face from her angle. She made note to keep an eye on the young man. Her attentions turned back to the presenter, when she suddenly spotted her target. Mr. Michael Hearst sat right were the museum's director should be, in the front row.

The presenter in the black suit was Frank Hendrix, the head of the FBI's art crime team. Saifa had recently heard about them, fourteen special agents charged with tracking down art thefts around the world. Must have been a nice job. From the way he sounded, she knew he was passionate about art, fanatical almost.

"They forgot to pull the data drives from the motion detectors in the security director's office. After the Rembrandt, they hit the prize of the haul, Vermeer's *Concert*. In about eighty minutes the thieves managed to swipe thirteen works of art valued at over half a billion dollars," he said, his words echoing along the back of the room.

Saifa couldn't fathom half a billion dollars. It was three and a half times that number in Israeli shekels. She could spend her entire salary every day for the next forty years and still not run out of money.

Who would ever pay that for something like this?

"And if you're wondering who would ever pay that much money for these paintings, you needn't look further than to men like Lefty Carlson and other members of the Boston and New England crime rings we've investigated over the past twenty-five years. There's an international black market for these stolen works, often sold, of course, for a fraction of their auction value. Funny thing was, the thieves didn't go after some of the more valuable works by Michelangelo, Titian, or Sargent that hung nearby."

"The thieves went after what their clients wanted," said a voice from the back of the hall.

The booming voice caught Saifa and everyone else's attention as they all turned toward the man who stood coolly at the entrance, hands in his pockets. He had been listening from where he stood beside the young man with the wild hair.

Saifa felt a sudden rush of cold sweat come over her skin. She remembered him from that night, that long-ago night in Crimea, the night of Anton Arlovsky, the monster with the crystal-gray eyes. He was the man with the briefcase. He was Peter Cole.

Saifa pulled back into the shadows to give her time to think. The poison had found its mark. The Pollard files had confirmed her kill. Peter Cole died that night. She was certain of it, because she'd done it. She quietly stepped away from the hall. Coming to the museum, coming to D.C., to this fool's errand, was much more dangerous than she had ever imagined.

Meanwhile, back across the room a new dance was unfolding.

"Apologies, I didn't mean to interrupt," said Richard, as Guillermo gave him a stern look.

"Sure you did, but no apologies needed," answered Hendrix, as he shifted to the next chart in the presentation.

"I thought you were one for anonymity. Talk about all kinds of unwanted attention," whispered Guillermo.

"I don't see Edvard here," said Richard.

"He flew out this morning, said it was urgent business."

Anja said she'd handle Edvard, yet made no mention of him leaving. Richard refused the thought any audience, the idea that she might be withholding truth from him. He refused fear its court and turned his attentions to the face out the corner of his eye.

Guillermo, too, noticed someone in the small crowd. A gentleman near the back of the audience with a salt-and-pepper twirly mustache, embroidered white jacket, and spectrum-colored umbrella for a cane, stared at the two of them.

"The munchkin Salvador Dali lookalike. He's the one from the night of the Pinacoteca."

"The Syndycate? We have to forget the Vermeers," said Guillermo, feeling his testes jingle.

"Don't get your panties in a knot, and let me listen to the presentation," said Richard, turning his attentions fully back to Agent Hendrix at the podium. Richard was terrified.

"Because of the fragments of paint and canvas on the scene, it was originally believed that the thieves cut the paintings away from the frames, but we've since discarded that theory. We suspect, in fact, they were removed intact and on their stretchers. They then made their way to the security director's office, snatched the surveillance video tape with the motion sensor readout, and left him the frame of Manet's *Chez Tortoni* in his chair as a parting gift. In an hour and twenty minutes, two supposed Boston police officers got away with the largest heist in American history…"

Fascinating, thought Richard, how the thieves had made away the night of the Gardner. He focused all his attention on the narrative from the FBI agent, sure of one thing: the munchkin Salvador Dali in the eccentric getup would find his way to them.

The lecture continued with varied questions from the audience, wrapping up with an introduction to the National Gallery's Vermeer exhibit and a cocktail reception for the guests thereafter. As the audience shifted over to the appetizers and drinks, Hendrix approached — exactly as Richard had hoped he would.

"Most people find who they know at a party and stick to them."

"Just like most people stick to *what* they know, when they open their mouths," replied Hendrix.

"You don't give people enough credit." Richard grinned.

"Then enlighten and deliver me from ignorance. Special Agent Frank Hendrix," he said, as he gripped Richard's hand in a firm shake. He stood head and shoulders over Richard.

"Richard Robles. Pleasure to meet you, special agent, and excellent presentation."

"Thank you," said Hendrix, eyeing Richard appraisingly.

"I'd heard about your program from Willie here," said Richard.

Guillermo gave him a not-so-comfortable smile.

"It's not the first you've heard of the Gardner Heist, I take it?"

"The only time I saw it, Vermeer's *Concert*, was March 17, 1990."

"The day before it was stolen?" asked Hendrix.

"It was a school field trip, my first ever to a place like that. The man in the painting with his back to me, the one with the brown sash over his shoulder, strumming his stringed instrument, and the two girls singing to the harpsichord's melody."

"That's quite a vivid memory. A bit too vivid, I would say. Sounds contrived."

"I was just a boy back then. Who am I to say? Anyway, the next day they were just empty frames."

"Not just empty frames," interjected the twirly-mustached gentleman as he approached the circle.

Richard noted the fine stitch to his suit, straight out of an Italian *sartoria*.

"They were pieces of a man's soul, taken by those who set their eyes on things never meant to be theirs. Giovanni Battista, head of security for the Vatican State," said the twirly-mustached gentlemen as he joined the circle, propping himself on his fanciful umbrella.

"Pleasure to meet you, Mr. Battista," said Richard with a casual grin, as Guillermo's eyes bulged from his head.

"Well, aren't we all the eccentric bunch," remarked Hendrix.

"Indeed, Agent Hendrix. Funny, Mr. Robles, we, too, have empty frames on our walls."

"In honor of the Gardner?" asked Richard.

"In honor of the Gardner, yes. Well, actually, they're not empty. But they might as well be, since the canvases in them aren't worth the frames that protect them."

"A bit harsh to say of such a fine collection, Mr. Battista. The Pinacoteca is one of my favorite," said Richard.

"I'm most sure it is. You know, a painting is like a memory. It is there, in your mind's eye, but is the memory, like the painting, real or a lie?" asked Giovanni.

"I'm not quite sure I understand what you're alluding to, Mr. Battista."

"Plucking out one's eyes does not blind a man to the truth."

"I suppose you're right," said Richard, taking in the awkward moment with that same grin. Giovanni had made his point while Guillermo blanched like death warmed over.

"Anyway, it is late. I'll be taking my leave now," said Giovanni, planting the end of his umbrella with a crack onto the laminate floor.

"I hope to have the pleasure of seeing you again soon," said Richard.

"It will be my pleasure—indeed, it will be," assured Giovanni, with a smirk that made his upturned whiskers twitch with delight.

"Good evening to you, sir."

"And to you, fine sir, who plays his game most enjoyably." Giovanni bowed, backing away with hand to chest, and left out the other end of hall.

"How are you for dinner tomorrow evening? My wife makes a great rack of lamb," said Richard, turning all his attentions suddenly to Agent Hendrix.

"I would be delighted," responded Hendrix with a furrowed brow.

"Seven, our place," concluded Richard, handing him a card.

"Now if you'll excuse me, I have to attend to another matter," said Richard, giving Guillermo a glance.

"Oh gosh, yes, the bathroom. I am so there," said Guillermo.

"Socially awkward, please understand," said Richard as he took Guillermo by the arm. "Seven, don't forget."

"Count on it," replied Hendrix, flipping the business card between his fingers. Richard took note of the curious card trick as he disappeared beyond the bend, leaving Hendrix to simmer in his own suspicions.

***

Guillermo and Richard descended the marble staircase beyond the glow of the museum lighting. The vault below was cold and desolate, filled with racks and stacks of old crates and pallets. Frames had been carefully draped with linens to protect the paintings hidden away from the crowds. Many of the works had never known the light of day in the museum, never having hung on her walls for the public to see. The smell of old wood and canvas filled the air with a musty taste known best to the museum curators and handlers who haunted the passageways below.

Richard hadn't uttered a word since encountering the twirly-mustached old man. Guillermo could taste the terror in his mouth, acrid and foul, the red wine from the event intent on revisiting his palate.

"We can't think too much on what just happened. We need to move quickly. The fact is that he knows," said Richard.

"So what do we do with the paintings?"

"They stay right where they are. They are our only leverage. This Giovanni Battista wants them back, and we're the only ones who know their whereabouts. We'd be dead otherwise, and until he has them, that won't do him much good," said Richard dryly.

Guillermo tried to swallow, but pain wouldn't let him. He stopped by one of the crates, leaning against it to steady himself. The musty air was making him more nauseous.

"Listen to me carefully. You'll do everything I tell you if you want to live. It's unlikely he knows what we are. But he's definitely one of them. He services the Syndycate. The head of Vatican security doesn't just show up here, not by himself. He's likely Sicaari, if not worse."

"What can be worse than Sicaari?" asked Guillermo in a high-pitched whisper.

"It's critical we stay focused to task. We must secure the Vermeers now. The exhibit opens in three days. We move in two."

"There's no way, Richard. Anja's preparations still need more work and I don't have the guards' schedule yet. I have a better idea. We run!"

"We do not run. We confront him. We make a deal. And we try to learn as much of him as he apparently knows of us."

"You think he killed Huygens?" asked Guillermo.

"I know he killed Huygens," said Richard.

Guillermo could no longer hold it in. The red wine from this evening paid his mouth a nasty visit.

***

Karl had seen enough for one day. So many dead, but it wasn't the dying he thought about. It was the how and why that seized him. Karl could feel the gentle slope of the grounds beneath his feet as he made his way along Arlington's Section 60, where those who fought were laid to rest. He had personally seen to the interment of dozens in this place. A part of him remained behind with each one of them. The oaks and sprawling greens with the thousands of headstones as far as his eye could see and the eternal guard at The Tomb of the Unknowns humbled him every time. This day was a quiet one at Arlington.

At the far edge, a horse-drawn carriage stood. A riderless horse, black like the night, stood next to the white stallions as the casket was lowered into the ground, surrounded by the mourners in black. A light breeze carried the bugler's melody as the procession stood at final salute. The 3rd Infantry honor guard in their white gloves and dark blues called out. The rifles turned to the sky. The clap cracked across the fields, then another, and a final one. Thirteen shots counted Karl as in the distance a lone woman held a folded American flag.

Please accept this flag as a symbol of our appreciation for your loved one's honorable and faithful service.

He knew those words well. They were etched in his mind. He stared down at one particular headstone. It looked no different from the rest except for the faith emblem and the name.

"There's never getting any used to it, is there?"

"No, there isn't," said Karl, turning to the raven-haired Katherine.

Her eyes were hidden behind large and just as dark sunglasses. She stood, in a black vest and pants, with purse slung over her shoulder. He hadn't heard her approach. He hadn't seen her since that day in his office. Something was different about her, a certain coldness. It did not surprise him. What was in those files would make anyone freeze over at the callousness of it all.

"Why'd you do it, Karl?"

"I thought it would help. No better service than defending our way of life while promoting medical breakthroughs, eradicating disease, prolonging life. We would redraw the canvas of what God had created was how we saw it; the audacity of the young and idealistic."

"You murdered hundreds with your experiments. Human trafficking subsidized by this government. Children, Karl, and you made sure to record every last gruesome detail."

Karl wished he could see her eyes behind those sunglasses. He turned his gaze back to the service at the far end of the grounds. The woman with the flag stood propped up by two 3rd Infantry Guard, their white-gloved hands beneath her arms and over shoulders. A young man led her back to the limousine. The sounds of taps had long faded with the wind. Only the rustling of the leaves remained.

"Many more will die."

"We all die, Karl. It's not the dying, but the how and the why," said Katherine.

Karl smiled, recognizing that very thought as his own. Perhaps he finally got something right.

"You're the one, Katherine."

"The one what, Karl?" asked Katherine, her ire approaching the limits of restraint.

"Secretary Bradford is en route to Beijing. The Chinese are blaming the *Amplify* on us. Calling her sinking an open act of war," said Karl.

"You framed me in your plots. You then give me access to files on heinous programs that I could never imagine you capable of. You tear at the very fabric of my humanity, everything I ever imagined of you. Death isn't recourse enough for what you did, for what's in those files."

"The R39 missiles were never found in the wreck of the *Amplify*. No evidence of anything except for the well-placed fragments of the two MK48 torpedoes."

"Are you listening to what I'm telling you? This was left on my desk," said Katherine, pulling the bloodstained file folder from her purse. She handed the folder to Karl. He gently ran a finger over the stained cover.

"It was Birkin's. I met with him over a week ago about a dead Russian admiral, Vasily Nygev. Birkin was killed in his home the day before yesterday with a garrote wire to the throat. It was you, wasn't it? You had him killed. You left me the file," said Katherine, demanding an answer.

"No."

"The truth for once, Karl!"

He silently paged through the folder. He turned back to the funeral procession. The groundskeepers collected the last of what remained of the service. The wind blew softly over the treetops at the edge of the grounds. The sky was a cold dark blue.

"The files contain everything on Nygev, including his final order releasing a Typhoon-class submarine, the *Simbirsk*. The same submarine shown in these pictures here," said Katherine, pulling another manila envelope from her purse and handing Karl the set of black-and-white prints. "She's the perfect platform for the R39s, a submarine that's no longer supposed to exist, released from a Russian naval yard, by a man, now dead, with direct ties to Viktor Kletnov, the man smeared across your repugnant files, the man you work for."

Karl bent down before the headstone, pressing his forefinger into the etching of the name in the granite. The faint, sweet smell of wood smoke hit his nose with the breeze. Somewhere beyond the distant tree line, a fire burned. She looked down at the headstone beneath their feet. Karl's stare was as cold as the morning wind, as cold as the name on the headstone that rolled off her tongue.

"Peter Cole."

"Two monsters of the same ilk," said Karl as he stared at the gravestone before him. "The Phoenix Program was a result of our eugenics program, kill groups created during the Vietnam War to eliminate high-value targets. Almost thirty-thousand killed, eighty-thousand neutralized, to put it nicely. It was our first program using Exohumans, men and women enhanced with the genome sequencing stolen from the Germans at the end of the war. The Program didn't end after the war. An offshoot of Special Activities Division, it grew into subspecialties—torture, high-value assassinations, other black ops directives— all funneled through the program, away from congressional oversight. Special access programs, all of the unacknowledged kind. In the mid-Eighties I became involved. That's when I met Viktor Kletnov. Peter Cole was a result of that eugenics program. He was just a young boy when I got him. The only one Viktor ever cared about."

Karl placed his hand on a knee as he painfully rose back to his feet. The arthritis ached through his right leg.

"I led the program for fifteen years. Peter Cole was like my son." Karl stared at the date on the headstone.

"Twelfth October 1999, his kill group had been sent to recover a rogue device critical to our efforts. There were others, deep inside our government, who gave the order, men also loyal to Viktor. So we went. We did as we were told. But a Mossad infiltration team turned up at the same time. The Israelis made their move, and so did we. It was a massacre. The device, along with the entire team, was lost."

"Why do you still lie to me, Karl, when we both know Peter Cole isn't dead," said Katherine.

"It's part of the game we play," said Karl with his most bitter smile. "No one else knew of Peter Cole but me. To every one else he died that night in Crimea. That's how Viktor had wanted it, and I agreed."

"Why so much intrigue over one man?"

"Peter Cole is no man. The only thing human about either Peter Cole or Viktor Kletnov is the flesh they inhabit. What you don't know is the true origin of the genome samples we recovered at the end of the war."

"They were seized from the Nazi Chancellery. Or is that another elaborate lie?" asked Katherine.

"The Nazis were the first to test on human subjects. But the genome, the 'Exohuman blueprint' came from a society few have ever known, creatures who control every aspect of our own society in ways you cannot imagine. They are called the Syndycate."

"You said creatures, Karl?"

"Some whisper of them as semi-humans, aliens, beings not of this world who, through technology, took on our human form, living among us, using us to further their own cause. They call themselves Exohumans."

"So these Exohumans, they manipulate our societies at, say, the highest levels of government, for example?"

"Business, science, education, religion. Everything you can name. They have a hand in it," said Karl.

"How convenient," said Katherine, her tone laced with disdain.

"You can sneer however much you wish. But you are as knee deep in this now as I am. They are aware of you. It's only a matter of time."

"A matter of time for what, Karl?"

"Viktor Kletnov is one of thirteen left among them. There were others, many more, but the war changed that. The National Socialists, the Nazis, were a result of a schism within their circles. A civil war broke out between them, manifesting itself in the governments and societies of humankind across the globe, what you and I grew up knowing as World War II."

"If what you say is true, and that's a big if, then everything, I mean everything we ever believed—the very basis of life—well, just throw that shit out the window and start over. Aliens, Karl, who live among us and manipulate our very realities? Even I find that pill hard to swallow."

"The Syndycate is the least of your worries. During the war, the Nazis exposed these transgenic genome sequences to human hosts, as did we years later, under my program. But the Nazis were more extreme, more aggressive. Their genomes went beyond the enhancement of the human body. Encoded in their specimens were entire lifetimes, memories — an awareness not of this world, alien creatures of terrible abilities they couldn't begin to fathom. When mutated with our own DNA, well, the results were unpredictable. Hundreds of them escaped into our world. They hid from us, procreated, lived as us. Many of them, likely not even knowing what they were, mutated over generations into things that not even the Syndycate could control."

"You knew all this, and yet you continued with your program?"

"A much more controlled version. Under careful supervision, for the benefit of what such transgenic advances might mean for humanity as a whole."

"You really believe your own bullshit? That your murdering and maiming experiments would help humanity?"

Karl gazed out across the countless headstones along the grassy slopes of Arlington. He turned to her with an icy stare. "You must find Viktor Kletnov. He's the only one who can help you now."

"I'm not the one here who needs help."

Karl was once again reminded just how much her words could carve out his heart like the dull blade of a knife.

310

"Exohumans walk among us. They can be anyone, any one of us. The dark storm clouds of war are once again on the horizon. Someone must stop them. That someone is you."

"Karl, I'm an analyst. I'm not one to stop anything."

"You're special, Katherine, always have been. Adversity and fate will conspire to make you what you will truly become. They must, for all our sakes."

Karl gazed at Katherine, seeing only the terrible sadness of his own reflection in her dark sunglasses, eyes that longed for the innocence of a simpler time.

"Take me to Peter Cole," she said, with a sudden gnawing hunger to know more of these Exohumans.

"So many dreams buried beneath these grounds," was all Karl could say, gazing back out across the headstones along the grassy slopes. "I'm sorry, Kat. I'm sorry for everything."

Karl never called her Kat. The pistol appeared in his right hand from somewhere in a trench coat pocket. "Shakespeare said it best. Cowards die many a death, the valiant taste of death but once."

"Karl, put the gun away," said Katherine with gentle sternness.

"Turn around and walk."

He lifted the gun to her face. His hand remained eerily still. "I said walk — please."

Karl saw so clearly. He could taste her from where he stood. He could feel her heart pounding in her chest.

"Please go."

XVI

THE STORM

The frogman approached from below deck, his wetsuit dripping with sea and sweat. With one hand, he desperately searched panels and compartments where a life preserver might hide, while with the other, he clenched the steel case strapped to his shoulder. His head snapped around at the clang of footfalls on steel grates. He mounted the steps, fighting to hang on as the sub churned from side to side. Popping open the porthole, he emerged into the violent sea storm above.

The seas crested, white foam frothing and winds howling across the bow. Rain pelted his face as he descended the sail. The sleek hull of the submarine dipped and peaked beneath his feet. He slipped his arms under the stair rails, wedging them between panels, bracing against the torrid force of the freezing sea. Stinging salt washed away the blood from the exposed bone of his knuckles. The metallic case hung heavy at his side, the strap biting deep into his shoulder. Skin and muscle were beginning to give.

"The boat is ready!" came the shout over the roaring wind. A young submariner hung to the side of the vessel, doubled over from the pain of something broken. This was the *Alrosa*, and as agreed, the young ensign, Dmitri Borei, had been waiting for him.

The frogman twisted about. The raft thrashed on the breaking waves, tugging on the bowline.

"Pull the raft!" he shouted.

"You won't survive, sir."

"Do it!"

Hand over hand, Dmitri pulled the raft to the *Alrosa*, as the freezing wind and water whipped it about. Agony cut through his side. He tasted blood in his mouth. It oozed out a nostril, washing away into the sea.

The frogman watched, still gripping the stair rail. A metallic object glistened in his fist.

"She's submerging!"

Dmitri twisted the raft upright onto the deck, as the foaming water rose over the hull.

"Get on!"

The frogman worked down the line, tethering the two of them to the sail, when his heel slid into the water. His hand reached from the spume and clamped onto Dmitri's vest. The weight of the steel case was too much.

"Pull!"

The frogman rolled over the side, landing flat on the raft, exhausted. The case thumped behind him on the rubbery bottom. Dmitri had pushed it over the edge.

"Release the line!" shouted the frogman to Dmitri, over the howling wind.

"I can't. Too much force."

Dmitri lost his footing on the hull. The cord that tethered him to the boat tugged him forward, as his eyes filled with terror. The submarine's sail had submerged beneath the waves.

Both men knew what the other was thinking. *Only one of them was meant to survive.* The frogman, Peter Cole, didn't give Dmitri a chance.

His heel smashed square onto the young man's exposed face, as his white-knuckled grip on the raft released. Dmitri vanished into the black murk below.

Ramin bolted upright, wheezing for air. He stared at the soft candle glowing in the corner. Clammy wetness soaked his sheets. He was drenched in a cold sweat. The nightmare had returned.

He looked over. Soraya lay fast asleep on her side, her pregnant belly propped on a pillow. He pulled off the covers and gingerly tiptoed his way out of the room, cringing with every creak of the wood beneath his feet.

The night draped herself over Tehran. An early fog covered the Alborz, feeling more like winter than spring. Ramin heated a kettle of cherry blossom tea and wondered about the nightmares that again haunted him like memories not his own.

The hour had been late when they first came — these nightmares — on a night much like this one. Ramin had been tasked to supervise the containment chamber to the fusion reactor, deep in the cellars of the university campus. Without warning, a sudden alarm chirped and whirred as the magnetic fields holding the helium plasma spiked beyond any measure their tesla scales could produce. A tiny liquid silver sphere, glowing a cobalt blue, appeared suspended beyond his nose and rippled through the air, as darkness itself rolled in like a fog, enveloping all light around him.

From that darkness, they had come — creatures, not men. They were tall and lithe, flowing with feminine grace. They were shrouded, eerie and out of place, cold when it should have been hot, desolate when there should have been others around. These things, they did not speak.

314

They clasped him with fingers like tendrils of cold stone, pressing deep into flesh. He roared for help, but his voice couldn't escape his vocal cords, muted by these creatures cloaked behind black niqabs.

A feminine hand of long gray bones and sharp black fingernails held something in its desiccated palm—a sickly green glow began to pulse. It was a ring, and on it was a script, a flowing language Ramin somehow read, somehow understood. The hand thrust into his chest. Agony twisted into his thorax.

Suddenly, the creatures were gone. The fusion reactor was as he remembered. The containment fields measured normal. What he witnessed had been a dream. But a tender wound remained where the hand had met his flesh—and there was something else, the briefcase at his feet. He released the clasps and pulled back the dented, bloodstained lid. In it was a centrifuge, but not like any he'd ever seen. The thing was made of technology and flesh. Ramin didn't know how, but the thing was alive.

First, there were the cold sweats and the gut-lurching pain, and the nightmares. But soon there was something more. His colleagues were the first to notice. He began to uncover improvements in their work, unwelcome improvements. Everything was clearer, simpler, slower. He first pointed out a few suggestions, some recommendations.

Before he knew it, he was proving theorems that yielded breakthroughs in nuclear development years ahead of even the most advanced programs. His colleagues began to talk among themselves, and the more they did, the more envy and jealousy turned them against him.

Kazem was the only one who stayed, the only one he could trust. But not even with him did Ramin share that which he saw, not as color and light, but as equations and impossible mathematics. He dared tell no one of the voices and images in his head. He didn't know where they came from or who they belonged to, other than that they were not his. He had the classic symptoms of a man gone mad, gone over the edge.

Tonight was cold and the garden lonely. Just a few more hours before Kazem would be by for their usual ride to work. Ramin bundled up on the bench beneath the cherry blossom tree and closed his eyes. Maybe this was all a bad nightmare too and he'd soon wake up with Soraya and the baby, and that alone would be enough. The feeling never left him though that someone, out there somewhere, was watching.

***

Saifa had made it back to the safe house. She stood in the courtyard, in the darkness, looking up at the windows. She considered disappearing. There were many places she could go to get away from all this. But this life would never let her. She had lived with the emptiness far too long. All she had left were her ghosts and her regrets.

"I've been pondering the many ways I can so easily murder you for what you've done," said Saifa, who was sitting at the kitchen under the lamplight when Ronen walked in. It was late at night and Ronen hadn't been able to sleep.

"Is that so," he said, no surprise in his voice.

He pulled up the bar stool opposite her at the counter.

"Once again, my intuition was right about you. Once again, I did not listen, and once again, my heart was wrong to trust you."

"No, Saifa, you were right. I did not have to tell you. You already knew why I called you. You're the only one who can do this."

"I found a business card at Birkin's residence this morning from a Michael Hearst, director at the National Gallery of Art. So I figured I'd go to the museum and have a closer look."

"Interesting how you failed to mention that to either of us," said Ronen, as he poured himself a new cup of the leftover Turkish coffee.

"There was a special program this evening about an art heist, the Isabella Stewart Gardner Museum. Half a billion of stolen art."

"The Gardner Heist. An FBI-sponsored program for VIP guests of the upcoming Vermeer exhibit," said Ronen.

"Peter Cole was there."

Ronen brought the cup of bitter cold coffee to his mouth. He did not utter a word.

"The same Peter Cole from the night in Crimea. You knew he was still alive. You knew he would be there."

Saifa waited for something from Ronen. But he only sipped his coffee and stared at her, through her, until finally, after a long silence, he spoke.

"You were correct about Andrei Birkin and the Hashishin. Maybe it was Anton who killed him. Maybe you should have killed me a long time ago. But you can't. Not because of anything else other than what you must do, what you were always meant to do. I did not bring you here for Anton. I brought you here for

317

the man you once knew as Peter Cole. His name is Richard Robles."

***

The bold headline read in stark contrast to the white background on the computer screen.

Consular Officer Murdered in His Home.

Anton sat at the coffee table beneath the high-vaulted ceiling of his room at the Quincy Adams Hotel, staring out the lancet window at the American Art Museum just across the street. The passersby went on their way, oblivious to who—or what—watched them. The black ink scripted into his forearm, a relic of a bygone time, burned as if a branding iron were fresh off his skin. Anton lived in a world that no longer needed or wanted his kind. But Viktor had found use for him, and the Lion of Ismael had been called upon to serve again. He did not need to know their purpose. Viktor and Salil were his masters. It was for them to decide. But he knew his.

Anton moved from the window to the mirror as he buttoned his shirt and fixed his sleeves. He laced his tie and slid into his pinstriped suit. He had arrived from London. That was what the documents on his table said. Everything had been set to draw attention from his true purpose. The survival of the Hashishin depended on this. This would be the last time.

Anton removed his briefcase from beneath the writing desk as the doorknob slowly turned. Anton thought to draw his pistol, but there was no need. The door swung open as Anton placed the case on the desk.

"It's been too long, old friend," said Anton.

318

The albino stared silently at Anton, quietly shutting the door behind him. There was nothing friendly about them. They each had something the other wanted, and over the centuries, their kind had learned to be practical.

"Ever pleasant to see you, Anton," said the albino, with the least of smiles.

The albino took a quick glance about the room. As expected, only Anton was present. Not that he doubted him. The Hashishin were an honorable lot even from the time before the schism. It was one of their less-redeeming qualities. If death were to come at the hands of this Hashishin, he would know of it before it descended. The albino was a Spectral, a species borne of their home worlds since even before the first schism. They were an ancient people, the closest to humans, and the only ones able to retain their form and still pass for one of them, even if bizarre to look at.

Spectrals existed before either Sicaari or Hashishin, and like the Guija, were seen as bitter enemies by the Argylians. Spectrals were feared for their cephalopodic capabilities to morph their bodies and limbs and their powers of psychotropic illusion. David was his master, but the albino, like Anton before him, was driven by a hunger that demanded beyond what even his loyalty could resist. The fact that they stared each other in the face was more betrayal than the albino could have ever imagined from himself or even one such as Anton. He had come in search of an alliance with a mortal enemy, in the hopes for a taste of freedom he had never known for himself and the few that remained of his kind. Perhaps a stitch in the fabric of time had indeed come undone.

319

"If our masters knew of this meeting, our existence would be snuffed from every permutation of reality," said the albino, with a yellow-toothed and sincere grin.

"We each have something the other wants," said Anton.

"Besides the desire to kill each other," joked the albino.

"Fortunately for you." Anton unlatched the briefcase on the table.

Many a Hashishin suffered that fate at the albino's hands, just as Hashishin murdered many of his own kind through their centuries of war. The albino considered Anton's threats. He despised threats. But in this case, he hated to admit that Anton could possibly make good on that statement.

"You seek the knowledge of the Fifth Discipline, of the *Pentathlos*," said Anton, as he produced an ancient, leather-bound tome from the case and placed it gently upon the table.

The albino gazed greedily upon the book. He quickly scanned the ancient tongue inscribed upon its face and the one-eyed obelisk at the cover's center. He never dreamed he would behold such a thing. The Hashishin were the keepers of the *Pentathlos* and Anton was its guardian.

Hundreds of Spectrals, his people, his kind, had met a terrible death in an attempt at a morsel of the ancient knowledge contained in its texts, and here it lay before him. But the albino had to make a sacrifice. He had to give something in return that never in all the existences he'd known had he considered possible. Indeed, a stitch to the tapestry had been undone.

"Very well," said the albino.

He drew an orincular dagger from its hilt and plunged its tip into his vein. The hollow blade filled with the black blood borne of his putrid flesh as Anton's mouth watered with desire. The albino ripped the blade from his arm and collapsed to his knees. He handed Anton the hilt. Anton clenched the haft, slicing the blade from the albino's clasped fingers.

The ritual had been done.

Anton held the blade known as *Kidir* in his hand, the one blade to master all, the blade meant for the true leader of all Hashishin, the one who would finally set them free.

***

Cars and mopeds of all types shoved their way through the metal throng that was Tehran's morning rush hour. Wheels and bumpers barely touched as the daily commute began to pick up. The heavy stench of burnt diesel filled the air, as the mopeds and their veiled riders puttered and weaved between cars.

"Why's the traffic so bad today?" asked Ramin, not touching his morning coffee in the cup holder.

"It's no worse than any other morning. Why are you in such a foul mood?" Kazem cut sharply in front of an old Datsun.

"I'm not in a bad mood."

"And I'm not my sister's brother," retorted Kazem.

"That makes no sense, what you just said."

"As much sense as you being in a foul mood," Kazem said.

"I couldn't sleep last night," answered Ramin.

"Soraya keep you up again with baby pains?"

"I'm the one with baby pains. Just bad nightmares," Ramin said.

"You're going to be a dad soon. It's called cold feet."

"If it were only," murmured Ramin. He looked out to the endless sea of metal that was this traffic jam. For some reason, the streets looked different this morning.

"Why are you taking a different way?" asked Ramin, suddenly curious.

"The exit on Hemat Highway is closed. So instead we breathe fumes and drink tar coffee," Kazem rattled off. It sounded to Ramin as if those words had been practiced.

Somewhere else in the city, at the mouth of a bustling alleyway, at the entrance to a local bazaar, a moped stood parked along the street's edge near the back door to a butcher shop. On the street beyond, a roundabout funneled the traffic as commuters trekked along their daily route to work.

This was his third morning cigarette and the day had barely begun. Darhab had pressing matters on his mind. Since their return from Kabul, Azar had been very different. He had always thought himself central to the Brotherhood, a movement he and Azar had founded together. But Azar's ambitions were growing and not in the direction he wished.

Darhab took a heavy drag and stared at Azar, who was busily working on something inside his black leather satchel. Every choice, every thing, had been Azar's. There was no room any longer for Darhab's voice, except for the one in his own head reminding him of the humiliation, of how far he'd fallen.

Salil had invited them to sit among the circle, that hot day in the clay hut in Kabul. They sat around that roast mutton as would lions and hyenas staking out a fresh kill, a circle where only the strongest would feast. They looked upon each other with veiled deference, hiding their salivating jowls, beasts starving to tear faces clean from skulls, gnaw bellies, and devour tripe. Those men despised in each other belief, faith, and flesh, and yet they conspired to a common end that justified their means. Darhab joined Azar at the edge of the circle, when Salil commanded him away.

"Leave us."

Darhab would not abandon his brother, and Salil would not ask again. Azar grabbed him by the arm and, with his eyes, excused him from the room. Darhab was struck silent before he could utter a word.

They had sworn a promise never to betray each other, and yet Azar had made him submit before these animals the moment he sided with them. The Pakistani, the Americans — especially the Americans — looked on with laughter in their eyes. In the silence, its echoes pummeled his entire being. The Chinese man didn't even bother to lend a look. He just laughed and nodded his head with pity.

Darhab's voice boomed from deep in his chest as his sinews came alive with fire and strength. But the hands that clenched him were too strong, and his will not strong enough. That booming voice never left his lips. He sat a penitent child, stood over by two Pashtun with AK-47s, spitting slimy chewed betel on his dirt-smeared feet.

The meeting had come and gone, he alone in the silence with those two goons. Azar finally came for him, not uttering a word, not looking him in the eye for the shame of what had been done, or perhaps the shame of what Darhab had allowed be done to himself.

That shame, like a filthy hand, reached into Darhab's belly; it twisted and pulled, it rubbed with pleasure where he felt most humiliated.

Azar ceased being his brother that night, and now here they were, Darhab again subject to Azar's bidding, playing an ever-more dangerous and foolish game. The streets of Tehran in morning rush hour were the last place they needed to be. The iron gate to the back door of the shop swung open, and Azar stepped through, the black duffel bag with a yellow stripe now slung and ready over his shoulder.

"Throw away the cigarette," ordered Azar as he carefully placed the bag into the rear harness of the bike.

"We foolishly strike the lion in his den. I smoke," said Darhab.

"The vehicle approaches. We ride," said Azar.

Azar had learned to not heed danger or warning. Hubris would yet teach him its lesson well. Darhab swung a leg over the bike, taking in a last drag, flicking the butt to the curb. The embers burnt what was left of the tobacco as the moped's whining motor came to life. Azar sat in the seat behind him, whipping the bag's strap snugly onto his shoulder. Azar needed to be careful. He needed to be very careful.

In the serpentine flow of rubber and metal that was Tehran's morning traffic jam, Ramin watched the stopped cars honking and blaring, calculating probabilities of success for the scooters winding and slanting through the tiny spaces that made up their current predicament. The sidewalks looked like ant hills, with moving heads in every direction. Beards and black hijabs were all he could make out among the crowds.

"There's something you need to know about me," said Ramin, turning to Kazem.

"Move, you stupid goat," shouted Kazem out the side window, as a blaring horn sounded in reply.

"What do you mean, something about you? I even know when you go to the bathroom. By Allah, I wish I didn't," said Kazem.

"The centrifuge is only a cover for my other work," said Ramin.

Back in the quagmire of the stalled traffic behind Ramin and Kazem, Darhab caught a glimpse of their white vehicle. How could he not, since theirs was the only utility vehicle built for a luxury unimaginable to most in this city—and none in this neighborhood. Darhab breathed the nauseous smell of benzene through a black scarf pulled over his nose and mouth. The taste of car made his stomach turn. He slammed the scooter to a stop, jolting off the seat.

"Keep focused. The white truck, five cars ahead, around on the right side," shouted Azar into Darhab's ear over the blaring traffic.

Darhab carefully balanced the bike around the metal fender in front. Azar unwound the strap from his shoulder, gripping the sack by a woven handle.

For the freedom of Balochistan. Where was the freedom in this?

Darhab balanced on his toes toward the target now three car-lengths away. Azar exposed them to what he called mad suicide and the extinction of the Brotherhood. They were pawns for the Americans and Salil Jawadi, the very enemies they detested most.

"Up along the truck, right side, now!" shouted Azar. Wobbling the bike, Darhab strained his shoulders and arms against the handlebars. The bike was about to topple.

From his place in the front seat, the scarf covered face looked like any other in the throng to Ramin, except for those black eyes. Eyes as hollow as death stared through him, past him from outside his window. The thumping in his chest skipped a beat. His bowels loosened and his groin shriveled.

Ramin was suddenly outside his body. He was standing on the street. Like a slow-moving picture, he saw two men on a bike, with the blaring horns a distant wail. The air was filthy with smoke and soot. Grainy dirt burned into his eyes. The black-scarfed man with those hollow eyes carried something. For some reason no one paid him any attention.

Ramin tried to scream, to tell himself to run, but the words failed to escape him. The man gripped the satchel from its handle and swung it up against the vehicle. The magnet at the base of the ticking bomb latched onto the door as the thump against metal pulled Ramin's awareness back into the car like a vortex. Ramin saw his reflection in the cavernous black eyes of the veiled rider. He saw Soraya, he saw his unborn baby, he saw death.

"Out the door!"

Ramin reached over Kazem with the strength of Heracles. The door kicked open, bending at the hinges, when the ticking black bag attached to the side hit zero. Fiberglass and leather tore into him, searing through his pants. A sharp burn shot up his spine. Ceramic ball bearings struck out in every direction as a fireball spewed into the morning sky, sending black ash into the air over the stalled traffic. Metal, plastic, and glass rained down from above. Panic-stricken passersby stampeded over each other, and drivers cowered frozen in their seats.

Ramin's soot-covered body and bloodstained face lay motionless atop his friend. He blinked once. He blinked again. But he was numb. The smell of burning flesh crept into his nose as the flames from the truck licked at his shredded jacket. He tried to scream, but all he knew was silence.

**

Ganesh couldn't take another minute of this. He had surfed the latest sports and news and played with all the social sites. His life right now was only more and more sad by the second and he needed a distraction from these endless hours of earphones and dashboards recording the latest deep-sea sonic wonders of the Reykjanes. Mike Freeman was as good a distraction as any.

"What do you mean, no midterm?" asked Ganesh, filled with disappointment.

"One day to the next, he just canceled it, wouldn't say why. Haven't seen him since. Last I ran into Mr. Robles was March Madness."

"Have they canceled the class?" asked Ganesh.

"Nope… There it goes again."

"There goes what again?"

"I'm picking it up, the same sound, this time from sensor 6233," said Mike.

"I don't hear shit!"

"That's because you don't have the gift," boasted Mike.

"It's called you smoking too much kahuna." Ganesh wished he could have himself some of that right about now.

"Isn't that what all you Indians do?" asked Mike, setting his terminal to record the sound.

"Hindus!"

"Whatever."

"I hope that teacher of yours shows back up and fails your ass."

"And I hope they deport your ass back to Bangladesh," said Mike, tossing a crumpled paper wad at Ganesh.

"India!"

"Did you say something?" asked Mike.

"Actually, he did" came a voice from behind, a sudden seriousness falling over them.

"Good morning, ma'am," said Mike as he stood to greet the arrivals, his earphones almost yanking off his head.

"You want to be careful there, son. That's an expensive piece of Navy equipment," said Lieutenant Larson.

"Yes, ma'am."

Ganesh watched without uttering a word from behind his cubicle space. The less they took notice of him, the better.

"So this is the one," said Robert, appearing alongside the lieutenant in his full commander's regalia.

"Yes, sir," said Lt. Larson.

"Is who the one?" asked Mike.

"May I have a few words with you, son?"

"About what?"

"I just have a few questions for you," said Robert.

"Man, I didn't do it," said Mike, all sense of formality escaping him.

"Neither did I. But my bosses never believe me," said Robert with a smile.

Mike followed the commander in his Navy blues with his three gold stripes on his lapels. He hated the feeling of being led, not knowing where, like a pig to slaughter. In his experience, being pulled aside and singled out was never a good thing. Robert opened a door into one of the many side conference rooms furnished with only a table, a few chairs, and a phone that probably didn't work.

"Please sit down," said Robert as he went around the lone table. With no windows to the outside world, it was one of the several conference rooms on this floor used by the research teams to review findings, just have lunch, or ask some personal questions. The padding on the walls made for a soundproof space. Mike sat down in the chair.

"They should have a coffee maker in every one of these rooms," said Robert.

"Not enough taxpayer dollars," said Mike.

"Oh, there's enough. The Navy just never makes good use of its money," said Robert, settling into a chair opposite Mike. "So I understand that you're conducting research, cataloging hydrothermal vents, for your Ph.D. in underwater topography, is that right?"

"Actually, I'm completing my masters in Naval Architecture and Marine Engineering, then a Ph.D."

"Wow, so you're going to be one of those guys who build our next-gen sub or something like that," said Robert, giving an air of being genuinely impressed.

"Something like that, yeah."

"So you are one sharp cookie."

"If you say so." Mike was feeling a bit on edge. He was being set up—*for what?* he wondered.

"In your report of 5th of May you cite a series of sounds, low frequency, on arrays 5721 and 5784 near the Azores Islands, quote, *'as if moving across the seafloor.'*"

"Did I do something wrong?"

"Not at all. You cited them again three days later on array 6234 over 150 kilometers distance, and if I'm not mistaken, you made mention of it again to your friend out there."

"Look, sir, if this is something we'd rather maybe ignore, I'd be more than happy to oblige."

"You're the only one who's noticed this sound, scuttling across the seafloor, to paraphrase you."

"I have no idea what you're talking about, sir," said Mike bouncing a foot and tapping his fingers.

"It's okay son, relax. What if I told you I wanted you to search for this sound across the seafloor with a more advanced system? Think you could do that?"

"Probably, I mean, yeah," said Mike, feeling suddenly a bit important.

"Good. I want you to get your stuff and come with me."

"Right now?"

"Yeah."

"Can I ask at least what it is I'm listening for?" Mike was unable to restrain his curiosity any longer.

"A submarine."

XVII

SECRETS LOST TO TIME

The pink flesh flaked off the bone as Hendrix carved into the rib. The taste of rosemary and Dijon with a touch of garlic melted in his mouth.

"You are one lucky man, sir," said Hendrix, trying his best to not speak with his mouth full. "If I'd known it was gonna be this good..."

"Thank you," said Anja as she cleared the empty plates of what once were tender lamb chops, but now were only picked-clean bones.

"You wouldn't have thought twice," said Richard, bringing his flute glass to his mouth, the remnants of a deep red Chianti swimming at its bottom. He downed it, placing the glass back on the table. He watched Anja walk back into the kitchen, radiant this evening with a joy he'd not felt from her in a long time. She was the Anja he remembered, so young, so full of life.

"Been a long time since I've eaten this good."

"And with such great company," added Richard snapping out of his reverie, as Hendrix finished the last of his chop.

"Speaking of company, what became of that strange gentleman from last night?"

"Was strange, wasn't he?"

"First time you two ever met?"

"First and hopefully last. Looked like one of those you don't want to get caught in a dark alley with." Richard poured Hendrix a bit more of the wine.

"Come on, a little old man with an upturned mustache and those wilder-than-crazy cross-eyes, what could he ever do to you?" chuckled Hendrix, wiping the Dijon sauce off his fingertips.

"That umbrella—did you see that umbrella? The strange leather straps and that carved bone handle, and the colors on the fabric?! There was a certain Daliesque madness about that man."

"Yeah, that umbrella was something to be scared of. Remember that novelist, Bulgarian I think, killed with a ricin pellet from the tip of an umbrella?"

"Georgi Markov," replied Richard with a tinge of angst in his voice.

"Yes, him! You should be scared. He seemed intent on you."

Anja returned to the table. "You two are perfect for each other. Gossip like two girls. Do either of you ever tire of talking about art and intrigue?"

"Never!" exclaimed Richard, pouring her a fresh glass of Chianti and then finishing off the bottle. He gave Anja a smile only to feel his heart flutter when she smiled at him in return. For an instant, he forgot the anguish at what he caused her. For the first time in a long time, he was happy.

"A match made in heaven, then," conceded Anja.

"It's good to relax with great company. Had a long week in Hartford."

"The wine helps," joked Richard.

"Most definitely." Hendrix folded his napkin to clean a corner of his lip.

"I heard that Hartford could be a break in the case," said Richard, alluding to the famous Gardner Heist.

"I see you keep tabs on the latest news."

"We want to collect that five-million-dollar reward for the paintings," said Anja.

"We did get some leads, but can't say more on the subject," said Hendrix.

"Oh come now, you can't leave us hanging on a thread like that." Even Richard's wife was getting into all this talk of stolen art and intrigue.

"I suspect Mr. Robles might know more as to their whereabouts than me," said Hendrix, taking a swig of the Chianti.

Like an empty canvas, not a hint of expression except for that boyish smile flashed across Richard's face.

"Come on, Frank. You guys have been trying to pin the thing on some mobster or other for the past twenty-five years, and zippo, zilcho," said Richard squinting his eye at Hendrix through his pinched thumb and forefinger.

"You think so?" asked Hendrix, finishing his wine rather quickly.

"You seem sharper than your average special agent. You gotta have a better lead than that by now."

"Actually, there is another lead—a tidbit, we'll call it," said Hendrix.

"Ooh, more gossip," chuckled Anja, pouring him more wine.

"Tell me about you and Viktor Kletnov."

The last of the Chianti dripped into the glass. A silence hung over the table.

***

The air was grainy with dust and heavy with the smell of death. Along the streets, men marched in olive-drab fatigues, rifles harnessed over their shoulders. They moved in a singular disarray past the skeletons of bombed-out buildings on a main city street.

The young man with thick black brows stared glossily down at the dark-bearded man before him. About a foot shorter than he was, the older man carried himself with the will of a giant.

"Do you believe in what is right?" asked the man of the young one.

"Yes," replied the young man, averting his gaze perhaps to escape the pain of answering the question and what would become of him for it.

The bearded man straightened the young man's tunic.

"As do I. So much that I give my only son."

"I love you, Dad."

"And I you, Daveed."

They each cracked a smile.

Artillery boomed in the distance as the young man extended his hand. The father clasped his son's.

"If you believe in what is right, then come back. For your mother... for me."

A bullhorn blew in the distance and a whistle screeched. The throng of men picked up their pace. Bellows and shouts rang along the crowd. Men surged headlong into a chaotic rush. The dust kicked up. The taste of feces and sweat caked the throat of the dark-bearded man. A shot rang out in the distance.

"Go," said the father, as the young man grabbed his shoulder harness and lifted his pack.

The dust shimmered through the sunlight. The chaos receded away in the silence. The father willed his hand to reach the boy. But there was only the taste of dust in his breath, as the clangor once again rang in his ears. Daveed gave a last look back at his father who stood, like him, in the olive-drab uniform of the Revolutionary Guard as the dust faded away to cold rock and windswept snow.

The young man had vanished and the beard had grayed. Lids had drooped, cheeks had wrinkled, eyes had grown a little cloudier. Those eyes of thirty-five years earlier now stared at a blooming cherry blossom tree along a sloping path in the foothills of the Alborz Mountains. All had paid a terrible price at Khorramshahr. For Salil, it was the last time he ever saw his son.

The pink blossoms swayed in the tree as the fresh scent of spring filled the air. His men had established a base camp somewhere deep in the mountains. The winds whispered the spirit of the place. Salil stared at the flowers; his stomach gnawed and twisted. In his hand was a flash drive.

His men had kept him from his home. They had found bloodstained stones in the garden, a ransacked house, blood on the bed sheets. They found the flash drive after they killed the assassins lying in wait for him. His would-be killers, VAJA, the Iranian Secret Police, hoped he would return. But he had been warned. His men had assured Salil that the ambushers had suffered a quick and very painful death. They had brought him this, a memory stick, and on it a recording from the one responsible for his Romina. It was a personal gift from Javeed.

Javeed had infiltrated his guard. He seduced his men, reached deep into his closest circle and ripped the innards from those he loved most. Javeed had waited for the opportune moment when Salil would be most vulnerable, when he could least respond. Only a few had known of his meeting with Viktor, few who could have opened a path to Javeed.

Javeed had not wanted to kill him. Instead he acted with an intent to punish. By comparison, death would have been a solace, and Javeed knew that. His Machiavellian sensibility knew that. Salil's hand trembled. His stomach turned and his knees weakened as he watched the recording over and over. Her voice, her gentle smile was replaced with wails of defiance, wails for clemency. He watched again and again what they'd done to her.

Parvin had warned him not to watch it. But he must. He witnessed these animals, their defilement, with his own eyes. Salil had an entire army at his fingertips. He had such power that none could ever imagine, not even the Syndycate. And yet still he was impotent to save her.

He denied himself, tried to live among them. He played their game, living in careful balance between humanity and the Syndycate. He had played their game long enough.

Parvin stood at his side, patiently waiting for him to emerge from his own mind. Their enemies were coming after what hurt most. Ominous dark clouds loomed in the distance. Salil turned and climbed the path in silence, coming to a tent somewhere deep in the camp.

"Any word of her?" asked Salil when he finally spoke.

"Nothing, sir," responded Parvin, standing at the tent's entrance.

The guards said there had been signs of a struggle: drag marks on the ground, a blood trail leading away, a shred of a garment, but no Romina. They returned to him what Salil recognized as Bousseh's silk riding pants. They violated his daughter over and over, before they proceeded to take her life-giving womb with the molten end of a wrought-iron spike thrust deep inside her.

"Please give me a moment," said Salil, with the faintest crack to his voice.

Parvin bowed in deference. He did not proceed past the entrance. Salil placed the memory stick into his breast coat pocket as he pulled back the flaps to the tent. His guest waited expectantly for him inside, already engaged in vibrant conversation.

He had played their game long enough.

"Israel has moved on Hamas and opened a front against the Caliphate," rang out the voice of James Fenway, in the crisp Vermont English Salil so remembered.

James sat with a water bottle in his hand and his American guards clad in tactical gear on either side of him. Outside, another handful waited at their armored vehicles. Salil's own men watched them warily, some in plain sight, others from the shadows.

"President McNeal will condemn the act initially, with the expected sanctions. We will also block the Security Council from unsightly measures, resolutions that don't further our cause. Once the government ministries are secure, you will announce your intentions for the formation of the new Republic. Back-channel military and political support from my government will soon follow. You will be offered humanitarian aid and other concessions in return for cessation of all hostilities, which you, of course, will politely refuse."

James kept flapping his tongue at the man dressed in the full rank and insignia of an Iranian army general. General Hasan Al Habar was the commanding officer to all regular army forces within Tehran's military district. He was a barrel-chested, upright, and proud man, with a thick mustache and full, gray-streaked hair. He was handsome and charismatic, admired by his men, adored by his women, and a lifelong friend to Salil Jawadi. Since the battle at Khorramshahr, they had quietly developed a network of loyal officers who would stand behind them when the time came, and that moment was soon upon them. Where Al Habar led, the army would follow. Salil gazed past the American as if he wasn't even there. James didn't even have the respect to direct his words at him, even if they were utterly useless and James an absolute fool.

"Of course, once Tehran falls, the rest of Iran will follow. The Security Council will move to recognize your new government with our backing and you will finally have what you always wanted," said James, looking past the general to Salil for the first time.

"Salil, so good to see you. Last we met, you spoke of your daughter. How is she? I brought you a gift for her," said James, revealing a small box in the palm of his hand.

"If you'll excuse me, Hasan, I will have words with this man. All of you," said Salil, his voice carrying across the whole of the massive tent. The men rose from their terminals and keyboards and exited by one of the many open slits along the edges.

Salil removed the amulet hanging from around his neck and released the clasp. Men in dark vestments that flowed loosely from their bodies emerged from the shadows. They were bald, dark-complected, slender, and tightly muscled. Up their forearms climbed the tattooed Lions of Ismael, disappearing beneath their long, black sleeves. They were his Hashishin. They were death. The six of them vanished back into the darkness. Even James's guards had left. He'd not commanded it, nor remembered them going. Salil and James remained in sudden and desolate solitude.

"Why? Why do you follow him?" asked Salil, opening the face to the amulet.

James sat in his place, unsure as to the question and his safety.

"David—why do you follow him? Did he promise you some great power? Does he satisfy your puerile ambitions, like an orgasm between your thighs?" asked Salil, taking a step toward James, holding something in his hand that made James rocket from his chair. Salil slipped the ring of reversion onto his finger.

The air began to haze as feeling began to leave James. Every breath he drew was harder, and with every breath, he thirsted for more. He was suffocating. His vision blurred. The tent vanished. A rolling field of undulating, tall, crimson grass on a sloping hill lay where they had been. Two cratered moons encroached the violet sky.

"Is this what you wish for? Is this what you wish to become?" asked the thing that stood before James in a hissing echo. James gasped, tripping over himself from the sight before him.

Flesh peeled away from Salil's face, his mouth and nose smoothed as if by windblown sand, his eyes vanished. Nose, mouth, even ears were gone. A skin of argent white covered his face and head as his body morphed into a cloak, a tapestry of color: orange and reds, violets and blues, folding and fluttering over and around the towering creature.

"I fought for so long to live as one of you. And all I was given in return was the vilest of what is human. Men like you took away what meant most to me. I allowed the Syndycate its dominion. I absconded my power, so that men like you could live with impunity. And in return, I was given only pain and death. You wish to be immortal? You wish to be omnipotent? You believe the Syndycate will grant your human flesh that wish? I will grant your flesh that wish such that you will rue the day you were born to this world."

Space fluttered and bent in fuchsia and indigo like a cloak around James, torso and limb, violating his nose and mouth, arresting his breath. James was suffocating alive, trapped in viscid air, suffering the agony of having every cell ruptured in his body without the luxury of dying.

"You will suffer. David Bradford will suffer. All of you will suffer as Romina suffered. I will be bound no longer!"

***

A fingertip brushed down the side of Richard's neck. Her nail lightly rasped over his chest, hooking into the first button of his shirt, resistance giving way like a warm knife through butter. The dark red, enameled fingernail made its way down, agonizingly pressing into his skin. His cheeks flushed. A tinge of pain shot through his chest. His hands gripped around the arms of the chair as he pushed off the floor. But the bindings held firm to his ankles. The rope bit slowly into his skin.

Sweetness escaped her mouth, her scent wafting through his nose. She wrapped her long fingers around his neck and began to squeeze his windpipe shut. The tip of her tongue slowly slid up the bridge of his nose. Her plush lips pressed a gentle kiss onto his beading forehead as she squeezed harder and harder. Tingling asphyxia rushed through his arms and legs into his thighs. Dark pleasure consumed Richard, body and soul.

The ecstasy left him strewn—broken on the bed. He lay on the king mattress, staring at the high-vaulted ceiling of his Quincy Adams Hotel room through the strands of hair that blanketed his face.

How could it all have come to this? He convinced Anja. Stealing those Vermeers was what must be done. They had planned. They had set all in motion. This night they would enter the National Gallery, just a few streets down from their hotel. They would get in, steal, and get out, as brazen as that. But Richard had not expected this from her, especially after that night at dinner with the FBI agent. The name, Viktor Kletnov, had been a death sentence in her eyes after all that happened, he was certain of it.

But instead, she opened up to him again as if lovers for the first time. Richard let the simplicity, the intensity of it all sweep him away. Nothing else really mattered. The little voice warned him at the perfectness of it all. It was all too convenient. But he didn't care. It would hurt too much if he did.

Shreds of undergarments and twisted clothes, remnants of the encounter, were tossed all about. Anja had lured him out of the house dressed in her knee-high boots, neck choker, and laced corset, with a purse full of play paraphernalia.

Richard slowly removed the ginger wig covering his face as he rolled onto his side, the fresh scrapes still burning over all of his body. The shower was running beyond the open door to the bathroom as the steam poured out along the ceiling, escaping into the vents above. He fell back onto the bed, the night still glistening on his skin and the pungent smell still fresh in his nose. And yet even with this delicious distraction, the memory of certain conversations crept back into his skull. The last people he needed to think about right now were a mini replica of Salvador Dali and a black man who looked more like an inside linebacker than an FBI agent.

"You always had a thing for this sort of shit," shouted Richard, sprawled naked and supine on the bed.

"Do I at least get a thank you?" asked Anja, as she strolled out of the bathroom, beads of water rolling off her skin. She passed the towel gently over her hips. His eyes slowly climbed up from her navel, catching her eyes shimmering in the twilight.

"At least there were no knives this time."

"I kind of like the knives," said Anja as she approached, the towel falling to the floor. She crawled into the bed, sliding onto Richard.

"You're the one who made me this way, lest we forget," she purred in his ear. She propped up on his chest, her hand getting close to his throat again. "Do you remember what you did to me that first night?"

"Should we walk away, Anja, from all this?" asked Richard, a sudden but not unexpected question. Richard pulled back from her, sitting upright on the bed. Anja followed the contours of his face, the light and shadow playing off his eyes and square unshaven jaw. His muscular lean frame silhouetted by the window, Richard looked like he bore the burden of the world on his shoulders. Anja grimaced, knowing this was their only choice.

"I thought the same thing, Richard. I fought you after what happened, I blamed you. But you were right. What was done, we cannot change. That world we had is gone to us. We must stand against them now. The Syndycate can't get their hands on those paintings."

"I've put us all in great peril, including our son. That Vatican inspector knew what we'd done: exactly what to ask, exactly what to look for, and exactly who to come looking for it. He killed Huygens, I know it, and suddenly that FBI agent comes asking about Viktor. How did he know to ask of me that name? Only one other knew that name, Karl Downing."

"Walking away will lead only to more suffering and pain. We can't give ourselves that choice, Richard. If they free the *Ilythiium*, we all die," said Anja.

Richard rolled from the bed and walked to the lancet window as passersby went about their Saturday night revelry on the street below.

"Karl came to see me." Richard knew the consequences of those words. But he had to say them. He begged her with his eyes, prayed she would prove his fears wrong.

"Why'd you keep that from me?" asked Anja.

"I was afraid, that would be the last straw. I was afraid you would blame me. That somehow I had guided him back to us. I was afraid I would lose Danny. That I would lose you. And without both of you there's nothing left for me."

A mesh of confusion and fury, sympathy and understanding, welled higher in Anja with every word from his lips. She could not help feeling the betrayal in his words.

How could it all have come to this?

It wasn't his transgressions that caused such confusion and loathing, it was hers. The betrayal lay buried deep in her own heart, at what she'd done, what Richard could never know: the dangerous entanglements she dragged them into. A vile enemy who murdered so many of her kind had come with a proposition — and an opportunity.

Salil Jawadi had found her; perhaps it was one of the consequences of altering the timeline. The Syndycate should never have discovered them. But they had, and Anja had no choice. She took matters into her own hands.

Salil asked her to bring him something locked away in a place only a Guija could find, a ring of reversion. Each member of the Syndycate had one forged for him, a perfect match to his DNA, one that would return him to what he was the day he first stepped foot onto this world. The thirteen rings had been cast away, beyond the reach of this physical world, to protect their masters from themselves. With his ring, Salil would be made whole again, powerful beyond anything this world could conjure.

But the ring brought its own torment. It would eat at him, destroy him from the inside out. He would not survive the inhospitable place this world would become to his body. If Salil alone possessed a ring, he would kill every one of them, every Argylian, just as the ring would kill him. Without the Syndycate, the *Ilythiium* would not matter. The creature would remain forever lost in the prison Richard and Anja had created for it in the two-dimensional world of a canvas, the fathomless world of a painter's imagination. The Guija would be finally free of their enslavement.

She did it for Richard and the son they'd borne. She granted Salil's wish. She invoked a magic long forbidden and even more powerful than what Richard had done the night of the Pinacoteca: a temporal bridge, channeled through one of the thirteen Armillary Spheres.

The harmonics of the Sphere's cross-rotating, opalescent bands amplified and captured energy like winds in a sail. They formed a micro curvature in space-time, a gateway beyond four-dimensional reality, a tunnel between two mirror universes. She bridged two worlds, two universes never meant to be brought together. All Guija knew such power was forbidden. To invoke it was to breach their most sacred vow, and Anja had done just that with Salil. She opened up infinite dimensionality into this four-dimensional universe. She found its hiding place—that ring of reversion. She brought it back for Salil. She brought it back here, tearing apart the fabric of time in exchange for chaos. There was no way she could know; she'd set the *Ilythiium* free.

Anja refocused her awareness on the present and channeled all her strength into what she would say and do next.

"The game we played with the Syndycate was a mistake. We should have never stolen those paintings," admitted Richard.

"The Richard I love does not wallow in regret. I won't let you start now," she said with a smile that betrayed nothing of the terror and rage churning in her soul.

"There is no such thing as coincidence. They know what we are. Viktor will stop at nothing to possess again what was once his," said Richard.

"We live because the Syndycate does not know, and they never will. The *Ilythiium* is a secret lost to time, and it will remain so. You always said the best place to hide it was right under their noses, in the very canvas of a Vermeer."

"We leave all this. We take Danny and we go, far away," he said, turning to her from the window.

His wife walked to him, her bare flesh silhouetted in the dark. The rain began to bead on the window. Her tender hand caressed his bare shoulders as her warm embrace pulled him from dark memories of a life so long ago.

"I'm sorry for everything I've ever said and done and for everything I *haven't* that has caused you such pain. But we can't leave any of this. Not now. We must take those paintings, and we must destroy them."

Richard gave her a gelid look. The terror of damaging even of fleck of those Vermeers blanched his face. He knew what she said was true. But his obsessions would never allow him.

Anja let him go. She knew where his priorities lay, and they weren't with her or their son. It was time they got a move on. She grabbed the satchel in the corner of the room and dressed the part for the evening, pulling the black bodysuit over her shoulders.

"I love you, Anja."

"And I you, Richard," she said. But there was no shaking the baleful winds of doubt and betrayal blowing in her own heavy heart.

***

The streetlights cast their amber glow over the pavement below. Droplets rippled in the puddles with the last of the rains. The black M-Class SUV appeared from its niche on a Washington, D.C., side street, its wipers clearing the beads on the windshield as the headlights flooded the desolate street.

Richard gripped the steering wheel as he drew in a hard breath, remembering Anja's every word, every caress. But he denied himself those thoughts and focused on the flashing semaphore to distract from the foreboding silence between them. They had reviewed their plan down to the last excruciating detail.

How many paces to the paintings; how much time to dismount and store; how many paces back?

They had the rhythm and timing of the guards and their rounds. Guillermo supplied all the insights; Anja and Richard verified.

Richard pulled the car out onto the street when that familiar distant buzz from that long-ago morning in the museum caught his ears. The phone buzzed again in Anja's hip pocket as she put the call on speaker.

"Hi mommy, it's meeeee," said the little voice on the other end of the line. "You're late. Daddy promised."

Richard felt the excitement in Danny's voice. They read together every Saturday night and tonight was Saturday, after all.

"Daddy promised *The House of Usher!*"

"You're supposed to be in bed, young man. Here, talk to your father," said Anja, hitting the mute button.

"You're reading our son Edgar Allen Poe?" Anja asked, lifting an eyebrow.

"Better than any comic."

Richard unmuted the call, fully prepared for a lashing at the tongue of his eight-year-old boy. "Hi, Danny," he said.

"Hi, Daddy." There was a long silence. Richard could hear his little boy's breaths as his heart sank. "Tonight was reading night..."

The pause knotted Richard's throat. "That's why we're — we're, I'm sorry Danny."

"Daddy, are you home already? Someone's at the door."

Richard and Anja traded glances.

"I'll go get it."

"Danny, no!"

A pair of high beams suddenly flooded his rearview mirror. Halogen lights charged toward them. His foot pressed the gas. The car lurched forward, sinking them both into their seats. His phone buzzed in his coat pocket. The rain slammed into the windshield. Buildings and streets blurred by. The phone kept buzzing. A BMW 750 roared up alongside them as its black tints lowered. With her Glock 9mm in hand, Anja took aim at the driver when she did a double take.

"I know her!"

Richard glanced through their open passenger window—Saifa.

She lifted a hand, showing them an illuminated screen. The phone buzzed again in Richard's coat pocket.

"Answer it," said Anja.

Back at the house, Clara heard a knock at the door. But that wasn't what caught her attention. She rushed into the living room.

"Danny, wait right there," admonished Clara, as she stopped the little boy in his tracks.

"Dad said he was coming."

"Your dad doesn't need to knock."

"I know that, Clara," said Danny with a little attitude.

"Who is it?" she demanded, as Danny rushed to the door.

"*Espera que te coja*. Just wait till I catch you," huffed Clara with exasperated breath, reaching the door first and peering through the peephole. A chiseled, pale face beneath a black fedora hat stared back at her. Whoever it was, he knew she was there.

"Danny—"

The door frame splintered like jagged shrapnel in every direction. The door came clear of its hinges.

The first pieces of wood and glass hit him before the roar of the world coming apart reached his ears. He couldn't hear his own screams as Clara smashed headlong into the table's edge. The floor was already pooled in blood before her body hit the ground. The man in the fedora hat and trench coat stepped over her. She lay limp and wide-eyed, her mouth twisted, staring lifelessly at Danny as a gloved hand came down over the little boy, and her eyes fell to darkness for the last time.

***

Richard palmed the phone, pressing the receiver to his ear.

"I want to help you. They know what you are. They know your —" said the voice over the receiver. But the connection broke. The pedal couldn't go any farther into the floor. Saifa was gone.

"Richard!" screamed Anja, as oncoming headlights neared.

The M-Class lurched right, tires skidding over freshly wet pavement. Shop windows quickly approached. He was headed straight for a woman on the street corner. He turned his wheel sharply and roared past, brushing right by her as the headlights in his rearview again caught up with them.

"What does she want? How did she find us?"

"I don't know, I don't know," shouted Richard, when the steering wheel gave way, and the phone slowly floated from his hand, hanging there, unaffected by gravity, right in front of his nose.

His head spun, streetlights streaking by, when rain and something sharper, colder, pelted his face where the windshield had been a moment before. He had not felt the impact. The M-Class had been crushed on the right side as it wrapped right around a pole.

His neck was stiff. Richard couldn't feel his hands. He couldn't feel anything. Anja's face was blurry. Blood trickled down her left cheek. They were drenched in rain, surrounded by bright white lights. He jammed open the car door, rolling onto the pavement. Shadows approached through the beams. He reached across, unclipping the belt, dragging Anja through the door with the last of his strength.

350

"Your driving sucks," said Anja, a slight slur to her speech.

He lifted her, limping down the sidewalk away from the lights, away from the shadows. He turned a corner, carrying her from the street into darkness. The narrow passage opened into a back parking lot where a couple of cars took up the spaces. He looked back. There was no one. They had not given chase.

Richard gently placed Anja against the door of a car. She smiled at him. Her pupils were dilated and her face pallid. The wetness was not rain; it was a cold sweat. Her right hand was twisted, her wrist broken, possibly in two places. He gently picked her up again.

"I appreciate the gesture, but her time is up — as is yours, Peter Cole."

Anton stood over them, as if carried by the wind itself. The lions inked on his forearms showed below the cuffs of his trench coat.

In an instant the air was viscid thick; Anton was trapped in a gelatinous placenta. Richard stopped time. But a steel grip clamped down on his psyche. Anja gazed at him with acceptance and a bitter smile.

Let him go, Richard. Let him go.

His hold on time collapsed and the roar of a raging torrent engulfed him. Anton lifted Richard clear off the ground and smashed him into the car door.

"You lost your edge, Peter. You were never this easy."

Anton raised his hand; a stainless-steel barrel glared beneath the streetlamp. He aimed the pistol at Anja. The hammer fell so slowly. The shell spiraled out the muzzle, the case sprung out the chamber, the little piece of lead cavitated through the air. In that moment, everything Richard had ever loved in this world was gone. Death would have been a mercy to Richard Robles. But it was not afforded him this night.

***

Zhen Xin strode along the jade path, the morning sun already peeking though the weeping willows, drying the pine needles of their morning dew. The air was crisp with a tinge of warmth. The swans swam gently at the edge of the lake. All was quiet except for the roar in his ears; the roar of blood pumping through his perturbed heart.

Zhen Xin climbed the worn steps, the *I Ching* manuscript wrapped tightly in a fine silk cloth in the crook of his arm. At the edge of the path, something caught the corner of his eye. A praying mantis lay in wait. Patiently waiting, it blended into its surroundings to bring death to its unsuspecting prey, not of malice, but of necessity.

Zhen Xin parted the heavy double doors carved of a serpentine dragon, returning to the scene of the crime as the *I Ching* demanded of him. The dried blood lay at his feet. The painting, the black canvas with the creature and her desiccated baby, towered at the far wall as it had that fateful night. He placed the tome on the floor and unfurled the silks, bending the cover open. The patterned hexagrams laid before him filled with knowledge, with sentience.

"The Lemniscate Paradox."

"The what?!" snapped Zhen Xin turning around.

"The secret to the *I Ching*." Jun Longwei stared at him with a toothless grin. "Do you remember how you got here?" he asked, with eyes of youthful lucidity that belied the gnarled limbs and withered skin of age.

"I was just in my study, a cup of tea in hand, the *I Ching* on my desk. I was staring at the swinging pendulum of Newton's cradle, the rhythmic sound of the spheres clacking into one another, when suddenly I was here."

"Where are your servants? Where are your guards?"

The usual personnel were nowhere to be seen. The rooms and corridors of the *Diaoyutai* were desolate, as if no human had ever laid foot upon her grounds. The blood at Zhen Xin's feet had vanished. Only the *I Ching* remained, opened to the page he had set.

Jun Longwei's grin gave way to a solemn countenance. There was no turning back now.

"Time is like the rhythmic sound of a swinging pendulum; it moves at a constant velocity. In one sudden moment, our awareness of it comes to a stop. We die. But for the *I Ching*, time is an intersecting loop with no beginning, no end. It is an eternal refraction, a prism of the infinite shades of reality. We are each a unique reflection of these realities, the *Taiyi*, the Great Oneness. Do you not sense the *si tseng xiang shi* of it all; that somewhere in time you've been here before?"

"Yes," whispered Zhen Xin looking at Jun Longwei, seeing past him, through him, as if discovering the awareness of the *Taiyi* for the first time.

Jun Longwei cast lingering doubt aside. The *I Ching* had never betrayed him. He recognized this awareness, the strange terror in Zhen Xin, when human eyes first opened to the truth of refracting time. No human had ever channeled the gift so strongly as Zhen Xin now did.

"The stones beneath our feet will come and go; the flowers and trees will bloom, and they will wither; the sun will rise, and the moon shall wane. We will live and die, according to the *Taiyi*, the Great Oneness. Every creature, living and dead, is part of this harmonious flow of nature and time, never meant to be fettered, never meant to be altered. But there are those among us who would disrupt this balance, those who would unravel our existence with the single tug of a thread. We are at the verge of the third great war, the war meant to destroy the cycle of time."

A glimmer of hope grew in Jun Longwei. *Perhaps Zhen Xin was everything he foresaw through the I Ching.* But with that hope there was a deep sadness. Zhen Xin's fate would be one he wished on no man.

***

Shi Ren left the partygoers to their revelry, lost to the obsessions that consumed her mind this evening. Her footfalls echoed along the walls as her long legs with their black high heels whisked between the slit of her dress. The fracas of the festivities was background noise already long forgotten. She stood alone in the grand hall of the *Diaoyutai*, its walls cast in shadows of eerie emptiness. The looming black canvas hung before her, the thing with its legs spread as always. The sharp-toothed fish head stared at her from between the legs of that mannequin, rotten and decayed like everything else in that painting.

How could anyone see anything of beauty in this thing?

Zhen Xin used to stare at it for hours. Shi Ren would find him here at times, when he needed a moment away or wanted some time to himself. He would come here and just stare at this thing of morbidity and death.

The baby in the painting fought to feed from its mother's breast, but there was nothing to be had.

Without death there could be no life.

Those were his words when he inspected every inch of that painting with lenses he donned only for the canvas. If he would only inspect her like so.

Only his thirst for power could rival what her husband felt for this grotesque thing. The more she considered how much she lost, how much he was lost to her now, the more she hated the painting for it.

She threw her glass at the canvas, the champagne splashing across the oil paint right where the fish-headed vagina dentate met her gaze.

She pulled the phone from the small pocket of her purse, trying her husband one more time. But there was no answer. The only reminders that she was the wife of Zhen Xin Liang were the guards at the door that kept her watch. She had no time alone, no peace, not a moment, not even for their grandson.

She threw the phone as hard as she could at the canvas, not caring what damage it would do, hoping it would do damage, indeed. She had fallen to her knees, sobbing into her hands, when she first felt it—the prickling skin on the back of her arms and neck.

The lamplight flickered. The air surrounding her undulated and bent, a prism of light, rippling through her and away in every direction. She rose slowly to her feet. She thought it might be the alcohol and her state of despair, but then she noticed her sleeve.

The dress she had worn this evening was black. The sleeve she now wore was white, the color of mourning. She looked about, trying to make sense of it all, before turning to the painting. The canvas hung, dark and ominous. But the black was different. The black was just that. The creature and her baby had vanished. Someone had set the *Ilythiium* free.

XVIII

THE LION OF ISMAEL

Richard pulled in a breath as if tasting air for the first time, trembling from the bitter cold beneath him. The memories began to trickle back in like deep crimson droplets through the cracks of an old sepulcher.

"Anja!" he roared, as the pain in his abdomen cut him short.

"Shhhhh," came the hush from the dark.

The cone lamp shade hung bright overhead, its heat quickly drying the splash of rubbing alcohol that had drenched Richard's body.

"You don't mind if I smoke, do you?" asked the silhouette just beyond the sphere of light.

A droplet of alcohol dripped from his nose, catching the prism from the halogen bulb. The chromatic sphere fell to the ground, splatting onto the cold stone surface. Richard sat stripped naked, contused all over. He shuddered and struggled to free his bonds.

"They will only bite into you more if you resist. Sometimes it's best to just let go."

Richard pulled with all his might against the bindings. The more he pulled, the more his wrists and ankles bled.

"Eventually, you'll stop."

Richard heaved, sobbing silently.

"My condolences for your loss, Peter. Anja served us well. It's a truth she hid from you far too long." Anton looked for a reaction in his eyes, something he might latch onto. But there was nothing, only the blank stare of a man struck suddenly by blunt force trauma. Anton had to plunge truth's blade further into his heart.

"Anja did what she promised you she never would. Viktor knew every step you took at the Vatican that night. She served the Syndycate. She served the Syndycate well."

The cavernous silence was broken with the tones of a dial pad echoing from the darkness. The sound brought Richard back to the world of the living. He recognized the sequence; it was permanently imprinted in his memory. A phone rang over a speaker. It was coming from the cell phone in the shadowed man's hand. It rang once... It rang again...

The chair's legs danced on the floor. He would tip over and break a shoulder. The shadowed man rose, slamming his foot down on the seat between Richard's legs.

"You're lucky I'm coordinated," said Anton.

The ringing ceased, replaced by a desperate breath.

"Hello?" said the high-pitched voice through the speaker.

The still image of a smiling redhead and little boy from a happier time filled the screen.

"Danny." Richard struggled to form his name.

"Daddy, help me!"

The cords again began to bite into him. This time he did not feel them.

"Speak up, he can't hear you," said Anton, bringing the phone closer to his battered face.

"Daddy, they hurt Clara. Daddy, help me! Mommy—"

The little boy's voice was cut short by Anton's thumb over the end button, the family photo replaced by the familiar screensaver of Richard's phone.

"A trick I learned from an old friend," said Anton.

"You motherfucker!"

Richard lunged at Anton, but the cords held.

"That will only serve to injure you more. And I don't want to injure you any more than I must."

Richard strained against the steel cords, his shoulders dangerously close to coming undone. He jetted bloody spit onto Anton's face. Anton wiped his eye clear of the red mucous. An open-handed slap caught Richard across the cheek, blood shooting into the air as his head snapped back.

"It's best you kill me now."

"If I kill you, so too shall your son die. An entire family, what a waste, all over a simple request."

Rage clenched Richard's mouth shut.

"It's strangely comforting to know that we all must die sometime," said Anton.

"Just let my boy go."

"Ah, that is good, Peter, a starting point for a negotiation. Or should I call you by the name you now go by?"

Richard bit his tongue. He would kill this asshole. He didn't care what he was.

"Your boy is safe. No harm will come to him. But there's something you must do first."

"I will cut out your tongue and feed you every last bit of your flesh, leaving your eyes last so you can see and feel everything I'm going to do to you."

"You're in no position for threats, or did my hit to your head cause that much damage?" asked Anton, as he gently rubbed his fingers over the gash on Richard's temple.

"The deal is simple, Richard, it really is. You will steal the Vermeers just as you were planning tonight. But not for yourself. You will steal them for Viktor, as you most masterfully performed at the Vatican for Christian Huygens. You do that in exchange for the safety of your family, your son. Is that clear?"

Only the sounds of his breath and beating heart reminded Richard he was still living.

"All this for a bunch of paintings? You fucking animal!"

"You don't have to be so pejorative. Hurting my feelings will get you nowhere. We both know they're much more than just a *bunch of paintings*. Thirty-five to be exact. And with the one on your phone, that makes thirty-six," said Anton, as he turned the phone back to Richard, *The Concert* displayed prominently on the screen saver.

"There was always a price to pay for playing with a man's dangerous obsessions. You should know best of all."

Richard's mind slammed the door shut on Anton. The force of it reverberated back into empty corridors behind him in a room of gilded walls and smooth volcanic black stone beneath his feet. He sat at his chair, suddenly untied.

Richard rose freely, as walls melted away to another place from so long ago. They had spindled time, he and Anja, against Viktor on a cold and lurid night when the Syndycate stood at the brink of conquest, the last of the Guija before them set for the slaughter. The *Ilythiium* lay at the verge of collapsing the multiverse, collapsing time into one, a reality where the Syndycate, where Viktor alone, held dominion over all.

Richard found a way, in an obscure corner of time's continuum. He lured the *Ilythiium* where Guija and only few humans could, beyond the limited dimensionality of the Argylian mind. He and Anja entrapped the creature in the last place Viktor or any of the Syndycate could ever conceive, the world of a human artist's imagination, brought to life in oil paint and canvas.

The Syndycate was ultimately defeated, and with time, both species, Argylian and Guija, learned to survive on this planet; preserving their essence, their memories, their awareness in the human flesh of this world.

Richard was just a boy when his own awareness of what he was first woke again in the corridors of the Isabella Stewart Gardner Museum. He was snatched from his mother's arms and shackled to the service of men he could not understand. But he found solace in the memories somehow inside him and in the care of Karl Downing.

Anton stood over him, waiting as if Richard had never left. His thoughts turned to Danny, a son born of two Guija. Richard didn't hesitate. Nobody would ever hurt his boy. It would be Anton instead who would soon know his pain.

"What assurance do I have that you won't kill my son?"

"You know our kind," said Anton pulling up a sleeve. The emblazoned Lion of Ismael stared at

Richard. "We stand by our agreements drawn in blood."

Anton pulled out a black blade, incising his tattooed forearm with its razor edge. Richard recognized it right away as ancient memory again flooded him. Anton held in his grasp an orincular dagger, the one known as *Kidir*. A gaping gash opened in Anton's arm, and carmine red flowed over his hand, droplets falling to the cold floor at their feet. He balled his fist, blood running between his fingers. It was the rite of the covenant, a concordat weaving two of their kind into one, the bond only broken by fulfillment of their pact—or mutual death. Anton placed the tip of the blade to the old wound in Richard's hand.

"You have my word. Do I have your agreement?"

Richard felt no pain, only numbness, resolute numbness.

"Yes," said Richard, never once blinking as the tip of the blade perforated his scarred hand, never once taking his eyes off his wife's murderer.

***

The Hummer rolled through the deep mud between the sycamores and firs, somewhere in the back hills outside Washington. The heavy truck came to a stop, shrouded in the blackness of an overcast, moonless night. A rear door opened, and a shadowed figure stepped out, his heavy boots sinking deep into the mud. He opened the rear hatch, pulling forth into the night's torrential downpour what remained of a half-dressed, broken man.

Richard collapsed into the mud, nothing to shield him from the rains, his clothes tossed to the side. The

362

shadowed figure approached, gently laying a large black plastic bag at his side. The figure stood over Richard as his shoulders strained to rise from the mud.

In that instant, the shadow vanished. The truck was gone. The rain washed over what was left of Richard as he turned to the sound of water hitting plastic. His sight adjusted to the darkness, the form of the body bag taking shape. His hand went to the zipper, his mind a blank slate, as though a switch had flipped in his head.

Richard pulled the tab back, and the bag revealed its contents. A lock of red hair fell out onto the mud. He gently placed the hair into his outstretched palm, the amber strands melting away with the rain. He pulled back the plastic.

"This can't be. They did not do this to you," whispered Richard, each word harder and harder until he choked on the last.

He cradled her burnt body, pressing her crushed face gently into his. He kissed her forehead as the flesh peeled away from her bones and the skies wept. He crumpled into the mud with what was left of his Anja in his arms. From among the trees, another's eyes watched. Even the coldest of stone hearts could bear not such a loss.

I am with you. I am with you.

Saifa's whispers were drowned out beneath the sounds of the falling rain and the beating of her own heavy heart.

Richard lay in that mud beneath the floodgates of the night sky, until somehow he rose to his feet, holding what remained of his Anja in his arms. Through trees and thicket, he carried her, his arms and legs giving way too many times to remember. He trekked for hours along the sloping streets and sidewalks of Massachusetts Avenue, cradling her to his chest as the night baptized him beneath a rain of pitiless absolution. No one noticed him along the side of the road. No one stopped for the man in mud-caked, torn clothes with a black plastic body bag draped across his arms.

The sun's first rays cracked through the trees as he made his way up Idaho Avenue and the last few steps. Passing the sign, he neared the building of the Metropolitan Police Department. He caught the reflection in the tinted glass doors of a haggard man who stared back at him. Richard pressed the handle and the door gave way into the reception area. He gently placed the bag onto the reception table and stared at the young female officer on duty. This was probably the first time she ever had someone lay a cadaver atop her desk. She fumbled for her gun.

"No need," he said, as he slowly lifted his hands and placed them behind his head.

***

"He hasn't said another word since he got here. Just the name Karl Downing," said Sergeant Mack Williamson as he approached Captain Sam Gartner, the commanding officer of the Washington, D.C., 2nd Police District, at the one-way looking glass.

He stared fixedly through the glass at Richard, cuffed and seated in the metal folding chair. The interrogating officer leaned forward and asked him the same question for the third time.

"Crazy son of a bitch kills a woman..."

"You don't know that," replied the sergeant.

"Fuck you, Mack. Guy dumps a cadaver on my front desk to kick off the week. Doesn't say a word, except that name."

"Karl Downing," repeated Mack.

"That one. You run the name yet? Fingerprints? Anything on the female?"

Mack pulled out a cigarette. "No fingerprints. Pathologist won't even let me get near the morgue," he said, lighting up in front of the non-smoking sign hanging prominently behind him.

"Figures. Always been that way with his dead bodies. Necrophiliac motherfucker! No match on this guy's prints?" asked Sam.

"He has no prints on his fingers, nothing," said Mack, wiggling his five before the captain.

"Get the fuck outta here."

"Maybe you should go in there and ask him yourself. Might tell you where he left them."

"Fuck you, Mack."

"There's someone here for him," said the sergeant.

"What do you mean?"

"A State Department type: suit, badge, the whole nine yards. See him coming from a mile away. He's at the front desk, asked to speak to you."

"Why didn't you fucking tell me?"

"I just did. He says he's Karl Downing."

Mack took a drag as the captain disappeared, leaving him with the nut job. A cigarette was the only way to relax so early in the morning.

***

Sam Gartner always knew he was a strange bird of sorts. He'd come to Washington with a Texas drawl

365

and the bawdy tongue of an angry New Yorker. No one really quite knew where or how to place him. Sam was usually up early, especially after a night of consumption and indulgence in his personal obsession. This morning's sky was crisp. The cool air breezed with the scent of spring bloom and the fresh rains of the night prior.

The black Suburban rolled into his back parking lot just like Sam might expect a suit to do. He stood, arms crossed and shoulders square, at the rear door to the station, while Mack leaned his heavyset ass against the wall and puffed down yet another cigarette. Karl Downing stepped out of the truck in his gray flannel and made his way toward them. Sam had a lot of anger in his heart and nothing boiled it over more than the likes of this man standing straight in front of him this very instant.

"You think yourself so high and mighty, don't ya? You have no idea just how low your type can fall," said Sam, blowing smoke in Karl's face from his burnt-out cigarette butt.

The Suburban was a bit low to the ground, as a matter of fact, noticed Sam. Must have been all the armor that bad boy was packing.

"There will be no trace of this in your records. Can I make myself any clearer?" asked Karl, as he approached Sam.

"Drop a cadaver on my front desk and just ignore it, just like that, matter of fucking fact," said Sam, his Texas twang finally making its way into the open. That only happened when Sam had had enough.

"What cadaver? You must be mistaken."

"You must be fuckin' shit-stock joking," said Sam.

"Don't dig yourself any deeper a hole. We wouldn't want to mistake the living for the dead."

"What's that supposed to mean there, big boy?" asked Sam, taking a step back from Karl.

"Good of you to keep your range. Hit first, hit twice," said Karl.

"You have no idea," replied Sam, longing to make good on that comment.

"Good day, gentlemen," said Karl, as he stepped back toward the truck and was gone before Sam could say another word.

"That son of a bitch fucking threatened me, twice."

Sam was halfway to the door by the time Mack was able to put out another cigarette.

"Where the hell you going?" asked Mack.

"The morgue, where else?"

Sam barreled through the steel door of the morgue's receiving area.

"I want to see the body!"

A technician behind a desk covered in a pile of file folders and an outdated computer stood quickly at attention, confusion running across his brow.

"Did you not understand me? The body."

The young man fumbled with the file folders stacked in a shaky pile. He rummaged across the desk, knocking over a cup, brushing aside a stale donut. Everything was suddenly soaked in creamed coffee. The tenuous pile fell over. Strawberry jelly splattered out from underneath across the floor. The stack had crushed the donut. He grabbed his badge, hastily going to the door. A swipe and they were in. The two examination tables stood empty.

"Where is she?"

"Who?"

367

"The cadaver brought in this morning," said Sam.

"No cadaver was brought in this morning, sir," said the young man, accenting the time line.

"Bullshit!"

Sam went to each of the freezer doors, pulling them back. The morgue was empty. Mack stood at the morgue's entrance.

"You're a popular man this morning," said Mack as a towering figure, this time in a black, tailored suit, stepped through the door.

"Captain Gartner, Special Agent Frank Hendrix. Mind if I have word with you?"

"Sure, if you don't mind telling me where the fuck your people took my dead body."

***

They had weaved and turned along rural streets onto the familiar roads of Old Georgetown. Richard gazed out the window at the sloping green grasses and headstones of a passing cemetery. Karl had not removed the handcuffs. Better Richard remained bound for the time being. Karl wasn't so concerned with Richard getting out of the car. The Suburban was made to keep its passengers inside. Karl was more concerned with the safety of those who accompanied him. Richard could do a lot of damage very quickly.

Richard sat stone-still, lost to another time. He stared through the window at the reflection of his resolute face, its only sign of life his grinding jaw.

He could see Anja again, her back against that car, her eyes wide, her mouth agape, her arms strewn at her sides, her body collapsed in the resignation of that moment. The cone-shaped piece of lead spiraled through the air, leaving its cavitation trail in its wake as it slowly cleaved through her forehead, burying itself deep into her brain. He watched her suck in a sudden breath at the surprise of it all.

Why would she stop him? He would have killed that Hashishin; would have let him suffocate in his own breath. But instead she willed him free, knowing what would come.

None of it could be real. Anja would have never betrayed him. No orb of sanctuary or anything else either he or Anja conjured could have done this. This was not the time tapestry he had woven. Only another Guija could have done this.

"What did you tell them?" asked Karl, shattering the silence.

"I knew those would be the first words out your mouth. Just like I knew it wouldn't take long for you to find me again, as soon as I talked to the cops," said Richard.

"I would have hoped for more fortunate circumstances."

"Save your breath, Karl. You're a whole lot more agreeable with your mouth shut."

"I will ask again. What did you tell them?"

"Nothing," said Richard.

Karl searched for that unspoken clue, a hint that might yield more answers than words ever could. His eyes narrowed on the wound still fresh on Richard's hand. Richard did not turn from the window. He focused only on the nothingness of it all as the neighborhoods blurred by.

"It was Anton."

"Yes."

"The Vermeers?" Karl asked.

"Maybe you should have killed me when you had the chance," said Richard.

"I thought about it."

The truck came to a stop at a neighborhood all too familiar to Richard. A police line circled an all too familiar house. The front door was open. Two men in black fatigues stood at the entrance, unarmed — at least to the casual observer. Richard was out of the truck before Karl could move. The two guards blocked his path. But a hand and a nod from the man in the gray flannel suit was enough, and the guards parted as quickly as they'd come together.

To Karl's surprise, the cuffs were off Richard's wrists. He left them laying on the back seat. Karl gave Richard a pained smirk. He hadn't expected that. Richard was still as dangerous and unpredictable as ever. He'd almost forgotten just how dangerous he was.

Richard strode past the guards without so much as a glance. The door had been torn clear off its hinges. He swept into the living room: the stain on the floor, the impact on the table, the blood still fresh in the air. His senses picked up every detail, every scent. Two more guards in similar uniforms and another man in a flannel suit, a younger version of Karl, crowded the far bedroom. He strode to them with purpose.

"Halt!" bellowed the young man in the flannel suit, gripping the pistol at his hip.

"Daddy!" came the cry of frightened joy from the room. Danny raced into his father's outstretched arms. "Where's mommy? Where's mommy?!"

"It will be some time before you see her again." The boy stood before him numbed in abandonment, speechless in despair.

Richard held him close as Karl stepped through the door and dismissed his younger doppelgänger. The men reluctantly departed, leaving them alone in the room. Rembrandt's painting hung at its place on the wall. The Stranger, the thirteenth apostle, gazed quietly at him from amid the storm.

"It is time."

Richard didn't say another word. He did not need to. The circle of thirteen had chosen. Somewhere in the firmament, the arcane revelation the young girl of Fatima had long ago witnessed had come to pass.

The Black Shadow descended from the east.

But the *Fourth Secret* missed one prescient detail. Richard was a master of time. The young Carmelite nun from Fatima could not foresee his own dark choice. The Syndycate would live their worst nightmares as he would do what only a Guija could. Like the pulling away of petals from a rosebud until only the bare stem was left, he would have his vengeance; he would know the truth. One by one, slowly and painfully, he would unravel time for every last one of them. He would tear every last one of them apart.

EPILOGUE

The last of the peddlers had gone home for the night. Tehran's bazaar was an empty maze of tents and tables. The remnants of the day littered the pavement of the deserted old city streets. Only the Basij and police roamed the night, vigilant in their paranoia.

Teymour Anjani bolted from his chair, feverously pacing across the Tabrizian rug beneath his bare feet. He glanced out the crack between the window shutters. He didn't see anyone. He didn't hear anyone on the creaky stairs. There were no shadows beneath the door. But they were coming.

He glanced back to his terminal screen. The camera on his laptop was covered. They could never know his face. He lifted the bandana around his neck and slipped on his moccasin shoes. The Exohumans were coming.

The Ashiyane had given him its orders. But Teymour had gone too far. Farther than they could have imagined. Farther than anyone, even the Ashiyane, would have wished. The Tor network had been cloaked so that even the Cyber Army could not find him. He found a chink in their armor with a simple cross-site script, a zero-day vulnerability he created in Python. The break-in was only the beginning.

His head spun from another lungful of poppy smoke as he stared at the description of these Exohumans and the creature they called the *Ilythiium*. The fans worked to the brink to ventilate the smoke from the room that would find him in Evin Prison, beneath her gallows, if he were discovered.

He slammed his laptop shut, tossed it recklessly into his carry bag, and stuffed the opium in the side pouches. He grabbed the memory key on the table when the wood in the old stairwell creaked. They found him. He must get to the scientist, the one named Ramin, before it was too late.

Chun Lai waited at the edge of the staircase landing. He felt the breeze from beneath the old wooden door. He welcomed the cool as he wiped a bead of sweat from his chin. He traveled far to find this one, on orders from those who wanted what the young man now possessed. Teymour found it just a step too soon; Chun Lai, a step too late. Still, he was patient. There was no way the young man could comprehend what he had. He approached the door, the breeze now blowing strong at his feet. The knob gave way to a soiled room barely wide enough to fit the mattress on the floor. The table was barren, the window open, the space empty. The young man was gone. But it was only a matter of time before Chun Lai would find him again.

Somewhere else, far away, Saifa stood at the edge of a rust-lit room, the walls lined with books. At the center of the room stood a table draped with a white fabric. Saifa knew who lay beneath the cloth. She followed the bends and creases in the fabric covering the form as she neared the table in step after silent step. The fabric rose slowly — the exhale of a breath. She stopped mid-step. Her eyes played tricks on her, they did. But there was no movement.

Saifa remembered the young woman she'd graded on her pathology exam, that *katsa* so determined to become what she now was. That young woman would have given anything for this moment. Saifa would have given anything to have it taken away.

She ripped back the cloth, expecting to find charred flesh, when she first felt it: the bend of the walls, the air convexing as the ripple pulsed right through her. The charred cadaver before her, the one she'd known as Anja, was suddenly gone.

Saifa stood in the middle of the street before the building she just entered moments prior, aware of what had never been, and what was yet to come. The voices grew loud again, voices of a long-ago place. Memories echoed of Ronen's betrayal at the hands of Anton Arlovsky, that monster with those crystal-gray eyes. The scar across her belly began to burn as she doubled over with the nausea of every cell in her body coming alive. Agony stole consciousness, but not the awareness of the transmogrification and the creature she once knew as *Ilythiia*.

Guillermo sat in the darkness, alone with his guilt. He had betrayed his friend and led the Hashishin to him. The fence had forsaken the thief. He, like Richard, was Guija, concealed in human flesh, born of seed not of this world. Their Argylian masters had enslaved them for so long as guardians of the *Ilythiium* until the Second Schism and diaspora changed all that. The Guija, believed extinct, were eventually forgotten.

But the Guija could not forget. Guillermo could not forget. He knew he must answer for what had been done, as he stood before the artifact, deep in that dungeon crypt. Only the candled wall sconces gave him light, enough to see the cloister the thing was set in. Its metallic bands, etched in an ancient script, interleaved and woven into a sphere atop a small stone dais, nestling a smooth, blue, radiant stone at its center.

"Forgive me," he whispered, as his trembling hand rose to the spherical artifact.

A glow slowly emanated from the sphere as it began to weave and rotate on itself. The runes burned a cobalt blue as light cast around the outline of his hand, engulfing his arm.

Two wrongs would make a right.

This was his penitence. He must find the *Ilythiium* first. It was the only way he could save Richard—save him from himself. In a roar of sheer agony, Guillermo's awareness vanished. The silver-white pulse of the Armillary Sphere rippled through time to the task Guillermo had set for it.